THE WITCH'S SPIRAL

M.K. Hancock

This book is dedicated to my husband, whose capacity for my questions never ceases. Without his help, much of the science in this book wouldn't work. And what's magic without the mysteries of science?

Part One

1

Judith Naismith turned 30 on May 30th, 1972. She would not turn 31, nor 30 and a day. She toasted the hour of her birth at 1 a.m., but kept drinking to celebrate. The smoky, wood paneled bar in midtown Memphis, Tennessee, still had plenty of eligible bachelors milling around. Her supposedly best friend Barbara had left around 2 a.m. with a real fox. Judith had thought about leaving then but had decided to keep celebrating until close. She'd find somebody good lookin' too. It was her goddamn birthday after all. Why couldn't Barbara have let ol' Judy have him?

She'd lost count of how many beers she downed after the fifth one, but she was sure she was going to find somebody to take home. She hadn't been laid since Tom had left the year before, and she was determined to ring in 30 with a bang. She had dolled up for the occasion, putting on false eyelashes and curling her hair. She had chosen the most flattering minidress and her best calf high boots, but when last call came, it was all for naught. It was her own fault, and she knew it, but she wasn't too bothered. None of them had really fit her standards, and so, alone and drunk, she walked the two blocks home.

She stuck to the main street, careful to avoid any places that were too dark and far from streetlights. She realized in a part of her brain that was somehow a little less drunk than the rest that she was being stupid for walking in this area by herself in the middle of the night. People got shot and killed for less than walking home alone at night. Hell, worse things happened to people walking home alone.

She quickened her pace as her mind began supplying reasons to be afraid. Someone she knew had been mugged on this street—a few miles down, but still. She remembered hearing about abductions and carjackings in this part of town, and her eyes scanned the long street in front of her. She had made this walk before, but usually on the other side of midnight and not often alone. But here it was, 3 a.m., and there wasn't a soul on the long street in front of her. She considered going back to the club and calling a cab, but she didn't want to turn around.

She thought she might have heard footsteps behind her, but she was sure it was just in her head. When she turned around, there wasn't anyone there. But her mental image was of one of the men she had turned away. He hadn't been her type at all, but she had spent about 10 minutes talking with him before realizing that was the case. He was charismatic, tall, and an older man. He looked to be in his 40s, but maybe older. He was handsome enough, but he had asked her if she was into the occult.

As soon as the word "occult" was spoken, Judith felt alarm bells ringing in her head. Mental red flags were hoisted and unfurled, flapping wild warnings. As a card carrying Catholic, she didn't want anything to do with anyone messing with the occult. She felt guilty enough being such a pervert, but it was a guilt she felt ready to combat. Men picked up women in bars all the time, so what was wrong with her doing the same? But she didn't want anything to do with that devil-worship shit, especially after what she had learned about her family.

Her aunt had told her last summer before she passed that she was a witch. She didn't believe it, of course. Aunt Mary had always been eccentric, with a house full of plants, crystals, and mirrors. She always seemed to be looking in mirrors. But she usually kept the weird stuff to herself. At least she had until she realized her time was getting close, Judith remembered. She had wanted to have a talk with Judith. Her parents had told her Aunt Mary was losing it in the head, and Judith believed it completely after the 3 hours she had spent on the porch with her in July. It had been hotter than hell, but she figured only Aunt Mary would know for sure. She supposed she should feel bad thinking ill of the dead, but she didn't. Not after what Mary had pulled.

For the entire visit, Aunt Mary had told her her theories about how the rules of the universe were knitted with magic. It was all pretty absurd, and to prove to her that it was real, her Aunt Mary had shown her a trick like one Judith had seen a magician do before on television. The magician had made a dove come out of a hat, but Aunt Mary had pulled Judith's diary out of her purse. Judith had been mortified that the woman had gotten it from her room, although Judith couldn't figure out how she had found the hiding place without her catching. She had been furious, but because her parents had told her Mary was going to pass soon, she had pretended to be delighted when she plucked her diary back from her aunt's thieving hands.

Aunt Mary had bored her for hours while she had sat and listened out of duty and politeness. At one point, Mary had made her take notes. She had scribbled down a few things, but she just couldn't believe any of it. Her mother had told her afterwards that she did a good job humoring her ill aunt, and that she was proud of her. She had said that it was the right thing to do, but Judith wasn't sure. Some of the things her Aunt had said had resonated with her, like about how Judith should always heed her intuition. Mary had said women in their family had a special sense for when they were in danger, and that she should always listen to her gut.

She had looked through some of the old books her Aunt had given her, but the images had disturbed her. The books looked like Aunt Mary had made them herself, since all the writing inside was handwritten. They had been filled with spells, potions, and incantations, but the sigils had been what creeped Judith out the most. There had been about 30 pages of different symbols, many of which she recognized as basic shapes—many different kinds of spirals, stars in circles called pentagrams, squares—but she recognized the evil inherent in the shapes. She knew they were intended to warp God's will.

She had thrown the books out after Mary died, feeling guilty as though she had sinned just by touching them. She'd washed her hands after and scrubbed hard, like the old books were more than just dusty but had some kind of spiritual grime that would stick to her. It seemed to her that witchcraft was the greatest sin of them all. Just thinking about it again on the walk home was enough to make her feel like she needed to wash her hands again. It'd been a while since she'd been to confession, but she wondered if talking to a priest about her aunt would make her feel better.

"It was a shame about the guy at the bar though," she thought, hastening her thoughts away from witchcraft. "Because he had carried himself with that way that just screams 'big dick.' I hope I didn't misread him."

After she told him she wasn't interested, he walked off to another table but he had continued eyeing her all night. Every time she saw him, he was looking at her. Sometimes it was over the rim of a glass while he was drinking at the bar and sometimes he'd be across the room, but she was sure his eyes were on her. She could feel it. It wasn't the first time a guy had stared at her, and at the time it had seemed like flirting and was only mildly creepy. But the further she got from the bar the more sinister his leering grew in her memory.

A news story floated to the top of her mind, and as she walked the dark street alone she remembered hearing on the news that there had been a spike in murders last year, and that 1972 was expected to be even more violent. She asked herself why she had walked home alone.

"Stop it," she told herself. "You're just scaring yourself. Maybe you should go back and call a cab."

It was then that Judith realized she was not alone. The certainty of the feeling seared her brain, catching her by surprise. She could sense there was someone else nearby, practically feel their presence. She felt her breath catch and she listened, not stopping but picking up her pace slightly. She heard footsteps, almost but not quite in time with hers. She turned around, not sure if he was right behind her or how far back he was. She was sure it was him. She couldn't shake the sudden and intense feeling that the occult man was following her. It felt like her intuition, which had become a lot sharper over the last year, although she had thought it was the confidence that comes with getting older. She tried not to use the word intuition, associating it with her Aunt Mary. She shivered, despite the heat, and kept walking toward home. She only had one more block to go.

She could hear the footsteps again. She was sure of it. She picked up the pace. The footsteps quickened too. They seemed louder, like they were getting closer. She sped up more, walking so swiftly that she was almost jogging.

Soon she thought she heard wheezing behind her. Hair raised on her neck and her skin prickled. She gripped her keys tightly in her hand and whirled around, determined to see some blood.

The street was vacant behind her, and the darkness of the alley she had passed a few yards before seemed sinister but unoccupied. When she turned back around, there was a woman in her path. A small woman with dark hair who looked scared too. Her pale blue eyes were big and under the streetlight they looked like they were shining. Judith halted in her path right in front of the woman.

"I saw him!" the woman said, "He dove behind that dumpster!"

She pointed and Judith turned around. She was sure she saw the shadow of a tall man behind the dumpster. She backed up, bumping into the woman before turning around again to face her, fear painted on her face.

"What do I do?" she said.

"Come with me," the woman said, and held out a hand.

Judith should have kept on her way home, but she took the woman's hand out of fear. They turned down an alley, and Judith wasn't seen again.

2

Rachel Ogden turned off Central Parkway onto Elm Street. She slowed down as she drove alongside Washington Park before turning into the steeply sloped entrance to the parking garage underneath the 6-acre park in downtown Cincinnati. She stopped at a machine that spat out a ticket and raised the gate. The garage was packed full of commuter cars, but she found a space near the bottom. She checked her reflection in the driver's side mirror, smoothing down a few wild auburn hairs that had escaped her braid before popping the trunk of her sedan and loading up with what she had brought to the Local Flavors and Crafts Festival.

Rachel took the elevator to the surface. The steel doors opened into the small glass and metal elevator lobby. Her arms full, she pushed open the glass door to the park with her back before stepping through to the sun. She had to squint until her eyes adjusted to the late May glare. Lately it seemed the weather only had two modes: soak or shine. Rachel was just happy it wasn't expected to rain until that evening, well after the festival.

She looked to the left, toward Cincinnati Music Hall, the massive Gothic Revival edifice roughly half the size of the park it loomed over. The conjoined red brick buildings radiated terracotta orange in the bright sun, creating a stark contrast where the peaks of its many pointed gables pierced the blue sky. Above rows of slim windows and glass entrance doors at the center of the building, gray iron tracery cut a massive clear glass circle into a bursting pattern of geometric shapes called a rose window. Rachel thought it looked more like an eye than a rose, and thinking of how they usually are on churches, reflected that was likely intentional.

She felt her phone buzz in her pocket with a text message, and she smiled. They'd been texting back and forth since Monday, when she'd given him her phone number after a week of sending messages back and forth online. She had just texted him when she parked in the garage underneath Washington Park. If he was answering that quickly, then he was probably already here. She'd respond once she got the extra supplies to the booth, she told herself, tamping down her excitement at meeting the man she'd been messaging with for the last two weeks.

"Today isn't a date," she told herself as she adjusted her load and marched around the cement path surrounding the Civic Lawn, a football field sized grass oval at the northern end of the park. "It's like a preview, just to make sure he's not a weirdo. He may not even have time to stop by."

Rachel felt sure she wasn't being catfished, but she had wanted to meet Mike for the first time in a public place during the day, just in case. She hadn't spent much time at Washington Park before and was glad to see the festival had a decent turnout, especially considering that it was during the day on a Thursday. There were plenty of families and potential new customers buzzing from tent to tent, pollinating local businesses with their money. The lunch hour was rapidly approaching, and that would bring all the downtown business people out in the sun on their lunch break for a cup of cold brew and a bite to eat from one of the food trucks parked around the perimeter of the park.

The green space was cluttered with pop-up tents and umbrella covered booths as local businesses and artists shared their wares. Rachel spotted the green banner draped on the front of their white popup tent, with "The Wise Bean" printed in black. The border around the edge of the banner was printed with a funky pattern made of different sized triangles joined closely together like a spider web. It had been Rachel's design, which her business partner Emily Jones had praised as "hip and hippie" enough to appeal to their free yoga class customers and the morning commute regulars.

They'd been in business for six years. Their shop had a loyal crowd in the northern Kentucky town of Highland Heights, 15 minutes across the Ohio River from downtown Cincinnati. They welcomed the commuters, college students, retirees and anyone else who wanted locally roasted coffee and cold drinks. They had renovated an old restaurant when they started and had been able to expand into the shop next door after the first three years. They had plenty of regulars but never missed an opportunity to meet new customers, volunteering as a vendor for most festivals they heard about in the northern Kentucky or Cincinnati area.

The Wise Bean's booth was sandwiched between a tent selling gourmet grilled cheese sandwiches and one selling tacos. Rachel walked behind her booth, where Emily was helping their newest barista, Mikaela Green, hand out pastries and coffee drinks. Cadence Williams, one of the shop's two third-key supervisors, was busy making multiple drinks at a time for the line of customers.

"I brought four more sleeves of cold cups, and two sleeves of hot," Rachel said as she walked into the booth.

She laid down the six long, plastic covered bundles of stacked cups in her arms on the white plastic foldout table at the back of the booth. She sat down the heavy blue tote bag that had been digging into her arm and started unpacking the bags of coffee beans where Cadence could reach them. The three women at the front of the booth were busy but in sync, and the line that had formed when Rachel stepped into the booth had already dwindled to a few customers by the time Rachel finished unpacking and staging the extra supplies.

"Do y'all need an extra set of hands? We're not too busy today at the shop," Rachel said.

"Thanks, Rach. We're fine now that we're restocked," Emily said. "Cadence and Mikaela could run this booth by themselves no problem, but I'm their backup for when it gets crazy. We're expecting a big lunch crowd from the downtown commuters."

"Excellent," said Rachel. "I may stick around for a half hour or so to meet with someone, so y'all just holler if you need me."

Emily had already been smiling while describing the money she expected to make that afternoon, but now her smile turned to a sly grin.

"Oooh, is it the boy?" Emily asked.

"Maybe," Rachel said. "We'll see."

She took out her phone and read the message. He was here. She described the location of their booth to him and hit send. A moment later, her phone dinged. He had responded immediately, saying he and his business partner would make their way over.

"Ok, yes," she said. "He's going to meet me here."

"Nice!" Mikaela said. "We can prescreen him for you if you want. Ask about his intentions with our boss."

"Yeah," Cadence said. "He better be intent on getting your workaholic butt somewhere aside from the shop on your days off."

"Funny, funny," Rachel said.

She reread the text he had sent. He was going to be over in just a few minutes. She wondered if he would look like his pictures and if he'd think she looked like hers. She pushed away the insecure thoughts and took a deep breath.

Emily walked to the back of the booth and stood nearly shoulder to shoulder with her. Emily's height usually meant she stood taller than most of her female friends, but Rachel was only a few inches shorter than Emily's long-legged 6'2". Emily bumped Rachel's shoulder lightly with her own. Rachel softly knocked her back, and the two chuckled.

"Nervous?" Emily asked quietly enough to where Mikaela and Cadence wouldn't overhear.

"A little," Rachel said. "The last guy I talked to online never showed up."

"I remember. Sean. What a turd."

"Agreed. It was just disappointing because we got to know each other so well online during the weeks we were talking, but then he just disappeared last month after standing me up. Profile and all. I thought about giving up online dating for a while, but then Mike and I connected. I'm just anxious, I guess."

"It's ok to be nervous, especially since you've been stood up before. But try to relax," Emily said. She patted her on the back and then grinned conspiratorially. "Besides, he already told you where he works, so it's not like you don't know where to find him. We'll totally key his car if he doesn't show."

Rachel nodded and laughed, knowing that Emily was joking but would help her get over it if Mike turned out to be awful. Probably not through petty vengeance—when Sean had disappeared, Emily had taken Rachel to the gun range to get out some of her anger. It had worked. The time at the range had been more expensive that the sushi dinner date Rachel had alone, but it had been exactly what she needed.

They'd been close friends since they met in a freshman business class at Northern Kentucky University, more than 10 years ago. Over the years since, they both focused all their attention on building their business. They had dated people, but most of their employees would say they were committed to their business more than anything else. Rachel's grandmother had been getting on to her about finding someone, so she had dived back into the world of online dating at the beginning of spring.

She'd never dated a club owner before and was hesitant at responding to his initial message. But since she and Mike had so much in common on their profiles, she had decided it would be fun to give it a try. Like Sean, they seemed to like the same music, books, and movies, but Mike was a much better communicator. Sometimes with Sean, it seemed like he had been interviewing her. He didn't give a lot. With Mike, it was a conversation at least. He had also been a gentleman, unlike a lot of other people that messaged her on dating websites.

Mike had told her he was the co-owner of a new club called Church that was opening just north of downtown. He and his business partner were handing out flyers at the festival to promote their opening weekend. Rachel had heard about the club first from Emily, who kept current with the local goth scene on Facebook. Emily had never given up her goth look, only making it more business professional—dark red lipstick, thick black eyeliner, and black button downs and blouses instead of t-shirts, which she saved for her off days.

Rachel herself didn't care too much about fashion. Most of the time she lived in her work uniform, all the way down to the black non-slip shoes. Today she had worn black trousers and a fitted black cotton blouse with a V-neck. The last three days it had been a different version of the same outfit. It struck Rachel as funny that Emily's favorite color to wear was also the color they had decided for uniforms.

There was nothing gothic about Wise Bean coffee. All black uniforms made it a lot easier to hide coffee stains. Emily, Cadence and Mikaela were all wearing the brown canvas aprons that Emily and Rachel had found from a supplier online. Rachel's was back at the store, where she'd be returning after her lunch hour was up. Even if business was slow, there was always something to work on.

Rachel was roused from her thoughts when she saw the man who was placing an order with Cadence. He looked just like his pictures. He was at least 6' 3" with well-coiffed black hair trimmed closer on the sides than on the top, where perfectly mussed black curls shone with product. A much shorter woman stood next to him. They were both dressed like they'd just come from a funeral. Mike wore an all black fitted suit. The woman wore a long black dress and a black pillbox hat with a birdcage veil that ended just at her cheeks. Emily followed Rachel's gaze and, putting the pieces together, stepped to the front of the booth to get a closer look.

"Can I have two medium cold brews with sugar-free vanilla?" Mike asked. He looked past Cadence and gave Rachel a small wave. "And a word with Rachel, if that's alright with y'all."

"Oh, you must be Mike," Emily said. "I'm Emily, Rachel's business partner. She'll be around to see you in just a sec."

Emily shook hands with Mike and the woman next to him whose name Rachel didn't catch as she walked around the outside of the tent to meet Mike. Mike started to go for a hug, but Rachel extended a hand at the same time. She was thankful he didn't make the moment awkward—he just shook her hand and smiled warmly. His thick black eyebrows raised over piercing pale blue eyes as he smiled at her, revealing two dimples on either side of his smile. They were barely visible in the growth of black beard ending just above his angled jawline.

"Mike Smith. So nice to meet you in person, Rachel," Mike said.

"It's nice to meet you, too," Rachel said.

He gestured to the woman next to him, who smiled politely at Rachel. Her shiny black hair was pulled back into an old fashioned roll on the back of her head in a rockabilly fashion. She moved the veil out of her eyes and looked at Rachel with a friendly smile. There was something strange about her that Rachel couldn't put her finger on right away, but finally it came to her when she moved the veil. She and Mike looked like cousins. She couldn't help but notice they had almost the same shade of icy blue eyes. They were so pale they were nearly white.

"Rachel, this is my business partner, Karen Staples," Mike said.

"Rachel Ogden. Nice to meet you, Karen," Rachel said.

Rachel extended her hand and shook the woman's hand with what she had always considered a professional amount of grip. But Karen had a very firm handshake—too much so. Rachel didn't want to be awkward, so she just smiled and shook the normal amount of time as the woman squeezed her hand. As she pulled her hand away, she felt something sharp piece her palm. She yanked her hand back in surprise.

A single drop of blood bubbled on the base of her middle finger. The dark red spot was tiny but Mike was quick to act, pulling a black handkerchief from his breast pocket. Rachel tried to refuse the handkerchief, but Mike insisted. She pressed the smooth cotton against the cut, feeling foolish. It had stung, but it wasn't a big deal. Just a prick. She supposed he was trying to be chivalrous.

"Oh no, I'm so sorry," Karen said with a conciliatory look. She pursed her lips. "That must have been my ring. It's a family heirloom so I can't get rid of it, but I swear it bites sometimes with all the little crannies it has. Jeez, I'm sorry. I thought it'd be nice to wear while promoting our club. Sorta spooky, right?"

She showed Rachel the ring she wore on her middle finger. Bronze had been worked into tight, striped knots that were studded with bumps. It reminded Rachel of a picture she had seen of snakes twisted together. Her skin must have been pinched between some of the yellow-brown knots, she decided. It didn't look comfortable to wear, and Rachel wondered how Karen wore it without cutting her hand up.

"It's ok," Rachel said, holding the handkerchief to the spot. "Accidents happen."

"Hardly the first impression I wanted to make," Mike said, and Rachel caught a quick look he gave Karen.

"Yes, wearing this old thing was a mistake," Karen said as she took off the ring and stowed it in her purse. "I forgot how it catches on things. Let me make it up to you two. Mike, if you want to take a break for a little bit while I keep handing out flyers, I wouldn't mind."

"That's a great idea," Mike said. "Rachel, want to take a walk with me?"

Karen walked off and quickly engaged with the owner of the grilled cheese booth. Rachel thought it was weird that she didn't say goodbye, but she didn't think too much of it.

"Sure," Rachel said, hesitating with the cloth in her hand. She wasn't even sure if there was blood on the black cloth. "I'm sorry—do you want me to wash this? Some meat tenderizer will get the stain right out if there is one. I promise I don't have any contagious illnesses or anything like that."

"That's ok," Mike said. "I'll take care of it. I'm so sorry about that again. I was hoping for a smoother introduction, not for my partner to stab you."

"It's ok. Karen seems nice," Rachel said. "Is she your cousin?"

"Good eye. We're third cousins," Mike said. "Or 4th? It's confusing. Big family, y'know. But don't worry about the blood. I like to keep the handkerchief because of nosebleeds, as sexy as that sounds. So it's ok. I've got it."

She shrugged and handed the handkerchief to Mike, who folded the napkin delicately and pocketed it. They walked a few feet apart through rows of tents selling newspaper subscriptions and homemade soaps. They wandered into a booth selling comic books in long white boxes and used records packed into milk crates. Rachel began looking through one milk crate while Mike looked through the one next to it. As they flipped through records, they picked up the conversation they had been having online the night before. Mike had been bragging about his record collection.

"Think you'll find any Blue Oyster Cult you don't have?" Rachel asked.

"Probably not," Mike said. "But maybe we'll find one for you. I can't believe all you know from them is 'Don't Fear the Reaper.' Did you listen to the other song I sent you?"

"I did, actually. I guess I know two songs of theirs," she said. She looked up at him when she said it, and mentioned how she had recognized "Burnin' for You" immediately upon hearing the chorus. "I liked it, although it's not what I usually listen to. I like some metal, but usually newer stuff like Ghost. I mean, obviously I like older stuff like Black Sabbath. I know Ghost was inspired by bands like them and Blue Oyster Cult. My spooky jam is definitely The Misfits though. I'm not a total purist—Michael Graves era is ok, but Glenn Danzig Misfits will always be my favorite."

Rachel felt like she was babbling and realizing that made her feel nervous. She was grateful that he just nodded sagely as he searched the box of records in front of him.

"Misfits are great," he said. "I used to listen to them a lot in high school. I've got a bit of an obsession with dark themed music. Give me skulls, death and monsters over love songs any day. Movies too."

"It's a whole lot more entertaining usually," Rachel said. "Can I guess that Halloween is your favorite holiday too?"

"I didn't get to celebrate growing up, but it's my favorite adult holiday now—Hey, look what you found!"

He reached in front of her, his arm brushing against hers. She caught a whiff of musky and clean smelling cologne. He pulled a record from the box she had been idly flipping through and put it in her hands. On the cover, a woman held a skull on a staff as she and two men dressed in robes stared out at the viewer. Even the empty dark sockets of the skull seemed to stare. Rachel read the name of the band and album as Mike spoke.

"That's Coven's 1969 debut album, 'Witchcraft Destroys Minds and Reaps Souls,'" Mike said. "It's a classic of the occult rock genre. These guys are actually the folks who introduced the 'sign of the horns' to metal fans in the US, although of course it's been used in cultures all over the world before then."

He made his left hand into a fist and then extended his pointer finger and pinky, then looked at her expectantly. She made the sign back and giggled.

"I remember a friend of my grandmother's said it's like giving the middle finger in Italy," she said.

"It probably means different things to different people. Symbols are funny like that. For Coven, it was about Satan. I know it doesn't look as spooky these days, but this album came out around the time of the Charles Manson murders. He really ruined occult rock for a lot of groups. This and a lot of other records got pulled from the shelves," he said.

He rubbed his hand on the back of his neck.

"Please tell me if I'm nerding out too much," he said, smiling. She thought his dimples were pretty cute.

"No, you're fine," she said. "Coven sounds pretty heavy. I dig it."

"Yes and no," Mike said. "Depending on who you're talking to, they wouldn't call it heavy. Lyrically, they don't pull any punches. But musically—well, think Jefferson Airplane, but if all the lyrics were about finding Satan instead of someone to love."

"Hmm," Rachel said. "That sounds interesting."

"It's definitely entertaining," Mike said. "They even recorded a Satanic mass for this record. My mom actually wouldn't let me listen to this album growing up. She said it was disrespectful. That's probably why I got so into occult rock."

A red flag shot up in her mind when Mike mentioned his mom, but she dismissed it. She certainly wasn't going to bring up her own mother. She usually waited at least a month or more into dating—until she was sure there was an emotional connection—before she brought up her family. It was a lot to lay on someone you just met.

But it wasn't like he had brought up his mother intentionally on a first date. He was just nervous. She could tell by his smile. She smiled, realizing that this did feel like a date, however informal. Rachel looked for another second at the album and then handed it to Mike.

"You should take this," she said.

"Are you sure you don't want it?" he said. "This is a great find."

"To be honest, I don't have a record player," she said. "I've been meaning to fix that, but I mostly stream music."

Mike shrugged.

"How about I buy this for you, and you come listen to it at my house sometime?"

Rachel opened her mouth but was unsure what to say, so she closed it again. She wanted to say "No" because she felt like he was trying to jump ahead too far ahead too soon. He sensed her hesitation, and quickly slid the record back into the box before holding his hands up.

"Sorry, I hope you don't think I'm trying to pull a fast one on you," he said. "No funny business, I promise. I just get excited about sharing my favorite music. Come on, let's grab a bite before I embarrass myself blathering on about Goblin and Jacula and the right brand of stereo speakers."

They exited the tent they were in and walked back to where they had walked from, where most of the food vendors were located on the outside ring of tents. Mike insisted on buying Rachel a slice of pizza, and the two stood near each other as they both tried to eat as cleanly as they could. Mike talked about the half-marathon he was considering training for, and they chatted some about running, the weather, and how much hillier northern Kentucky was than West Tennessee. They finished their cheesy slices and threw away their napkins and greasy plates.

"This has been really nice," Rachel said. "But I've got to get back to the shop."

"It has been nice. I'd like to see you again. Maybe this weekend? You're welcome to come check out the club tomorrow. Let me know, and I'll put your name and whoever you want to bring on the list. Wear black."

"Sure!" Rachel said. "Emily has been dying to check out Church. She'll be thrilled."

"Good," he said. "I've got to find my partner but I'll text you, ok?"

"That sounds great," Rachel said.

They hugged very briefly, and he smiled at her before walking away. She turned around, deciding to go the opposite way to avoid any awkwardness. She looked back only once and saw that he was still walking through the crowd but was texting on his phone.

"*He's worth another date,*" Rachel thought.

She looked at her own phone and realized she had taken fifteen minutes longer than she planned. Amorous thoughts vanished. She felt antsy to get back to the store, in case they needed her. It was unlikely. Between Mikaela and their other third-key supervisor, the store was pretty well managed even when Emily and Rachel weren't there. They had the capital to expand, but they were running into issues finding a suitable second location. Rachel had done some research, but there wasn't any urgency to it.

She started walking faster, stretching her long legs out for their full stride as she turned the corner. It was a longer walk back to the car this way around, but she would stop by the Wise Bean booth to make sure they were all set for the rest of the day. She was halfway back to the booth when something shining at the next booth in her path caught her eye. The table at the next booth was covered in crystals, fossils and rocks.

One in particular, a large milky pink ball, struck Rachel as beautiful. Before she knew it, she was right in front of the beautiful rose quartz sphere, which rested on a plain wooden stand. It was surrounded by glittering crystals, but something about the pink orb was alluring. It was small enough to fit in her hand but was bigger than her fist. The pale rose color was striped with blush pink veins that were almost white. It gleamed in the sun, polished to an almost mirror finish.

Rachel lingered, gazing at the milky pink ball for a couple minutes before she realized she herself was being examined. She looked up from the stone that had caught her to the short, blonde and blue-eyed clerk standing behind the booth. The woman was smiling at Rachel with a knowing look. For a moment, Rachel was certain she knew the woman's name. Then, the feeling was gone, replaced by the unsteady feeling that she had been in this exact situation before, despite all evidence to the contrary.

"That's a lovely piece you've found there," the clerk said.

"I, uh—Yeah, it sure is!" Rachel said, taken by surprise. She decided to pretend she hadn't been entranced by a rock. Regaining her professionalism, she stuck out her hand and the clerk took it and shook warmly.

"Rachel Ogden," Rachel said. "I'm one of the owners of Wise Bean coffee in Highland Heights. We've got a booth here ourselves if you need a caffeine boost."

"Morgan Wilson," the woman said. "I'm the owner of Crystal Crescent in Columbia-Tusculum. What you see here is just a small selection of what we carry in the store. In addition to crystals and jewelry, we also carry a very large selection of metaphysical supplies."

"Tarot cards and stuff like that?" Rachel asked politely. Her gaze had returned to the rose quartz ball. She wondered how much nonsense the woman was about to tell her—maybe she was going to offer her a hokey palm reading for a nominal fee. Rachel swatted the thought away and tried to listen with an open mind.

"Yes, ma'am," Morgan said. "I do my best to run an ethical shop. All our crystals are ethically sourced, hence the pricing. This one here is $70, including the hand-carved stand. Metaphysically speaking, many people associate this stone with love and emotional healing."

"Hmm," Rachel said. "To be honest, I think I just like it because it's beautiful."

"That's as good a reason as any," Morgan said, nodding. "Even if you aren't spiritual or religious at all, crystal collecting can still bring joy and beauty to your home."

"Spoken like a true saleswoman," Rachel said and grinned. "I may be an atheist, but I think you just sold me a crystal ball."

Morgan nodded and pulled tissue paper out of a box from below the table. She removed the ball from its wooden stand, wrapped it and placed it in the bag. As she wrapped the stand she looked up at Rachel with a slight smile.

"Have I met you before?" Morgan said. "You seem so familiar."

"I was about to ask you the same," Rachel said. "I'm having some Deja vu right now."

"Same here. Something like that anyway," Morgan said. "Tell you what. I'm throwing a few promotional things in here in case you decide to come look at our wares. We carry a lot of materials for witchcraft, but we also have a lot of pieces that can look very hip in a home or a coffee shop. Just last week, I received a 40-pound amethyst geode. Quite a showpiece."

Rachel nodded while she dug through her purse, thinking that she had no intention of buying more than one crystal. She wasn't even sure what she was going to do with this one, only that she had to have it. She would place it somewhere at home where she would see it every day. Maybe in the office, she thought. She handed Morgan her debit card, and Morgan swiped it on her smartphone's card reader attachment.

"Would you like a receipt?" Morgan asked.

"I'm ok," Rachel said. "Thank you though."

"Anytime!" Morgan said. "I hope we see you again."

"*Unlikely*," Rachel thought as she walked back to the Wise Bean booth to check in before walking back to her car.

3

"Fuck yeah!" Emily said, pumping her fist up and down. "We are gonna get so gothed up your Meemaw won't even recognize you."

"I don't know about that," Rachel said. Cadence and Mikaela were talking with a customer, so she had pulled Emily to the back of the tent.

"No corpse paint?" Emily said playfully. "You sure?"

Rachel laughed, picturing herself with white face paint with black around the eyes. Maybe a few stripes on the cheeks, like a member of KISS or a black metal band.

"You do what you like," Rachel said. "But I might try to get laid, so no. No corpse paint."

Emily shook her head, smiling.

"You're trying to lay the wrong kind of people," she joked. "Nothing says love like smeared paint. But for real, let's get a game plan going for tomorrow. Neither of us are closing. Since I have all the goth goodies at my house, let's get ready there."

"Sounds good. I'm going to head back to the shop and help close. I've got the mid-morning shift tomorrow so I'll probably hit the hay early tonight to make sure I'm rested."

"Good thinking," Emily said. "Are you sleeping better?"

"Not really," Rachel said. "I did go to the doctor yesterday. They said it's likely stress dreams."

"I'm sorry, bud," Emily said. "Maybe take a sleeping pill?"

"He prescribed me one. I just hate being groggy. Besides, it's not like I remember the dreams. I'd rather feel tense than muzzy in the morning. I'm gonna run, but let's text about tomorrow's plans."

"Sounds good," Emily said. "I'll holler if we need anything else here."

Rachel headed for the parking garage elevator ensconced in its glass booth. For the last month, she'd awoken multiple times during the night with her heart racing, covered in sweat. Her doctor had found nothing wrong with her and had suggested it was stress related. She'd tried a few things, like meditation and more exercise, but nothing had stopped the nightly disturbances. She'd go to sleep, then bolt awake, sometimes leaping from her bed as she awoke. Sometimes she was screaming.

She couldn't remember anything she had been dreaming about, but whenever she woke up like this, she felt sick to her stomach. The feeling seemed to linger on the next day if she focused on it. Mostly she tried not to think about it. She'd tried to remember what had happened in the nightmares, but found it made her feel worse. She didn't like to think about it.

"*Tonight I'm taking a sleeping pill,*" she thought as she pulled out of the parking garage. "*Just so I'm totally rested tomorrow. It'll be a big day.*"

Driving back to the shop, she reached for her drink in the cupholder. She took a sip of water from her reusable bottle. Her eyes widened as her mind offered up something it hadn't yet. She swallowed her water awkwardly and started to cough.

"*There was a cup in my nightmare,*" she thought. She couldn't picture the cup from her dream, but only knew with an unsettling certainty that it had been there. She tried hard to think, but nothing more would come.

She suddenly felt ill, like she had just woken up from the nightmare again. Her stomach whined as it struggled with the greasy pizza in it. Rachel turned her thoughts away from the nightmares.

"Why make myself sick over nothing?" Rachel said aloud. "At least you aren't still having nightmares about the fire anymore. Just be thankful for that."

She pushed the thoughts aside and focused on the road.

***

The front of Church looked like a miniature black stone cathedral. It was at least three stories high, with skinny windows crammed into tall towers that flanked the broad face of the building. Below the steeply pitched roof and between the turret capped towers, a red glass window shone with fierce light through black iron tracery shaped into a pentagram. Below it, underneath decorative stone molding and a set of beautiful arched windows, the words "CHURCH" protruded in brick from the front of the building. Red lights just under the letters cast long shadows that stretched the word out above it.

The drive from Kentucky had been just under half an hour. It was easy to get to Church from most places in the area since it was right off Central Parkway, one of the main boulevards running north and south. The location had initially raised some doubts, as it was mostly warehouses and churches nearby.

A local columnist suggested the business would fail since there wasn't anything else for people to do in that area, but it was clear to Emily and Rachel that Church was starting off well. The pointed archway of the building's entrance had a line of dark clothed people waiting that wrapped around the right corner of the building. Rachel and Emily only found parking in a pay lot on the street behind the building.

They walked from the back toward the front of the building, but it was obvious that Church was meant to be viewed from the front. A loading dock and a set of gray metal doors marked the back, while the sides and back of the buildings were mostly windowless, featuring just a couple of plain exit doors. The few windows on the sides were arched and paneled with stained glass, but their patterns were not as ornate as the building's stone front.

It was only when they were in line and close enough to the face of the building that Rachel realized it wasn't stone at all but some kind of plastic composite. She ran her hand over one of the rock shaped panels, feeling the manufactured roughness. They had made the material look ancient, and it reminded Rachel of a haunted house she'd been to a few years prior.

"Excited?" Emily asked. She had turned to face Rachel toward the back of the line.

"I'm jazzed to get my dance on," Rachel said, taking her hand from the building. "I don't think I've been to a club for years. Wasn't the last time we went to one for Cadence's bachelorette party?"

"Oh man," Emily said. "I forgot about that. That was only a few years ago. I can't get that hungover anymore."

"Me either," Rachel said, faking a gag. "No jello shots."

"No. Definitely not."

The line moved quickly, and soon they were ushered into the archway and through the double doors into the club. When they entered, the main dance floor was to their right. Through the crowd, Rachel could see the floor was lit up with blue light. The ceilings were much higher than she had imagined from the outside. She turned her attention back to her right, handing her driver's license to the woman at the ticket counter. After she and Emily had their hands stamped, they headed toward the bar.

There were two bars on the main floor—one just past the dance floor and one toward the back surrounded by high top tables. They walked to the bar at the back, ordering drinks from a thin red headed man wearing a black polo. His hair was buzzed on the sides but long on top, pulled back into a bun on the top of his crown. The style showed off the tattoos on his neck. They were all minimalist and geometric in nature, but the tattoo behind his ear caught Rachel's attention. It looked like a single striped chevron.

"My name's Kevin. What can I get you two beautiful young ladies?" he asked, winking at Emily.

"Two gin and tonics," Emily said.

"Coming right up, gorgeous," Kevin said.

He scooped ice into two plastic cups, measured out and added gin before filling the cups with tonic water from a hose. He put straws in the cups and then handed them to Emily. Rachel thought he looked kind of cute although cheesy. She looked at his tattoo again.

It was made up of five letter V's stacked almost right on top of each other. A straight line ran a stem through the center of the four larger V's, and a small V bloomed on top of the stem. This little V was the only V that did not have two tiny V's attached to each of its arms. At first she had thought it was a rune, but it looked more like a bug.

"Two gin and tonics for two beautiful women," he said.

Emily handed him her card. After starting her tab, she and Rachel walked to a high top table closer to the dance floor. The music was loud but good, an aggressively urgent electronic beat with a grinding groove to it. She was pretty sure she heard the sound of a whip crack repeating somewhere in the mix. The floor was packed with bodies moving and sweating, but even outside the dance floor the club was busy.

"He was flirting with you," Rachel said as they made their way through the crowd.

"If I wanted to fuck a bartender, I'd get on Tindr," Emily said and then laughed.

Rachel sipped her drink and raised as eyebrow.

"I'm not interested in dating anyone right now is what I mean," Emily said. "I don't feel like it."

"That's cool," said Rachel. "I don't feel like I need to date anybody. I wouldn't mind it. I dunno. It's been a long time."

"I hope Mike's nice," Emily said after another sip of her drink.

"Me too," Rachel said. "I texted him when we parked. I hope he's as into his work as I am, but that we see him at least a little bit tonight."

"I'm sure we will," Emily said and smiled at her friend. "His eyes were glued to you the whole time he was visiting the booth yesterday."

"Yeah, he seems a little inexperienced but sweet," Rachel said. She finished her drink. "Wanna dance?"

Emily finished her drink and the two worked their way into the crowded dance floor. Rachel had noticed it was lit from underneath when they walked in, but walking on the brightly-colored floor, she saw it was designed to look like stained glass. She looked up and saw people on the second floor peering over a glass balcony, drinking and dancing.

The DJ was dressed as Jack the Ripper or a Victorian vampire. Rachel wasn't sure. He had on a large top hat and a black cloak. He kept the cape wrapped around his shoulders except for when he dramatically shrugged it aside to raise his hands in the air.

"Get your hands up!" he whooped into the microphone. "Get your hands up!"

Rachel and Emily put their hands in the air as the song built up and up to a climax. The crowd around them was a sea of raised hands and gyrating bodies as the song changed. The bassline dropped out, before a distorted choir began whispering a chant punctuated by rapid drums. Then the music changed to whispering, with clicking and hissing as percussion.

"Get those hands in the air!" the DJ cried. "Here we go!"

All instruments kicked back in at full force, and everyone on the floor writhed in time to the beat. Space cleared around a break dancing man in a black jumpsuit, gas mask and black high top shoes. The crowd pushed Rachel and Emily further back on the dance floor. After dancing until she felt like a break, Rachel pointed upstairs and looked at Emily, who nodded.

They climbed a black staircase with neon purple lights built into the handrail, following two women in matching Wednesday Adams dresses. Rachel was glad she had borrowed some of Emily's more elaborate black clothes. She had brought what she thought was a nice blouse and skirt to Emily's house to get ready, but Emily had set her up with a different outfit, dark eye makeup and dark red lipstick. They both wore all black, with Rachel wearing a black A-line dress layered with black lace that was snugly flattering around her waist and fluttered around her knees. Emily wore fishnet stockings and a black halter dress that hugged her curves.

She felt they both looked like models and insisted on taking several photos together before they left Emily's house. She couldn't deny she was excited for Mike to see her dressed up like this. As if on cue, her phone buzzed in her pocket. Mike was taking a break in a few minutes. She texted that they would be at the upstairs bar.

They walked past the balcony that overlooked the main dance floor, but not before Rachel snuck a peek, stepping around the black wooden pews that edged around the balcony. The throng on the dance floor seemed to have multiplied in the time it took them to get upstairs. There were so many bodies that Rachel couldn't even see the dance floor except in snatches of light. Pulses of blue, orange, red and white shone occasionally through the crook of someone's elbow or between dancers. She hoped she got a look at it when it was less crowded.

Rachel and Emily found a second, much smaller dance floor on the second floor, along with several rows of booths separated by white gauze hung from the ceiling. Different black and white horror movies were projected on the fabric. Rachel caught a glimpse of a scene where a woman was kneeling on the floor next to a bed. She moved a rug aside to reveal a trap door, and she leaned down to listen to something going on underneath.

Rachel felt a hand on her elbow and jumped.

"Sorry, I didn't mean to startle you," Mike said in her ear. "That scene's from *The City of the Dead* with Christopher Lee. Rachel, I thought you might like it since the Misfit's song "Horror Hotel" is based on it. Sorry—Can I get you two a round of drinks? You look thirsty."

"Sure!" Emily said.

"Thank you," Rachel said. She knew she was blushing. He had picked a movie to play for her?

They grabbed three chairs at the end of the big bar that wrapped around the back right corner of the room. The bar itself was made of clear acrylic cast over piles of crystals, strange coins, tarot cards and occult trinkets, backlit by neon purple light that made the strange objects look even weirder. Behind the bar, three women in black polos mixed drinks.

"I'll take a water, and whatever they want is on me," he told one of the bartenders, who nodded and looked at Emily and Rachel.

"Gin and tonic, please," Emily said.

"I'll take a Jack and Coke please," Rachel said.

"Are y'all having a good time?" Mike asked.

"Absolutely," Rachel said. "This place is gorgeous."

"Congrats on the packed house for opening night," Emily said. "I'm sure you and your partner are very pleased."

"Oh, we are," Mike said. "This was a much better turn out than we expected. The social media campaign our PR people launched has been like magic. The analyst said a night club wouldn't do well here, but we're proving him wrong."

"Man, I want PR people," Rachel said.

"Me too. Maybe once we've got more than one store," Emily said.

Rachel nodded and then looked at Mike. She had been putting off research on the second location, but she didn't want to think about that right now.

"Are the clubs in Memphis this popular?" Rachel asked, remembering Mike's company had two other locations in the south.

"Oh, yes," Mike said. "We have a semi-goth club in Memphis. Not as elaborate as this one, but it's packed to the gills every time we do a goth night. The more mainstream club regularly goes over capacity. They're the right kind of problem to have for a club, but my partner wanted to branch out to a different city instead of opening another Memphis club."

"Makes sense," Rachel said. "Cannibalization."

"What?" Mike said. He smirked, showing just his left dimple.

"You know," Rachel said, "Eating into your own profits by having too many sites near each other. It's the same reason we haven't opened a second shop yet. I'm in charge of the research, but I haven't found anywhere yet that fits. If we open one in downtown, our northern Kentucky store might lose some of its commuter customers to the new store, which doesn't make more money for us."

"Yeah, I forgot that term," Mike said. "I hate marketing. I leave a lot of that stuff up to the higher-ups."

"I thought you were a partner?" Emily said.

"I am," Mike said. "I'm part-owner of this club. You met the other owner, Karen. She's a lot better at the business end, and I'm a lot better at people management. Sorry, I didn't mean to get y'all into a business conversation. Can I get you two some shots?"

"No, I'm ok," Rachel said. "And I never mind talking about business."

"Me either," Emily said, smiling. "But I will take that shot."

Mike ordered a shot for Emily, which she tapped on the bar and then downed.

"I'm going to check out the dance floor up here," she said and moved away before Rachel could reply, leaving her there with Mike.

"*That sneak,*" Rachel thought.

She looked over at Mike, who was already looking at her. He smiled, and Rachel grinned when she saw his dimples. He was wearing a black button-down shirt with the club's logo stitched into the left breast pocket. It was a pentagram with the word "Church" sewn below it in white.

"I'm glad you came out," he said.

"Me too," Rachel said. "I haven't been to a club in forever, but this is a lot of fun."

"You look beautiful," Mike said.

"Thanks. I wore black," Rachel said and winked.

Mike flashed an abashed smile. He looked away, scanning the crowd on the second floor.

"Yeah, I kicked myself later for saying that," Mike said. "Like you were gonna show up in any other color to a goth club."

"I mean, I do as I like," Rachel said. "So you never know."

Mike looked at her now and grinned.

"Would you maybe like to get dinner with me soon?" Mike said.

"Yeah," Rachel said, smiling. "That sounds nice. Got anywhere in mind?"

"I have a few places I want to check out next week," Mike said. "I'll text you and we'll set it up."

"Cool," Rachel said.

"I've got to get back to work, but save me a dance?" Mike said. "I'll come check on you in a while to see if you need anything."

"Thank you," Rachel said. "You're so sweet."

Mike moved to give her a hug, and this time they embraced without hesitation. It was a comfortable hug, and Mike gave her a squeeze before letting her go. He walked behind the bar and disappeared behind a black swinging door. Rachel finished her drink before searching for Emily on the dance floor.

4

Around 2 a.m., the crowd began to dwindle. Rachel looked down from one of the wooden black pews lining the second-floor glass balcony. There were fewer people on the blue dance floor now, so she was able to see the stained glass pattern of the floor.

Different colored plastic panels in geometric shapes joined to form a hypnotic spiral that spun out from the center of the dance floor. A thin black coil twisted in field of glowing blue, white, red, and orange shapes. The panes were cut and placed so they appeared to follow along with the spiral, which doubled in size with each quarter turn. The effect on the eye was mesmerizing, and Rachel looked up only when Emily returned with plastic cups of ice water for them.

Emily let out a long sigh as she sat down on the bench next to her. She stretched her legs out in front of her, tapping the clear balcony with her feet.

"I'm pooped," Emily said, smiling.

"Me too," Rachel said. "I'm gonna text Mike and tell him we're about to head out."

She got out her phone and sent him the message, then took a sip of her ice water. Emily rubbed on her calves.

"I'm gonna have to do some stretches before bed," Emily said. "I'll be sore from all this dancing tomorrow."

"It's been a really good workout. Although I think we should stop by White Castle on the way back. What do you think?"

Emily nodded and took another sip of water. Rachel's phone buzzed with Mike saying he'd be right up, and he hoped she saved a dance for him. She texted him back saying she felt up to the challenge. He was soon with them at the pews, asking Emily if he could borrow Rachel.

She laughed and shooed them away. Rachel promised she'd be back soon, and then Mike took her hand and led her downstairs. They went to the main dance floor, where the DJ was playing a dance track with gloomy synthesizers and a heavy beat.

They danced close to each other at first, not touching each other but moving on their own to the beat. But after a few moments, Mike put one of his hands on her waist, and she put an arm on his shoulders. They moved closer together as they danced, and she felt his other hand wrap around her waist and pull her near.

Pressed against him, she felt more aroused than she had in a long time. It felt good to be this close to someone. She had joked with Emily about trying to get laid tonight, but she saw it happening pretty soon if things kept up. They kept good rhythm with the beat, and she put her other arm around his shoulders and looked up at him, daring him in her mind. It worked. He kissed her, a gentle kiss with no tongue. She kissed him back just a little harder, and afterwards Mike looked at her with what she thought looked like just enough restraint in his eyes.

"Would you like to have a nightcap in my office?"

"Sure," she said, grinning.

Mike led her off the dance floor, around the ticket booth to the door next to the stairs. He tapped his nametag on the gray scanner panel next to the door's handle. The red light on the top of the scanner box blinked green. Mike opened the door, and she followed him downstairs.

It was lit much brighter than the dim club, and it took her eyes a moment to adjust. She kept her hand on the handrail as they walked down the flight of steps to another door with a badge scanner. He tapped his badge again and pushed the door open when the light turned green, leading the way into the lower floor.

A security guard in a black polo eyed them, then nodded at Mike. He was an older man with buzzed white hair who obviously spent a lot of time on the weights. He crossed his thickly muscled arms as he watched them pass. He stood in front of one of three rooms with closed doors locked with ID scanners, which Rachel assumed contained their safe and other security equipment.

Mike led her past the guard, past open conference rooms and more closed doors with ID scanners. They walked all the way to the back of the building. The conference rooms on the left continued all the way to the back of the building, but the right side emptied into an open loading zone ending with the closed metal dock door. There were shelves with supplies in labeled boxes on the other side of the guarded rooms. A few wooden pallets were stacked next to a second stairwell, but otherwise the back right side of the building was swept clean. She turned to her left and saw Mike tap his ID on the scanner for the room closest to the back door.

"Welcome to my office," he said. "It's not much yet, but it's my home away from home lately."

She stepped in after him, and the door swung shut behind her. The room was soundproofed. It was so quiet compared to the loud club above them that Rachel could hear her ears ringing. It almost felt like she was in a different place entirely. She felt a whisper of apprehension creep up in her brain.

"*I just met this guy and am now locked in a basement with him in a nightclub,*" she thought before she could stop herself. "*No, no, no. Stop that. It's fine. This is your second time meeting him in person, and Emily knows where you are. This guy is harmless anyway. And hot! Just relax.*"

She watched as he poured each of them a finger of bourbon into two lowball glasses from a tray in the corner of his office. It was sparsely decorated, with a large black desk and a few upholstered chairs. A framed poster for the Robert Eggers movie *The Witch* hung on the wall behind the desk, showing the silhouette of a woman in a moonlit forest grove, surrounded by the outstretched branches of the trees around her.

Mike turned around and handed her a glass.

"Have you seen it?" Mike asked.

"I did not," Rachel said. "I'll be honest, I haven't seen a lot of horror movies, aside from slasher flicks."

"Jason and Freddy?"

"Yup, I love those," she said. "Emily and I joke about what a good employee Jason Voorhees would be."

"Really?" Mike said and raised an eyebrow.

"Think about it," she said. "He's creative. He never kills the same way twice. And that drive! When Jason puts his mind to something, it gets done. There's literally no stopping him."

"I like it," he laughed. "But you should see *The Witch*. It's nothing like *Friday the 13th*, but it is intense. Slow-building, but so worth it."

"Maybe you can show it to me," she said. "I'm down for more horror. I know a lot of Misfit's songs are based on old horror movies, but I haven't seen any of them. Except for part of *The City of the Dead* now, thanks to you."

"Yeah, the Misfits' song is 'Horror Hotel' and Danzig's version doesn't really spoil anything."

"What's it about?"

"Hmm," Mike thought. "Without me ruining it for you? Let's see. A woman goes to a small town to learn about its history with witchcraft. Things get creepier from there. The atmosphere is so suspenseful, so creepy."

He blew a chef's kiss, and they both giggled.

"I'll have to check it out," she said.

Rachel sipped her bourbon and was impressed. It was heavy on rye, giving it an almost floral spicy taste. Much better than the Old Grand-dad she kept above the fridge. She noticed him looking at her.

"This is great," she said. "Thank you."

"Of course," he said. "Thank you for gracing my office with your company. It's not often I have a beautiful woman in here, let alone one that likes bourbon."

Rachel rolled her eyes and smiled.

"What? Is that a thing?" he said.

"Yeah," she said. "Thank you, but the idea that only certain genders can enjoy such basic pleasures as whiskey is pretty silly."

Mike chuckled and then nodded.

"Fair," he said. "Either way, I'm glad you're here."

"Me too," she said, taking another sip. "This has been a lot of fun."

"Good," he said. "I'm glad you've had a good time."

He finished his bourbon and set his glass down on the desk. Rachel finished hers and set it next to his. He took one look at her and pulled her in his arms. They kissed gently at first, but things quickly grew more passionate. Rachel felt him slip his tongue in her mouth and went with it. She ran a hand across his chest and kissed him again before pulling her head away.

They were pressed up against the edge of the desk, and he had one arm wrapped around her waist. She could feel a bulge pressed against her, and the realization made her literally step back from him. She smoothed down the skirt of her dress, even though it wasn't wrinkled.

"Phew," she said, biting her lip. "This is a little fast for me. I should get back to Emily. But I'd like to see you again."

"Same here," he said. "Are you free on Tuesday night? I've got the evening off if you'd like to help me explore some of the good food in Highland Heights."

They made plans for a dinner date, and then Mike led Rachel out of the office and back up the hall. Before they reached the stairs, the white-haired security guard raised a fist to his mouth and cleared his throat. She and Mike continued past him and were at the door to the stairs when the guard spoke.

"Sir?" he said to Mike. "A word, please."

"Rachel, go on ahead," Mike said. "I'll text you."

Mike gave Rachel a quick peck of a kiss before she could react. She grinned, kind of glad that he was always ready to jump into work. He had bragged about his people management skills online, and she hadn't seen much of them yet. She started upstairs slowly with the intention of eavesdropping. Then she rolled her eyes at herself for being weird and hurried upstairs to find Emily. It was time to go home.

***

Mike and the guard listened for the door to close, cutting off the muffled club noise and bringing the basement floor to silence once again. Once it was quiet, the guard fixed Mike with an unfriendly stare.

"Did she have clearance to be down here?"

"I gave her clearance Wayne," Mike said. "Please don't start with me today."

"Did Karen?"

Mike rolled his eyes and turned toward the door, twisting the handle.

"I'll be letting her know," the guard said.

"Fine," Mike said, closing the door behind him and walking heavily up the stairs to the top level.

***

Emily reached into the paper bag for another cheese slider. Finding the last one, she slipped it out of its package. She finished off the burger in a few bites, then took another sip of soda. She looked over at Rachel, who had fallen asleep on the drive back after scarfing down three sliders. Her head was resting against the window in a way that did not look comfortable.

Emily turned onto the highway leading back to Kentucky. They'd be at her house in 10 minutes probably, with traffic this light. Only a few other cars were out on the road once she got out of downtown. She wondered idly how long Church would stay in business.

"That was too fun," she thought. *"But there's no way they're going to get that much turnout after the first few weeks. I don't get why they opened a location here and not somewhere with a stronger goth or nightclub scene, but I'm really glad they did."*

Rachel snorted and then started awake, gasping and panting.

"Hey, hey," Emily said. "It's ok. Holy crap."

Rachel looked around, her eyes wide. She sat up straight and sighed heavily. Then she put her hands to her face and pressed, rubbing outward. She was trying to wipe away the dreadful feeling she had but only succeeded in smearing black eye makeup on the outer sides of her eyes.

"Damn," she said, then took a deep breath. "I don't remember what was happening, but it was awful."

"I'm sorry," Emily said. "At least you don't remember? That's better than being stuck with a bunch of bad memories, right?"

Emily realized what she said could be taken the wrong way. She didn't mean it in that particular way. She knew Rachel knew she didn't mean it that way, but she couldn't help but feel bad.

"Shit, let me rephrase: It's good that you don't remember the dream, right?"

"It's ok," Rachel said. "You're right. I mean about the dream and about the fire. It means my brain is protecting me. Thank you for remembering."

"I'm sorry," Emily said. "I really only meant about the nightmare."

"No, you're right," Rachel said. "Don't be sorry. I'm glad you remember that I think I'm missing some memories. A therapist actually told me I thought about it too much while fucked up in high school and warped the memories somehow."

"That's depressing."

"Tell me about it," Rachel said. "It's ok. I like my version better anyway. Less painful to think about."

"I'm always here if you want to talk about that night," Emily said. "I mean it. I'm here for you."

"Thanks," Rachel said. "It'd probably be good. I know last time we talked about it, I felt better. But I just don't like to remember it. I'll let you know if I change my mind."

Emily pulled into her driveway, and they both got out of the car. They hugged before Rachel got into her own car. Rachel waited until Emily was in her house before driving off. It started to drizzle on the 5-minute drive to her own house and had begun to rain in earnest when Rachel was unlocking her door.

She scrubbed off her makeup, changed into her pajamas and crawled into bed. It had been a good day. She let her mind drift, thinking about how Mike's arms had felt wrapped around her. Exhausting from dancing all night, she fell asleep to the sound of rain on the roof and thunder in the distance.

5

The storm worsened as Rachel slept. Rain lashed at roofs, and wind whipped through the streets, houses and trees so fast that if anyone had been awake in Rachel's neighborhood, they would have shivered at the sounds and pulled their covers tighter. Pea sized hail pellets pinged and bounced wildly off cars and homes until they melted in the deluge. Lighting struck a transformer down the street from where Rachel slept soundly, dowsing the area in darkness.

Rachel woke up only when lightning struck close enough to her house that the sound of thunder shook her awake. She opened her eyes in time for a blinding flash of lightning that filled her room with light. She sat up in bed, rubbing her eyes and wondering why she needed to go to her office. She knew she had to go there, but she couldn't explain the impulse.

"*Why?*" Rachel thought, even as she pushed the covers aside and slid her legs off the bed.

She stood up, grumbling but shuffling toward her bedroom door. Flashes of lightning illuminated the handle as she grabbed it before the house went dark again. She palmed the wall as she walked down the hall, still asking herself why she was walking to her office. She couldn't think of an answer, but she didn't stop.

She pushed open the door to her office, stepped in and closed it behind her. In the dark, she saw little except the silhouette of her cluttered desk. On top of stacks of paper and junk was the bag she had bought from Crystal Crescent. Ignoring the rest of the bag's contents, she had pulled out the rose quartz orb when she had returned home from the fair. She had put on the windowsill in her office, so that it would be to her left when she worked from home in the mornings. She liked looking at it, and so far its presence brought her a cheer she couldn't explain with its looks alone.

But now something was different. She felt pulled toward the orb, knowing something was about to happen. The feeling was so visceral she stopped questioning it. She had to be closer to it. She hurried around her desk, pulled out her desk chair and sat in front of the window to watch the pink ball.

Raising her hand, she reached out to touch it. She could feel a strong prickling sensation when her hand was a few inches away. It felt like what she could only think of as energy crackling around the orb, like the lightning outside. It wasn't visible energy, but she could feel it just the same, like a powerful static electricity. She pulled her hand back when a crash of thunder outside shook her nerve. She knew it wouldn't hurt her, but she didn't know why this was so.

Abruptly, another strange thought came to her: The orb was gathering energy, or something was putting energy into it. This made her feel strange, as though she was still dreaming. Suddenly she felt the tips of her toes begin to tingle, almost like the top joints of her feet fell asleep. She sat back in the chair and shook her feet, weirded out.

Instead of fading, the prickling feeling spread upwards from her toe tips to her ankles. Rachel bent over in the chair and rubbed at her feet, telling herself it was something to do with all the dancing. But she knew that wasn't true. The feeling spread up to her knees. Lightning flashed outside, and Rachel shivered. Up to her stomach now felt like frozen pins and needles were tapping on her nerves. It didn't hurt, but she didn't like it. She also didn't like how she knew it was almost over.

The creeping sensation rushed up her spine and into her arms and head. She felt it all the way to the tips of her fingers. Her head felt like it was crackling, and she stood up. Her rational brain tried to tell her she needed to call 911. She pushed the thoughts away easily. She had goosebumps and felt strange, but she wasn't in pain and she felt safe.

The tingling feeling evaporated, and Rachel felt normal again. At least physically. She looked at her hands, but then jerked her head up. There was a soft pink light in the room now. It was coming from the rose quartz sphere. As she watched it seemed to grow brighter.

She told herself it was flashes of lightning reflecting in the orb, but she knew that wasn't true. Her eyes went to the window to look at the storm. Rachel jumped as a bolt of lightning arced out of the sky and down into her backyard, striking the towering birch tree at the back of her yard with a roaring boom.

Light seemed to fill the branches and then quickly disappear, and Rachel felt the ground tremble. Lightning struck again, but this time there was no noise. The bright white light filled up the room, and Rachel could see a woman standing outside the window in the flashes of light. Her hand was reaching at the glass. As quickly as it had come, the apparition disappeared, but the face of the woman was seared into Rachel's memory. She knew that face. She would never, could never forget that face, even if there had been nights when she was terrified she would.

Rachel gasped and pushed away from the window and the orb. The back of her chair hit the long part of her L-shaped desk, upsetting the junk pile. The bag from Crystal Healing toppled over, and a small book slid off and smacked onto the floor. Rachel had not looked at it when it was given to her, nor had she bothered to take it out of the bag once she had the rose quartz orb out. But the book seemed different to her now in a way that she couldn't place.

There was nothing special about it, but the impulse to pick it up was strong. She got on her knees on the floor, picked up the book and turned it over in her hands. It was a promotional notebook, bound with a purple matte cover. "Crystal Crescent" was embossed on the cover underneath a crescent moon. She flipped through the wide-ruled pages quickly. All of it was blank except for the first page, on which someone with excellent penmanship had written the following strange words:

"You must protect yourself! Life or DEATH. Enemies may come and go unless you barricade against them. Create a barrier to protect your home and mind.

BEWARE - All magic comes at a cost!

The cost for this spell is one drop of your blood and three bronze coins. If bronze is not attainable, look to the elements.

Materials: Blackened birch wand, Kitchen salt and black rope

Stand in a hexagon of salt and knot the cord. While creating each knot, think only of protecting yourself and your home. Use visuals in your mind to help cement your intention. Picture something sheltering you and your area.

STAY SAFE! Practice magic only if necessary and only if you have material to cover the cost."

Rachel took the book back to her bed, but it was a long time before she fell back asleep. Every time she felt herself start to drift into slumber, she would start awake and grab the purple book off the nightstand. She'd stare aghast at the page, not believing it to be real. She'd put it back, close her eyes and try to relax, telling herself that she'd be able to think about all this clearly after a full night's rest. Sleep mercifully took her around 6 a.m.

***

Rachel woke up with a start, which she had almost become used to at this point. She took a few deep breaths to calm her racing heart. Her hand brushed against the thin notebook laying on her covers, and she looked down at it and remembered. She swung out of bed and ran out of her room to the office, through the door to the rose quartz orb on the windowsill. She put her hand on the pink crystal ball.

There was no prickling energy. It felt cold, but not unusually cold. Just the same chill touch any piece of glass might have after an evening of air conditioning. She looked at her hands, remembering the prickling sensation that had worked its way up her body. That had been real, she was certain of it. It had been so strange, but she hadn't been scared.

"Maybe I was struck by lightning," she suggested to herself. "And that's why I think I saw her. That's not anymore ridiculous. Except that you're here, thinking and breathing. Nothing's burnt."

She looked around the window, hoping to find some charred marks that would mean something explainable. She then looked up at the birch tree at the back of her yard. It had been split at the top, but it wasn't severed all the way through. The branches there were blackened, but it looked like it hadn't cut through the tree completely. Rachel figured it might live. Charred and broken branches dangled in the crooked eaves of the tree, and many more were flung all around the yard.

"I didn't imagine anything," she thought, confused but sure of that much.

None of it felt like a dream in the morning light. Not that she'd remembered a dream in months. She knew she had to do something, otherwise she'd think herself into a panic attack. It would be best to do some work, she decided.

She put her reddish-brown hair in a ponytail, pulled on her boots and went out to see the storm damage. In the backyard, the birch tree seemed mostly intact. The side facing the house had been struck, but there was no damage on the other side of the tree. Scattered across the ground were the debris and sticks that had been blown off by the wind or shot off by the lighting. Rachel got a contractor bag from the garage and walked around the yard picking up fallen branches.

She wiped her brow on the back of her arm and then reached for the next branch, an almost arm length stick of charred black birch. She felt a sudden flood of certainty as her hand wrapped around the wood, which faintly prickled against her palm. She dropped the stick, and the feeling vanished.

She squatted down and picked up the stick again. It was as though there was a distant rumble deep within the bough. As she looked at the burnt branch she understood that this was the birch wand she needed for the spell, and that it needed to be placed next to the rose quartz orb. She stared for a moment at the stick in her hand and tried to reject the thought. It didn't work. The wand simply needed to be with the orb.

Rachel felt peculiar but brushed the feelings away. She decided she was just feeling inspired. She also felt moved to put the orb and wand on a purple silk scarf she took out of the top drawer of her dresser. The scarf was special to her, as it was one of the few items her mother had left her with it when she had left her at her paternal grandparents. Her father had died when she was very young, and her mother had left her with Grandma and Grandpa to be raised when she was eight years old.

They seemed to blame her mother for the loss of their son, but never out loud around Rachel, at least at first. But however they tried, the blame lived with them, and they never had a kind word to say about Rachel's mother. It tore Rachel's heart for years, but she understood and tried to be compassionate. She knew they missed their son, just like she missed her father and her mother. She was mostly behaved, but she was at their throats whenever they made snide guesses about where her mother went.

They fought more often about it as she got older, until eventually they learned to keep their remarks to themselves.

They used to say to each other that Rachel's mother Theresa was too messed up on drugs to make time for her daughter anymore. That she wasn't even writing letters. She had though. The letters had come almost as soon as she had left.

They had been sporadic throughout her youth, with gaps of months and even a year in between with no letters. She didn't always respond to the letters Rachel sent, but she always had advice that had helped Rachel as she struggled through her teens without her mother. But the letters stopped before Rachel graduated high school. No letters or any communication had come from her mother after she turned 17.

Rachel spent her late teens determined to mourn in a self-destructive way, sneaking out to party and returning home late at night only to sleep through her morning classes. Her grandparents were concerned and did their best by her, but she realized for herself the futility of her self-imposed misery when it was time to choose a college. Her grades were ok, but she had not done well enough in high school to get into any of the schools she had wanted. She went to the closest college, where she worked hard toward the goal of owning her own business.

She was lucky enough to meet Emily her freshman year. The fire of Emily's drive was contagious, and soon Rachel was spending most days studying with Emily. They were roommates for several years while they worked to get the business off the ground. Now they were doing so well they'd had to hire an accountant to manage their growing finances.

Rachel was no longer that troubled teenage girl, but she had never stopped missing her mom. Until last night, when the lightning struck the tree and she saw her. Her face was older, but she had the same kind, dark eyes. In her memories of the flash, she could see her clearly. She knew that it was her mother who had stood in the light outside her window. It was her mother who had given her the spell to protect herself. But against what?

6

"You're getting ahead of yourself," Rachel told herself. "This is nuts. You need to find the rational explanation. There's always been one before."

She reread the note 30 times that morning, sitting in her desk chair in her office with a cup of coffee. Occasionally she looked up with suspicion at the black birch wand and rose quartz orb laying on the purple scarf, half expecting them to skitter off the windowsill. But she couldn't explain their strangeness, so she tried to focus on the note.

For a moment, she saw herself with skeptical eyes. There was a truth in her now, it felt like. She didn't want to call it intuition, because intuition had always sounded like bullshit to her. Wasn't it just another word for truth? But if intuition was just a survival mechanism for safety, maybe it too had been heightened when she received her power.

"The note could be a prank," Rachel said, hoping it sounded real out loud and knowing the alternative wouldn't. "The Crystal Crescent woman could have played a really disturbing prank on me. Morgan gave me the book, after all."

She closed her eyes and replayed the purchase from two days before. It hadn't been that unusual. And Morgan hadn't been too pushy. But there had been something off, hadn't there? Hadn't she recognized Morgan from somewhere before?

It wasn't that her face looked familiar, or her name or business. It was her. There was something familiar about her that Rachel had picked up on that had given her the weirdest Deja vu. Morgan had said something about it too.

"*What if she knows me and I forgot her?*" Rachel thought. "*Maybe this is a prank on me for forgetting her name. We probably met at another*

Cincinnati festival, maybe one of the ones in Fountain Square. It seems like we're always there."

She could see her mother's face in her mind, the way she had looked last night. She had only seen her for an instant, but it had been her high cheekbones and her eyes. That hadn't been a prank, and she knew it with such a weird certainty that she tried to talk herself out of it.

"That could have been your reflection," she tried.

It hadn't been the first time she thought it. For just a moment last night, her mind had told her that the woman on the other side of the glass had been her reflection. But she had seen her own likeness on the glass too. No, she knew it hadn't been her mirror image last night.

"Ok, so you saw your mother's ghost. That's not such a big deal, right? There's all kinds of shows online and on TV about people seeing ghosts. Just because you got this note at the same time doesn't mean it's from your mom or that you even have to do anything it says."

Rachel furrowed her eyebrows, thinking again about how Morgan had looked so familiar. Had she been in the shop before? It was easy enough to picture her standing in front of the wooden counter at Wise Bean. Probably ordering an herbal tea. Talking to Emily?

But there was no way Emily was involved. She was sure of it. Rachel thought about the dark language of the note, with death in all capitals. This wasn't a prank. It was a warning from her mother, she was sure of it. It couldn't be from anyone else. She suddenly knew what she needed to see to really believe it.

Rachel jumped out of her office chair and went to her filing cabinet. She tore open the top drawer and riffled through some files before coming up with a handful of white envelopes. They were some of the letters her mother had sent her from when she was 8 to when she was 17. She closed the filing cabinet and turned on her heel, holding the letters to her chest.

She walked back to her chair and sat down before opening one of the envelope's flaps and pulling out a folded letter. She placed it on the desk next to the purple notebook. Taking a deep breath, she unfolded the letter. She pressed down the seams of the old paper so that it would stay flat. Then she opened the purple book to its first page and compared the two.

The handwriting was the same. There was no doubt about it. Both were written in the same neat, tidy lettering. Her mother, who had disappeared entirely 13 years ago, had written her a note from the other side of the grave. A note instructing her to perform witchcraft in order to protect herself from an ominous unnamed threat. The only things preventing Rachel from picking up her phone and calling her therapist's office was the bizarre touch of the orb and wand. That and the electric certainty that she had imagined nothing when she saw her outside the window.

She thought for a while on what she should do. Clearly the spell was the top priority, if she were to accept what was written in the book as real. No matter how much she tried to push the thought away, it persisted. She tried to do other errands around the house, but her mind kept returning to the first page of the purple book.

She came back to her office after lunch. She cleaned, filing papers that needed to be kept and throwing others away. She wiped her desk clean and vacuumed until all the spots in the carpet were gone. She put up the letters from her mother and hid the purple notebook out of her sight. Then she opened up her laptop and started to research witchcraft.

"*If I'm going to do this, I need to know what I'm getting into,*" she thought. "*Before I make any decisions.*"

She started with free online encyclopedia entries, reading on Wikipedia. She didn't stop reading for hours. She knew the basics about the Salem witch trials from school, but she hadn't heard about the trials in other countries. She tried to absorb as much information as she could before coming to a decision. It seemed inevitable that she would cast the spell, but she was damned if she wasn't going to try to talk herself out of it.

By far the scariest possibility was that the kind of witchcraft her mother meant was the evil kind. There was blood involved. It sounded like less than the amount a diabetic person needs to test their blood sugar, but it was blood. Rachel wasn't ignorant of the significance. What was next? Was she going to have to sign her name in a book under the red eyes of a black goat? Cannibalism? Were they the sort of sadistic witches that sniff out children and virgins for torture or meat pies? The kind that's always making blood sacrifices and inviting small children into her oven?

But that didn't seem right at all. Rachel's senses felt heightened, and her sense of certainty told her nothing was certain about her family's magic but one thing: it seemed grounded in pain. She wondered why blood was necessary at first, but she let go of her fear and examined it instead.

Nothing in the letter gave it any kind of malevolent intent. It was scary, but it was a warning to protect herself. There was no mention of the devil or any dark being to whom she would need to pledge herself. It said she just needed the branch, orb, salt, and some black rope. She was weirded out by the drop of her blood required, but it seemed such a small amount that she was ok with it. She would be the only one handling the blood, and she could keep things sterile.

There were other kinds of witches, of course. Rachel had heard about Wicca and modern Pagan religions, so she did some light reading on those online. Emily had tried out Wicca in college, so she remembered some from then and that didn't seem right either. She went to Facebook, finding many groups for self-proclaimed witches. These groups were full of friendly people sharing spells like recipes, but there was nothing dangerous about the magic they were performing. It seemed to be a kind of self-care for some people and a religious experience for others, but it comforted Rachel to see that in some families it was normal to practice witchcraft.

Rachel closed her laptop, deciding to go ahead with the spell. The purple notebook was open to the first page right behind her computer. She looked at it for a second, positive that she had put it in her desk drawer. Then the book flapped closed as easily as if it had been held open. Rachel stood up quickly and looked around. She didn't need to see her mother's ghost to feel her presence this time.

It was a calm feeling, calmer than Rachel had felt all morning. Just as suddenly, it was gone. But it was all Rachel had needed. She plucked the rose quartz orb from its stand and brought it and the scarf and wand with her to the kitchen. She dug around in junk drawers before finding a bundle of black paracord rope and a knife. She cut off a few feet of rope and grabbed the canister of salt from the pantry.

She returned to her office to do some online searching about bronze coins. There were some available for sale, but performing the spell felt urgent. It had to be done today. She knew she could find some at the metaphysical store, but she didn't think she could look at Morgan without accusing her of something insane. She found a local coin dealer online and was disheartened to not see anything about bronze coins on their website.

"'Look to the elements'," Rachel said out loud. It sounded mystical, but that didn't feel right.

She searched for the Wikipedia entry for bronze and read it idly while trying to think. Based on her reading earlier, she wanted to think her mother meant the elements that metaphysical circles usually talked about—water, earth, fire, air. She read that bronze was an alloy of copper, one of the chemical elements. That was enough for her. She made a quick jaunt to the nearest coin collector store. The coin dealer in town had plenty of bronze and copper coins, and she was back at home with a bag full of both before long.

She thought for a while on where to do the spell. Comfortable with the idea of picturing her house, she thought it would help even more to look at it during the spell with a purposeful gaze. The thick ring of trees around her backyard had always provided privacy in the past when the leaves were in bloom, so Rachel decided to perform her first spell in her backyard. She put the materials in a tote bag and walked to the back of the yard, underneath the birch tree with its singed crown.

She took a deep breath before she started. Then she set the rope, wand and orb on the damp grass before pouring salt around her in the shape of a hexagon. She pricked her finger with a safety pin she had dipped in rubbing alcohol. It stung sharply. She pressed her thumb against her forefinger, squeezing out a small drop of blood that she dabbed on the three copper coins before bending down to place them next to the wand and orb.

She picked up the rope and stood back up, focusing on the house. She pictured a crackling shield of energy rising around her property. Her heart trebled when it formed before her eyes, made of strings of light that emerged from the ground individually, but she pressed on and found it easy to will the lines to weave their way up into the sky above the house.

Each line weaved its way up, extending further into the sky. She imagined it humming as the edges of the shield joined to form a dome encasing her house and yard in a net of lightning.

"*No harm will come to my home*," she thought as she pulled the first knot tight.

She held the vision of the protective dome as she prepared the next knot, looping the black cord around her thumb and pointer fingers on her left hand. With her right, she slowly pulled the loose end through the circle she made.

"*My home and mind are protected from those that wish me harm*," she thought, firmly pulling the knot together.

She readied the next knot, concentrating on creating the shelter with her mind. Thin cords of light raised out of the ground to join with the others as she worked. With each knot, the spaces between the strands grew thinner.

"*No one with ill intent can penetrate this protection.*"

The dome seemed more real to her with each knot. The streaks of light had knitted together tightly. By the time she was at the end of the rope, the vault around her property was so thick that she couldn't see through it. It was a thick layer of light, one only she could see. The spell was done, and as soon as she tied the last knot, the dome vanished from her sight.

It was done.

She stooped down and put the rose quartz orb back in the bag. She looked at the wand, wondering what role it had played in the spell. She put it in the bag, noticing the faint tingle as her hand wrapped around it. She didn't see the coins in the grass. She felt around the ground, even getting up to search from a different angle. The coins were gone.

7

"Everything ok?" Mike asked. "You're awfully quiet."

Rachel looked up from her chicken satay, which she'd been nibbling on in silence. Mike had ordered way too much food in what Rachel figured was an effort to look generous. She didn't mind. He was handsome, and the restaurant in the shopping center near Northern Kentucky University had the best Cambodian food for miles. The table in front of them was covered in small plates of pork belly, pot stickers, spring rolls and fried shrimp.

She had been too quiet, she figured. It was hard not to get caught up in her thoughts about everything that had happened since the Friday before. She had cancelled their Tuesday date so that she could continue her research binge. She had checked out a copy of Christopher Dell's *The Occult, Witchcraft, and Magic: An Illustrated History* from the library and was only halfway through it. He convinced her to take a break from the work project she said she was working on. It wasn't difficult. He talked her into a Thursday night dinner in Highland Heights. She was sure she'd been a dull companion so far.

"Sorry, I've got a lot on my mind with work," she said. "You know how it is."

Mike nodded. She was glad he wasn't giving her too hard a time. She had shown up to the restaurant a few minutes late after debating whether or not to cancel. He hadn't even mentioned it.

"I'm glad you came out," Mike said. "I thought I might have scared you off after last Friday."

"No, nothing like that," she said. "I'm glad I came out too."

It wasn't a lie. She had spent the five days since Saturday alternating between frantically Googling everything she could find about witchcraft and pretending everything was normal at work. When she was home, she was stressed trying to figure out what she needed to do next. When she was at work, she pressured herself not to think about what was going on at home. This had been the first hour all week that Rachel felt anywhere near relaxed.

She had barely responded to Mike's text messages all week and had felt guilty about it. Finally deciding it would be good for her to get out of the house, she had agreed to the Thursday dinner. Anything was better than another night spent wondering what happened to the coins.

She hadn't been able to find anything like it online. She had found plenty of stories about people performing magical acts, but nothing like this. It was so simple it was almost sinister. They had vanished, and so had her nightmares. She had been sleeping better than she had in months, but she felt so torn about it. Had she really paid the cost? Was there more to be paid?

She realized she was starting to drift back into the rat hole she had dug in her mind. She reminded herself that she was out on a date with Mike in order to feel at least a little normal. She looked up at him. If she could keep engaged, maybe she'd relax.

"How's opening week been?" she asked.

"It's been busier than anticipated," Mike said. "We're hoping to keep these crowds coming with different promotions, but it sure is great being the popular new club in town."

"Y'all deserve it," Rachel said. "The decorations alone. I can't imagine how much work went into building that club."

"Yes, it's been in the works for a while now," Mike said. "We're all very happy with how close the final product came to its design. Did you see the candelabra made out of bones?

"I did. Very spooky," Rachel said. "Which is the point, right?"

"That's right. It's all about atmosphere with a goth club," Mike said. "People like to dress up for all kinds of reasons. If the price is good and you play the right music with the right background, people will show up. We make more off drinks and food than we do off entry because people like to stay once they get there. We keep them drinking, and there's an arcade in one of the rooms upstairs. Of course we worked with the in-house agency, so there's lots of consistency with the other clubs under our umbrella as well."

"What'd you do before this?" Rachel asked before nibbling on her chicken satay.

"I managed one of the clubs in Memphis for a few years after college," Mike said. "So I was already familiar with a lot of the higher ups. They said it was a natural choice for me, and I agreed."

"Certainly seems to suit you," Rachel said.

"My turn to ask a question. Would you like to go to the club again with me this weekend?"

Rachel looked down at her plate. There was so much to learn, and she didn't even know where to start. She gave an uneasy grin when she lifted her eyes back up at him.

"I would, but not this weekend," she said. "Pencil me in for something next week. But I've got a big project I'm taking on and need to do more research this weekend."

"I work most nights next week. Could you do breakfast?" he asked.

"I could on Tuesday," she said. "There's a nice greasy spoon not far from the coffee shop if you're interested."

"I love greasy food in all varieties," Mike said. "Spoon or no spoon."

Rachel laughed. She felt herself loosening up a little. Mike didn't seem like he was putting any pressure on her, which was great. He was sweet, in his own way. He had opened the car door for her and the restaurant door, which felt unnecessary but flattering.

Although she felt it was a low bar, he hadn't also made any lewd comments at all, nor had he blown up her phone when she ignored him. He was respectful. The last thing she could stand right now would be someone demanding her time. Not until she knew what happened to the coins.

***

Something felt different at home. Rachel felt it as soon as she walked in the house. It was quiet, except for the normal grunts from the refrigerator and the drumming of the rain, patchy with peals of thunder. It wasn't something about the house itself that had changed, but the atmosphere in the house. She had felt in the last few days as though her mother was with her, that feeling she had only known in dreams for decades. An almost palpable feeling of comfort. And it wasn't there when she got home.

"*She'll be gone soon,*" she thought as she set down her purse and keys on the table next to the door. "*It's got to be tonight.*"

At first she had thought it was the protection spell wearing off. On Thursday morning before work she tried to see the barrier, and it had appeared for her just as she had left it. There were no holes among the golden seams of the shield. She looked as quickly as she could, walking the perimeter of her yard, but the protection hadn't failed in any way.

But after the date with Mike, it was unmistakable. Her mother's spirit was fading away. She was sure of it now. The thoughts she'd been pushing away all week about what to do about it couldn't be ignored anymore. She was going to have to use magic again. If what she had seen so far was possible, there had to be a way to communicate with her. That part was certain. What worried Rachel was that there was no way for her to know what the cost would be.

She sat in her office looking at the rose quartz orb and the wand on the windowsill as rain streamed down the window. She took a deep breath, stretched and sighed. She'd thought many times about calling Emily since the Friday before. She'd dodged her questions all week, but Emily knew something was up.

Now she wished she had told Emily so someone could talk her out of this. She hadn't done a very good job herself, clearly. If there was anyone that could talk her out of trying to talk to her dead mother, it was Emily. Rachel wished she could be skeptical again. No matter how much she didn't want to believe in ghosts, she had only to look at the handwriting in the purple notebook.

She had read a lot about communicating with spirits during the week while trying to sketch out in her mind what she needed to do. There didn't seem to be such a thing as an authentic séance. People had been caught rapping the bottoms of tables, moving objects on sticks and spitting out cheesecloth for ages. Mediums used all kinds of tricks to convince gullible grieving people out of their money, and they'd been doing it a long time. But it didn't seem to matter how many times such schemes were revealed throughout history, people wanted to talk to the dead.

"*Scam or not, I've got to try. I have to know something only my mother can tell me,*" Rachel thought with a sigh.

She turned around in her chair and made sure she had enough space cleared off on her desk. Then she fetched two candles, the bag of coins, rubbing alcohol and a safety pin and placed them on the desk, switching off the lights as she walked back into her office. Lightning flashed outside, brightening the room before thunder crashed with a boom.

She clustered the candles on the opposite side of her desk before she lit them. She wasn't sure how long this would work or how much her mother would be able to do. Keeping the room dim would make it easier for her, she thought. The flickering light of the candles provided just enough low lightning to make the shadows dance, but she could see enough. She set the Crystal Crescent notebook and a pen next to the candles, folding the book open to a new page.

Rachel placed the pink crystal ball on its wooden stand on her desk. She dumped out the bag of coins and pushed them all around the orb. She'd given it a lot of thought, and since she didn't know how many to use, she figured it was better to be safe than sorry. She pricked her finger with the pin after sterilizing it, pushing a droplet of blood up from her finger before letting it fall on the top of the rose quartz orb.

Lighting leapt across the sky outside. In the brief glare, Rachel could see the garnet drop drip down the pink ball. The red streak clung to the surface halfway down the ball before losing its fight with gravity. In the darkness, the afterimage hung in her eyes. Thunder clapped, setting off her spell with a crack. When her eyes adjusted, she saw that the blood was gone, leaving just the smooth rosy surface of the ball.

"Mom," Rachel called out. "I feel you slipping away. I don't how much energy you have left to give, but I want you to illuminate the orb again so we can talk. Can you give me two winks for no and one for yes?"

Rachel paused and waited. She had pushed aside these thoughts all week. There were dark notions brooding in her mind, and only her mother could tell her for certain. She held her breath as she waited. For a moment she wondered if it was too late or if she had truly lost it. Then the rose quartz orb glowed with a faint pink light before darkening again. Rachel breathed a sigh of relief and thought hard about her next question.

"Are we devil witches?" Rachel said.

The orb brightened and grew dark before glowing and dimming again. Rachel felt relief but it was only temporary. If this power didn't come from a divine power, then where did it originate? Did this mean there were no gods or devils?

"Is there a god or devil that these powers originate from?"

The orb was silent. Rachel waited, but there was no light. She counted up to a minute, but she was sure this was wasting precious time. The energy it took for her mother to communicate this way had to be exorbitant.

"Of course she wouldn't know either," Rachel thought. *"Figures."*

"Are there many of us?" she asked.

The orb brightened and grew dim, brightened and grew dim. The two winks didn't surprise Rachel. She had thought that if it were more common she would have found out about it by now. But how was a secret as big as witchcraft kept hidden from the world all this time? Rachel wanted to ask so many questions, but few fit in the yes or no answer framework. She knew she didn't have much time either. She wanted to know what had happened to her mother, where she had gone all these years. What should she do now?

The flickering light of the candles extinguished, and the orb went dark. In the pitch black, Rachel thought she saw her mother's face again, right before her own. It was just the contours of her face, an impression made in light like a tragic mask. Then its luminous quality paled until it was gone.

But when the visage faded into darkness, a new understanding dawned in Rachel's mind. She knew with uncanny certainty that her mother had been murdered. She raised a trembling hand to her own throat, startled by the vivid feeling that a blade had been pressed against her neck. The skin there was cold, as though stroked with an ice cold knife. It was here when her mother's throat had been slit, and the certainty of this thought startled her.

The discovery of this foreign knowledge made Rachel feel lightheaded. She braced herself on the desk and drew a few deep breaths. Then she shuddered and relit the candles on her desk with shaking hands, and in the wan light she peered at the ghost's writing left on the notebook. Cold dread filled her as she read the new message. It was written in her mother's neat handwriting, lettered the same way as the page before and just as dire.

"Our kind are hunted. They killed me, they killed Rosemary Crantz, and they'll come for you next."

8

The Ohio River snakes between northern Kentucky and southern Ohio, marking the boundary between the states. It was proximity to the river that nourished Cincinnati into the metropolis is today. The city was first established in 1788 on the northern shore of the Ohio River as three settlements nestled between the Little Miami and Great Miami rivers.

In those days, trade in and out of Ohio was notoriously difficult unless you lived near the river. Sending goods down to Mississippi and New Orleans was expensive and slow, and returning upriver against the Ohio was worse. Construction on major canal systems to open up new trade routes in Ohio started in 1825.

Man-made waterways like the Erie Canal in New York had a remarkable effect on the economy of New York. After decades of political effort, Ohio made two canals: one running from Toledo to Cincinnati on the western side of the state and one from Akron to Portsmouth on the eastern side. The expense of constructing hundreds of miles of canals nearly bankrupted the state, but the routes helped the cities and towns along them grow and prosper.

The portion of the canal that ran through Cincinnati was completed early on, and the transit and shipping opportunities it brought helped Cincinnati grow to a city of over 100,000 people by 1850. But canals fell out of favor before the end of the 19th century as railroads and cars provided cheaper and quicker means of moving people and goods. Most of the canal was filled in, except for a portion that had been used to build a subway tunnel and a boulevard. The subway project was put on hiatus in 1928, but the boulevard was opened and is still in operation.

Central Parkway was built on top of the former canal route, cutting from north to south through Cincinnati, where it turned sharply east below Washington Park to go through a neighborhood German immigrants had named Over the Rhine. Drivers following the route of the old canal would turn off Central Parkway onto what's now Eggleston Avenue, a long southeastern stretch where a flight of locks once fed boats straight into the Ohio River.

Traffic on Eggleston Avenue today flows into Columbia Parkway, U.S. Route 50 and East Pete Rose Way, which becomes Riverside Drive. All three of these run alongside the Ohio River as it winds its way south. Further east along the river is Columbia-Tusculum, the oldest neighborhood in Cincinnati. It's on the southern edge of Columbia-Tusculum that Morgan Wilson's family originally settled in a white clapboard house they built in 1815.

The Wilsons were a large family once, and the house was full for the first few generations. But keeping secrets in large families was much harder in a city than out in the country. Those who thought they couldn't keep the secret were asked to move when they were old enough so they wouldn't have to live with the burden. Those branches of the family tree withered the further they moved from the one with power in the family, but it was a price paid willingly.

Some left because they found religion, since the books in the library said that religion was only allowed to be studied, never followed. Others left because they couldn't take lying to neighbors and friends who asked questions about things they had seen. The witches in the Wilson family were very cautious, but the results of their secret work could still bring suspicion from time to time. The size of the family changed as those who had mourned the flight of their siblings chose to have smaller families. Morgan was an only child, as her mother and grandmother had been.

Real estate agents had come by the Crystal Crescent from time to time to marvel at the massive old white clapboard house and try to convince Morgan to put it on the market. It had six bedrooms at one point, in addition to the library, kitchen and living room. The Wilson house had seen its share of renovations, but like many of the houses in the historic district it didn't stray far from its original design.

The roof of the house was flat, except for the chimney that stuck out like a plug, the only red brick on the exterior. The house was painted white, with black shutters. There had been perfect symmetry in the way the windows were originally installed on the face of the home. There were three sash windows evenly spaced on the second floor, each with 18 panes of glass. Beneath the middle window was the front door, painted black to match the shutters.

The windows on the right side of the house were parallel to each other, as the windows on the left side had once been. The bottom left window had been moved to the right to install a second entrance for the shop. The door on the left was painted a muted purple, the same color as the modest wooden sign reading "Crystal Crescent" staked in the yard. The letter Cs in the logo were waning crescent moons. Morgan didn't get many customers at the physical store these days to see it on the sign. Usually they saw the logo on the store's website. The store's local popularity had peaked in the '90s, but its internet presence was stronger than ever.

***

Rachel had searched online for Rosemary Crantz using every search engine she could think of, but she had found nothing by Saturday morning. Nothing that felt right, at least. When she started, she was sure she would know when she found the Rosemary her mother had meant. She had also felt confident that she'd be able to find Rosemary online. But by the time she went to bed late Friday evening, she had started to think differently.

She wanted to talk to Emily. They had always talked about everything. If one of them needed to vent or bounce an idea off the other, they had never hesitated. But now was different. The things Rachel had seen since the night of the club had been unexplainable, and she wasn't sure Emily would believe her. She wasn't sure she even believed it herself sometimes.

Whenever the reality of what she had seen was too much, she tried to convince herself Morgan had played a prank on her. Late at night after a few drinks, she'd change her research subject to Morgan and her store, but she couldn't find much evidence.

There wasn't much online about her personally, but she had an online store that sold crystals, incense, candles, and herbs. She offered tarot card and palm readings by appointment.

After the frustration of her unfruitful search for Rosemary Crantz, Rachel started picking at her theory about Morgan. No matter how many holes she poked in the idea, she kept popping up in her head. After all, Morgan had mentioned witchcraft, given her the book and sold her the orb. She decided it wouldn't hurt to take a look in her store. She looked up Crystal Crescent on Google one more time to make sure they were open before grabbing her keys.

***

Morgan was at the front counter of the store, sitting in a desk chair in a collared white shirt and blue jean skirt. She was reading from an old leatherbound book. It didn't look like one of the books on the shelves of her store, which lined the left side of the front room of the shop. It was much older, with worn binding and frail pages that smelled almost sweet. She heard the black beads in the curtain behind her shift, but Morgan didn't turn in her chair to see who had entered from the resident side of the house. She knew it was time.

She felt the head-butt first. He rubbed his head on her leg before turning around and bumping her gently again with the flat part of his head. When that didn't work, he stood on his back two legs and put his front paws on Morgan's right knee. He stared at her with his large green eyes.

"You're always on time, Randi," Morgan said. "How do you do that without a watch? Must be that good conditioning."

Her black cat, a long muscular tom, only licked his lips in response. Morgan looked at her phone. It wasn't exactly lunch time, but it was close enough. She stood up and flipped over the closed sign on the window before walking through the beaded curtain into the foyer she hated. The scarlet walls and mahogany stairs she had grown up running up and down felt overbearing, not to mention the dour portraits of past matriarchs and patriarchs that frowned at you no matter which direction you looked. Sometimes she thought something bad had happened on those stairs, but she wouldn't let herself remember what.

After feeding Randi, she walked upstairs to the office across from the library and checked her email. Most of the work for the online shop was done early in the morning, so there were no more packages to take to the post office today. There hadn't been any new orders in the last few days, but Morgan wasn't worried. She had a way of making things work out. There was always someone online willing to buy something she had, whether it was through the regular channels or not.

She was surprised to see the woman from the festival waiting on the porch when she walked back into the shop. It was definitely her: Morgan felt a thrill of Deja vu when she saw her, much stronger than the last time. She was standing on the other side of the purple door, wearing jean shorts and a black t-shirt and peeking through the window with her hands cupped around her face. When she saw Morgan enter she waved enthusiastically. Morgan went to unlock the purple door.

"We're open, we're open," she said, eyeing Rachel carefully as she stepped over the threshold. "Come on in."

"Your store is beautiful," Rachel said as she walked in. She felt like she had already failed as a spy, so she looked up and smiled at Morgan, meeting her eyes. That strange Deja vu feeling had been simmering the back of her brain since Morgan came into her line of sight, but now it boiled over. The Deja vu was so intense Rachel felt stunned and momentarily dizzy. She looked away, sure more now than ever that Morgan was like her and that she didn't know what to say to her without freaking out. She was thankful Morgan spoke first, as it made her feel a little less obvious.

"Thank you," Morgan said. "Feel free to peruse."

Morgan sat down at the counter next to the shop door and window without another word, so Rachel moved toward the back of the store, opting to delay the inevitable. There was a round table with a purple tablecloth that had a display of giant crystals, including a large amethyst geode half the size of Rachel. The left side of the store was lined with display cases containing many of the crystals and gems that Rachel had seen at the festival. The stones were sorted by color. Rachel walked past rows of purple amethyst, blue lapis lazuli and radical labradorite, gray but with streaks of oil sheen luminescence that winked blue, green, red as she passed.

She walked into the next room, deeper in the house. There were racks of books here on mindfulness, witchcraft, botany, astrology and astronomy. A bookcase in the left corner of the room held dozens of variations of tarot cards and boxes full of incense and small multicolored candles. There were cast iron cauldrons in different sizes, altar coverings, pendulums, and ceremonial knives.

Rachel stopped in front of the case of ceremonial daggers. There was an assortment of knives displayed on black velvet cloth. Strings of fairy lights were arranged in loose circles around the knives, twinkling with pale copper light on top of the black fabric. There were double sided blades, knives with runes and pentagrams emblazoned on their hilts, plus a few knives made from polished bone. Some were dull and obviously ornamental, but a few looked very sharp. A few were carved from obsidian, and they looked as sharp as scalpels.

Rachel's fingers were touching her throat before she realized she had raised her hand. Had it been a blade like one of these? She moved to touch the glass case as her eyes fell on a black knife. A shadow fell across the knife case as Morgan walked to the other side. Rachel flinched.

"Are you alright?" Morgan asked.

She looked up and was confused and embarrassed by Morgan's concerned expression. She opened her mouth to brush aside the concern, but was stopped by Morgan continuing to speak.

"It's just that I felt that, just now. You're very scared. When I read your aura when you walked in I thought you were angry. It's like a thundercloud around you. But now I see you're frightened. Maybe it's not any of my business to ask, but why are you going out without any wards if you're so scared?"

"Wards?"

"Protections. Talismans, amulets, shit, even just a protective ring. You're walking around like a babe in the woods," Morgan said.

"I have a protection spell on my home and mind," Rachel said. She felt out of her depth at the woman's questioning.

"It's not good enough when you're out of your home," Morgan said. "Magic is bound to location or object. Everyone knows that. What sort of witch goes out without some kind of protection or cloaking?"

"I'm sorry, am I being too forward? I haven't met any like us aside from my own mother," Morgan said, "I had read about that strange Deja vu feeling in the library after the festival. There's lots of theories, of course, but witches aren't much for scientists. They described it more like heat stroke than vertigo."

Rachel's eyes opened wide and she stepped back from the counter. She stuttered, uncertain what to say, but grasping for the first time at the blind hope that Morgan was like her.

"Ah, that settles it then. I wasn't sure at the festival, but I had an inkling you were like me," Morgan said, her eyes softening into a motherly gaze. "That explains why you're so scared. You're all alone. I'm so sorry for your loss. Was it your mother or your father?"

At the revelation that there were others like her, the weight of the secrets she'd borne collapsed on her. Rachel burst into tears.

9

Morgan sat a hot mug of chamomile tea in front of Rachel, who sniffed and blew her nose again before taking a small sip. They were sitting at Morgan's kitchen table, where Rachel had just poured her heart out. She had told her about everything magical that had happened since she purchased the orb from Morgan. She told her about the ghost of her mother, including the name she'd been given. She gave as little background as possible, telling her only what seemed relevant to witchcraft.

Morgan had listened patiently at first. But as Rachel summarized her side of the experience at Crystal Crescent, she began to cry. Rachel stopped, but Morgan asked her to finish. She did. When she was done, Morgan took a moment to compose herself and then spoke.

"This is not supposed to happen like this. I didn't know. I'm so sorry," Morgan said. "I'll do everything I can to help you. But you must not do anything to put yourself at risk. It's an unsafe world for witches."

"I thought she had died when I was in high school," Rachel said.

"She died the first night you saw the orb glow," Morgan said. "You only gain the power when the forebear dies. It may not feel like it, but you're very lucky to have seen her like you did. Not many people get a chance to say goodbye."

"I'd hardly call seeing a ghost lucky, but I know what you mean."

"I don't know about ghosts. I believe spirits move on when they pass to the next life. But from what you've described, it sounds like you witnessed your mother's astral projection," Morgan said. "Since that timed with your receiving your power, it's easy to conclude that your mother died while she was astral projecting. You did the right thing by getting her to expend the rest of her energy. The soul can linger on the astral plane for a long time if disconnected from the body. What happened is very rare, but not unheard of."

"So we are really witches?" Rachel asked. "Is it like Harry Potter?"

"No," Morgan said. "Witch is the word my family uses. It works well enough. Did your mother really never tell you anything about your heritage growing up?"

Rachel sipped her tea, then took in a deep breath of the steam. Talking about the magic was one thing. It felt uncomfortable to talk about her childhood with anyone she barely knew. She didn't even like talking about it with her therapist. She'd waited years to tell Emily. She decided to give Morgan the shortest version.

"No," she said. "I had no idea. My mother left when I was 8, but I didn't hear from her after I was 17."

"I'm so sorry. I can teach you, if you want. I'd be honored, actually. Just know that—well, saying there's 'a lot' doesn't really cover it," she said. "I'll show you the library in a few minutes. But the basics are pretty simple. The power passes in families. It's only ever in one person at a time, and when the one with the power dies it moves on."

Rachel thought about this for a moment and was horrified.

"What happens if I don't want to have children?"

"No one knows," Morgan said. "I'm sorry I don't have answers for you. These are high level questions and deserve more time to answer than we have this afternoon. There's a few obscure texts in the library, but I was taught that some mysteries are best left unexplored. My great-uncle lost his mind trying to decipher old screeds about the afterlife for witches. I find reincarnation to be a comfort. My life as a witch in the Wilson family has been lonesome. Reminders of death abound everywhere in my home. Surely the next life I live won't be this isolated."

Morgan's eyes clouded over as she looked away from Rachel. Rachel leaned forward and put a comforting hand over Morgan's without saying a word.

"It's speculated the power may go to a different family or just disappear. We don't have any way to know and obviously, we try not to find out. My own mother got a sperm donor, and I'll probably do the same. But I'm not in any rush. She, like my grandmother and myself, led a modest life. I don't go out unless I must. I stay here in my house that's covered in protection spells. I study, and I sell goods to make my way. Once I have a child, my life will be devoted to teaching them everything I can about our gift, as I was taught."

"What do you mean you don't go out? I have a business I have to run that's not in my house."

"I plan all my excursions from the house and take every precaution to ensure I'm protected. Only you can decide what chances you want to take. All I can tell you is that it's dangerous out there for us."

"But we have powers."

"Yes, powers that come at a great cost," Morgan said. "You were right to be scared of using magic to talk to your mother. How many coins were gone where you were done?"

"Nearly half of them," she said. "Those don't come cheap either. But it was a relief that there were coins left at all."

"I'll give you more to take home. My family has been stockpiling copper for ages. And other supplies you'll need as well. But back to my point. The more effect a spell will have, the greater the cost. Moving small objects, manipulating small amounts of the elements, those are small cost magic. But say you tried to move a skyscraper or a mountain—that might actually kill you immediately.

"It's never an exact science. I've done what you did many times myself and overpaid as a precaution. But it's clear that over time, it affects your health. This is why I said I don't need tarot cards to tell you your fortune. There hasn't been a witch in my family that's made it to 70. And those were the lucky ones."

"What happens?" Rachel asked. She picked back up her tea and took a small sip. Her phone buzzed with a text message, and she ignored it. It didn't matter who it was, this was more important.

"Most die of health complications in their 60s, at least these days. That's longer than the life expectancy used to be, but you can thank modern medicine for that. In the old days people died a lot younger. Some chose to martyr themselves by giving up their lives so that a major spell would work. There's books in the library if you're interested, but those stories are incredibly depressing. There have been murders, of course. Especially in the earlier days, when the family was very religious. There are also outside threats, like groups who will kidnap or extort witches to use them for their magic. You should always, always be careful about groups. It's best to be alone.

"I've met many witches that aren't like us over the years. Most don't know that we even exist, which is by design. Witch families survive by keeping to themselves. But the ones who do know about us know about our blood. You don't always have to use your blood in your own spells. Most of the time you don't for smaller magic. But if a witch who isn't like us uses our blood in a spell, that spell will work if it's not something impossible."

"How do I avoid people like that without closing myself off to the world?" Rachel said. She had hoped to come away from the store less paranoid, but that was looking less likely by the minute.

"I don't know the answer, clearly, but I've had a close call. Learn from my mistake. I get lonely here sometimes, so I made friends with a woman who came in the shop all the time. She had a coven that sounded very low key, with lots of meditation and a focus on mindfulness. She told me they did lots of volunteer work. And they didn't require any deity worship, which I don't believe in."

Rachel nodded.

"My grandmother raised me Catholic, but I'm an atheist too," Rachel said. "They say there's no way to know either, and that's what faith is. Believing in something without proof."

"I definitely would not say I'm an atheist," Morgan said. "Religion has its purposes. There is simply no way to know to know if a divine power exists."

"Oh, I'm not against religion. I just don't believe in deities. I was a lot firmer about this just a few weeks ago."

"Yes, my family was very much atheist for a long time. There were decades of trials and tests to see if we could reach a higher being. There weren't any conclusive results, but they did discover something interesting. We'll go up there in a little bit, although I don't want to overwhelm you. But back to my story, because it's important that you know the kind of threats that are out there. This friend of mine, we'll call her Janet, convinced me to come check out her group in Covington. It was fine at first. They were very friendly. Until they started doing blood drives. I wasn't the only one they were asking to donate every time, but I was the only one who could use magic to see what they were doing with my blood. I can teach you that spell. There's many ways to look into unprotected spaces."

"What'd you do?"

"I had the weirdest feeling that Janet was up to something. I'm sure you know the kind of feeling I'm talking about. When I did the spell, I saw Janet pouring my blood into glass jars she kept in the freezer of her apartment. We usually had the meetings there. There weren't many of us, probably about seven total. I waited until our potluck meeting at the solstice to confront her.

"I made some special brownies that everyone sampled. I had enchanted them so that anyone who ate them would be compelled to tell the truth. I had a bag of copper coins in my purse, so I wasn't scared at all. I spoke with each witch individually and asked what they knew until I was sure it was just Janet who was involved. I stayed late and told her I wanted to speak with her alone about a spell I was working on.

"I still remember how wide her eyes got when she heard her door lock by itself behind her. There's no cost to such small magic as that, or at least it's a cost I'm willing to live with. Like cigarettes, I guess. Anyway, I asked her point blank if she had been stealing my blood.

"She answered truthfully, thanks to the brownies. She told me she had snuck up to my library a few times while visiting me at the store. I had trusted her enough to allow her on this side of the house. You're the only person I've let on this side since then. I usually tell people we don't have a restroom now.

"She had repaid my trust by sneaking into the library and reading enough to twist her mind. She found a book on dimensional travel and read about some of the attempts using blood magic. The rest she filled in with information she found online or I guess her imagination. She wanted to try to reach a parallel dimension and thought it would work if she had enough of my blood. It wouldn't have worked. It's never worked, and many good witches have died trying. Multidimensional travel is almost entirely speculation.

"Anyway, I made her think I turned into a giant snake. A crimson snake, thick as a fire hydrant and so long it couldn't fit in her living room without coiling in on itself dozens of times. I gave it realistic scales that shifted as it slithered. I made the eyes glowing red and the fangs covered in green venom.

I watched unmoving from the front door as it slithered around Janet, winding around her legs. I had it raise itself all the way up to face her. Its glowing red eyes stared into hers before it hissed again.

'You will speak of what you have seen to no one.' I told her. 'You will never do this again.'

Since she heard me but saw only the monstrous snake in her living room, which hissed at her, she assumed the snake was speaking to her telepathically.

'I promise!' she cried. 'Please!'

'I will know if you break your promise, and I will find you. That is my promise.'

Then I made her fall asleep and I left," Morgan finished.

Rachel was stunned and wondered if she should be scared of Morgan, but for the first time since she saw the spirit of her mother, she felt optimism penetrate her heart. If Morgan had done something like that to someone that had crossed her, surely she understood why Rachel wanted to find her mother's killer.

"I have so many questions," Rachel said. "But would you help me do something like that to whoever killed my mom? Or would you at least help me find them?"

Morgan looked at her watch.

"Let's go upstairs. I want to show you the library. Wait here, and I'll check to see if I've got any customers."

She got up and left Rachel in the kitchen.

"*Fuck*," Rachel thought. "*Why is she dodging my question?*"

Her phone buzzed with another text message. She looked to see three missed texts from Mike and two from Emily. She slipped her phone back in her pocket.

10

"Sorry to keep you waiting. Let's go upstairs."

Rachel pushed back from the table and followed Morgan back out into the foyer. Morgan was ahead of her with her hand on the dark wood railing. She was about to walk up the stairs when Rachel's phone rang. She rolled her eyes and apologized to Morgan.

"I'm sorry, just a sec," she said, taking the phone out of her pocket. She had assumed it would be Mike calling, but it was Emily. "I've got to take this."

"Go ahead," Morgan said.

Rachel stepped into the kitchen and answered the phone.

"Hey, I'm sorry I missed your texts, I was busy," she said. "What's up?"

"I was just wondering what you were up to. I feel like we haven't had a chance to hang out since we went to the club."

Rachel felt a pang of guilt. She had been avoiding Emily out of fear that her friend wouldn't understand. After everything she'd learned from Morgan, that fear didn't seem unreasonable. But she had always trusted Emily in the past, more than anyone.

"I'm running an errand across the river right now but I can come over afterward," Rachel said. "I've been really distracted lately. We'll talk about it tonight."

"I'll be here," Emily said.

Rachel hung up and went back into the foyer where Morgan was leaning against the banister. She stood up and swept her blonde hair off her shoulder when Rachel walked back in. Then she clapped her hands together briskly.

"I want to make sure you know I'm making an exception for you," Morgan said. "No one that's not in the Wilson line has ever looked at these books."

"I can't begin to thank you enough." Rachel said.

"What I'm saying is, everything I've told you must stay between us," Morgan said.

Rachel held up her phone. She thought about smiling, but she didn't.

"That was my business partner, Emily," Rachel said. "I trust her more than anyone, even my own grandmother."

"If you choose to share your secret with her, that's your business. But you must keep my secret," Morgan said. "Can you promise me that?"

"Can you promise me that you'll help me? You keep dodging my question about what happened to my mother and whether or not you'll help me find out."

Morgan sighed and ran her hands through her hair.

"No, I can't promise you anything that involves me leaving this house," she said. "I won't take any unnecessary risks. I'm happy to let you have access to my library and to read what you like while you're here. You're welcome to move here if you'd like more frequent access. I could probably turn the meditation room into a spare bedroom. I certainly wouldn't mind the company."

Rachel tried not to react too strongly. She realized Morgan lived in the house alone, and likely didn't see people often. Her intentions seemed good though. Morgan seemed to notice her discomfort.

"I'm sorry," Morgan said. "It's just that this house has so many protection spells on it, I don't feel safe anywhere else. You said you cast a protection spell on your house, but this house has been secured for more than 200 years. A witch died to ensure this house would always be protected. Nothing is getting through here without me letting it. You would have access to all of my resources. You would be safe. It's an option."

"I can't promise you anything either then, except that I'm going to talk with Emily about what's happened to me," Rachel said. "She and I are good at putting together plans. If I tell her everything and she doesn't send me away, can I bring her here?"

"What? Why?"

"Because I think you'll trust her too once you get to meet her," Rachel said. "And because if you want me involved in your life at all, you have to get used to Emily. She's amazing, and if you have a problem with her you have a problem with me."

Morgan considered this and then raised her hands to her chest, palms facing Rachel.

"Fine," she said. "But if I don't trust her I'm not letting her see anything outside of the shop. Maybe she can talk some sense into you. If you try to go after whoever killed your mother, you may end up dead. That'd be the end of your family line."

"Do you think I don't know that?" Rachel said. "I'll be careful. But I have to know."

"Do you agree to my terms? Tell her what you like if you trust her. But if I do not trust her, she will not be allowed anywhere in my home outside the storefront."

"Understood," Rachel said.

"So do you want to see the library or not?" Morgan asked, gesturing upwards.

"Let me come back," Rachel said. "I don't want to get overwhelmed. This has been a lot. But do you have any suggestions for finding Rosemary? Maybe a spell?"

"Magic is easy, Rachel. It's just dangerous and needs to be exact. Every time you cast a spell, you're gambling. Just remember that." Morgan said and then sighed. "The way your mother had you cast the protection spell was essentially a witch's ladder. It's an old folk magic way of concentrating your intention for a spell.

"Knot magic is simple, but if you don't have rope all you need is yourself and a firm intention, plus material for the cost. It's about force of will. If you want to change the universe, even in the tiniest way possible, you have to mean it. Now, wait right here and I'll get you some more coins."

Morgan went upstairs and Rachel wondered if she should follow her. The allure of the library was strong. If everything Morgan had told her was true, then she was far behind in the education she was meant to receive. She didn't like that feeling. But Rachel had already learned today that she would likely die young, or at least never make it to be a strong senior citizen like her grandmother. That had been shocking enough. If there were books in there that would twist a woman to steal blood, what other hidden dangers could lurk there?

Morgan reappeared at the head of the stairs with a purple tote bag with her logo on it. She walked down to Rachel with a smile. Rachel tried her best to look grateful. It wasn't hard.

"Thank you for everything today," Rachel said. "I'll be back soon. It's so good to know I'm not alone."

"Please do come back soon," Morgan said. "I put my cell phone number on a card in here, plus coins and some minerals on the house. You'll want to supplement coins with minerals whenever you can. Oh, and I'm giving you a loan. I put a book in there that might be helpful. Take care of it, and bring it back next time."

"Thank you so much," Rachel said.

She hugged Morgan. It felt like she had found a long lost cousin. She was sure that Morgan and Emily would get on just as well. But before that could happen, Rachel had to think about how she was going to explain everything to Emily. It had all just poured out of her with Morgan. She hoped she could tell Emily without both of them freaking out.

***

Emily was hanging an art print on the wall above the black leather couch in her living room. The entire image was black and white, in order to match with Emily's decor. The walls were white except for the black framed photographs and festival posters. There were some pops of reds and purples, but her living room was predominantly monochromatic.

This poster had a hypnotic black and white tie dye background that spiraled around the insect at its center. The focus was the top half of a cicada with wide set bulbous compound eyes and two thin antennae. Six thin arms were folded in a crooked tangle over its striped thorax. Veined, translucent wings were spread behind it, shimmering with a thin layer of rainbow iridescent paint. Where the end of its abdomen should have been was a bumpy plug of soft white powder.

She had designed the poster in a program on her computer after being inspired by an article in *The Atlantic* about Massospora Cicadina, a parasitic fungus that preys only on periodical cicadas.

These insects evolved to spend most of their lives underground before they dig their way up to the sun, only living as an adult for up to a month or so before reaching its natural demise.

In an insidious example of coevolution, the Massospora Cicadina evolved to target juvenile cicadas while they slept in the earth. When it was time for the cicadas to break through and mate, the infected bugs acted as though nothing was wrong. They didn't seem to mind the loss, instead becoming hypersexual and frenetic with energy despite half their body being replaced by a plug of white fungal spores.

Scientists had discovered the fungus pumped the bugs with khat and psilocybin, mind altering drugs that fueled the cicadas as they flew over their uninfected friends, shedding spores like deadly snow. One scientist quoted in the article had called the infected bugs "flying saltshakers of death," which Emily thought made the art print suitably gothic. The bugs were doomed once infected, forced to march to the fungus's orders until they died of exhaustion.

Emily raised her hammer and tapped the nail on the head until it drove into the wall. She sat the hammer down on the back of the couch before picking up the print, which she had put in a black poster frame. She had just secured it on the nail when she heard Rachel knock at the door.

She answered with apprehension. It had taken a few days after the club for her to realize that Rachel was ignoring her. Usually they talked out their issues, but this time was different. Emily had given it a lot of thought over the week.

Rachel hadn't seemed that upset when she had left her house on Friday night. But she dodged talking about anything that didn't have to do with work. She'd barely responded to texts, so Emily had been glad she'd answered the phone. When Emily opened the door, Rachel looked at her with a thin smile before sighing.

"I'm ready to talk if you're still interested," Rachel said.

"Of course," Emily said. "Come inside."

Emily reached forward and brushed at the hair on top of Rachel's hair with her hand as she walked through the door. Rachel looked at her questioningly.

"Sorry, I thought I saw a lightning bug's butt light up on your head," Emily said. "It must have flew off."

Rachel chuckled, although it wasn't dark enough out for lightning bugs. She bent down and unlaced her shoes. Emily's black carpets showed every speck of dirt, so she slipped off her shoes once she was finished and put them in the organizer near the door.

"Thanks for doing that," Emily said. "And look, I'm here for you. That's what friends do. You and I are business partners, but we've always been friends first. Friends talk to each other. I understand if I upset you on Friday. My comment about it being good that you didn't remember something must have sounded flippant, but I only meant about your nightmare. Even still, I'm really sorry. It sucks. It sucks more than I can put into words."

Rachel sighed and sat down on Emily's leather couch. Emily sat on the black chaise lounge across from her and put her hands in her lap. She waited for Rachel to speak.

"I'm not mad at you. A lot has happened, and I didn't know if you would believe me. I still don't."

Emily sat up straight and looked alarmed.

"Are you ok? Did something happen with Mike?"

"No, no. Nothing like that. I'll start with the night of the fire. I fired the therapist that told me I messed up my memories. I went a long time without, but then I started seeing a new one a few years ago," Rachel said. "It was great and helped me with closure about that night. I had a lot of trouble letting go of my version of what had happened, and she helped me with that. I don't have to be right, but now I know I was right. I was right all along about what happened that night.

"I had woken up because I could hear my mom crying out my name," she said. "There was smoke whispering out of the top corner of the door frame like a grey ghost in the dark. And the way she was screaming my name."

Rachel paused and drew a long, shaky breath. Emily put her arm around her friend and hugged her in silence, waiting for Rachel to continue when she felt ready.

"It was the most desperate sound I'd ever heard. And then there was silence. I panicked but then I remembered we had talked about fire safety in school, so I knew to feel the door. It wasn't hot, so I slowly opened it with a towel on the door knob.

"Black smoke streamed in, filling the ceiling until it was just blackness above me. I remember thinking it looked like an evil cloud. I army crawled into the hallway, where I saw my mom was laying with her eyes closed. I thought she was dead at first, and I screamed. She called my name again and started coughing, so I crawled as low on the floor and as fast as I could to her. I remember crying so hard that I was gasping, but that it was hard to breathe because the air was so hot. I was...I thought it was the end. But then we were outside, and then we were at my grandmother's house.

"The parts my therapist thinks I'm missing are everything between the hallway and my grandmother's house. I swore up and down as a kid that we 'popped' outside. I remembered that much. One moment we were in the hall, the next we were outside. I remembered gasping in the night air and how it was so cold. Then we were at my grandmothers. I think it really happened. I think my mom teleported us out of the fire and then to my grandmother's house."

Emily's eyes widened as she listened. She had heard about the night of the fire before, but not this version. Rachel had never mentioned teleporting before, and Emily could see why. It made her feel sad to think that Rachel was missing her mother this much. She wished she had tried harder to talk to her this week when she was pushing her away.

"That's an interesting theory," she said gently. "Although people do tend to forget or misremember traumatic events, especially children. Why don't you think that's what happened?"

"Because I just found out I'm a witch," she said. "I went to Crystal Crescent in Columbia-Tuluscum to see the woman who sold me a pink crystal ball at the festival at Washington Park. I talked to my mom's spirit with it. Twice. She's gone now."

Emily opened her mouth and then shut it again, considering her options before she spoke.

"Who is this? And I thought you were an atheist? Since when do you believe in ghosts or crystal balls?"

"I am an atheist. Maybe agnostic. I don't know. No one knows," Rachel said. "I'm sorry, I'm kind of overwhelmed. Her name is Morgan Wilson, and she runs a metaphysical supply store out of her house. Tarot cards and crystals and things. She told me that there are witches like me all over the world. That we keep to ourselves and study witchcraft all the time. I can use magic, but I shouldn't since it shortens my life."

"So you can't prove it to me?" Emily asked, hoping calling her bluff would help her snap out of it. "Whoever Morgan Wilson is, she sounds like a scam artist. Did you see her do real magic? You said she sells tarot cards, and you know those are a scam. It's the Forer Effect, your brain just can't help making up stories. Con artists like her take advantage of that."

"I'm telling you, it sounds deadlier than huffing gas," she said. "I can prove it to you if you want, but it's got to be something small. She might be a con artist with other people but..."

Rachel stopped talking and thought about it. Morgan made a good point. She hadn't seen Morgan do anything supernatural, nothing like what she'd seen herself do. Why had she been so quick to trust her? She remembered how Morgan mentioned putting a spell on brownies before, and how she had calmed down after that cup of tea.

"*It was chamomile,*" she thought. "*Stop it. You were certain a minute ago, and now you're doubting yourself and coming up with new weird theories. You felt it when you were near her. That was real. She's definitely like you.*"

Rachel took a deep breath.

"I don't know how ethical her work is, but she didn't seem like she was conning me at the shop," she said.

"That's how that works Rachel," Emily said. "If you knew you were being conned, they wouldn't be very good at it would they?"

Rachel dug into her purse and pulled out a fistful of copper coins.

"Let me prove it to you," she said. "I've got a lot more to tell you, and it'll be much easier if you believe me. I want you to find something small and hold it in your hand," Rachel said.

Emily got up and walked to the side table next to the front door. She took a key from a white ceramic bowl on the black table. It was a plain house key, a copy of the one on her keyring. She brought it to Rachel.

"No, I want you to hold onto it," she said. "I want you to go outside with it in your hand and then come back inside. Look at it while you're out there, then close it up in your fist and come in here."

Emily made a skeptical face, but she did as she was told. She took the key outside and looked at it in her palm. Nothing special about it still, just a metal key with ridges and a hole for a key ring.

She closed her hand into a fist and walked back inside to the living room where Rachel was sitting on the couch.

"Now what?" Emily said. "Do I open my hand?"

"Yes."

Emily opened her hand. The key was gone. She thought it might be a trick but she didn't know how Rachel had done it. She was sure she'd seen a magician do something similar before. Rachel read the look on her face.

"You don't believe me," Rachel said.

"I'm sorry," Emily said. "I want to believe you. It'd be wonderful if magic was real."

"What do you need to see?" Rachel said. "The key is back in the bowl by the way."

Emily walked back over to the bowl. The key rested at the bottom, as if she'd never picked it up in the first place. She looked back up at Rachel, who was gazing at Emily's new print over the couch.

"Ok," Emily said. "That's a neat trick. I don't know how you did it, but I don't think that's really proof of anything."

"Look again," Rachel said. "Just a warning: this is an illusion. It's not going to be a key this time."

She looked down into the bowl. It was full of cicadas now, all half eaten with Massospora Cicadina. The bugs were black and white like in her painting, and they were squirming and rubbing all over each other in a pile. She could see the thickly veined wings glitter with different colors as the cicadas struggled.

One crawled out of the bowl and landed on the table with a soft tap. It fell on its back, exposing the powder soft white plug that made up its bottom half. The vulnerable insect reached out its long jointed arms at Emily before it began rocking wildly in an effort to right itself. The six shiny black tapered legs thrashed erratically outward.

At once, all of the cicadas vanished, leaving the bowl empty except for the key.

"Ok," Emily said. "I'm ready to listen."

Rachel started again, this time with buying the orb at the fair and ending with a detailed description of her experience at Morgan's shop.

11

"This is crazy. Are you sure there are people looking for you?" Emily said. "Wouldn't you have seen some sign of that by now?"

"What if I have and just haven't noticed?" Rachel said.

"That sounds paranoid."

"Maybe. But the night I talked with my mom through the orb, that feeling that someone murdered her was so real. I've never been so certain of something, especially after what Morgan told me about that coven."

"I still don't trust this Morgan person," Emily said. "You need to try to think rationally. Do you know how ridiculous it sounds to say there's some conspiracy to kill you?"

"Look, I don't know what's going on. But I think if I can find out what happened to Rosemary, I'll have a starting point at least."

"I'll take your shifts if you need to take time off to do research," Emily said. "And I can do some searching online too. Just please don't do anything rash."

"I won't. I'm going to go check out public records in person tomorrow to see if I can find anything," Rachel said. "Come over Monday night after work, and we'll compare notes and see."

"So what happens if you find something?" Emily said. "What will you do then?"

"If I find evidence, I'll go to the police," Rachel said.

"And if you don't?" Emily said.

"If I find the truth, but not evidence? Or if there's nothing?" Rachel asked. She shrugged. "I'll cross that bridge when I come to it."

"Just promise me you won't do anything crazy. That you'll at least talk to me," Emily said.

"Of course," Rachel said. "Will you come with me to meet Morgan later this week?"

"Sure, it couldn't hurt. Just text me, we'll figure it out."

Her phone buzzed with a text message. She ignored it. It wasn't that she didn't like Mike. He seemed like a nice guy, but finding Rosemary Crantz was her priority. She needed to find out who killed her mother before they found her.

Her phone buzzed again, so she took a look. He had sent her six text messages, most of which were asking what she was doing this weekend. She remembered telling him she was unavailable all weekend at the restaurant just a few days ago. She started to text back, and then put her phone up. She'd worry about it later.

***

Rachel's doorbell rang just after 9 a.m. on Sunday morning. She had slept in, grateful for the good rest after an intense week. She had felt so alone since the first night the orb glowed. She had doubted her own sanity at times. But now she had two other women involved who believed her, even if they didn't want to believe each other. And she had genuine resources she could use, like the book Morgan had lent her.

The moleskin notebook was the size of her hand, and its pages were full of magical inventions. According to the book, creating magical objects was high cost magic if the magic effects weren't set in parameters. A box with a hole cut in it could be turned into a weather forecasting device with only a few coins, if the effect was only meant to last a day.

Witches had been using magic to enhance tools since the very first witch, according to the book. Rachel thought about how helpful that would have been back when they were renovating the coffee shop. It had taken days just to do the demolition of a cement wall, but a super powered sledgehammer would have done the trick in an instant.

She was stirred from her thoughts by the doorbell.

"*That's weird,*" she thought. "*Shouldn't be any packages on Sunday. And I'm not expecting anyone.*"

She thought it unlikely that someone out to kill her would ring her doorbell, but she peeked through the blinds in the living room anyway to see if there was a car in the driveway. There was.

It was Mike's black BMW. She had given him her address to pick her up for date the week before that she had cancelled. She relaxed some but also got annoyed. Why hadn't he called first?

Mike stood on the porch, dressed in a pale gray collared shirt and black slacks that looked tailored to his legs. One arm was behind his back. He laughed as soon as he saw the look on her face.

"I know, I should have called, but that would have ruined the surprise," he said before handing her the bouquet of flowers he'd been hiding. They were large red hydrangeas, big bushy clumps of petals on thick green stems. "I wanted to apologize if I've come on too strong. I think you're really special, and I'm willing to go as slow as you'd like to go."

"So to tell me you want to go slow you show up at my house uninvited with flowers?" Rachel thought to herself. She didn't take the flowers from him. She didn't want to hurt his feelings, so she phrased it as gently as she could.

"I'm really busy right now, Mike. A new project just landed in my lap that has to be done as soon as possible," Rachel said. "I don't really have time to date anyone right now. I'm sorry."

"Like I said, I can go as slow as you'd like to go," he said. "If right now isn't good, that's fine. I can wait for you."

Rachel was sure he meant to be romantic, but he was creeping her out. He bent down and picked up a brown paper bag she hadn't noticed by his feet.

"I brought you biscuits and gravy, but you probably don't want that if you're working. It's basically nap fuel."

"No, not really," she said. She felt guilty. It wasn't that she wasn't attracted to him. "I'll tell you what, I can still do breakfast on Tuesday if you're interested."

He grinned, and Rachel saw the dimples and wondered why a guy as hot as Mike had to come along at the worst possible time for her. She smiled back and gave him a hug before sending him on his way, taking the flowers at the last minute after he insisted.

***

Mike drove back to his apartment alone. He pulled into the parking deck so quickly that the tires squealed when he stomped on the brakes. He let himself ride the inertia of the sudden stop, going limp above the waist so that the seatbelt caught him hard in the clavicle before sending him back to the headrest.

He was stressed. This wasn't going well. He had to put all his effort into planning the best date ever on Tuesday morning. He would surprise her with another gift like Mom had suggested. Clearly she wasn't impressed with flowers.

He was thinking about jewelry when his phone rang. He answered using the car's Bluetooth system. It was Karen.

"Hi Mom," he said.

"Is anyone with you?" Karen's irritated voice said from the car speakers.

He knew it annoyed her, but he still called her mom whenever he had the chance. After all, he'd grown up calling her mom until he went to college. He'd done so until she had a talk with him the summer before he moved to the dorm at the University of Memphis.

They had been fighting because Karen had wanted him to go to school where his father had gone, Xavier University in Cincinnati. Mike had wanted to go somewhere closer to home in Memphis, so he had never even applied at Xavier. He let this information slip while they were packing up his room, and his mother immediately went on one of her tirades.

She had been packing a box of books from his desk when he had told her. Her immediate response was to sweep the box off the desk and onto the floor with a quick and angry swipe. She whirled around to look at him, and he noticed her hands were clenched into fists.

She could be caring, but her temper was quick. As long as things were going how she wanted, she was almost sweet to him. She had been very encouraging of his studies, and she had enrolled him in after school programs that his babysitters would pick him up from.

They used to go camping at least once a month when he was in elementary and middle school, but when he started high school the organization demanded a lot more from her. She'd return home late at night, often after he went to bed. He would sometimes see her in the morning before the driver took him to school. She had taken off a few days to help him get ready for college, and this was how he had repaid her—by telling her how he hadn't done what she told him to do.

He had always wanted to help her, so that she would have more time for him and for herself. He knew she was stressed. She was always working, constantly on business trips or at the office. When she was home lately, it sometimes seemed like she wasn't even there. He had seen her the night before staring in the mirror and touching her face like she was looking for wrinkles.

There weren't any on her face. Her smooth skin hadn't aged since before he was born, and she was still as slim as she was in her wedding pictures. He had said she looked beautiful, and when she had looked at him, she had seemed so far away in her eyes that it had unnerved him. He had started to wonder then if she knew he hadn't applied to Xavier. The thought kept him up all night and tugged at him the next day until he confessed halfway through packing up his room.

He thought these things as soon as she shoved the books off his desk. He felt a rush of guilt. Her reaction spelled it out for him—she hadn't known, but it was clear it was a betrayal to her. He knew it was no use arguing with his mom, especially since she was paying for his school. If he didn't get a degree he didn't know what he could do, so he sat down on the edge of his bed and looked up at her.

She looked disgusted at the books spilled on the floor, and then she moved her gaze to him. Her expression didn't change. He thought her gaze was like a spotlight, only you were frozen by it on a stage where you didn't know any of the lines. Only she did. And if all her attention was on you, there wasn't much you could do but sit there and take it. Maybe it was more like being in a firing squad, he thought before he realized he hadn't been listening. He was going to pay for that, he knew it.

"You're not even listening! All the things I've done for you, and you couldn't do one simple thing for your mother?" she had cried out. Sometimes she yelled so loud it hurt his ears. "I ought to make you live at home instead of sending you off to the dorms. Clearly you can't be trusted with even simple things. How do you think that makes me feel? Do you think it makes me feel like you're ready to join the organization?"

He had shook his head. He had sometimes wondered if he ever wanted to be part of her organization, but those thoughts made him feel terrible. She wouldn't tell him much about it, saying that he wasn't ready and that it wasn't time yet, but sometimes she'd tell him about the kind of people they hired. He thought it was great that they hired people who were down on their luck, and he wondered if giving people second chances made it all worth it for her. She was gone most nights of the week, and based on how often she yelled at him, it seemed like stressful work.

He knew his mom didn't mean the things she said to him sometimes. It couldn't just be the work, he had thought. His father had passed when he was seven years old, and he thought his mom carried that with her sometimes.

"She doesn't mean it, he thought, she's just overstressed and alone. And I've been bad—I've been making my own plans when she's already made plans for me. I'm ungrateful. She's giving me a dorm for four years, a checking account, and a job right out of school. An even better job if I graduate with honors. And I didn't even apply to the school she wanted me to go to, because I wanted to what? To be closer to home? To help her? Is this what I want life to be?"

"I should have known you'd be a liar," she had said, and the hate in her voice was so sharp it cut right through his thoughts. "Just like your father."

He knew she didn't mean it. He only ever heard bad things about his father when she was mad. The Frank she talked about when she was in a good mood sounded like a completely different person. Sometimes she just exploded, he thought. She couldn't help it. He got up and moved to the box of books she had knocked over. He got down on his knees and started putting the books back into the box, trying not to look up at her.

Mike took his gaze to the floor, where he studied the fibers in carpet while she yelled at him, as though maybe he could learn how to be like them. They were tough. They got stepped on and mashed all the time, but they were fine in the end. It occurred to him that carpet sometimes has to be replaced. He finished putting the books back in the box while she stood over him ranting with her hands on her hips.

"Are you listening to me?" Karen had asked. He could tell by her voice that she was winding down. She sounded tired. He sat back down on the edge of the bed, holding the box on his lap.

"Yes, Mom," he said, looking up at her. "I just wanted to be closer to home so I can help you. That's all."

She had smiled then and came close to him. She sat next to him on the bed and put her arm around him. When she spoke, her voice was so calm and kind that it scared him. He never forgot what she told him.

"There are many things I have not told you because you have not yet earned my trust. You are going to have to earn my trust to be part of this organization. That and graduating with honors should be your only mission over the next four years. To show you that I can trust you, I'm going to tell you one secret. Will you keep a secret for your mother?"

"Yes, ma'am," he said.

"Not long from now," she had told him then, "You will continue to grow, and I will continue to look the same, as I always have. It will look strange to people when they see you call a woman who is your age or who looks younger than you 'Mom.' They won't understand. To protect us both, you need to call me Karen when we're in public. Is that understood?"

Mike wasn't as surprised as he felt he should have been. The lack of surprise felt like a strange void in his feelings. He wasn't sure he understood how she did it, but he had noticed his mother looked the same now as she in photographs from when his parents were young. He had always thought it was just good genetics. Hearing her acknowledge her youthful appearance felt strange. He wanted to ask her why or how, but the timing didn't feel right. It never felt right. She was quick to fly into a mood when it was just the two of them alone.

"Yes ma'am," he said.

"And the next time I give you an order, are you going to ignore it?" she said.

"No, ma'am," he said.

"Good," she said. "Because I want you to take over the organization when it's the right time, but I won't even take you on unless you follow my orders without questioning. I also won't pay for your school if you can't follow instructions. If you fuck up again, you'll live at home and use the dorm as an office, do you understand? You know the rule."

He knew the rule, and she knew he knew the rule. He recited it because he knew she wanted to hear it. They had done this routine as far back as he could remember.

"She who has the gold makes the rules," he said.

"That's right," she said and smiled.

***

It had taken him a few years to get used to it. He liked to call her mom every now and then because it seemed to irritate her now. Usually though, he called her Karen. He had an idea of how much money was at stake based on his mother's luxurious houses and apartments. She had staff, and he wanted to have staff one day of his own. He sometimes thought about this when he was getting ready in the morning—the idea of someone who was paid to make him breakfast or bring him fresh towels. It gave him something to look forward to, whenever she retired and put him in charge. Things would be easier then.

But as much as he loved riling up his mother in the ways she tolerated, he didn't want to be the one to spoil the group's plans with a careless tongue. He only chose to call her Mom since he was alone in the car.

"No Mom, it's just me."

"How's progress with Rachel?" she asked.

"I really like her, Mom," he said. "She's really nice and smart. She listens to great music and is funny. But she's not interested in me. She was at first, but she's been really distant for the last week."

"Since Friday?"

"Yeah, how'd you know?"

"Mike, I told you this is a top priority for the group. You didn't pay attention to the briefing video I sent you?"

"I know you want her to join the group as soon as possible. I've got her interests down. It's not that."

Karen's response came in sickly sweet tones.

"I know it's not that. If you had been paying attention you'd know that the night of your little rendezvous at the club was when she received her powers. She just found out her mom died. You were meant to comfort her during this time. Is that not what you've been doing?"

"Why can't I tell her that we helped her mom?"

"Because she'll think we killed her. How is that not obvious to you?" Karen said. "Theresa left our group, and we don't know where she went. We know she died because Rachel's got her power now, but if we tell Rachel that she will not trust us. It's too much. Now, have you been keeping the handkerchief on you?"

"Yes, ma'am," he said.

"It might not be strong enough. I'll see what I can do, but you have to bring her to the solstice gathering on the 21st. I'll gently break everything down for her then."

"I have been trying! I wish you would tell me why I can't just tell her about the organization before the solstice. This would be so much easier if I could just be honest," Mike said.

Karen was silent. When she responded, her voice was calm and measured.

"Mike, when you say stupid shit like this, it makes me think there's something wrong with you," she said. "Think. What have I told you hundreds of times about information?"

"That control of information is the only way the organization works, and that I'll have access to Level 5 info when I'm a Level 5," Mike said. "But I've been a Level 4 for six years, Mom!"

"You wouldn't even be Level 4 if I wasn't the leader of this organization," Karen said. "Whining isn't going to help you. Getting Rachel to join our group next week will. I promise you. Now, are you coming over for dinner tonight? Chef is preparing a vegetarian meal since I'm abstaining from meat ahead of the solstice."

"I'll be there," Mike said.

12

Susan Murphy was ready for Halloween 1983 to hurry up and get here. It was late September, and her favorite month was right around the corner. She had already started thinking about her Halloween costume options all month and hadn't made a decision yet. She planned on going to at least one of the parties on fraternity row, but she didn't know that she wouldn't make it to any party, let alone October.

She had been debating being either a witch or a Martian. Since her grandmother had died and left her with the ability to perform complicated spells, the witch costume seemed boring. Almost stereotypical. Her grandmother had never worn a cape or a conical hat, and she hadn't collected any crystals either. Susan had grown up thinking she was a doctor, but her mother had told her she was a medical botanist.

She'd had a greenhouse that she sometimes let Susan into, where the plants never stopped thriving no matter what season it was. The greenhouse was empty now. Most of the plants were slowly dying at her mother's house, but one of the snake plants stood in front of her bed at the dorm. It had grown an extra foot since she took it with her.

She had been studying big dusty books of old spells all summer. Her mom had been at her every chance she could get to study her "family history" more. There were books dating back to before America was settled, books translated from forgotten foreign languages, and dusty tomes full of instructions on herbs and sigils. Susan found it incredibly boring. She loved the magic, but hated the studying. She figured it was taking college courses on top of studying magic that was causing her burnout, but she hadn't figured out yet how to work around her seemingly finite amount of attention.

"Halloween costumes," Susan said to herself, trying to get her train of thought back on track. She tripped over an uneven piece of sidewalk, stumbled but kept her footing. She kept walking, thinking about how she would go about dressing up as a Martian.

It was September 23rd, and the weather was beginning to chill. It was after midnight, she knew, but she didn't think it was too late to be out. She was walking home to the dormitories from a party near the University of Memphis campus. She had gotten bored at the party after attempts to start conversations failed to take off. But the beer was fueling her imagination, and as she walked down the dark, car lined street, her thoughts returned to her seasonal obsession. She wanted to dress up as a Martian, with as many eyes as possible, she decided. At least 20 eyeballs, she thought as she started humming "20 Eyes" by The Misfits.

As she was thinking for the 5th time about how to make fake eyeballs, she heard a woman's voice from a parked car as she passed. She turned to see where it had come from. There was a woman leaning out of a car window one car down.

"I said, do you need a ride?" the woman repeated.

She looked nice enough, but Susan only had another block to walk. She told the woman so, and the woman had smiled back at her.

"Well, that's alright. I don't mind helping a student," the woman said.

She smiled at Susan with such maternal kindness that Susan walked around the front of her car and got into the passenger seat. The woman driving was small, with a polite face and large pale blue eyes. If Susan had been more sober or more studious, she might have noticed the bronze pendulum in the woman's lap. The bronze point was covered with tiny markings and symbols that aided the pendulum in pointing out witches. In her research, Karen had discovered some of the bronze implements that were used during the witch hunts in ancient Rome. It had taken her researchers a few years to replicate some of the designs, but thanks be to Nephilor and witch's blood, they worked for at least a week at a time.

But Susan didn't notice the bronze pendulum that had led Karen to her. She only looked at Karen's face as she got into the car and buckled in. Then she just looked ahead and pointed down the street.

"You just have to go straight. This street dead ends at the dorms," she told the woman. "I'm Susan. Thank you for the ride."

"Pleased to meet you."

The woman nodded her head, smiled at her and then faced the front again. Susan thought she seemed a little weird, but nice enough. Karen started the car, reversed, cranked the wheel and then turned her car out of the parallel parking spot where she and Frank had been waiting for Susan for two hours. They had watched her walk into the party, and had sat waiting in the dark for her eventual return to the dorms.

Susan leaned back and closed her eyes for a moment, feeling dizzy from the beer. She didn't see the man in the back of the car uncover himself. She also didn't see him wet a cloth. She felt something cold and wet and strong smelling on her face. Then there was nothing.

***

She felt the ground underneath her. She felt groggy, and her head hurt. She couldn't see. As she tried to move, she realized she was bound with rough feeling rope. She felt a rag in her mouth, and realized she had been gagged and blindfolded. She wriggled around, but froze when she heard a voice. It was the same woman that had picked her up.

"She's waking up. We'll begin soon."

She felt hands at her head, and cringed. She tried to kick out her legs, but she had been bound so tightly she couldn't move. The hands removed her blindfold, and as her eyes adjusted to the light, Susan saw that she was in a dark room with stone walls, almost like a cave of some kind. The dank smell and darkness reminded her of her grandmother's basement.

Eight hooded figures were around her in a circle wearing shapeless dark green cloaks with hoods pulled up to cover their faces. In front of her, holding her blindfold, was another similarly cloaked stranger. In the hand that wasn't holding her blindfold, Susan saw a glint of metal.

Susan looked at the person closest to her. Tears began streaming down her face. She could not see the details of their face in the dark shadows of their cowl. She felt with every ounce of her intuition that nothing she said or did would convince them to let her go, but she could not stop herself from begging for her life.

"What's going on? Please let me go," Susan said. "I'll give you anything you want. I'm a witch. I can give you anything. Just please let me go."

Her pleas were muffled by the gag. Karen almost laughed at how absurdly pitiful Susan was acting. She had expected more of a struggle, and she almost felt bad for the little witchling. This was to be her second witch sacrifice, and if she had a conscience left, it was calling out to her. With the last bit of her compassion, Karen spoke.

"I'll remove the gag if you promise not to scream or fuss. No one can hear you down here anyway. Do you have any last words you want to speak?" Karen said.

Susan nodded, sniffing. She looked so weak and pitiful that Karen untied the gag. Holding the fabric in her hand with the blindfold, Karen looked at Susan expectantly.

"Go on then," she said.

Susan closed her eyes, and her brows scrunched together, wrinkling her forehead. Then she released all tension in her face, and the skin went smooth. She opened her eyes. There were no fresh tears, and the wet streaks of snot on her face did nothing to undermine the pure malice that shone through her eyes.

"With my forebears, I curse you. You will be found, and you will be punished," Susan said with a tone of grave finality.

Karen rolled her eyes. With a sigh, she spoke the words, then took the knife and slit the girl's throat. The blood sprayed across her, painting the front of her robe slick red. Frank stepped close to Karen and handed her a chalice. Karen filled up the cup with the blood, and then stood up, holding the chalice high over her head. She prayed to Nephilor for the necessary requests, and when that was completed she took the first sip.

"Nephilor!" she shouted.

"Nephilor!" shouted the hooded figures together. "Praised be his name!"

Karen took another sip from the cup, and the chanting and sipping went on for seven rounds before cleanup and blood preservation could begin. They'd been experimenting with different stabilizers, but it would be years before they had funds to upgrade their storage technology, barring a miracle. She smiled with wet red lips as she looked down from her altar to her cloaked followers. There was plenty of time.

13

Emily had only found one thing online, and it was a birth certificate from 1933 in Memphis. The name was a match, but when she texted her about it on Sunday, Rachel had told her she was certain Rosemary was in Kentucky or Ohio. Emily brought a printed copy of it to Rachel's house anyway after work on Monday evening. They were sitting at the counter on red metal bar stools in Rachel's kitchen waiting for a frozen pizza to bake in the oven and discussing how their days had gone.

While Emily was at the shop that morning, Rachel had driven across the river into Cincinnati, where she went through public records at the courthouse downtown. After not finding anything there with the name Rosemary Ellen Crantz, she went to the main library. She told a librarian she was looking into genealogy of her grandparents, and that she only had a name. They helped her find the same certificate Emily had, and she had also printed it out.

Rachel took the pizza out and slid it onto a cutting board. While she waited for it to cool, she looked at the two printed certificates next to each other on the counter. She wondered if maybe she was wrong. She had been certain that Rosemary was in Ohio or Kentucky, but she supposed she could have been born in Memphis.

"There's no matching death certificate, which could mean she's still alive. But it could also mean that she went missing, like my mom. I think the only way we're going to find out if this is her is if I use magic," Rachel said.

"I think so too," Emily said. "But I don't want you hurting yourself."

"This is one of those chances I have to take," Rachel said. "If I don't figure out soon who it is that's killed my mom, they're going to find me first."

"Let's see what we find out," Emily said. "I'm here to help, but just remember that it could be nothing."

Rachel and Emily talked about what sort of spell Rachel should do while they ate dinner. While Rachel cleaned the plates afterward, Emily drove to the nearest gas station and bought maps of the greater Cincinnati area, including Northern Kentucky. She brought them back to Rachel's house, and the two of them unfolded all of the maps and laid them across the living room floor.

They placed the maps so that they lined up correctly geographically, leaving a foot of space between each map. Rachel stood in the middle of the arrangement with the maps spread around her. She wore the eye mask she used for sleeping on top of her head and held a copy of Rosemary's birth certificate in each hand.

"Are you ready?" she asked Emily, who stood in front of Rachel on the other side of the map quilt.

"Sure," Emily said. "I've got the marker ready."

Emily raised her marker in salute. Rachel pulled the black eye mask over her eyes, which she closed anyway. She thought about what it was she hoped to accomplish with this and how to phrase it.

"I'm going to spin. Where I land is where Rosemary Crantz is if she's on these maps."

Rachel spun around, again and again, until she lost count. She spun more, until she felt ill. She had no idea which direction she was pointing in. She spun once more slowly, and then stepped forward. She felt paper crunch under her bare feet. She leaned forward and then lowered herself to her knees. She could hear some of the paper tear, but it wasn't the important area. She let go of the birth certificates and held her hands with her palms down before reaching down with her right pointer finger. She pressed a spot on the paper map that she couldn't see.

"Here," Rachel said. "Mark here."

She smelled the permanent marker stench and lifted her eye mask. Emily had drawn a spot exactly where her finger was. It was in Kentucky, right on a town named Hearth. Rachel went to her office and searched until she found the biggest map of Hearth she could find with roads included.

She printed off a copy of the road map of Hearth, and they repeated the process. They blew up the map to make it as large as possible, printing it off in 6 sheets of paper. This time when Emily marked the spot Rachel landed on, they had a street location they could look up.

Emily was already looking up the location on her phone when Rachel took off her eye mask. When she found what she was looking for, she looked up at Rachel, feeling trepidation for the first time. For a moment she thought she saw two or three points of light flicker high over Rachel's head, but there was nothing there. She rubbed her eyes.

"What is it?" Rachel asked.

Emily showed the screen to Rachel. They were both sitting cross legged on the floor in Rachel's living room. The blue-white light of the screen made them both pale, but any color in Rachel's face drained away when she saw what Emily had found.

"No," Rachel whispered.

"It's a cemetery," Emily said. "I'm sorry. Maybe this isn't her. The birth certificate says she was born in '33, so this doesn't mean anything special. She'd be 86. That's older than what Morgan said witches usually live to see. That's not such an unusual age to die."

"It's strange that there's no death certificate though. I can keep looking," Rachel said. "But the only way I'm going to know if this is her is if I go to Hearth and see. You don't have to go with me."

"Nuh uh, I was in Girl Scouts. We use the buddy system. There's no way I'm letting you go there alone," Emily said. "What if you're right and there's someone there? I'm going with you. I'm working tomorrow and Wednesday but am off Thursday."

"Let's go on Thursday. We'll go after they open," Rachel said. "I've got dinner with Grandma on Wednesday, so I'm going to ask her about Mom to see if she has anything I haven't seen that might help. I've been putting that off."

"Understandable," Emily said. "Let me know if you want me to come with."

"Thanks," Rachel said. "Just keep believing me."

"Of course," Emily said. "You know I'm here if you need to talk about what Morgan told you. There's no way we're going to Hearth without talking about it."

"About how I'm gonna die before 60?"

"Yeah. Which I don't buy," Emily said.

"To tell you the truth, I never thought I'd make it to 30. I mean, I told you about some of the stupid shit I did in high school. When I was 17 and hadn't heard anything from my mom in so long that my grandmother filed a missing person's report, I tried to binge on anything I could find that would make me feel different. I thought about death a lot."

"I'm so sorry," Emily said.

"I didn't want to die, but I couldn't help thinking about death. It was just part of my life. I mean, it's part of everyone's life," Rachel said. "No one gets out alive. My dad died when I was six, and I don't remember anything about him. I don't even have any pictures. So naturally, when Grandma took me to mass I was eager to be Catholic. It seemed like the only chance to see my Dad again was in Heaven. It seemed like magic.

"So when Mom stopped writing and Grandma filed the report, I returned to those thoughts. But they didn't bring the same comfort they did when I was a child. I had already begun to question a lot of what I had learned in church. I didn't know what to believe or do anymore, and that's not a good place to be when you're 17. I'm lucky Grandma noticed. It took a lot of therapy and being honest with myself about how I was being self-destructive, but the best thing that came out of that time period was the way I started thinking about death. I had it all twisted up.

"I stopped thinking about the afterlife and accepted that I was going to die. That's just part of life. No one gets a say in when their time comes, and no one knows if there's anything after this. I found it easier to assume that there's not anything after this. That this is all the time we have, so we have to make it count. I do the best that I can for myself and those that came before me. Every day. That view hasn't changed just because of what Morgan said."

Emily unfolded her legs and got on her knees. She wrapped her arms around Rachel and hugged her tightly. Rachel leaned her head against Emily and put a hand on her arm, squeezing her back before letting go.

"I'm glad you try to be optimistic with your nihilism," Emily said. "I know that can be hard. I've got a similar view on death, which might be why we've always gotten along so well. Neither of us like to waste the precious time we've got."

"That's right," Rachel said. "Which is why I have to figure this out."

"As long as we take what we find to the right authorities, I'm with you every step of the way."

Rachel nodded and smiled wearily.

"We'll do everything we can by the books and see where this goes," Rachel said. "But don't worry about me. Worry about whoever murdered my mother."

"Telling me that doesn't make me worry any less about you," Emily said. "You're my best friend, and I'm not going to let you lose yourself to a revenge fantasy."

Emily put her hand on Rachel's while she said this, but Rachel withdrew her hand when she responded.

"I don't have a revenge fantasy. I want to know what happened to my mom. If it turns out that she was really murdered, then I'm going to do everything I can to get justice for her. Please believe me. If there's a way to do it legally, that's what I'll do. I just don't know if that's going to be the case."

"Fair enough."

14

At the beginning of the 20th century, plans were made and construction was started on a subway system below Cincinnati. The once-popular canal running through downtown had become disused and dirty. Few boats trafficked the waterway. Railroads and cars had made the waterway obsolete, but it could still serve a purpose if drained.

Construction was underway for years as tunnels and stations were built using sections of the canal bed. It was an expensive endeavor, and the timing proved to be its demise. Inflation after World War I caused the project to rapidly outgrow its budget, as the cost of materials alone was twice as much as the initial budget in the post-War economy. There were efforts at revival, but the subway was put on hiatus in 1928. The Great Depression, World War II, and political squabbling ensured the project's death.

Roughly two and a half miles of subway were built using the remains of the canal system, but no tracks were ever laid down. Stations built above ground were demolished, and entrances were sealed off. Grates for venting along Central Parkway, the boulevard built on top of the tunnels, remain one of the few signs above ground of the tunnels. Some of the tunnels were used by the city to run water mains and fiber optic cables, but most efforts at rapid transit have been above ground.

The city maintains the tunnels in order to keep Central Parkway operational, as it quickly became vital for North-South passage, running like an artery through the heart of downtown. The Cincinnati police patrol the tunnels and stations using secured steel entrances along the highway. They check the tunnels to make sure they remain empty, but they only inspect four of the six stations. The Linn Street and Trettle Street stations are ignored on these patrols because they are hidden, bricked up like Montresor's friend in Poe's "The Cask of Amontillado."

Karen had heard tales of the subway from her parents growing up in Cincinnati. They didn't tear down the above ground stations until the '60s. Her father had been against building the subway when it was proposed in 1920. He thought it was a mistake that was going to take jobs from those that lived in the city, like they did. She remembered his stories and the potential of the tunnels when they decided to expand into Cincinnati.

Building in access to a walled off station had been nearly impossible to keep under cover, but money went a long way in keeping people quiet. The club property was purchased in 1994 under a shell company. After significant sound proofing, construction had been done under cover of night to gain access to the tunnels. Once a door and tunnel had been constructed to gain access to the underground station, the property was made to look abandoned. When Mike was given the property in late 2017, there was still substantial work that had to be done before it could be opened.

The location of Church had been chosen specifically for the access point it gave to the Trettle Street station. The station was walled off from the rest of the subway system, and Karen made sure the walls that lined the platform were reinforced and soundproofed. Exactly nine people knew about the secret chamber under Church, by Karen's design. It was a secret one had to work through the club's level system all the way to the top in order to find out. The space was used only a handful of times and otherwise remained empty. It was a sacred space, after all.

On Monday night at the station under Trettle Street, the northernmost station and the last one built, Karen knelt before a white marble altar. She clasped her hands together above her head before laying her head on the ground, spreading her forest green cloak out around her. She whispered into the earth a long string of curses and gibbering, repeating them over and over. This wasn't always how she performed this ritual. Normally she would have called the other level 5 members, but this required urgency. This particular spell was going to require a lot of power. The witch's blood would work, but she needed as much of Nephilor's magic as he could give her.

She scratched his name onto the ground with a piece of white chalk. She wrote the name carefully, scooted on her knees to the left and writing it again, over and over to form a circle around the altar. She was not alone in the cavernous station. A young dark haired witch named Megan was on the other side of the altar, although not of her own will. She was tied to a wooden armchair with Para cord rope.

She had been visiting a club in Memphis a week ago when she was invited home by a handsome young man. He had been all over her on the dance floor, and said he wanted to get to know her in private. They had spent an hour in a dark booth, where he had entertained her and gotten her drunk before he suggested they get out of there.

She had gone with him, but she noticed she was stumbling more than she should have been when she left the club. She passed out soon after getting in a car. When she awoke, she was in a cage in the tunnels with only a bucket and a roll of toilet paper. The cage was made of chain link fencing, but the cuffs they placed on her hands were made of bronze covered in inscriptions. She figured out quickly that she couldn't cast any spells with the cuffs on. They had fed her nothing but eggs all week, standing over her with a lantern in the dark. They had drugged her before they bound her to the chair with rope and gagged her. She was awakening in time to witness Karen's dark ceremony. She tried to speak and to call for help, but her voice was muffled by the gag in her mouth.

Karen heard her rustling, but didn't let it distract her. She was confident in the binds she had placed her in. They strengthened the enchantment on the bronze bindings with each sacrifice. Finished with her whispering ritual, Karen sat up onto her heels in a squat in the middle of her chalk circle, and raised her hands in the air.

"Oh Nephilor, eternal father, you who would give us magic despite our imperfections, you who would give us eternal life to serve you, I plead to you to show us direction during this our time of trial. The girl will be among us soon, but we want to ensure she will be under our thumb.

"Her power is growing stronger, I can feel it," Karen said. "Oh eternal one, please guide me."

She stood, walked back to the altar, and looked at the tools she had brought and placed lovingly on the altar before she prayed: A silver chalice and a sharp silver knife. They never seemed enough, but she knew they pleased Nephilor since he always granted her what she asked when she used them. She would use them today to renew Nephilor's gift, but also to enchant something to assist her son. She slipped on a pair of black leather gloves.

"It is clear we must continue our course, but that we are not pleasing you, Lord. We will increase our gifts to you. Nephilor be praised."

She picked up the cup and plucked the knife off the altar and turned to face the bound witch, whose eyes widened upon seeing the blade. Karen smiled at the woman, and stepped closer. Megan began to throw her body around in the chair as much as she could, but it was useless. The chair barely budged, its legs scraping lightly on the concrete platform. She tried to throw her weight to the left, then to the right, and back again, tears streaming from her wide blue eyes.

"With this kiss I seal this sacrifice to you, Nephilor. May it sustain you, and may you see to it that Rachel falls in love with my son. May this love put her under our thumb. Grant me the continued strength and youth you have been giving me all these years, so that I may continue our mission to bring you into this world so you can cleanse it as you see fit."

Megan's rocking succeeding in putting so much weight on the front right leg of the chair that it splintered. It was useless, since she was still bound. Laying on her side on the dusty platform, she realized the futility of her efforts and began to weep, her cries muffled by the gag.

Karen knelt down next to her, putting the knife inside the chalice and setting it on the ground behind her so that it was out of Megan's sight. She made calming shushing sounds and wiped away Megan's tears. Tracing the curve of her jawline with her thumb, Karen knelt down and kissed Megan's forehead. Megan quieted and looked up at Karen, unsure what this meant, and desperate enough to hope that it meant a change of heart. She didn't see Karen pick up the knife, but felt it when Karen placed the blade against her neck.

Karen pulled the hood of her cloak over her head. Megan looked up at her, screaming into her gag and with eyes bulging as Karen cut open her throat. The red hot blood splattered on the green cloak like a Jackson Pollock painting, and Karen filled the chalice as it came gushing out in spurts from Megan's throat. Once the cup was full, Karen rose and returned to the altar.

She raised the cup, and took a long sip from it. The hot iron taste filled her mouth, and when she opened her mouth to say his name again, some of it dribbled out onto her chin.

"Nephilor!" she intoned.

She took another sip, sucking down the blood like she had so many times before.

"Nephilor!"

She slurped from the cup, blood hot on her lips.

"Nephilor!"

The taste was disgusting, like drinking molten pennies, but she knew it was worth it. She did this seven times. It felt better than ever. She could feel the magic coursing through her. She could feel Nephilor's strength in her.

When the cup was almost drained, she dropped two small objects into it and rolled them around in the blood before plucking them out and rinsing them with rubbing alcohol. After they dried, she placed them in a small black jewelry box.

She wiped her face with the sleeve of the cloak before pulling it off over her head. She tossed the robe on top of the dead witch and pulled off her gloves, tossing them on top of the cloak. She checked her hands for signs of blood. They were clean. She left, using the steel door at the far left side of the platform. The door led to a very narrow staircase at the top of which was a trap door. She pushed open the door and walked up the steps into one of the secured basement spaces in Church.

The walls of the room were lined with monitors that two level 5 employees were watching from their desks. Wayne, head of security, nodded deferentially at her when she looked up at them. Lisa, a bespectacled woman with long brown hair, pulled a sandwich bag out of her purse with a wet piece of cloth in it and handed it to Karen.

"What is this?" Karen asked.

"Makeup remover wipe," she said. She touched her hand to her own cheek. "You've got some here."

Karen nodded and opened the bag. She wiped her face with the wipe before speaking again. She put the now pink wipe back in the sandwich bag and handed it back to Lisa, who put it in the trash can next to her chair.

"Thank you, Lisa. I need you to go clean up a mess in the ritual room. You may take another Level 5 if you need assistance. Save what blood you can, but make sure you completely dispose of the body per standard protocol. Nephilor shall be pleased with your efforts if you do this quickly but with care."

"Yes ma'am," Lisa said, bowing her head. "I'm grateful for the opportunity to please our lord."

Lisa went to a cabinet at the back of the room and pulled out a bucket of cleaning supplies. She draped a long black bag and thin yellow biohazard suit over her shoulder. She walked toward the stairs but waited. It was never acceptable to leave the room before Karen did.

"I thank you both for your diligence. I know there's been some whispers among the 5's about involving my son, but Nephilor's plans will not be challenged. He has revealed to me that we will meet our goal the night of the solstice. The sacrifice provided by the Memphis branch has sealed it."

"Praise be to Nephilor," Lisa said.

"Praise be to Nephilor," Karen and the white haired man at the computer desk responded.

Karen turned and left, stopping in her office to pick up her purse before exiting through the back door of the club. She got in the backseat of the car that had been waiting for her. Her driver closed his book when he saw her. Once he opened the door for her and offered her a bottle of water, he maneuvered the black luxury sedan out the back of the crowded parking lot and onto the highway.

"*Nephilor will be returned to corporeal form. With me by his side, everyone will face our judgement,*" she thought as she watched the billboards pass as they drove to her Covington apartment. "*Let the rapture begin.*"

15

Tuesday morning, ten days before the summer solstice, Rachel woke up to the sound of her phone ringing on her bedside table. It was Mike. The clock said 7:05 a.m. She groaned.

"*Fuck*," Rachel thought as she sat up in bed. She had forgotten about their date, staying up late the night before to check online for Rosemary Crantz's death certificate. She hadn't had any luck. She rubbed her eyes and answered the phone before sitting up in bed.

"Hi Mike," she said with as much cheer as she could muster.

"Hey, just showing up didn't go so hot, so I'm calling first this time." Mike said. "Are we still on for pancakes at 9 am? I believe a greasy spoon was mentioned?"

The last thing she wanted to do was look away from the project in front of her. She had thought about going to Hearth by herself to find the grave, but the call from Mike changed her mind. Rachel smiled in spite of herself. She would wait for Emily. She'd been burning the candle at both ends, and it would be good to get a change of scenery.

"Sure, that sounds great," Rachel said. "Want to pick me up around then? We can carpool."

"Perfect," Mike said. "I'll see you then."

***

He had shown up dressed the most casual she'd seen him, with black jeans and a faded black t-shirt with a skull on it. He brought red roses this time and had waited patiently in the living room while she put them in a vase. Then they drove to the Side Street Diner and talked over cups of coffee, piles of hash browns and fried eggs. Conversation flowed easily, and Rachel was having a great time. She had to admit to herself that she enjoyed his company.

Mike waited until all the plates were cleared before he slid a black jewelry box across the booth of the diner to Rachel. She looked down at it with big eyes, feeling the butterflies in her stomach suddenly settle. She had felt like a schoolgirl all morning, but the feeling fled as she looked at the too serious box.

"Um, what is this?" Rachel said.

"I wanted to give you something special, because I think you're special," Mike said.

"You didn't have to do that. You don't have to buy me things," Rachel said. "Especially not this soon. Mike, it hasn't even been a month since we started talking."

"Please, just open it," Mike said.

Rachel looked at him with hesitation before opening the box. Inside was a pair of rose quartz earrings. Small diamonds were set on either side of the rose quartz, which had been carved into the shape of a rose. The diamonds felt inappropriate, but the rose quartz shocked Rachel. She had to combat a wave of paranoia that crashed down on her as she looked in the box.

"*How does he know?*" she thought.

"That's your birthstone right? Your profile said you were a Libra so I took a guess," Mike said, smiling. "I can return it and get pink tourmaline if you'd prefer, but I thought that'd be a bit much this early."

"Mike," Rachel said. "I can't take this."

"At least try them on," he said. "I picked them out just for you. I noticed your ears were pierced, but I've yet to see you wear earrings. Please?"

Rachel was conflicted. They were very pretty, but it felt like a red flag for Mike to give her an expensive gift this early. She wondered if maybe this was just Mike's method of courtship, like how he kept over ordering at restaurants and texting her compliments all the time. She took the earrings out of the box and looked at them in her hand. They were very pretty, and she found she did want them.

She slipped on the earrings. The way he looked at her once she had them on made her feel beautiful. She stretched her left leg out under the table until her foot was touching his. He reached under the table and squeezed above her knee gently before leaving his hand there.

"Thank you," she said. "They're lovely."

He looked so handsome in that moment that Rachel thought about suggesting they head back to her place. She was just starting to fight that impulse when her phone rang. It was Morgan. She had texted her the night before about what she had found with Emily.

"I'll be right back," Rachel said, slipping out of the booth before Mike could respond. She took the call outside, walking around the corner of the diner near the dumpster so that she wouldn't be overheard.

"You need to be careful if you go to Hearth," Morgan said. "You don't know who this Rosemary is or whether her grave is being watched."

"That's the weird thing, Morgan. There are indexes of graves online. We searched and didn't find a match for her for this cemetery. And I couldn't find a copy of her death certificate anywhere online. I'm starting to think the spell I made up to find her didn't work. Maybe it landed where it did on accident."

"That's pretty unlikely, unless you didn't want it to work," Morgan said.

"Going there is the only I'm going to find out anything," Rachel said. I'm hoping my grandmother held onto some things of my mom's that might give me a clue, but I doubt it. Hearth is the best lead I've got. But we'll go prepared, don't worry."

"Good. I hope for your sake she did. Go see her before you go to the cemetery."

"I am. I've got dinner with her tomorrow night. We have a monthly thing."

"That sounds nice," Morgan said. "I miss that kind of thing sometimes. Are you coming back to see me this week?"

"Yes, and I'm bringing Emily, who I did tell everything. You can trust her, I promise."

"We'll see. Come over Friday after 5. I'll make dinner."

"That sounds great," Rachel said. "Thanks."

She hung up and went back inside. Mike was at the counter paying the check. She picked up her purse from the booth, got cash out and left a tip on the table. He turned and smirked at her when she sidled up next to him at the register.

"You never take off work all the way, huh?" he said with a wink.

"Business never sleeps," Rachel said. "Or eats breakfast. Something like that."

"That's what I learned in school too."

Rachel laughed. It wasn't even that funny, but she felt giggly around him. They walked out to their cars, talking for a while between them. Rachel leaned against her car, and Mike stood in front of her with his hand planted on the car behind her. Their chemistry felt especially intense today.

"It's so hard not to kiss him. You've got to stay focused," Rachel thought. *"You don't need to fall for anyone right now."*

"I've got to go to work, but would you like to do something this weekend?" she said.

"Yeah, I was looking at getting tickets to the Reds game on Saturday if you're interested," Mike said as he moved his elbow closer to the car, bringing his face closer to hers by an inch.

"Oh, I'm interested," she said. They were so close to each other that she couldn't help flirting. Fuck it, she thought.

Mike kissed her then, and she kissed him back. It was only through sheer willpower that she was able to stop herself from inviting him back to her house before work. She pulled back, and he gazed into her eyes.

"We have so much in common," he said. "Do you want to come listen to records and hangout tomorrow?"

"I can't. I have plans with my grandmother after work. But the baseball game would be great," Rachel said.

"Do you have any plans for next Friday?"

"No, nothing yet."

"We're doing a private event at Church. I'd be honored if you'd be my date," he said. "It's open bar and kind of formal, so you'll need to wear a nice dress. But it doesn't have to be black."

"What is it for?"

"It's an annual party the parent company throws every summer to celebrate our founding. Usually it's at the first club in Memphis, but there's a lot of talk about making Church the flagship location. I think they're going to announce it then."

"Sounds like a big night for you then," she said.

"Oh yeah, it will be if that happens," he said. "I'd love to celebrate with you. If it gets too stuffy or they run out of drink tickets, we can always cut out early. Usually though it's a big party."

Rachel thought about it, but couldn't see any reason to say no. She thought he moved a little too fast, but maybe that was their pace. She wondered if maybe she moved too slowly.

"Sure, I'll come," Rachel said. "Sounds fun."

"Great!" Mike said, grinning widely. "I'll text you about the game, but let me know what you're thinking about wearing next Friday. There's sort of a dress code. I can let you know if it's formal enough if you want."

They kissed goodbye, and Mike hugged her tightly before letting her go.

***

Every muscle in her body was screaming at her to run or fight. She tried to move her hands and her feet, but felt only layers of thin rope tied tight enough around her wrists and ankles to cut off circulation to her fingers and feet. Even if she could get loose she wouldn't be able to stand up. She tried to scream, but there was a rubber ball in her mouth, so her cries produced nothing but useless murmuring and spittle. It made it hard to breathe the more she struggled to do something. She tried to curse the person. She'd rather kill herself murdering her attacker than die by their hand. But she couldn't speak, couldn't even move her fingers. She couldn't do anything but die.

Rachel woke up screaming, covered in a cold sweat. When she realized she was awake and alive, she was panting. She moaned and pulled herself into a ball under the blanket. Then she released and breathed in and out slowly, trying to meter her breath to slow down her heart, which was threatening to jump out of her chest. She could feel the memory of the nightmare quickly fading away, just as it had every morning as soon as she opened her eyes. Her stomach turned as she held onto the gruesome dream, determined to know what had been haunting her sleep.

She grabbed her phone, opened a blank note, and wrote down everything she could remember before her mind blocked it away. There had been a person standing over her with a silver cup in their black gloved hand. They were wearing a dark hooded cloak that hung shapeless on them like a bedsheet. They had pulled the hood down low over their face so she couldn't see them. She had felt something cold and sharp against her throat. She knew she was being murdered. Even if she was blindfolded in the dream she would have known. The certainty of her death was still evaporating. She could taste bile threatening to rise.

She slipped out of bed and checked the protection spell. She found a loose area near the front and repaired it before returning to her bedroom, weaving the golden threads without knotting the rope this time. She focused her will as strongly as she could and watched them join together again. She tried not to think about Morgan's offer of a stronghold too seriously, but she couldn't deny it was frightening that the barrier was already coming apart.

After depositing the extra coins she hadn't needed back in her office, she returned to her bedroom. She laid in bed staring at the ceiling for another hour before she was able to fall asleep. She hoped her grandmother knew something that would help. If she didn't and there wasn't anything in Hearth, Rachel was afraid she'd seen a vision of her future.

16

The second Wednesday of each month, Rachel had dinner with her paternal grandmother, Melissa Ogden. They'd tried different arrangements, but this worked best for both of them. The 72 year old widow kept a busy social calendar in addition to working 30 hours a week. She had saved enough to retire but was determined not to do so, even telling Rachel at dinner last month that she had no plans of slowing down anytime soon.

She still lived in the two bedroom brick ranch house Rachel had grown up in, although she had talked of selling it for a condo. Rachel was sure she loved it too much to ever move. The house was tucked away in a wooded neighborhood in Alexandria, about 20 minutes from Rachel's place. Most of the neighbors were retirees, although there were a few young families.

Grandma was walking Ace when Rachel showed up. Ace was Grandma's long legged black poodle. Grandma had trained him since he was a spastic little puppy to be as sure in his footing as she was in hers, and the two regularly marched around the block with their heads high and shoulders back.

"Sweet girl, I'm so glad to see you," Grandma said, giving her a big hug.

Ace was excited too. When she stepped back, the big dog jumped up at her with its paws in the air, landing them on Rachel's hips and looking up at her, with his tongue rolling out of his black snout. His tail wagged enthusiastically, shaking the black puff of fur on the end of his tail.

"Down! Sit. Good boy," Grandma said, smiling down at her dog. Ace knew all the tricks. She turned to Rachel. "Let's go inside before he loses his manners again."

Ace followed Grandma inside and so did Rachel. Rachel watched as Grandma detached the leash from the dog's red collar, wrapped it around her arm to form a loop and then hung it on a hook next to the front door beside a golden crucifix. Grandma went to hug Rachel, who squeezed her back. Grandma was shorter than Rachel, around 5' 6" with golden blonde hair that was shorter in the back than it was in the front. She clasped her hands together and smiled at Rachel.

"Are you ready to get cooking?" she asked.

"I sure am. I brought the lard you asked for," Rachel said as she unloaded two tote bags onto the counter.

She and Grandma worked together in the kitchen to make fried pork chops, potato salad, and roasted broccoli. They talked while they cooked. Grandma caught her up on the office gossip and Rachel told her how business was going and a new drink they were launching.

They talked about the bad storms that had been rolling through. This year seemed worse than ever, but storm season was almost over. By the time they sat down at the kitchen table to eat, Rachel knew there was one topic her grandmother hadn't brought up yet. It always came up.

"So, how's your love life?" Grandma said, "You said you were talking to someone. Sean?"

"No, I moved on from Sean a while back. He stood me up."

Grandma grimaced.

"That's why I'll never try online dating," Grandma said. "But you're not giving up are you?"

"No, I'm dating a man named Mike Smith right now. He runs a nightclub in Cincinnati. He just gave me a present this week actually."

Rachel tilted her head, showing her grandmother the new earrings. She hadn't taken them off since breakfast the day before. She liked the way the pink rose quartz looked with her skin. It was a softer look than she usually wore, but she thought it was a nice change. Mike had sent her a picture of the kind of dress he wanted her to wear to the event, a white wrap dress. The earrings would look amazing with it. She liked that he had good taste.

"That's sweet. He sounds like an old fashioned gentleman. I'm glad you found one you like."

"I do like him, but I'm not sure I'm ready for anything serious. There's a lot going on. As busy as work is."

"Work will always be busy, Rachel," Grandma said, "You've got to make time for everything else in life."

They ate quietly for a while. The only sound aside from the scraping of forks on plates was Ace panting in the living room. If one of them looked at Ace, he would turn away, but he was watching. He was a good boy, but Grandma always gave him her scraps.

"I guess it's not work," Rachel said. "I just think he's moving kind of fast for me. We've barely known each other a month, and he gave me these earrings yesterday. I really like them, but there's diamonds in them. Doesn't that seem like too much?"

Grandma shrugged. She set down her fork and looked at Rachel seriously.

"You're wearing them, so you seem to like the earrings," Grandma said. "You said he's a nightclub owner. I'm sure he makes decent money. Maybe he just likes to give nice gifts. That's not so bad. Is he pressuring you about other stuff?"

"No," she said. "Not at all. He's really nice. He likes good music, and he's really attractive. He's always complimenting me, and he's polite. Funny, too."

"What are you worried about?"

She thought of the lightning striking the tree in her backyard. Twice. She thought about how she was worried that someone was going to come after her. Someone that murdered her mother. She wondered if she was just projecting the stress onto Mike.

"I just don't feel like I know him," she said. "I guess that's it."

"Well, that's an easy enough problem to solve, isn't it?" Grandma said. "Talk to him, ask him questions. Don't get scared off because he likes you so much he can't help showing it. At least give him more time before you decide you don't like him."

Grandma made no secret that she wanted Rachel to start a family. Rachel wasn't surprised she was in support of Mike. She had been after Rachel to get back into dating for years before Rachel had finally signed up for an online dating website. She didn't want to get into the great-grandchildren discussion, which cropped up every few months now. She had something far more important to talk about.

"Grandma, do you have any old things of my mom's?"

Grandma put her fork down. Rachel wasn't sure what to expect. When she had rehearsed this all week in her mind at home, at work, at the grocery store, and on the way to her Grandma's house, she had planned on building up to asking. But a swerve from talking about how Grandma expected her to have kids was better than nothing.

"What brings this up?" Grandma asked. She crossed her arms.

"Well," Rachel launched into her prepared explanation, skipping parts, dancing across it like it hot coals. She hated lying to Grandma. "It was just Mother's Day last month, and it occurred to me all I have of hers are the letters she stopped sending when I was a teen. There's not a grave I can visit, and I don't have any pictures."

Grandma didn't look convinced. She had picked back up her fork and was twiddling with it out of what Rachel figured was impatience, stirring chunks of the potato salad on her plate. Rachel decided to be blunt.

"Look, I know you didn't like her. And if you don't have anything, that's fine too. I just figured I'd ask, because, you know, she was my mom."

Grandma looked back up at her. Rachel couldn't help but notice how different she looked from just moments before. She looked resigned, as though she knew this was coming. Rachel tried not to smile. She had thought there would be nothing. How bad could it be?

"I do have some things, but we need to talk about them first before I give them to you," Grandma said. She sighed deeply. "I always figured this day would come. Help me pick up, and then we'll talk."

Rachel gathered their plates and started washing them in the sink while Grandma put up the leftovers. Grandma then excused herself and went down the hall to her bedroom. Rachel was wiping down the table when Grandma walked back into the kitchen. Rachel's heart fluttered when she saw white envelopes in Grandma's hand.

"Have a seat," Grandma said. "I always knew this day would come, but after a while I thought maybe it wouldn't. I've always felt awful about this, but we did what we did because we love you. I know you love your mother, and I don't want to break any illusions you have of her, dear, but there were some things me and your Grandpa did to keep you safe."

"What do you mean?"

"Well, we always read the letters your Mom sent. I don't know if you knew that. We figured you did, but we'd reseal them anyway."

Rachel felt anger but quickly pushed it aside. She didn't want to waste any time with her Grandma being mad about something that happened when she was a teen. It was pointless anyway. She was 30 years old now. Besides, she couldn't take her gaze from the envelopes.

"What are those in your hand Grandma?" Rachel asked.

Grandma sighed, and then pushed the letters across the table to Rachel. Rachel picked them up. She ran her hand over the front, feeling the smooth white paper. Her name was written in her mother's neat handwriting.

"There were three more letters. We didn't give these to you because she was so drug-addled that she was writing dangerous, weird things to you. We kept these from you to keep you safe. That may have been wrong, and it may have been wrong to read your letters, but we weren't going to let her ruin you. Looking at you now, I know we did the right thing."

Rachel didn't know what to say. She opened her mouth to talk, but then nothing came out. It seemed unbelievable to her that her mother had written her more than she knew. It was almost more unbelievable that Grandma had held onto the letters all this time. Why would she have done that, Rachel thought, if she hated my mother so much? She looked at her Grandma, at the letters, and back at her Grandma.

"Close your mouth, dear. There's those three letters, and a trunk in the attic. I almost tossed all of the stuff out so many times, but I didn't think I could live with the guilt. I could never get the trunk open, but we were pretty sure it was empty on account of how light it is. And it looked antique. I figured that might be some kind of family heirloom. My plan was for you to get all this after I was dead, but, well…"

She waved her hand open-palmed toward Rachel. Rachel realized her Grandma really would have taken this all to the grave if she hadn't of asked. She was angry and disappointed that these things had been kept from her, but she wasn't surprised. Grandma had always had trouble with boundaries.

"All these years, and all I had to do was ask," Rachel thought. "She didn't hang onto them for my mother. She held onto these things for me. Even though she didn't want to."

She got up from her chair and walked around the table. She hugged her Grandma tightly.

"It's ok, Grandma. Thank y'all for protecting me. I'm glad I have y'all."

It was the truth. No matter how disappointing it was to find out that she had been held out on, she loved her grandparents and were glad they had tried to keep her safe. If she hadn't had them, she wouldn't have had anyone. Her mother had told her all of their relatives in Memphis had died.

In the attic, a dusty old space lit by a single hanging bulb, Rachel found the trunk buried in a corner under cardboard boxes of Christmas decorations. It was a dark blue steamer trunk, and much larger than Rachel expected. It looked big enough that someone could curl up in it. Rachel tried the handle but couldn't get it open. She laughed a little to herself.

"*Of course it won't open,*" she thought to herself. "*After everything that had happened so far, I wouldn't have been surprised if the trunk had danced across the attic to me and opened itself.*"

She pushed the trunk across the floor, but it turned out to be much lighter than she had thought. The worn leather handles didn't give, so she was able to pick it up. She managed it bulkily down the attic stairs, and was just barely able to get it loaded into the backseat of her car without too much trouble. She put the letters in her glovebox, deciding to read them at home.

To prove that she wasn't too upset, she stuck around for another hour longer than usual, until Grandma was ready to go to bed. They watched the late show and chatted about Grandma's garden. After the emotional evening, they didn't want to return to the topic of the trunk or the letters. They hugged when Rachel left, and Rachel told her again that it was ok, that she loved her, and thanked her. Grandma sent her home with some strawberries from her garden.

Rachel could understand why they had wanted to protect her, so she couldn't stay mad. They acted the way they always had. Putting herself in their shoes helped. They thought her mother had been dangerous, they'd made that clear over the years. She thought about it on the way home, wondering what she was going to find in the letters. What could have been so strange they had felt compelled to hide it from her?

17

She brought the trunk into the living room and tried to open it first. It sat taller than it was wide, and she was able to learn online that it was probably as old as it looked. It was the kind of trunk people used to take on trains and steamboats. Any logo or branding had long worn off, although there was a lighter patch where Rachel assumed a tag had once been.

The leather was worn away in some parts, flaking off navy blue chips to reveal the brown dried hide underneath. She dug around in junk drawers until she came up with a skeleton key. It should have worked, but it didn't turn the lock. It only stuck out of the lock, refusing to turn. Thinking it was her only chance, she decided to use magic. She brought the sack of coins from her office and placed it on top of the trunk before trying to will it open.

There was no clicking of tumblers in the lock. The trunk soundlessly and slowly cracked open along its hinges like a book. The small sack of coins fell down onto the carpet with a thump. Rachel got down on her knees and looked inside. The right half of the trunk was all drawers, and the left was an empty space with only wooden hangers attached at the top for clothing. The inside had once been papered with a patterned lining, some of which clung halfway to the surface of the walls of the trunk, but the rest lay in a tattered pile at the bottom of the case.

She started going through the drawers. One of the handles came off in her hands. She set it down and started back at the task with a more delicate touch. She gently opened drawer after drawer, but found nothing that seemed useful. The only object in the case was what looked to her like a dog tag kept in a miniature leather wallet.

It was rectangular piece of metal smaller than her thumb, with a paper card inset on one side. A loping signature read "Eleanor M. Crantz" below the logo for Goldsmith's. Beneath "Goldsmith's" it read "Memphis' Greatest Store." On the other side Eleanor's name and a Memphis address was punched into the metal plate.

Rachel did some searching online and found the tag was a charge plate, an early kind of credit card. The name seemed like a coincidence. She knew her mother's maiden name was Miller, not Crantz. She didn't know her grandmother's first name, or any of her relatives beyond her mother. But she had some vague memories of the woman she had called Zaza. Could her grandmother's mother have been Eleanor?

"Could I be related to Rosemary?" she wondered.

It seemed possible. The address on the trunk was in Memphis, where Rachel had heard all her family on her mother's side was from. She wondered if it was the house that burned down, but after searching online found it was still standing. She couldn't find any information online about who owned the house. Finally, she left the charge plate on her desk, deciding to talk with Emily about it in the morning. She still had the letters to get to, which she couldn't put off anymore.

She wasn't sure what the content of the letters would be, but after her grandmother's warning she thought something dark and stiff might help dampen any shocks. She went into the kitchen and poured herself a couple fingers of bourbon. She took the glass back to her office, wishing for a minute she had a cat or any kind of companion that could comfort her. She thought of Mike, but she was sure he wouldn't understand any of this.

"There's no use wishing I had someone else here. This is something I'll have to face alone. The bourbon won't help, but it will be tasty," Rachel thought, opening the door to her office.

She took a sip of bourbon, and then she fanned out the letters on her desk. They looked identical, but the postmarks were each a week apart. Rachel did the math in her head—these had all been mailed to her when she was 18. A full year after Rachel thought her mom had stopped writing.

Rachel pushed back at the thoughts that swarmed her head, but old resentment bubbled back up to the surface—how she'd really needed her mom at that time, when she was sneaking out to get blackout drunk with clumsy handed and dull tongued boys, just to feel like she was living her own life without the watchful eye of her grandparents. At the time, she had been full of bitter anger toward everyone she was related to—to her grandparents for smothering her and talking shit about her mom, to her mother for disappearing, to her father for dying so young. She had worked through most of her issues as she had gotten older, but learning there had been other letters had made the old wounds feel soft again, and threatened to reopen scars Rachel thought had long since healed.

The unknown was very threatening, and Rachel was almost sure there would be something in these letters that would break her heart all over again. Taking another sip of bourbon, she reminded herself that something had taken her mother. She knew this in that secret part of herself, but even that witch part of her struggled against her own painful memories.

For a long time after her mother had left her at her grandparents' house, she had wondered if it was her fault. The mind fills in the unknown with the worst possibilities it can find. She found herself surrounded by emotional memories of self-sabotage, incalculable loss, and endless mourning.

She pushed back at the part of herself that had cried long mornings alone, when she was 18 and would wake up before anyone else to get ready before the bus came. Sometimes she would dream that her Mom was there to pick her up, that she had swept into Rachel's room, and how they'd get everything all packed. Rachel would swing open the door to her room so they could leave, only to find she was in a different dream, and when she turned around, her mom and her room had been replaced by something else. She was alone again. She'd wake up, and cry silently, the pain fresh again.

Rachel reproached herself. She should be well past this, she told herself. She'd certainly worked hard enough to get over being that sad little girl. In her senior year of high school, she decided she had to stop mourning, or she'd be mourning the rest of her life. It took realizing that her parents wouldn't want her to be miserable, wasting her life crying over people that either couldn't or wouldn't be part of her life. It was a realization that opened a lot of doors in her life that she thought had long been closed. She felt it was ok to be happy, and that she didn't have to drag around this burden all her life just because it had been handed to her.

For a long time after that, she felt she was ok. And holding the letters, rubbing her fingers over her name on the outside, she realized she was still going to be ok. Because it was still true. No matter what was in the letters, her parents never would have wanted anything for her but success and happiness. They would be so proud of where she had worked her way to in life—a business owner, college graduate, and now a witch. There couldn't be anything in the letters that would hurt her in some way she hadn't already hurt herself. Nothing that would confirm any of her worst suspicions and ruminations about why her mother had left. And anything that tried to hurt her—well, she was a lot stronger now.

She finished the bourbon and. set the glass aside. Then she picked up the earliest letter, holding it in her hands before opening it. Her eyes teared up at the salutation, and she cried while reading it:

Dearest Rachel,

I'm so sorry I haven't written in so long. I've wanted to, but they've kept me very busy, whether I've liked it or not. I'll be back with you soon. I'm doing everything they want, and they seem happy. We've made a lot of progress. They've given me special privileges, like sending you letters again.

When I come home to you, I'm going to teach you all about your gift. I hope you've noticed it by now, but you are very special. And one day, you'll receive my gift too.

There are things in your blood that make you special. There are people who will want to use you when they know how special you are. Stay away from these people: they will flatter you, but it's all empty praise. I hope you never end up in a situation like the one I am in.

Please be good. I know being a young adult is tough, especially one without their mother. I promise I'm doing whatever it takes to come home. I'll see you soon.

The second letter was shorter but cryptic:

Dear Rachel,

Look for the wolves. They've adapted to survive, and hide their long teeth and claws. When they're done with me, they'll come after you. Find them before they find you.

Try not to be afraid, for as long as you know who the wolves are, you'll be safe.

It's the wolves who should worry.

The third letter was even stranger:

Dear Rachel,

They've promised me that if I do something very big and special for them that they will let me go home. They've made a lot of promises, so if you don't see me in a month, we'll know.

Do you remember the fun games we used to play when you were little? I spy, with my little eye, something green. You loved that one.

I want you to remember some things as you grow:

Remember, not everything is as it appears. Many important things are unseen.

Remember, you are strong and powerful.

Remember, they are watching.

Protect yourself.

I love you, my darling Rachel.

Rachel understood why her grandmother hadn't passed on the letters. She ran her hands over the pages, feeling how deeply the words were dug into the paper. It looked like her mom had written each letter over and over until the letters all looked bold and thick. Grandma had surely seen the strange appearance, ominous and vague pronouns and references to wolves, and assumed it was drug induced madness. Rachel was just thankful Grandma had held onto the letters.

"But what's up with the spy game?" Rachel thought. "All three letters are written in green ink, signed with Mom's big cursive signature. It seems like too easy of a solve."

There was another possible solution. On each letter in a different spot was a small symbol that looked almost like an errant doodle. It was a black line, like a slit, in the middle of a six pointed star. The star was itself contained in a larger six pointed star, which was contained in a circle. It looked similar to the symbols Rachel herself often doodled, of overlapping geometric shapes.

Rachel sat looking for a few minutes at the symbol. She got out other letters of her mothers, but none had this symbol on them. She couldn't understand why her mom would draw her attention to the symbols. She racked her brain trying to think of any instance in which she'd seen it before, but she couldn't place it.

She figured the wolves were whoever had her mom. It definitely sounded like she had been kept somewhere, and not of her own volition. Rachel had to assume that she had been kidnapped or otherwise taken, as she couldn't think of any reason why her mother would willingly be captive. Who were the wolves? If they were watching her, surely she would have noticed. Also, what happened between the last letter her mom sent her and these letters? The old letters didn't talk about wolves, a mysterious "They," or any promises of coming home.

The old letters had all been short, but only talked about growing up, and mostly were motherly advice. Rachel smiled while thinking of how her mother had managed to parent from afar, until it occurred to her that her mother may have been in a cage or similarly locked up while she was writing those letters. She looked at the clock, and decided it was too late to be angry. She couldn't figure out what the symbol was or who the wolves were. There wasn't anything useful. The charge plate felt like a distraction. She wasn't sure if she would find any answers in Hearth, but she knew it was her last hope.

18

The next morning, her head a little fuzzy from the late night bourbon and troubled sleep, Rachel lingered in bed. Emily would be over in an hour or so, as they decided going to the cemetery right when it opened would look strange. They would get there around 11 a.m.

She knew she needed to get up and get dressed, but she was thinking about the wolves, Rosemary, and Eleanor Crantz. Who were they? She felt like she wasn't seeing the whole picture. There just weren't any answers that felt right. She finally got up and started getting ready, but her train of thought didn't change tracks.

She pulled on gray shorts and a black blouse, brushed her hair and did her makeup. All throughout her morning routine, she wondered who the wolves were. What kind of people kept another person from communicating with their daughter? Was Rosemary Crantz one of the wolves? The thought made her bristle. Maybe her mother had to use coded language in the letters, and that's why she had named Rosemary when she was communicating with her as a spirit.

Her phone buzzed. She jumped, mussing her eyeliner. Sighing, she fixed her mistake with makeup remover and then looked at her phone. It was Mike. She smiled, glad she was at least certain in her affection for him.

"Good morning, beautiful :)" he had texted her.

The application indicated that he was still typing.

"I got us the best tickets I could find for the Reds game. I was thinking after the game I could grill us some steaks at my place?"

Rachel read the message and thought about how to respond. She wasn't sure what today was going to bring. Emily would be

coming over soon so they could head to the cemetery she was
sure a woman she'd never met was buried. They were hoping to
find some kind of clue about the people her mother had called
wolves. She wondered if she'd be up for going out on Saturday or
if they would find her before then.

"*Unless he's with them,*" she thought, but pushed the thought
away as she checked her earrings in the mirror. "*That's crazy. Don't
be ridiculous. That's too paranoid. You know you can trust him, otherwise
you'd know something was up when you were around him. What's the point
of intuition otherwise?*"

"Sounds great :)" she texted back.

***

Emily looked out the window of Rachel's car, watching the
cattle graze in the pastures they passed. Hearth was nearly an
hour south of Highland Heights, tucked away in the knobby
bluegrass hills. She wasn't sure what she expected to find in
Hearth, but she hoped desperately it was something that would
help her friend.

Rachel had shown her the charge plate when she arrived that
morning. Emily pulled back up Rosemary's birth certificate online
and compared the mother's names. It was a match. Rachel was
stunned but refused to believe that they were related. There was
no way to confirm that Eleanor and Rosemary were related to
Rachel since she didn't remember or have any records of her
mother's side of the family. She didn't want to ask her
grandmother, confident that she had spilled all the beans she had.

They had fought for the first few minutes of the drive after
Emily had suggested that Rachel go to Memphis to check out the
house. It had felt like a crazy suggestion to Rachel, but each day
that passed since Rachel showed her the powers she had, Emily
had grown more convinced that there really was something going
on. Even if no one was really after Rachel, getting out of town
seemed like a smart idea to Emily. At best, it would give Rachel
some time to relax. At worst, it would buy them some time to
figure out what the threat was they were dealing with.

Rachel had refused. She was determined to find out what
happened and thought the charge plate was a red herring. They
stopped talking after Rachel's response to Emily's suggestion that

Rachel was the one who was distracted with Mike: the Reds game and a fancy dress event next week were the first things Rachel had brought up in the car. Rachel had shouted at her that she was allowed some happiness, and then she went cold, focusing on the road.

Hearth was a home rule-class city with a population of less than 1,000, according to the sign posted on the side of the two lane road that Emily and Morgan were driving down. It was 40 minutes south of Alexandria, and Emily couldn't take the quiet anymore. But she wasn't going to acknowledge Rachel's tantrum. She wasn't listening to sense, that much was clear.

"Maybe we should go to Crystal Crescent after we check out the cemetery," Emily said, breaking the silence. She hoped Morgan might be able to point out the obvious to her if she wasn't going to listen to her. It was a gamble, but she had time to think up a plan during the quiet drive.

"Fine," Rachel said in a sigh.

"Take some deep breaths," Emily said. "We don't know what we're going to find, but we're prepared for the worst. You've got a bag of coins, and I've got my handgun, absolute worst case. Hopefully it doesn't come to that."

Rachel slowed the car and put on her right turn signal. They had come to an old road at the base of a hill. There was a granite sign with gray river stones embedded along the edges. "Memorial Hill Cemetery" was engraved in the slab. The gate was open, so they drove past parcels of evenly planted tombstones up another hill until they came to the office building. The land gently rolled for acres into the surrounding woodland, a green sea dotted sparsely with graves, monuments and mausoleums.

Rachel walked into the office first, with Emily after her. They both felt nervous but wouldn't admit it to each other. The office opened onto a lobby, a spacious seating room with cream colored sofas and tawny brown leather chairs. There were three sets of tall brown doors set in the off-white wall at the back of the lobby, presumably leading to viewing rooms, and a hallway to the left that trailed off elsewhere. It was a large, well furnished room with one employee in it. He was a thin, gray haired man who looked up at them from the computer on his large walnut desk.

"Hello, how may I help you?" he asked in hushed tones.

"We were looking for my grandmother's plot," said Emily. They had decided during the drive that this was the best tactic. They figured two women just walking around looking for a random grave might seem suspicious.

"What's her name?" he asked.

"Francine Jones," she said. They had found her on the grave index. Unlike Rosemary, she had a death certificate. They didn't think he'd ask for ID, but Emily was thankful to have such a common last name. He didn't even blink, just scribbled the name on a piece of paper and then stood up from the desk.

"Give me a few minutes," he said before walking away and down the hall.

Rachel and Emily sat on one of the couches and waited in silence. Rachel started to feel uncomfortable. This place seemed expensive for such a small town. She had a bad feeling she was going to find what she was looking for here. She wondered if she wasn't also uncomfortable because she hadn't been in a place like this since she was six years old. She tried to remember the last time she had visited her father's grave and couldn't remember the year. She took a deep breath, reminding herself there wasn't time to be sad. She already felt all over the place. She decided when all this was over, she'd make sure her mother had a marker next to her father's.

The man emerged from the backroom with a few sheets of white paper. He gave them a map of the cemetery and marked where the grave would be. They thanked him and then walked out of the office.

"Well, here we go," said Emily.

They got back in the car. Rachel unfolded the map on her lap. She held a coin in her hand. She took a deep breath, and then closed her eyes. She held her hand over the map for a moment.

"Rosemary is buried here," she said, and pointed to a spot on the cemetery map. It was in a cluster of graves near the back of the cemetery, which butted against the surrounding forest. By a stroke of luck, it wasn't far from the site the man in the office had marked.

She drove slowly through the cemetery, which had a paved road looping through the well maintained grass. They were the only car on the path. They parked on the gravel shoulder once they got to the section that had been circled on the map. Rachel turned off the car. She started to get out, and then Emily grabbed her wrist.

"I'm sorry we were fighting. I'm scared. I think we both are. But I want us to be on the same page with this. After whatever happens today, no matter what, let's go see your friend Morgan. I think we need to tell her what we've learned. She's the closest thing you've got to an expert."

"You're right," Rachel said. "I'm sorry for fighting, too."

Rachel squeezed Emily's hand. They hugged. Rachel texted Morgan that they'd be coming by after the cemetery, and she hoped it wouldn't interfere with her work hours.

"See you soon. Be careful," Morgan responded.

"Are you ready?" Rachel said.

Emily picked up her black leather purse from the floor. She unzipped one of the outer pockets so Rachel could see where her handgun was stored in a holster built into the bag. She checked to make sure her weapon was secure in its holster. She didn't rezip the pocket, putting the purse strap on over her shoulder so she could access it.

"Ready to go but hoping I don't have to," she said.

Rachel nodded then checked the heavy bag of coins in her own purse. They got out of the car and walked. They passed many different headstones, from simple markers and slabs to ornate sculptures. Many of the graves had flowers or wreaths laid on them, some artificial and some wilting or beginning to nod under the weight of their blooms. Finally, just past a 6-foot weeping angel sculpture, they came to the spot the caretaker had circled on the map.

There were significantly less graves in the back of the cemetery. Rachel was uneasy, but remembering the copper coins in her purse made her feel better. Remembering Emily's superior marksmanship helped too, but she hoped it would never come to that.

They stood and looked at Francine Jones's grave for a little while. They did this so that if there were people watching, they would have their story. They didn't know who she was, but she had lived her own life, and a very long life judging from the dates on the grave. Rachel wondered when her own time was going to end.

She pushed away the thoughts and looked up toward the back of the cemetery, where the manicured grass and polished tombstones ended, butting with a dense wall of tall, thin trees. On the map, the forest around the cemetery looked only to be a few acres, but the dense green leaves made the foliage look endless. The bright midday sun struggled to penetrate the shade between branches, making it difficult to see if anything or anyone lurked further in the woods.

She nodded at Emily, and they walked further toward the back. The graves went all the way to the woods, but the markers were sparsely plotted. Wide spaces stretched between the graves at the back. Feeling like she was being watched, Rachel paused in front of the final resting place of another stranger. This person was buried in the row in front of what was supposedly Rosemary's grave. Emily paused too, before they moved to the next row.

She didn't let herself look at the headstone until she was right in front of it. It was alone, with empty plots on all sides. Rachel felt chills when she saw the inscription. Staring at the writing on the grave and the weird symbol, she was certain they'd found Rosemary far too late. She looked unsteadily past the grave into the forest, certain there was an unseen voyeur. It felt like the hair on the back of her neck was standing up.

The grave didn't have Rosemary's name on it, but it had something else. Engraved into the pale gray marble was a loosely wound, thin spiral. It turned only once before trailing off the face of the tombstone. Below the image, the inscription read:

"FRANK MAPLES 1930-1995. Devoted husband, loving father, eternal brother."

"I have the surest feeling there's two bodies in this grave," she whispered through gritted teeth. Her stomach felt like it was going to turn over. She was glad she hadn't eaten breakfast.

"We should go," Emily whispered.

Rachel took a picture with her phone at discreetly as she could. She turned around, terrified at the prospect of the woods being at her back. She wasn't sure if anyone was watching her, but she knew why they would be. Whoever Frank Maples was, Rosemary Crantz was buried with him. Emily volunteered to take over driving, and she headed for Crystal Crescent without a word.

***

When Rachel and Emily were in Hearth, Mike was visiting his mother. He wanted to tell her the good news in person so he could see her reaction. He was sure if she was really going to make him a Level 5, this was going to be it. She was going to come to the Solstice. He needed to know the rest of the plan now.

Karen was staying at an apartment she kept in Covington in a complex on the bank of the Ohio River. She had picked the apartment it entirely based on the view. The apartment faced downtown Cincinnati. She was on the patio when he got there, watching the Cincinnati cityscape from her white outdoor sectional and smoking a cigarette.

"I wish you wouldn't do that," he said. "I've got good news to give you. She's coming to the solstice. She agreed."

The smoke drifted between them as he looked down at his mother, who seemed much calmer than he had seen her in weeks. She smiled up at him, and the smile reached her eyes, showing off the dimples in her cheeks.

"Good. I knew you could do it. And you know smoking doesn't make a difference to my health," she said. "I haven't had a cold since '58. But fine, if it bothers you."

She put out the cigarette, crushing the ember in a cut glass ashtray on the coffee table next to her. It held many more cigarette butts, the only litter on Karen's pristine patio.

"So what next? Will you tell me more of the plan?"

"Soon," she said. Mike nodded.

That was the best he was going to get, and he knew it. Mike went to the barrier of the balcony and took a deep breath.

She watched as her son looked out over the glass patio railing at the dark river and the skyscrapers beyond it. He had grown into a handsome, intelligent man, even if he was untrustworthy, occasionally worthless and prone to disobedience. He had his uses.

She had tried to raise him with a normal life, keeping the group secret from him until he had graduated high school. That hadn't always been easy, but she had done her best. She hoped he remembered his youth as fondly as she did.

"Do you remember how often we used to go camping?" she asked.

"Of course. We went practically monthly when I was young," he said. "My favorite was the Crystal Creek near Hearth. Do you remember the fish we ate?"

"Yeah, we couldn't catch a thing, so I left you to tend the fire while I made a McDonald's run," Karen said.

"Those were probably the freshest fish filet sandwiches. Or at least the closest they've been eaten near actual fish."

Karen laughed. Being so close to nature had made Karen feel more attuned with Nephilor back then. He would whisper to her what he wanted, and to please him she would sneak out of camp after midnight and go as far into the woods as she could without getting lost. Then she would strip down and dance for as long as she could, humming and cursing and singing songs and praises for him. When she was exhausted, she would check for ticks, put on her clothes, and get back to camp. Sometimes it was dawn when she got back, so she would get the fire going and wait for Mike to wake up.

Mike never told her if he had seen her at night on any of the camping trips, but she was sure he hadn't. He had never asked her about any of her absences. He had always been asleep when she had returned to camp. Sometimes she wondered how much he knew. She thought he liked all those occult albums because he'd seen them in robes at least once. They'd never talk about it.

Nowadays she always felt Nephilor was close. Even closer now after she killed that witch for the love spell. She could feel his presence all the time now, and he had grown even stronger. It thrilled her that they were so close to completing the big plan.

"Thank you, Mike," she said. "You're doing a good job."

He turned and looked at her with joy. She'd never said that before. He decided to leave on a high note.

"Thanks, Mom," he said before closing the door. "You'll love Rachel. You'll see."

He went inside. Karen watched him leave through the glass. Then she stood up and walked to the glass railing. The sacrifice had worked. Rachel trusted Mike now, she thought, and that would help move things along.

She lit another cigarette, and as she blew out the smoke she marveled how she never would have made it to where she was if

it hadn't been for Rosemary Crantz. She remembered she had
been 25 when she met Rosemary. She had been living in
Cincinnati her whole life to that point. The Cincinnati skyline
didn't have quite as many skyscrapers as it does now, with the
metal and glass behemoths clustered over the bridges that
connected the city to Kentucky. She still recognized the tallest
buildings from her youth, although now they were overshadowed
by buildings three times their height. She let her eyes drift over
the monolithic towers, and she savored her memories of
Rosemary.

Part Two

19

She met Rosemary on the bus on the ride home from the bank. It was 1955, two years after she had been married. She was working part time as a teller at a bank downtown. The math never troubled her, but she was quite bored. She was not a complainer though, so she worked her shifts and saved the money she made for their nest egg.

She took the bus to save the extra money, and she would often go to the library on the way home to pick up something to read. Sometimes she would look up books on New York City, just to look at the pictures of the busy streets. She'd imagine herself there, part of something huge. Cincinnati was a big city with more than 500,000 residents in the last census.

She had looked up the number and thought it was a lot until she found out more than 7 million people lived in New York City at the same time. Something that huge seemed unfathomable. Frank told her that when they could afford it, that they would make a special trip up there for her. But after Rosemary left, her interests shifted sharply.

The first time she saw Rosemary she was struck by her beauty. Instead of people watching, all Karen could do was steal glances at Rosemary. Karen thought she looked like a model, and that she dressed like one as well. Rosemary was long and lithe, but with strong shoulders and shapely legs hugged by a red pencil skirt. She was wearing a matching red suit jacket that was tapered at the waist, and Karen marveled at how fashionable she looked with her bobbed red hair. Her heels and purse matched her suit, and she wore a single pearl on a gold chain around her neck. She had walked past Karen when boarding, and Karen had been embarrassed to realize she had stared at her butt.

After watching her from a distance for a week, Karen knew she couldn't wait any longer. So Karen had gone to talk to the woman on the bus, lured in by her beauty and the serene expression on her face as she read her book. Karen had never felt this attracted to a woman before. She had crushes every now and then, but nothing this strong. She was nervous but sure that at the very least she had to experience the pleasure of talking with her. She moved when the bus came to its next stop. She sat across from her and had timidly asked what she was reading.

Rosemary had looked up at her from her book, and for a moment Karen wasn't sure if she was going to speak or not. The woman's face didn't reflect annoyance though. She smiled at Karen. Her eyes were a dusty green, like the sage plant in Karen's garden.

"Oh, it's no bother at all," Rosemary had said, sliding a bookmark into her book and closing it. "It's a fascinating book on magic."

She had handed the book to Karen to look through, and her hand had touched Karen's just barely, but Karen smiled and blushed.

"Magic, huh?" Karen said.

Expecting card tricks, she opened the book and flipped through some of the pages. Instead of white rabbits peeking out of hats, pictures of knives, spirals and crystals greeted her. She had never seen anything like it before. Her thrill at the woman's presence was magnified somehow by the occult images in the book. She smiled at Rosemary and looked through the book once more, finding a page on knot spells.

"This looks pretty interesting. I'm guessing you didn't get this at the library?" Karen asked.

"No, it's from home. I had a feeling you'd be interested. I'm Rosemary," said the woman, reaching out her hand to shake Karen's. "Rosemary Crantz."

"I'm Karen Maples," said Karen. She shook the woman's hand and smiled at her.

The two started talking, and conversation flowed easily. They found out they lived in the same neighborhood. Rosemary had just moved to town from Memphis, Tennessee and was living at a boarding house two blocks from Karen and Frank's house.

"I'm still new in town. I only moved here a month ago. I'm still getting settled, but I found a job as a secretary downtown, so things are looking up," Rosemary said.

"Would you like to join myself and my husband for dinner tomorrow night? That is, if you don't have plans," Karen said.

Karen hadn't planned on asking her to come over, but surprised herself. She wanted to ask her but was afraid, and yet, it had come out of her mouth anyway. She and Frank didn't have a lot of friends and rarely entertained, but she didn't want to lose the vibrancy this woman radiated. When Rosemary smiled at her and accepted the invitation, Karen was delighted. She wrote her address down and gave her the slip of paper.

***

Frank listened to Karen's story of meeting the woman on the bus as they snuggled in bed that night. She had told him about it over dinner, and then again while he was reading the evening paper. He told her she had nothing to worry about, but when she brought it up again, he knew what she needed to hear.

"Do you remember *The Black Castle*?"

"'The Count has already made arrangements for you,'" she quoted as ominously as she could manage before giggling. She hugged against him. "You know I'll never forget that night."

She kissed him, and he kissed her back before laying his head down again.

"Well, do you remember how nervous you were?"

"Yes," she said, feeling heat in her cheeks.

He had proposed to her after the movie. They had been going steady for two years, since they met on a blind date in '50. She remembered the walk back to his car, when he had asked her to marry him. It was late December, nearly January. He had gotten down on one knee, and she had felt faint, like everything was about to change.

"I knew it was coming because we had talked about marriage, but you surprised me. I wasn't expecting it after that movie."

"A buddy of mine had told me it was more of a romance than a horror movie," Frank said with a shrug. "I almost waited. I just knew if I had asked you on New Year's Eve, you'd have known it was coming. But do you remember what else happened that night? Before that?"

She remembered that he had slipped the knit glove off her left hand after she said yes. And how the reflection of the street light in his dark brown eyes looked like the night sky, and the cold wind chilled her hand as he put the ring on her finger. They had slept together that night at the boarding house where he lodged, sneaking her in with help from his roommates. She didn't remember much of the movie at all aside from the parts that made her laugh.

"What?" she asked.

"When they opened the door to the room full of thrashing alligators, you grabbed the hand of the woman sitting next to you by accident," he said.

"I did?"

"You did," he said. "I never brought it up, because you seemed embarrassed. But your smile afterwards...it didn't need words. Even in the dark, it lit up your face."

Karen felt embarrassed, and Frank sensed it. He sat up in bed, and she followed suit. He took her hands in his.

"We've always been open about your crushes before, like on Miss Anderson next door at our first place. Don't you remember what fun we'd have thinking about Miss Anderson together?"

"This is different," Karen said. "That was fantasy. I actually talked to Rosemary and invited her home."

Karen looked at her hands in his, feeling like she had betrayed him.

"When you told me about it when I got home...I haven't seen you this lit up in years. Don't get glum now."

"You aren't mad?" Karen asked, looking up at him.

"Am I mad that you met a beautiful woman you're attracted to? That's a silly question, Karen. It makes me happy to see you happy. Besides, why shouldn't you have feelings?" Frank said. "It's good that we're talking about it. I think it's perfectly natural. Sweet, even. Do you think you'd ever act on your desires?"

Karen shook her head. She took one of her hands from Frank's and held the back of her neck.

"No, I'd prefer to be friends," she said, looking down. "Anything else is much too complicated."

Frank smirked.

"You do what you like," Frank said. "Just remember that. You're a Maples. We're a team, and we'll always have each other's backs."

***

The first dinner was lovely, and the three of them stayed up late playing poker after dinner. Rosemary brought the book she was reading on the bus and read from it to them. Frank and Karen were mesmerized by her. She told them about runes and crystals, and how rainwater could be used in moonlight to see things that were faraway.

Frank was skeptical at first, but Karen was not. Frank teased her that Rosemary could have told her she could turn into a horse, and Karen would have believed it. Karen felt this to be a weakness, and so she began studying. At least once a week, Karen would turn her library trips into occult study sessions. She read up on the Hermetic Order of the Golden Dawn, finding the group especially fascinating.

They were a secret society that had bloomed and withered decades before she was born. The group had fractured into many smaller groups, including one started by the infamous Aleister Crowley. She had heard that man's name, remembering her father's denunciations after reading about him in the paper. She read everything she could find about the groups and their attempts at contacting deities, wondering the whole time if anyone in the group knew anyone like Rosemary.

Rosemary was soon their regular dinner companion. The three would sit at the dinner table for hours after the meal was over while Rosemary taught them everything she knew about magic. Karen and Frank listened to their beautiful guest with rapt attention. They studied her smooth hands as she used a branch to unlock cabinets and move small objects short distances. Karen and Frank couldn't replicate her results, but they were fascinated nevertheless. Frank began to order occult books out of magazines, and he and Karen would study together in the evenings.

She was happy being her friend, but Karen's romantic interest in Rosemary refused to fade. In her dreams, they were lovers. Sometimes she'd remember her dreams while talking with her and would blush, thankful that Rosemary had told her telepathy was impossible.

But Rosemary was not without intuition. After a few months, she began to flirt with Karen and Frank, always finding an opportunity to compliment or touch one or both of them. When she was sure they were interested in her and that she was interested in both of them, she decided to have an honest conversation.

She waited until one evening when they had been playing poker. She found poker too easy with her intuition, but it didn't always work. This evening in particular, she was having a tough time reading Frank and Karen, and she knew why. She'd been putting off addressing it, but now was as good a time as any. She set her cards down and ground out her cigarette in the ashtray between her and Karen.

"What is it?" Karen asked.

"I think we should talk openly," Rosemary said. "About us."

Frank raised an eyebrow, and then looked at Karen.

"What do you mean?" Karen said.

"You know I'm a witch, so you know I sometimes have certain feelings. Well, right now I can't help but feel both of your attraction to me."

Karen set down her cards. Her face was flushed.

"I'm sorry," Karen said.

"It's ok," Rosemary said. "I'm interested. But let's talk about it."

So they did. The threesome's friendship soon became a relationship. They decided to proceed with what they were feeling, cautiously at first, and then more confidently as they came to know each other in a new way. They established rules for their relationship, prioritizing communication and openly discussing feelings so that no one felt left out or unheard. In public, discretion was the name of the game, and in private, it was teamwork.

Rosemary had one hard rule from the start: She did not want to have children. She explained it was a family tradition that she would have to return to her family home if she was ever with child. Frank and Karen told her they understood, and so they often took precautions, using contraceptives and other methods.

The three were inseparable. In the fall of 1956, Rosemary moved in with them. Frank built a special bed frame, and they ordered the largest mattress they could find. They set up a room just for Rosemary as well, converting Frank's office into a bedroom so that she could have her own space whenever she needed it, without question.

Their small coven practiced daily. They meditated together in the mornings and at night. In the evening, Rosemary would teach them what she had learned and read to them from her books. Rosemary did not worship a particular god, as she believed magic existed on its own, separate from religion. She told them it was connected to nature and life, running under everything all the time.

Karen felt that a deity was missing from their group. She fixated on this, and would bring it up weekly at first, then daily. She would participate in rituals and magic, and while the spells they cast with Rosemary always worked, she felt they weren't accomplishing anything lasting unless they chose a deity to honor. Her library sessions turned into studies of gods from different folklore.

She obsessed over thoughts of gods, explaining to Rosemary and Frank that she believed their power would be magnified if spells were executed under the name of a god, but that it had to be a real god. Karen was sure that she would know when she found the right one.

Rosemary didn't believe it was necessary to worship any being, but she wanted to make Karen happy and didn't think worshipping a deity would have any effect on her magic. She thought Karen wanted something to believe in, so she joined Karen in her trips to the library. They'd taken to sleeping on either side of Frank in the oversized king bed. At night, the lamps on both nightstands would be turned on, and Frank had his option of reading from his own book, turning to his right to read from Karen's book or turning to his left to read from Rosemary's.

Frank had been promoted into a management role at the factory at the end of 1957, so there was a general sense of relief in the home. Money hadn't been tight before since all members of the house worked, but the increase in funds brought by

Frank's work let a substantial amount of breathing room in their finances.

In January of 1957, the Maples and Crantz planned a family trip to the beach for June of that year. They had chosen a beach in North Carolina that Frank had gone to as a youth, Topsail Island. Frank and Karen worked on the beach plan obsessively, charting routes to take in their Chevrolet through the West Virginia and Virginia mountains. They planned a grocery list and meal plans so that they would not have to leave the beach once they arrived. The most exciting parts of the plans to Karen were the rituals they planned.

In an effort to impress the women in his life, Frank had chosen the beach house as a surprise. Rosemary and Karen had agreed to be surprised, and both were nervously excited to see what Frank had chosen. They had speculated together on what Frank may have booked, expecting from their pragmatic lover a small seaside shanty with just enough room for the three of them.

They consulted star maps when Frank had told them the dates of the trip and memorized all the constellations they could so that they could stargaze every night during the trip. They were especially excited as they would be arriving on a Friday on the day of the Summer Solstice, June 21, 1957.

The anticipation built over the months of planning, until finally the day arrived. They left at 6 am, driving as the sun rose to greet fog covered fields and placid lakes sipped on by drowsy horses. Karen turned from the passenger seat window to smile at her lovers, feeling a sense of peace and contentment she would never know again. She had no way of knowing she was on her way to meet the god who would drive her on a decades-long journey to madness.

20

The roads turned narrow as they wrapped through gaps and passes where the mountain peaks grew higher and the pine trees more plentiful. Mountains gradually gave way to flatter land, until dirt turned to sand. The drive was peaceful, with good conversation and a packed lunch. When Rosemary mentioned she had a surprise for them this evening, Karen had smiled and told her she had brought some surprises as well. Frank smiled and said nothing, his eyes on the road.

He revealed his surprise when he pulled into the driveway of the house. The car was quiet as Frank pulled into the oceanfront house's driveway. The house loomed over them, two stories built on stilts that made it seem even larger.

"Is this really it?" Karen said, her voice giddy, knowing the answer. She clutched Frank's hand.

"Is that a roof deck?" Rosemary said, smiling widely, leaning over from the back seat with a hand on Frank's left shoulder, craning her neck to look up at the house.

"Yes to both questions," Frank said. Frank grinned broadly at the touch of the two women he adored, loving the excitement in their voices and knowing that he caused it. He was sure he was in for the best week of his life to date. "Let's go in and check it out."

And so they did. Frank had rented a four bedroom house with a roof deck from which you could see the ocean and the tops of most of the other houses. When asked why he rented such a large house, Frank explained he rented the house especially for the roof deck. The booking agent had assured him it was very private with a glorious view of the sunrise and sunset, which sounded perfect to Frank for stargazing.

The house had two rooms on each floor. They unpacked their things in the master bedroom on the first floor, putting their clothes and makeup up into the shelves and drawers there. Above their bedroom, in the second story room that opened onto the roof deck, they pushed the furniture aside to make as much floor room as possible. After they had made the space, they agreed to wait until the moon rose to set up materials for a ritual for prosperity. While they were at the beach, they would spend as much time relaxing in the sun as possible and would only study or perform magic at night. So they put on their bathing suits, slathered on sunscreen, and walked down the worn wood walkway that cut through the dunes to the beach.

When Karen stepped onto the soft white sand for the first time and saw the great expanse of ocean in front of her crashing onto the shore, she felt a sense of peace unlike any she'd ever known. She felt connected to nature, and as she looked up to the sky, she took a deep breath, imagining herself absorbing the beauty and calm.

She walked straight to the shoreline and stood at its edge, watching the bubbling waves rush to meet her. As the cold water lapped at her feet, she looked at the horizon where the sea met the sky. She smiled thinking about the week in store for them. That night was to be a full moon, and she had surprises of her own in store.

Rosemary helped Frank set up their umbrella, then used a church key to open two beers. She walked to the waterline, and handed one to Karen. They drank cold beer and watched the waves come in.

"I brought a surprise for us tonight," Rosemary said. "Something I got from a coworker. It should be helpful if we would like to do some magic under the moonlight tonight."

"Perfect," Karen said. "I have some surprises as well for this evening."

Frank walked up to the two women, drinking from a beer of his own.

"I'm looking forward to whatever magical surprises you two have in store for us," Frank said. He lifted up his beer can and said, "To Topsail Island!"

The three of them brushed their cans together.

"To Topsail Island!" Rosemary and Karen echoed.

They all drank. Finishing the beers, they put the cans in a canvas bag they brought for trash, and then dove into the waves. They swam all day, alternating between playing in the waves and drinking on the beach. Rosemary and Karen walked south on the beach, gathering large shells they found to add to their altar at home.

That night they ate a small dinner of roast chicken sandwiches and chips. Afterward Rosemary revealed her surprise, dropping an envelope dramatically on the coffee table in front of Frank and Karen as they drank their after dinner coffee. Karen opened the envelope and found three small tablets. She looked up at Rosemary, who explained that she had brought with her three doses of Delysid brand LSD. Rosemary gave them a rundown of what to expect.

She had gotten the LSD from a coworker, a bright young woman who was married to a psychiatrist. The woman had told Rosemary about her experience over three lunch hours, and Rosemary had listened each day with rapt attention as the woman described the effects. In the books she had destroyed before she left Memphis, there had been many accounts of experiences with hallucinogens. Time and time again, her ancestors had tried to contact deities, and many of the later accounts involved the use of such drugs.

Rosemary was certain no such hidden beings existed, for the records of those failures had been very clear. The most that ever happened was changes in perception. It wasn't prescribed, but this was medicine from a psychiatrist. She had been assured by his wife that it was a milder experience than mescaline or ayahuasca, two drugs named in the books. She didn't want her loved ones to have an experience like her ancestors had, but she thought a slight change in perception might help them be more open minded about some things. She wouldn't say it to herself, but she hoped Karen might find a new way to think about her theurgical thirst, and then they would all find relief.

"In about an hour to an hour and a half, we'll start to feel it. You'll feel giddy and maybe a little drunk, and the effects should peak after around three to four hours. However, this can last a lot longer, up to 12 hours or more, so we will be up all night long but we're in good company," Rosemary said. "But from what I've read, this stuff opens up the mind. You will see unbelievable colors and patterns. I think we'll be more receptive to the universe, and our magic should be even more effective."

They discussed it, and then they all took the small pills that Rosemary had bought. Then Karen brought out her surprises. She had sewn three hooded green cloaks for the three of them, and had packed quite an assortment from their home crystal collection. She put the box of crystals and the cloaks in the upstairs room that led to the roof deck.

They then took to the roof deck to watch the sunset, and as they watched the sky's color change from bright blue to pink and orange, Karen began to see the clouds move in strange ways. She found herself struck dumb at the beauty of the sunset, and when she tried to talk found she could not find her voice. She laughed, watching the clouds wiggles on the horizon and form weird shapes.

For a moment, the clouds seemed to merge, and the face of a horned god appeared to her. Its quavering face shifted as the wind moved the clouds, and its mouth turned from a rounded O into a wide grin. Then its jaw split down the middle into two equal halves. The eyes bulged out under its horns, which curled and unfurled again. It seemed to look into her. She gasped, but it seemed the wind had been knocked out of her. She found it hard to speak.

"Do you see that?" she managed to ask Rosemary after a few breaths.

Rosemary looked up from the book she brought onto the porch, a heavily illustrated book on Irish mythology. Karen saw that the pupils in her eyes had grown larger. The sage green rim around the black pupils of her eyes had thinned considerably, and the effect was startlingly beautiful to Karen. She noticed the light freckles on Rosemary's face seemed to move in a strange dance as she looked at her face, and the movement reminded Karen of the stars and the rotations of planets. Karen had longed all day on the beach to touch Rosemary, but had held off in case of outside observation. Seeing her now, Karen's thoughts of the face she had seen in the sky were obliterated, and she looked at Rosemary with the same kind of wonder she had given the sunset.

"See what?" Rosemary asked, but the questioning gaze was soon replaced by a smoldering look when she saw the love in Karen's eyes. She too noticed Karen's wide pupils. Karen's skin seemed luminous to Rosemary, and the way the wind tousled Karen's long black hair stuck Rosemary as wild and witchy.

Serotonin continued to pour into the women's brains, and they giggled looking at each other as they sat on the wooden bench on the roof deck. Karen leaned over to Rosemary, and she kissed her gently.

"I love you," Karen said.

"I love you too," said Rosemary.

Frank came upstairs with a small cooler. Karen and Rosemary both turned and smiled widely at Frank as he walked up to them. He sat on the other side of Karen and handed the two women cold cans of beer after he opened them.

"We love you Frank," said Rosemary.

"Yes," said Karen. "So much. Thank you for this Frank."

"I love you both so much," Frank said.

Karen leaned over and kissed her husband, and the two spent a moment with their foreheads pressed together. Rosemary looked over at them and smiled. The three felt the most content they would ever feel together.

They sat for hours and watched as the sun set and the moon rose, chatting vigorously about magic and the ritual to be performed that night. Karen was sure that tonight was going to be the night they found the god she was looking for. She had never felt so certain about anything. When it was 11 pm, she got up to prepare the ritual room. Rosemary followed her.

Karen laid out a very large green blanket on the floor. She got down on her knees and Rosemary joined her. The two of them placed crystals on the perimeter of the fabric, Karen observed the patterns she had never noticed in the fabric and in the facets of the crystals. She spread the seashells they had gathered that day between the crystals, admiring the beautiful spirals in some of the shells. It seemed like everything was perfect for the ritual this evening. Except for one thing that never seemed right.

Karen blurted out a question she had wanted to ask Rosemary for a long time.

"Rosemary, why aren't you serious about the spells we perform? You never seem sincere, especially when we're trying to invoke a god. The spells we do for prosperity...if you really believed in them, wouldn't we be rich?"

Rosemary didn't respond right away. She took another crystal out of the box and laid it down with the others. She looked strained.

"Talk to me," Karen said. "Please. You tell me you don't believe in gods, but I feel like you're not telling me the whole truth. Sometimes it feels like you're hiding something. I look at you during our spells, and I can tell you don't mean it as much as I do."

"Let me think about what I want to say," Rosemary said, frowning slightly. She looked away from Karen. "Hold on. I'll be right back."

She got up abruptly and went downstairs. Karen stared at the open door to the room as she left. She wondered if she had crossed the line she had been gently prodding for months. But then Rosemary came back up the stairs with a composition notebook. She opened it up to a blank page and sat next to Karen on the floor.

She drew a loose spiral on the page. It was a shape Karen had seen before, like a nautilus shell. The spiral she had drawn looped a few times tightly in the center of the page, growing with each turn until it curved off the page.

"Do you see how the spiral grows more with each quarter turn? The shape stays the same, but the scale changes at a constant rate as it rotates around the center. It grows. Eventually it runs right off the page. It's called a logarithmic spiral. Do you know who Jacob Bernoulli is?"

"The last name sounds familiar," Karen said.

"Well, he's one of the many people who have studied the shape over time. Jacob Bernoulli was a Swiss mathematician, one of many gifted academics from a large family of influential scholars. He wanted a spiral like this on his grave, along with the motto 'Eadem mutata resurgo.' That's Latin for 'I rise again changed but the same.'

"It's a reference to the self-similarity of logarithmic spirals. This pattern of increased growth from a small start but always staying the same form can be taken many different ways, metaphorically speaking. Bernoulli said it could be a symbol for resurrection after death or for fortitude in the face of life's many adversities.

"It's found all over the universe. There are galaxies that spiral just like this. But you can also see its shape in pinecones and paper nautiluses. Spider webs too. I prefer to think of it as a symbol for life. There will always be change. We must embrace change, learn and grow as much as we can while we're here."

"You don't think the recurrence of the shape all over the universe is a sign of a god?"

"I think it's acceptable to use a symbol to metaphorically process emotions and beliefs, but to attribute more than that to a geometrical shape is taking things too far," Rosemary said. "But I don't believe in gods, as I've told you before. I think if there were such things as gods, they wouldn't allow women like me and those that came before me to have the power that we do have.

"We already know that man will kill us if they learn of our strengths, so we hide. We even hide from each other, keeping secrets confined within families. Secrecy is what has kept us alive. That's why I'll have to leave if I'm ever with child. I have to tend to the secrets of my family.

"The growth spiral can also serve as a metaphor for magic. Things have a way of getting out of hand when magic is used. Caution and moderation are always best, because we don't have any way of knowing what we're really dealing with. It's difficult to establish parameters when experimenting with magic. All of my ancestors refused to think about it that way. The records of their short lives were full of greed, pride, and arrogance, which is why I destroyed their records. The books were all the same anyway. They thought they were gods among men, and abuse of the power drove them into madness. I had to break the pattern. I had to start anew on my own.

"That's why I encourage us to be mostly academic in our pursuit of witchcraft. I won't hold you back in your search for higher meaning, but I've heard the stories from women in my family about the kinds of things that happen when magic is used recklessly. They're the same stories I will have to tell my child if I decide to have one."

"We should check on Frank," Karen said, wanting to avoid any further discussion. She hated when Rosemary got on her high horse. Maybe it was jealousy, she thought, but to be so calm and certain about not believing in gods made Karen feel frustrated. Sometimes it made her mad even, knowing that Rosemary was so sure gods weren't real even though she had these incredible gifts. She knew she ought to be open about her feelings because talking about feelings was how they made their relationship work, but the topic of religion always felt too tense with Rosemary.

Sometimes, when Karen was really frustrated with Rosemary, she thought that Rosemary believed herself to be better than her because of her power. Rosemary's pledge to leave if she ever became pregnant worried Karen along these lines as well, as though Karen and Frank couldn't help her raise her baby in the kind of home that Rosemary thought was appropriate. She wondered if Rosemary planned to leave one day, regardless of whether she was pregnant.

Rosemary must have sensed her hesitation, because she set down the shell and took Karen's hands.

"I love you Karen," Rosemary said. "I want you to be happy, so I'll help you as much as I can, but I think eventually you're going to give up on this search for a god to invoke and worship. You'll be a lot happier then."

Rosemary smiled at Karen, and Karen smiled back at her vacantly, her resentment suddenly gone as she realized the freckles on Rosemary's face were dancing even faster than before.

"Let's talk about this at home," Karen said. "Let's go see if Frank is ready for this prosperity ritual."

So they went through the screen door onto the wooden steps that led up to the roof deck. Frank was meditating and watching the moon rise. He turned to face the women at they climbed the steps stepped onto the deck, and in the moonlight they could see his pupils had grown.

"It's beautiful up there," he said.

"Wow," Rosemary said, looking up at the sky. It seemed she could see more stars than she had ever seen in her life.

Karen looked up too, just in time to witness a meteor cut a slash of light through the night sky. The shooting star happened quickly, and then was gone.

"In about half an hour, it will be midnight. The witching hour," Frank said. "I think if we're very quiet, we could go do our magic down on the beach. I've been watching, and there's no one down there. It's very windy today, so I doubt anyone would be able to hear us down there either."

And so the three discussed a rudimentary plan for a ritual. They stripped down to their underwear and then put on the green hooded cloaks that Karen had prepared. At that point, there was no denying the acid's effect. It affected each of them differently, but they did not notice the differences. Frank became a monk of sorts, quiet and observant, he rarely left the roof deck. He laid on top of the wooden slats on the deck floor and watched the skies above, rarely talking except to point out different constellations. Rosemary became more scholarly, spending most of her time looking at the books she had brought.

Karen became something else. She knew she'd never be the kind of witch Rosemary was, but that evening she felt like more of a witch than she had ever felt before. She felt like she was brimming with magic and might overflow. She agreed to wait until midnight, but she was the first with her cloak on. As midnight crept closer, she recognized in Frank and Rosemary signs of intoxication and decided that only she could see clearly what the universe was presenting to her.

She could feel the magic in the air, so palpable to her that it brought goosebumps. Rosemary and Frank giggled and spun around in their cloaks, dancing and hanging onto each other. At ten until midnight, Karen decided to head down to the beach, leaving her sandals behind. Rosemary and Frank started to follow her but kept stopping, whispering and shushing each other about sounds they thought they heard.

21

Karen walked without worry of stones or splinters as she trod barefoot down the boardwalk. She felt like she was floating down to the beach, as if the moon was pulling her like the tide. Halfway down the long wooden walkway, she noticed the bushes and plants on either side of the boardwalk were reaching out to her from the dark. She couldn't help but remember the beginning of Amos Tutuola's *My Life in the Bush of Ghosts*, where the novel's narrator fled slave traders by escaping into the bush only to lose themselves for decades in a haunted wilderness swarming with nightmare creatures, spirits and supernatural beings.

In the moonlight, the black silhouettes of overgrown limbs and branches spilling onto the walkway became hands, groping blindly to catch her. A breeze wafted over the dunes from the ocean, rustling the fabric of her cape and making the growth in the dunes appear wild. The hands reached frantically for her, and even though she was sure it was an illusion caused by the drug Rosemary had given her, she ran down the rest of the boardwalk quickly.

She was the first to step foot onto the soft sand that night. Frank and Rosemary were delayed at the house. They had come down the wooden deck stairs to the footwash with Karen, but Frank had heard a sound he thought came from inside. When he mentioned it, Rosemary suggested they stick together to investigate. They did not realize Karen had gone ahead to the beach for almost half an hour, as time under LSD became an abstract concept.

They went upstairs and found that the oven timer was beeping. They had set a timer based on the time that Rosemary had said the acid would reach its maximum level, but they forgot this. They laughed over the timer after they turned it off, suggesting other things the timer might have been for: maybe it was the end of time, the alarm clock for humanity, or maybe there was something in the oven. There wasn't. They soon forgot about the timer.

Rosemary rummaged in the fridge for an apple, which she then tried to cut into pieces. She found it very difficult to do, which Frank thought was funny. They gave up on the knife and took turns eating the apple, and then, giggling, made out for a few minutes against the refrigerator. It was only when Rosemary reached her hand out for Karen that the two realized she was not there. They looked out the window at the bright quarter moon over the beach, and then remembered they were supposed to walk down.

***

When Karen stepped onto the soft sand and saw the dark waves crashing onto the shore, she felt overcome by the beauty of the beach at night. The sand looked white in the dark, and the ocean looked black. She walked to the shoreline. She turned up to face the moon, closing her eyes under the bright light. She felt the light of the moon upon her and thought about how the moon had been worshipped at different times by different groups. She tried to feel that power.

She felt herself open and become receptive to the universe. She wasn't sure if it was the LSD or all her studying and prayers. She felt in tune with the skies, looking up and searching for the constellations she had memorized. Her eyes traced across Hercules, Lyra and Draco, and she was relieved to see she recognized them.

It was then that she saw the bright purple star under the moon, a star she did not recognize from any of the maps she had memorized. The star was unusual not because it wasn't familiar to Karen. There were many stars in the sky above her that she didn't recognize. But it was brighter than Jupiter, whose light appeared dim next to it. It seemed brighter than any other star in the sky, and the more Karen looked at it, the more she was sure it did not belong. And yet, she could not look away.

It did not look like the other star. Its light was clearer and brighter. It seemed to flare out instead of flicker, and her brain thought it looked as though someone had poked a hole in the night sky and was shining a purple spotlight down at her. Her rational mind tried to tell her there was something wrong with it, but the more she held the star in her gaze, the more it seemed right to her. It seemed right for her. She felt an intoxicating energy that seemed to pull her.

She found herself drawn to the star and began walking toward it, walking at the tideline swiftly over the sand with the star in her eyes. As her green cloak flapped in the wind behind her, she walked over smooth white hills of sand uncovered by the tide. She did not realize how alone she was on the beach until she thought to turn around.

There was no one behind her, but she did not feel scared as long as she kept her gaze up. She did not feel alone when she looked at the star. It felt like it was calling her closer. She gazed in wonder as thoughts of gods began to eddy in her head.

"This is it," she thought, "I'm ready."

Karen felt the power of the unknown star surge. As she watched, pearly whorls of clouds swam out from the star like glowing fingers. They grew longer as they stretched and pulled away from the star, leaving a perfectly circular space around the now searing purple light. Iridescent wisps wound down out of the bubbling clouds, reaching toward Earth, braiding rapidly through the sky toward her. Flashes of light blinked and winked in the vaporous feelers, like small fireflies were signaling to her as they made their way down from the heavens to meet her.

"Are you the god I have been looking for?" Karen asked the star in an awed whisper. She could barely hear herself over the whip of the wind and the roar of the ocean, but was sure she was heard. She barely noticed the flickering golden lights dancing around her on the beach.

She received her answer in the form of a push. She felt a force from above pushing her down hard, and she was forced to her hands and knees in the sand at the shoreline. On her knees in the shallow tide, the water soaked through the bottom of her cape, making the green fabric appear black. The soaked fabric clung to her knees even as the tide tried to pull it into the ocean, but she did not notice. She had been waiting for something like this to happen since she had started learning about magic.

She had been sure that gods were real, and now she was seeing and feeling the proof. She was afraid, but it was a holy fear. This was not like the boardwalk brush, whose ghostly hands had tried to grab her on her way down to the beach. She was sure that had been the LSD. This, she thought as she was forced deeper into the sand by some unseen hand, was real. She could feel the rough sand scraping at her hands and knees as she sank, and she winced in pain.

The fear deepened as the force on her pressed her deeper still into the sand, and she could feel as her feet, shins, knees and hands sank deep into the sand. For a moment, she saw herself in her mind's eye, buried in the sand with only her head above the surface. Some little boy with a bucket looking for shells in the morning would find her cold dead head, eyes still searching the sky for the purple star. She realized the tide would smother her before then. She might never be found.

She knew she had to say something, to let the god know she recognized his great power and that she would worship him. Maybe then he would have mercy. As she felt the pressure on her back pushing her deeper into the sand, covering the backs of her calves and knees, coming up to her elbows and to her thighs, she dug deep within herself for her voice and begged for her life.

"Please spare me, my god. I've been waiting for you, my god. Please, come to me. Show me how to be. Show me everything," she yelled. "I will worship you until the day I die. Please!"

The wind on the beach was fierce, and whipped her words away from her as she cried out, but the presence behind the star must have heard. She felt the force pushing down on her dissolve until it was gone. She blinked and found she was no longer half buried in the sand, but on top of it again. The sand under her hands was firm.

Grinning wildly, her pupils expanded to the point where her eyes looked like two black stones, Karen craned her head up, showing as much of her face to the star as she could. She watched as the milky white opalescent tendrils finally reached her, trailing all the way from the now blindingly bright purple star. The sand around her was lilac in the light. She sat back on her heels and opened her arms wide, holding her palms up, offering herself to the star. The tendrils took to her, connecting like an iridescent vein between the star and herself.

She felt the power wrap around her, into her, consuming her. She felt more alive than she had ever known was possible. She could feel the tendrils working inside of her, pulling strings, shifting cells and atoms, making room in her soul. She noticed the flickering of the star began to fade, and the strings of the cloud began to dissolve around her, into her. She watched as the star grew dim, and the nacreous threads detached slowly around the star, one by one like picked flower petals. The purple star vanished as the last string detached. They flowed slowly down to earth, chasing the same path down to Karen. As she watched, the shimmering ends pulled into her as though they were being reeled.

An idea came to her so suddenly she knew it was a gift from the god. Several symbols appeared at once in her head, and she set immediately to work drawing these on a large scale in the sand, to be washed over by the ocean once the tide came in. Rosemary and Frank finally came over the dunes hand in hand to find her on her knees near the shore, finishing a 20 foot circle of strange sigils dug into the sand.

Frank was amazed at the work Karen had done, and he was so full of pride that he broke from Rosemary and rushed ahead to help her dig. Rosemary gasped and shivered upon entering the circle, as she felt echoes of a cold, unknown power lap over her.

She felt with her mind for where the power came from and then looked in surprise at Karen, who stood then and wiped sand from her hands on her cloak. Karen's black hair had been whipped wildly by the wind, her cloak was soaked from the bottom up to her waist, and at some point she had removed her clothes so that she was naked.

Karen and Frank spoke, but Rosemary could not hear them from her position on the other side of the 20 foot circle. Karen motioned for Rosemary to come closer, and when Rosemary met her eyes she found for the first time that she was afraid of her lover. She thought it was the LSD, but Karen's eyes looked as large and round as silver dollars, the whites around her eyes as luminous the moon. Her grin seemed crazed as she beckoned for Rosemary to come to her, but she told herself it had to be the LSD affecting her perception.

Rosemary joined with Frank and Karen at the shoreline, where Karen ran them through a ritual she had come up with, she said, by divine inspiration. They removed their undergarments and at Karen's instruction, began walking one at a time clockwise around the perimeter of the circle. As each witch made their turn, they moved one at a time to the center of the pentacle, where they tasted of each other and laid hands on one another in as solemn a way as they could. At the point of climax, each repeated a phrase in their heads that Karen had given them. When they were done, they rinsed off in the tide and walked back up the boardwalk back to the beach house, where they showered off in the outdoors shower before returning upstairs.

They watched the moonset, and performed the ritual they had planned earlier in the evening on the roof deck. They prayed for continued prosperity, spiritually and financially. Afterwards, they all laid down and tried to go to sleep. Karen closed her eyes, and in the swirling spirals circling in her mind, she saw the purple star. She put her prayers to her new god and hoped she could explain to her lovers in the morning.

22

Morning came and went, and it was afternoon before the three awoke. It was raining, but the sun was shining. The three drank coffee on the screened porch, watching the ocean on the horizon over the dunes. For the first time in months, Karen didn't feel compelled to bring up her search for their god. She had been successful, so she decided to wait to tell them.

Her memories of the previous night's events were fuzzy, but not those of her encounter with the star. Replaying the memory of being buried in the sand, Karen felt a flicker of worry as she realized Rosemary and Frank were going to be concerned.

"They didn't feel it," Karen thought. *"They're going to think I hallucinated the whole thing. Or if they believe me, they might think it's dangerous."*

She knew it was dangerous. A new voice in her head began to speak, she told herself. No, it was her voice, she was sure of it. She had never heard herself with the tone before, and the thoughts came into her head before she realized she had collected them.

"Of course it was dangerous," she thought, *"It's a fucking god. My god. The one I've been looking for almost six months. He's come to me."*

"It's a he?" she thought.

"Yes," she thought. *"And I will have to work to earn his name. I will have to prove myself to this god, and he will reward me for it. Frank and Rosemary will understand, but it might be best to present it to them differently. I should wait. Maybe not this week. Have fun with your lovers, praise your god in secret, and when you get back, present it to them in a way they will not fear."*

Karen nodded to herself. Frank stood up to go inside, holding his empty coffee cup.

"Anyone else want more coffee?" he asked.

Rosemary held out her empty cup, and he took it from her. Karen looked down at her nearly full cup. She smiled up at Frank and shook her head, and he grinned at her before walking inside. Rosemary scooted closer to Karen on the couch.

"How are you feeling?" Rosemary asked. She was sure that she had been mistaken about the night before, but something seemed different about Karen this morning. It was hard to tell. Rosemary cursed her intuition in her mind. Anxiety about their relationship seemed to cloud her intuition to the point of worthlessness.

"Is Karen mad because I dismissed her search for religion?" Rosemary thought, replaying last night's conversation in her mind. *"Or because I brought up leaving again?"*

Lately the thoughts of returning to her ancestral home had been dogging Rosemary's thoughts. Things had become serious with Karen and Frank, and Rosemary often fantasized about staying with them forever. They would never have children, and the family line would end with Rosemary. She didn't know what would happen to the gift after she passed. Her mother had told her that it would simply end, as things did sometimes.

The idea of wasting such power seemed immoral and selfish, and lately her body seemed determined to have children. She'd have dreams that she was pregnant, and when she saw young children in public she couldn't help but wish for a child of her own. Someone she could teach everything she had learned so that they could grow even more than she had in her life. She'd fantasize about starting a family with Frank and Karen, but she couldn't stand the idea of denying her child their heritage.

If Rosemary became pregnant, she knew her child would gain her power when she died, just as she had upon her own mother's death. She would have to return home, to Memphis where the family home was locked up and empty. She had hoped never to return, burning most of the ancient library in a fit of passion. She didn't want to be chained to the legacy anymore, but even hundreds of miles away it still felt as inescapable as the march of time.

After her mother had passed, Rosemary hadn't been able to stand the empty home, filled with the ghosts of a hundred years' worth of her relatives. She had left to see the world, taking only what she could in her mother's steamer trunk and leaving the few remaining ancient books and writings that survived. Those secrets were only meant for witches like her, and keeping them contained in that house was the only way to keep them safe.

Rosemary remembered the warnings of her mother Eleanor about magic. It consumed slowly, her mother said, if you were a natural witch. Some magic spells were too strong for anyone but natural witches to perform, she had been warned, as they would flay the soul of any normal mortal. Natural witches had to be taught to harness this power, and her mother had told her of those in the family line who had overreached and lost their minds as a result.

If Rosemary were ever pregnant, the only safe place for her and her child was at the house in Memphis, protected long ago against outsiders. Anyone with harm in mind for a member of the family would find themselves unable to enter the home. It would be there that she could teach her child everything that could be taught, and she was sure of that more than she was sure of anything else, including her love for Karen and Frank.

Wrinkle after wrinkle appeared in her mind whenever she thought about what would happen if they had children. Questions piled up until they formed an impenetrable barrier in her mind. She did not obsess over the thoughts, but knew them with a certainty she could only attribute to intuition and her own stubbornness. She knew from the beginning that she would have to leave if one of them found themselves pregnant.

She had expressed her concerns before and after the first few times she had sex with the two of them. Karen had assured her at the beginning that Frank and Karen had no plans for procreating, and they were careful to monitor both of their cycles. Frank had surgery to ensure he couldn't impregnate them, but nothing felt certain. Rosemary was careful not to let the worry consume her, but she knew that one day their happy story would come to an end.

Looking at Karen, Rosemary wondered if their story was winding down. Karen looked over to her, meeting her eyes and smiling. Rosemary saw the same peaceful pale blue eyes she had fallen for, and she smiled back at her lover. She was sure suddenly that Karen was not angry with her, and she felt such relief that she had forgotten her worries from the night before by the time Frank returned with two hot cups of coffee.

The rest of the week was the most peaceful time the three would ever experience. In the mornings they would pack drinks, sandwiches and snacks into a cooler. They'd trek down to the beach and swim all day, until the sun started to set or they were exhausted. They'd cook dinner together at the beach house, eat and drink together, play board games and read after the sun went down.

23

When they returned home, Karen returned to conversations about finding their god. Over the course of a few weeks spent at the kitchen table with several books spread in front of her, she wrote a spell that she told Frank and Karen would help them find their deity. The spell would actually strengthen her connection with the god she had already found. She painted symbols on their bodies with black and red paint, and the three of them performed a sex magic ritual on a tarp on the floor of their living room, working their way through specific poses that Karen had mapped out.

She remembered it very clearly. Frank was pushing into her from behind, while she had her head between Rosemary's thighs. They all heard it then. It was a whisper, but it was a name. The name of her god. It was Nephilor.

Karen dreamed that night that Nephilor came to her. In the dream, she was standing alone in her bedroom in front of the window. There was only space outside, pinwheeling galaxies and stars. The window began to glow orange, like a molten heat eating the frame, and the glass frosted over. She backed away, and that's when she heard his voice.

He told her he had been waiting for someone that could hear him, and he asked her to build a church for him. He said he was a god that was not known to others, but that he had been watching the earth since it was formed, waiting for someone like her. He had told her that to lead his church, she must make a sacrifice, but that she will be paid back tenfold. He told her the sacrificial lamb would present itself to her, and that he would be back to tell her more.

Rosemary and Frank had listened to her dream over breakfast. The three of them were very excited to have made contact with a divine being. They had been sure the sacrifice was going to be some kind of animal. They discussed it as though it was going to be something as simple as cleaning a fish.

After the dream, months passed with no other word from Nephilor. They continued to praise Nephilor with sex magic once a month, but he was quiet. Karen began to wonder if he had gone, or if she had imagined it all.

One afternoon during her smoke break at work, a young teller came up to her. Her name was Emma. She had seen some of the symbols in Karen's books and wanted to talk with her. The young woman was interested in magic, but she wasn't inexperienced. She told Karen that she was a witch looking for a coven. The two talked excitedly, and Karen invited her over for dinner the following night.

That night, Rosemary, Frank and Karen talked it over. They were sure that the young witch was not the lamb that Nephilor had asked for. They also weren't sure they could go through with it if she was. They performed the ritual again to call to him, covered in red and black paint and writhing together on the floor.

"She is the lamb," Nephilor whispered in her ear. "You will need to bring her close to the earth. Write my name on the ground in a circle with white chalk. Sacrifice her there, and leave no trace behind. Drink her blood seven times. I will grant you youth, and you will lead my church until I am ready to walk the earth."

"Are you ok?" Rosemary asked.

Karen had pulled away while listening to the voice. She told them what it had told her.

"I don't know about this," said Frank.

"This feels wrong and seems beyond risky. It was one thing when we were talking about small animals. And why does a god need help killing?" Rosemary said.

"What if he's not a god?" said Frank.

"You mean like a demon?" Rosemary said. "A ghost? What? No one's ever made contact with something like this. We need to be cautious. We don't know what we're dealing with."

"He's not a demon," said Karen. "I've talked to him."

"Have you seen him?" Frank asked.

"He's only talked. But who's seen God with a capital G? Maybe gods aren't how we think. Maybe they don't always have bodies. Maybe his body is incomprehensible, and that's why he hasn't shown himself. He told me he is an unknown god. He wants me to lead his church," Karen said.

"He told you that last time. Look, we're just saying maybe we should think on this before we do anything rash," Frank said. "That's not unreasonable."

"Don't get us wrong, Karen. We love you, and we believe in you. We just want to make sure we want to follow this Nephilor before we jump down this rabbit hole," said Rosemary. "I don't think we do. Human sacrifice is incredibly powerful magic, more powerful than I think you realize. It would tear you apart. You would never be the same."

Karen loved both Frank and Rosemary, so she listened to them. She wondered if it should worry her that she did not hold the same concerns. The voice in her head told her they must obey Nephilor, and the memory of her near burial in the sand underscored that belief. If he could do that, he could do anything, she thought. Especially if she disobeyed him.

"*It's not murder,*" she thought. "*It'd be murder if it wasn't an order from a god.*"

She thought long and hard about the potential consequences, not just from the law if they were caught, but with her partners. She decided that if they could not stomach it then she would have to wait. Nephilor would have to wait, consequences be damned.

They decided to get to know Emma. She and Rosemary quickly became friends, as though they'd known each other for years. They had her over for dinner a few times before she became interested in their rituals. She had never performed sex magic before, but after hearing their stories was intrigued. Karen had shown her books Frank had ordered from California that detailed different sex magic rituals, and Emma had taken time to go through the book herself.

Nephilor was displeased with their lack of belief. He began appearing as animals in her dreams, sometimes complete creatures but more often chimera. The form he took would always be made of shimmering, iridescent light. The first time he had the body of a horse and the neck and head of a wolf. In her dreams, she would be standing at the gate of a wide field of grain at night. The sky was black, with the exception of a blazing purple star. The beast would trot up to her through the field and bring his face close to hers. No matter what animal form he took, his mouth would never move when it spoke to her. He urged her to make the sacrifice like this for four months.

He did not threaten her, but only seemed disappointed that she would not follow this first command. Finally, the dreams shifted as the god changed his demand. He told Karen he required praise, and that sacrifice was the highest form of praise. If they would not sacrifice to him, he needed more praise to sustain him. He wanted Emma involved in the sex magic ritual they had been using to praise Nephilor. He demanded more praise, and the more people involved, the better.

Karen told her lovers about the new dream over breakfast the next morning. The three of them were sitting around the kitchen table, drinking their coffee and eating scrambled eggs and grapefruit.

"I'm at least glad that he's not trying to get us to murder someone anymore," Rosemary said.

"Me too," said Karen, and then she told a lie she supposed was meant to comfort both of them. "I don't think I could have gone through with it."

Rosemary grabbed Karen's hand and held it tight. She looked at Karen with concerned eyes. Karen couldn't help feeling she was being dramatic.

"You never had to," Rosemary said. "We don't have to continue down this path if you don't want to. We don't have to worship a god. I know we discovered one, but we don't have to praise him if you don't want to. I've told you before, but magic exists separately from gods. It's as natural as gravity."

Karen had already considered it. She had decided Rosemary didn't know what she was talking about. She was sure that Nephilor was lonely, and that's why he was mad sometimes. She knew there was a gentle side to her god, the one she found, the one that only called to her. She also wasn't sure Nephilor would ever let her go. He appeared in her dreams most nights.

Sometimes the edges of the creatures would blur, and it would look to Karen as though they were made of the milky white tendrils she had seen that night on the beach. In these dreams when she saw the animals as opalescent, when it seemed that the tendrils might break from the animal and reach for her again, she would awake, covered in a cold sweat, but wide awake.

Her heart beating rapidly in her chest, so loud she could feel it in her head, she would chide herself for her fear in her dreams. She knew with a certainty she wanted to call intuition that she should not be afraid of Nephilor. He would never hurt her again. He just didn't know how to act sometimes, she thought, and then she would feel guilty for her fear.

"I think it must have been maddeningly lonely to be an unknown god," Karen said. "I think the more praise he receives, the gentler he will become. I can hear it when we talk at night. He has told me that for millions of years, no one could hear him at all. I can't even imagine."

"What do you talk about with him, darling?" Frank said, stirring eggs in a frying pan.

"He tells me about the birth of the universe, about the power that runs through everything. He gets angry that we won't make sacrifices to him, but he won't leave because we're the only ones who can hear him. He's getting softer on that though. He finally told me that the reason for the sacrifice is that it's the highest form of praise. If we can get him more praise, that will suffice. I want us to bring Emma in on the ritual we do for Nephilor."

"Well, she was definitely interested in sex magic the other night when you were showing her that book. Why don't you talk to her directly?" Frank said.

"You've got no problems with it?" Rosemary said. She sounded surprised.

Frank and Karen looked at Rosemary.

"What's the matter?" Karen said.

"This is just a big unknown, that's all," Rosemary said. "I mean, what's Nephilor going to do once we get more people to praise him? What comes after that?"

"He hasn't told me yet. But I think he just wants a following. He seems very concerned with praise. I really don't think he could do much. I think the sacrifice stuff is very 'old god.' If we start his following, we can make sure it's much more modern and humane."

Rosemary nodded. She could see Karen was happy to go along this path, and so decided she would be as well. For now.

She had never heard of anything like this happening before, but was sure she could stop things from going too far.

"I think that would be much better if that's the case," Rosemary said. "All of the sacrifice business has been making me nervous."

"I'll talk to Emma and see if she's interested," Karen said.

24

Emma was very interested. She had read about sex magic but had lots of questions when Rosemary told her they practiced it as a form of praise for a god they had found. She wasn't sure about their god, but wanted to find out more. She and Rosemary were similar in their abilities, and the two had spent time over the past months discussing how their families had referred to different practices. She thought that it was going to be safe because she trusted Rosemary.

They agreed to meet that night for dinner and what they began referring to as "praise" when discussing aloud at work. Emma showed up early with a casserole and a box of rolls. Karen asked Rosemary to take Emma's dishes to the kitchen. Karen had prepared a large meal, starting with appetizers and cocktails, followed by a pork crown roast served with green beans, mashed potatoes, and baked beans.

"Why, we've practically got enough dishes tonight to hold a church potluck," said Rosemary to Karen as she brought Emma's dishes into the kitchen. She had made two pies for dessert.

Karen had laughed at Rosemary's joke and agreed there was indeed going to be a feast that night, and then took the box of rolls from her. Rosemary set down the casserole. Karen turned to Rosemary and took her hand.

"Are you ready? I know you said you were feeling nervous earlier," Karen said.

Rosemary squeezed Karen's hand back and looked into her pale blue eyes.

"It's really the sacrifice talk that makes me nervous. I've got a feeling we haven't heard anywhere near the end of that line of request," Rosemary said.

"Well, that's not what he's told me. I think he'll find the other forms of praise just as satisfying," Karen said, and she squeezed Rosemary's hand. "I know I do."

At that, Rosemary blushed. Karen leaned over and kissed her on the cheek, and then let go of her hand. Now that their guest had arrived, it was time to begin.

Karen brought out a tray of cucumber and salmon mousse canapes. They chatted and drank vodka gimlets before everyone helped carry the dinner dishes to the table to eat. Karen looked proudly at the spread of dishes once they were laid on the dining room table. Nephilor had told her it was important that they feast before the ceremony that evening, and she had spent her spare time that week in the kitchen preparing dishes ahead of time. It had paid off. The dining room table was covered in dishes of different foods, and everyone ate until they were unable to eat anymore.

After dinner, they undressed in the living room, folding their clothes and setting them on the sofa. Karen brought out the black and red paint and painted the required symbols on everyone's bodies. She instructed them on the chants to be spoken, several positions they would need to use, and the need to keep praising Nephilor as they worked. Then they chanted his name, and began laying hands on one another.

In the heat of things, Karen looked into Frank's eyes and was surprised to see a look there that she had never seen in her husband. His eyes looked brighter than she'd ever seen, like a fire was lit on the inside. They seemed to reflect light that wasn't in the room. Frank also was working with a stamina Karen hadn't seen in him before. She knew it had to be Nephilor, and as she thought so she felt a chill work through her. She brushed it off, focusing her mind on praising him.

The four of them worked and writhed together with a new energy. They moved slowly, focusing only on each other. Karen felt a feeling like a fog coming in and became so absorbed in the religious group sex that before she knew it three hours had passed. They had spent the time enraptured in praise for Nephilor and in each other. Frank finished in each woman, his back arching and his eyes rolling backwards. When he was done, finishing in Karen last, he collapsed after pulling out. He was asleep, and he wouldn't remember most of the night's activities after the praise began.

At the end, when he was in Karen, she heard Nephilor in her head.

"One of you women shall carry my child. She shall have many gifts and will help lead the church. You have planted my seed tonight, and you will see to it that my fruit grows strong."

"Did everyone hear that voice?" Emma said, her voice cracking. She had covered herself with a pillow from the couch, and there was fear in her eyes.

"Y-yes," said Rosemary.

Rosemary also looked shaken, and Karen wanted to comfort her but at the same time felt like she had been vindicated. Yes, the three of them had heard him whisper his name before, but Rosemary had never seemed convinced. What he had spoken to the four of them was unmistakable. She looked at her husband's clammy pallor as he lay on the floor next to her. She felt a chill that she quickly suppressed.

"I think he possessed Frank," said Karen, her face white. "He had a vasectomy though. Please don't worry. I'm sure it's nothing."

Nevertheless, Emma got dressed and left. Rosemary and Karen washed the paint off of the sleeping Frank, and roused him enough to get him to bed. He felt exhausted and slept soundly through the night. The two women climbed into bed after cleaning themselves up. They didn't talk while they cleaned up the mess from the ritual, and Rosemary slept in her own room.

Karen's dreams that night were intense. Nephilor was overjoyed, and in her dreams he took the shape of a white monkey, high in the branches of a magnolia tree. The monkey swung from branch to branch, talking to her continuously. He paused to pull a white magnolia from the tree, buried his face in the petals to smell deeply and then threw the flower away.

"You've done a great thing, my child. You joined together two witches in union to praise me. I can see into your thoughts, and I know that you don't see the significance of this. It will be many decades before you do. I promised you a reward, and that is now given to you. It will take time before you realize what I have given you. When you see what you have wrought, you will wish you had chosen to make the sacrifice. But all will be well, in time. You'll come around once you accept more sacrifices will be required to maintain your reward."

For a moment, Karen wondered if she had betrayed Rosemary and Frank, but the thought vanished. The white monkey whooped, and then swung back into the branches of tree before climbing up until Karen couldn't see him anymore. She woke smelling magnolias.

Emma didn't show back up at the bank. Karen didn't know for sure, but intuition told her that Emma had probably skipped town. Karen never heard from her again, but once Rosemary left, she didn't care to spare Emma another thought.

A month after the ritual with Emma, Rosemary found that she was pregnant. Without saying a word to anyone, she left in the night, going back to Memphis to return to her family's home. She was alone, but in her home she had everything she needed to raise her child how she knew she must be raised. She found herself relieved to be away from the Maples, and especially from Nephilor.

Things hadn't felt right to her after their return from the beach. The month after the ritual with Emma had been tense. Something seemed different about Karen. When she found herself pregnant, she decided she did not need to explain anything to anyone. She only needed to leave, so she did.

Karen was heartbroken. She thought Rosemary had abandoned her, and this made her angry. She felt hate fill her heart, and she let it happen. Karen used her anger as a driving force. She threw everything of Rosemary's away and turned the room that had been Rosemary's into her own office. She worked constantly on a new project, wallpapering the room with notes and maps.

Frank soon got involved as well once he realized what she was doing. He had thought she had seemed different as well, but he had known when they had married that they would both change over the years. She was still his Karen to him, no matter what god they worshipped, and he loved her just the same. The new drive she was showing made her even more attractive to him, and he did everything he could to help her with her new project.

By 1965, they had plans laid out for a large organization dedicated to Nephilor. They called the business Church, as everything was done in the name of praise for Nephilor. They would never name the group in public, referring to it only vaguely. On tax documents, it was the RFW Company. Frank went to Memphis to scout out property for a club and to see if he could find Rosemary. He couldn't find her, but he found a large plot of land near the university that seemed perfect.

Construction started in 1968 after years of dispute over how the land could be developed. This was a learning time for Karen and Frank, and the experience taught them knowledge that they used when they purchased property for the group going forward. They learned to wait until after all inspections to start on the necessary underground rooms for worship. They learned to dig the tunnels at night and to soundproof so that the construction wouldn't be noticed. They sourced the smallest construction equipment and the most bribable workers they could find.

Around 1969, Frank realized his wife hadn't aged a day in 10 years. They celebrated this as more proof of Nephilor's power. By that time, the clubs in Memphis had gained some popularity. Their plan of hiring potential church members worked amazingly well, as did the level system Karen created. They had studied how other religions recruited, and cherry picked some of the tactics. They hired from shelters and halfway houses, outside of employment agencies and at soup kitchens. They found those who needed someone to lean on, and they gave them training and wages that would help them get on their feet again. They could not cure their problems, but they could make it easier with Nephilor's help. The employees would attribute their improvements to Church, not knowing just how much they had been helped.

They didn't present themselves publicly as a religion, of course. They were a charitable organization, but only in their hiring practices. As far as the government was concerned, they were just nightclub owners that paid their taxes. The people that ran the shelters and halfway houses thought they were giving people chances they wouldn't get anywhere else.

Once they had helped an employee back into society, earning their trust and loyalty in the process, they chose those that had potential and put them through the level system. Employees that didn't make it to the level system often didn't make it very long at the clubs. Turnover was high, except once they were in the level system. The employees that were chosen for the group had the longest tenure at the clubs.

Level 1 employees received an introduction to magic in nature. They were required to complete a set amount of volunteer hours cleaning up the environment. They also learned entry level magic, such as reading tarot cards. Recruits often stayed at this level for a year at least before being exposed to Level 2, where they were shown more supernatural proof.

Level 2 members also participated in paranormal research and were sometimes sent on fact finding missions. They were required to write reports on the missions, and those reports were edited and archived by Level 3 members. Level 2 members that proved themselves worthy were promoted to Level 3, where they gained access to the group's archives, which they were required to maintain.

Those in Level 3 who showed good leadership skills were promoted to Level 4, which emphasized magic and leadership. These members were usually in management in the clubs. Level 5 was a small group, selected and led by Karen and Frank. These were the chosen few who proved themselves worthy of learning about Nephilor. All levels before 5 had activities they did where they praised Nephilor in minor ways, without knowing his name. Karen had found other ways to get praise for the hungry god by installing symbols under the dance floors of the clubs and by having the level 5 members perform honorary rituals and daily prayers.

It still wasn't enough for Nephilor. He came to Karen in her dreams and instructed her on who and how to sacrifice so that she would not be caught. He told her that her youth would only be sustained if she did these things for him. She tried to ignore him and to continue to find other venues of praise for him.

He had brought great wealth to their family, and the praise he received from the clubs and level 5 ceremonies gave him strength. But he persisted in telling her it wasn't enough, and that sacrifice was needed. By 1972, she begun to notice that she was starting to age. Between that and the dreams every night, she could no longer think of any reason not to do as he asked.

The first sacrifice was a young woman in Memphis. Frank had been instructed to lure her out of the bar where they found her, but she wasn't falling for it. She seemed scared of him. Nephilor told Karen where to be in the woman's path so they would not be seen. Karen convinced her to run with her to safety, knowing the dark alley ended in a dead-end as Nephilor had shown her. She knocked the girl out with ether and then Frank helped load her in their waiting car. They carried her to the underground space beneath the first club in Memphis. Karen slit her throat and sang the words Nephilor gave her. When all was done, she burned the body. She kept the ashes and used them and the remaining bones for spells. It seemed that magic done to help their employees worked even better when the remains of witches were used. It wasn't until the next sacrifice that she learned how potent their blood was for spells.

Frank helped her secure the witches and clean up, but he never had the stomach for the act of sacrifice. Fortunately, Nephilor was very clear that Karen would be the only one to touch witch's blood. Frank never touched a knife, but he was present during the ceremonies by his wife's side.

In 1995, Frank had a heart attack during the weekly sex ritual. All the Level 5s were involved, but Frank was with Karen when it happened. Karen watched in shock as he grabbed his arm, his eyes rolling back in his head. He had collapsed on top of her, and she heard his last breath in her ear. Frank left her with a seven year old boy, Mike, but Karen felt alone and empty.

She found light in Nephilor and filled more of her time with praise for him. She thought sometimes that she had lost her mind, but instead of fearing for herself she laughed at those thoughts. She felt like she could truly see what He had in mind for the world, and that not only was it right, but it was the ideal.

He would bring about a rapture, and all that would be left uncharred would be those in her group. He would bring back a few chosen souls from the dead, including Frank. When she realized this, she redoubled her efforts at expanding membership. She raised her son as best as she could, and as he grew into a handsome young man, she realized a plan for him. She wanted to return to Cincinnati, but she would wait until he was old enough. Nephilor would tell her when it was time.

Rosemary came back to her in 1997. She was surprised to see that Karen looked just as beautiful as the day that she had left. Karen told her of the good that Nephilor had brought her, and the good that was yet to come. He had grown in power over the years, and now he could speak to her at any time.

Rosemary needed Karen's help. Her daughter, Theresa, had begun to show powers that had never been seen in her family. Usually magic did not manifest until the previous witch had died, but Theresa had startling abilities that she couldn't control. With just a glance, Theresa had created a fire that had almost killed herself and her daughter and had destroyed her own home. Theresa didn't feel safe around herself anymore. She didn't feel safe to even open her eyes. Rosemary had understood that Nephilor had something to do with the uncontrollable powers. She had known she had to return to Karen.

Theresa had wanted help too. She wanted to go back to her daughter and to raise her with a normal life, or as normal as witches may live. Her mother had taught her since she was born about the gifts she would receive upon Rosemary's death, but nothing had prepared them for the chaos that started when Theresa's powers began to manifest.

Karen had never forgotten how Rosemary had abandoned her, but she agreed to try to help. Memories of the love she had for Rosemary had always stayed with her, even though the choices Karen had made in the intervening years had made her into a completely different person. Karen had wanted to help Theresa for Rosemary. Nephilor had different plans.

***

Karen flicked ash off her cigarette over the railing of the patio. Rosemary taught them everything she knew. She gave everything she could to the group when it had been just the three of them. If only she could see where it was now.

"We're so close to proving you wrong, Rosemary," she said aloud to herself on the empty patio.

She crushed her cigarette out in her ashtray and went inside.

Part Three

25

Neither of them spoke until they were pulled into Crystal Crescent. Emily felt uneasy. She had felt like someone was watching them the entire time they were in the graveyard. That weird, creepy, almost tingly feeling started when they met the caretaker and hadn't stopped. She tried not to think about it, but dismissing it as paranoia was tough. Something was going on.

The main strip of the town had vacant storefronts, and they'd barely seen a soul that morning on the road. It was a tiny town, but it had the kind of cemetery found in rich suburbs. She wondered if the woods and the cemetery weren't owned by the same group. All the surrounding land had largely been developed into farmland.

And then there was the symbol on the graves. They had seen a spiral just like it on the dance floor at the nightclub. It was obvious Mike had to be involved in some way. She didn't know how, but it wasn't easy to dismiss. Could his company be killing witches for money?

Rachel hadn't said a word since they got back in the car. Emily had never seen her act like this before. She did tend to go quiet about things she was conflicted about, but never for this long. Emily knew if she brought it up first, Rachel would fight back. She'd already blown up about Mike on the way to the graveyard, and she'd said nothing the whole drive up from Hearth except the occasional sigh.

She wanted to see what Morgan's advice would be. If Morgan pushed Rachel anywhere aside from getting out of town, Emily would be certain that Morgan was involved in all of this. They had zero evidence to take to the police, and "I've got a feeling there's two bodies in that grave" would at best get them kicked out of the police station. If Morgan was involved, Emily would have to get Rachel out of there without alerting Morgan that she knew what was up.

Her eyes went to her purse as she thought about the worst case scenario again. It felt hard to swallow, but she managed before taking a deep breath. She pulled into the parking lot, shifted into park, and turned off the car.

"There she is," Rachel said.

Morgan was sitting on the steps of the porch before they pulled up. She was smiling and waving until they pulled in. Once they pulled into the parking lot, it was like a cloud passed over the sun. She crossed her arms and looked grim as she stood up to greet them, her brow tensed. Morgan met Emily's eyes for only a moment and then looked at Rachel.

They got out of the car and walked up to the cement steps. Morgan stepped back into the shade under the columns. Emily didn't like her body language. Her arms were still crossed, and she wasn't looking at her. As she stood in the sun looking at the woman on the porch, she couldn't help but read this standoffish body language as a bad sign.

"Hello," Morgan said.

"Morgan, this is Emily. Emily, this is Morgan," Rachel said.

Morgan looked at her long enough for them to nod to each other before she turned around.

"Come quickly," she said. "Let's go inside."

She walked through the purple door on the left of the building. Rachel looked back at Emily with a confused look on her face. She shrugged as if to say, "I don't know why she's being weird." Then she walked up the steps and followed Morgan into the store. Emily walked up the steps with hesitation, then she unzipped the outside pocket on her purse. Just in case.

She walked across the porch and into the store. Or at least, she tried to. As soon as one toe of her black leather slip-proof sneakers crossed the threshold, she stumbled backward. Her foot felt like she had been burned. Painful heat seared from the tips of her toes. But as she stepped back the pain faded away to nothing.

"What the fuck was that?" she said, trying to keep her voice low.

Rachel looked at Morgan with wide eyes.

"What'd you do?" Rachel said.

Morgan narrowed her eyes and uncrossed her arms.

"I didn't do anything. Your friend has ill intentions for me. That's the only reason she wouldn't be able to cross the threshold."

Emily felt her anxiety click over into clear anger. She felt vindicated in her suspicion.

"Clearly you're involved with all of this," she said. "Rachel, we need to go. Now."

"Morgan, explain yourself," Rachel said.

"Me?" Morgan said. "Are you kidding? This spell is logic based. She can't come in if she has any intent to harm me. It's simple. Your friend here is bad news. What do you want to do about her?"

She addressed this last question to Rachel almost like a mobster. Emily's thoughts flickered to her weapon, but she recognized that as paranoia amplified by fear. She let out an exasperated sigh.

"Good idea. Everyone take a deep breath," Rachel said.

Morgan looked dubious, but they all took a deep breath together.

"Another one."

The three women breathed in and then sighed out.

"Now you two shut the fuck up," Rachel said. "I need you both to be honest and work together. It could literally make the difference between life or death. I wouldn't have brought you here if I didn't trust Morgan. Emily, you know I trust you, but I need you to explain why you have ill intent."

"I don't. I have a weapon on me but I don't know if I will have to use it. I hope not. Just like I hoped I wouldn't have to this morning. But that doesn't mean I shouldn't be prepared. Something is going on, and you're in danger.

You don't seem to be thinking clearly, especially about Mike and Morgan. You don't know this woman. She could be part of this whole conspiracy against your family. I think she's unscrupulous; there's nothing moral about conning people. And there's nothing right about an atheist running a metaphysical store, let alone doing tarot readings. Why sell something you don't believe in to people that do? I don't trust her."

Morgan's eyes had been distrustful until Rachel finished speaking. Now she just looked angry. She walked to the door frame and held her hand in the air as though there was a sheet hanging in the doorway.

"Get in here if you're going to say anything else," she said. "I can see you're fiercely protective of your friend, and I can't fault you for that. But you don't understand anything about my business."

"Tell me why I should trust you," Emily said as she eased past Morgan into the store.

"I want to help your friend because it's the right thing to do. It's good that you recognize the severity of the situation, but you're misplacing your anger when it comes to me. I'm just trying to help."

"What's reasonable about conning people?" Emily said with a smirk.

Morgan scoffed and started to respond before Rachel interrupted.

"I wish Mike were here. He's a good people manager. Maybe he'd be able to manage to get you two to act like fucking adults," Rachel said.

"What?" Emily and Morgan said at the same time. They looked uneasily at each other.

"You're acting like children."

"I don't disagree, but why did you just bring up Mike?" Emily said.

"Who is Mike?" Morgan said.

"My boyfriend," Rachel said. "Honestly, I think he's the only person keeping me sane right now. My life feels like a broken boat in a storm lately. You two being bitches to each other isn't helping. We're wasting time."

Morgan looked at Emily, but her expression was different now. The anger was gone. Emily felt a flutter of hope.

"How long has she been with this guy?" Morgan said.

"Since everything started with this witch business," Emily said. "There was a spiral on the grave we just went to that looked just like the one on the dance floor of the night club he owns. Not one of those tight spirals, but the one that starts small and then loops out."

She drew in the air with her finger to illustrate the spiral. Rachel turned to face Emily.

"Symbols mean different things to different people," Rachel said. "It's just a coincidence. I would know if Mike was involved when I'm around him."

Emily saw as Morgan's eyes went wide behind Rachel. Catching Emily's eye, Morgan pulled at her earlobe, winked and nodded toward Rachel. But when Rachel turned around, Morgan resumed a normal expression as though she'd been listening and not signaling like a baseball catcher.

"Right Morgan? Wouldn't intuition warn me I was in danger?"

"Yes, you're absolutely right. You'd know if he was involved, unless he tampered with your cognition with magic. And he would never do that, right?" Morgan said in motherly tones. "Can't you see Emily? Doubting Mike is the wrong way to go."

Emily's jaw dropped. She closed her mouth when Rachel looked back at her and smiled uneasily. She thought Morgan was a bitch, but she was onto something.

"Yeah," Emily said, managing to sound friendlier. "Maybe you're right. Maybe I just don't know him like you do, Rachel. Why don't you tell us about him?"

Rachel started talking and didn't stop for several minutes about how perfect she and Mike were for each other. Emily noticed she touched her earrings twice while she gushed. Morgan saw it too. Morgan stepped closer to her, putting her arm around her.

"Those are beautiful earrings," she said. "Did he give those to you?"

Rachel nodded and blushed. She shrugged out of Morgan's hug and stepped back from both of them.

"Yeah, I never really cared for jewelry as gifts. I was weirded out at first, but he has great taste. They're going to look beautiful with the dress he wants me to wear next Friday."

"The solstice?" Morgan asked gently. Emily had to work hard to restrain her own reaction. She was positive now about Mike's intentions.

"No, he said it's a work event," Rachel said. "That's just a coincidence that it's on the solstice. There's no way he's involved. He's just a sweet goofball."

"You're right, Rachel," Emily said. "I'm sorry I wasn't listening earlier. I'm glad you have someone like that right now."

"Could I see those earrings? Call it an occupational obsession, but I can't help but admire the quality of that rose quartz. I have to know where it rates on the Rose Quartz Purity Index."

"The what?" Rachel asked, holding her hand to her ear. There was just a hint of suspicion in her eyes.

"It's a metric for gemstones, specifically rose quartz," Morgan said. "I promise it won't damage your darling's gift. I just swipe a wet cotton swab on each earring, and the color of the fluid changes depending on the purity. You don't even have to take them off."

"Uh, ok. But then we need to get back to business. I'm just glad you guys are acting like adults now. We need to tell you all about what's happened since I came to see you last."

"This will only take a second, and then we'll get back to what's important," Morgan said.

Morgan quickly exited the shop through the beaded curtain on the other side of her desk. Emily could hear her run upstairs and then back down. She thought she heard the sound of water moving through pipes, but Rachel didn't seem to notice. Emily didn't believe in prayer, but she found herself praying anyway that she and Morgan were on the same page she thought they were.

Morgan came back down with a black cat trailing behind her. She had a large white microfiber cloth bundled in her right hand. The wet part of the cloth covered her pointer finger, and she was grasping the rest of the bundled fabric with a clenched fist. Emily wondered what she was hiding in the cloth and whether Rachel would notice. She had a blue plastic bucket in her other hand.

"Couldn't find cotton swabs, so this will have to do," Morgan said. "Let's see now. This cleanses the enchantment permanently."

She rubbed both sides of Rachel's earrings with the wet cloth before she could react to Morgan's last sentence. Rachel started to pull back from her when she reached for the left earring, but Emily had moved to Rachel's side and held onto her.

Rachel dropped to all fours and started retching. Morgan nudged the bucket with her foot in front of Rachel, who started throwing up. Her bile was a runny black liquid before it turned clear. Rachel coughed and spat until she was gasping for breath.

"What'd you do?" Emily said, getting down on her knees and rubbing her friends back.

"Exactly what I said," Morgan said. "Give her a minute. She was under a love spell. By the looks of it, a very strong one. That black vomit is sure sign a witch was murdered for the spell on those earrings."

Rachel sat back on her knees and took deep breaths until her breathing was near regular again. Her heart was hammering at her chest wall. Morgan handed her the cloth, and she wiped her face. Emily had thought there was something in the cloth, but whatever it was gone now. Rachel groaned, then ran her hands through her hair. Emily turned her attention back to her friend, patting her left shoulder and trying to make comforting sounds.

"Don't move," Morgan said. "I'll get you some water."

The black cat rubbed against Rachel, who petted it until Morgan came back with water. Emily was glad Morgan's store had no traffic, because the three of them were sitting on the ground just inside the door of the store. Rachel downed the glass of water and then wiped off her face again. She looked pale but some of her color was starting to return. Randi meowed next to her, and she petted his soft black fur with a shaking hand.

"I'm guessing there's no such thing as the Rose Quartz Purity Index?"

"No," Morgan said. "There are identification and classification systems for gemstones, but my customers usually aren't into geology at that level. I'm sorry I had to trick you, but I'm guessing you didn't consent to that love spell. You would have wandered right into their hands if we didn't figure it out. Great teamwork, Emily. I could tell you didn't trust me, but now I see why Rachel trusts you so much."

Rachel nodded and started to get up. She stumbled, but Emily put an arm around her to keep her upright. Rachel shrugged it off. She seemed steady on her feet so Emily gave her space.

"I'm fine. Let's talk in your library," she said. "We don't have any time to waste."

26

They talked through everything, planning for hours. It was dark by the time Rachel got home. After she locked the front door and checked her protection spell, she went around the house and shut all the blinds and curtains. Then she went to her bedroom. She didn't pack a suitcase. She picked out a few shirts and pants, rolled them up tightly and stuffed them in her oversized purse along with some toiletries. Then she went to her office and packed a few more things.

The letters were still laid out on the desk as she had left them. When Morgan had told her what she needed to do with them, she had felt foolish for not thinking of it sooner. Not as foolish as Mike had made her feel, but they'd make sure he paid for it. There wasn't time to feel sorry for herself, even if she still felt sick to her stomach. She got to work, picking up the black birch wand from its spot on her desk and holding it over the letters.

"I want to unlock these letters and see what's been hidden," she said with all the confidence and finality she could muster as she pointed the tip of the wand down onto the symbol on the first letter, then the second letter, and finally she rested the tip on the symbol on the third letter.

As she began to draw the wand's tip away from the symbol on the third letter, she found she couldn't pull it away easily. The tip of the black branch was stuck to the page. She felt the resistance and pulled back the wand, adding more muscle than she thought necessary for lifting a stick. It felt like a heavy weight had been attached to the wand's end under the surface of the paper. The weight reminded her of the time she had gone fishing in the lake at the community park and had caught what felt like a choice filet dinner but turned out to be a reusable canvas bag filled with old cans.

She adjusted her footing so that both of her feet were flat on the ground, about shoulder width apart. She rolled her shoulders back, took a deep breath and bracing her stomach muscles like she was about to be hit in the stomach. Then she put both hands on the wand and pulled back slowly but firmly.

The grounding helped her fight the wand's resistance. As she freed the wand from the surface of the paper, she saw the green ink pull up from the paper like a taut line of thread connecting the wand tip to the page. The words on the page—the very ink disappeared from the pages of all three letters as she tugged. The words peeled away and up into the smooth green line that connected the letter to her wand like string pulled from embroidery.

She stepped back, surprised to find the paper on the desk stayed flat and still while she pulled what was feeling more and more like a struggling hooked fish. Backed against the wall, she hauled the wand up as high as she could.

The green line suddenly snapped away from the tip. The thread of ink sucked back into the page, finishing with the end that had been attached to the tip of Rachel's wand. The line's end disappeared into the blank page with a whispery popping sound.

Green ink poured out of the spot the line had disappeared into, spilling first onto the third letter. As the ink slowly spread, words had begun appearing where the line had disappeared into the third letter. The words followed the wave of ink, rippling across the page. As the ink spread and moved outward, words were left behind like shells in the tide, appearing as the ink worked from the third letter to the second and finally to the first.

Rachel set down the wand and sat in her chair. She picked up the first letter and began to read.

Dearest Rachel,

I do not know if you will ever read this letter this way, but if you have, things have changed for the worse. I had hoped it would never come to this, but had prepared all the same. I have wanted to speak plainly to you for so long, so please read carefully as I have only enchanted three pages worth of ink.

I am filled with regret that I ever left you. With every day that passes, I know more and more that this has been a grave mistake. I do not think they will ever let me leave here, and I don't think they'll let me write anymore after this last letter. I enchanted these last few letters so that I could write plainly to you in secret. I hope you find this before I reach my end here, but I think it's unlikely. Still, I will write to you just the same, if not for you, then for me. It gives me hope to think you may find this while I'm alive, and if you find this after I'm dead, then at least you will have an explanation.

You must understand the state I was in when my mother and I left you with your Memaw and Pawpaw. Before I moved you to your grandparents, I had begun to manifest powers I could not control. It happened very suddenly. Items I wanted would find their way into my possession, whether I wanted them to or not. It was fun for the first few days, something I thought might happen to young witchlings. I took to carrying a large purse.

A blouse or a jacket I wanted in a store would be in my purse when I got home, without security tags and without my hands ever touching it. Makeup, food, anything I wanted. But then it started happening with things I didn't want. Items my eyes just lingered on, like mens shirts, batteries, canned cat food. It was when I was looking at handguns at a store and felt my purse suddenly slouch with new, heavy weight that I realized this was a problem, and not one I could control.

I had tucked you into bed that night at our quiet house in Memphis, and I had meditated over my altar with an intention of inner peace, for an end to the strange madness. I lit a black candle to symbolize the goal of my meditation that night: the destruction of negative energy. It was that night that I learned of another power that I could not control. I meditated on the flame, picturing myself casting off negative energy and whatever internal disquiet that was causing these strange powers.

The flame lept from the candle, and it went where my eyes went. It leapt to the floor, catching the carpet ablaze. When I looked at the wall, flames grew there. I looked back at the window of my bedroom, and flames caught there as well. I'm still not sure how I managed to get out and get you out, but the house burnt to the ground. We lost everything but each other and my Honda Accord.

We went to your grandmother Rosemary after the firemen left, and she told me about the manner of my conception. She had belonged to a small coven that she said had found a deity, and I was conceived during a sex magic ritual. After that ritual, your grandmother said the deity spoke to them, and said that there would be a child conceived. After she realized she was pregnant, she fled to raise me as she was raised. Witches like us have to stick to our own kind. It can be incredibly dangerous if the wrong kind of people want to take advantage of your abilities. We changed our last name to Miller once she returned to Memphis. Before then, it was Crantz.

She told me that night that she had been waiting a long time for the other shoe to drop. We stayed with her while she got in touch with someone in the organization. They must have convinced her that things were better than they are, because we left for Cincinnati the next day and arrived at a mansion in a wealthy neighborhood. They gave me a physical and a room to stay in. I never left my room without supervision after that day, even during the years when I fooled them into thinking I was helping them.

In my letter, I called them wolves because I do not know what they call themselves. I know it's a coven of some kind that worships a god. I don't think I was supposed to, but I've heard his name. They call him Nephilor. I believe they do everything in his name. I think they have made contact with something, but I've never believed gods to be real. I'm not sure what it is that they speak to.

I know they're up to something, even though they tell me they're not, otherwise they'd never do this to a person. They keep me sedated, mostly I guess so I'll play along. Every week, they put brass chains on me and trundle me downstairs to a laboratory. There are tests where I move things they ask me to move or change the shape of a flame in a glass box. They put blinders on me so that I cannot see who or what else is in the room, but I always hear their murmuring and the scribble of their busy pens. I always feel it when they stick needles in me. They told me if I played along, they'd release me once I was stable. The tests, they said, were to help me gain control of the abilities. I don't think they'll ever judge me as stable as long as I'm able to do what they ask.

At first, I believed I'd be able to escape. But your grandmother asked me not to. She told me she trusted the person running the organization, and that they'd be the only ones able to help us. That was in 1997, the last time I saw her. They won't tell me where she went, but I know that she passed because other powers came to me in that year. I am sure that they took her. I know it with the certainty you may now be becoming familiar with. We use the word intuition to describe this, but it's something stronger than that for us. I'm sure you know yourself now how electric the certainty is.

I'm saving all the magic I can for when they are done with me. When I die, the power will come to you. I don't want to die without seeing you again, and I want to make sure you're prepared since after I pass they will come after you. I plan on using astral projection at the moment of my death. I will come to you then, and do everything I can to help you before I fade away.

We all have our own theories as to where the power comes from. Since families tend to stick to themselves for safety, we don't have a lot of resources aside from our own. My mother burnt most of our resources when she was young, but she and I worked together to write down as much as she could remember from her studies growing up.

I had wanted to tell you my theory of magic in person, I had hoped for it every day, but if you are reading this, I was never able to. Let me do my best here to tell you in writing:

We are conduits for the universe. Carl Sagan said we are all made of star stuff, and he was right. I hope you learned about this in school, but let me try to summarize: Long before the big bang, far from Earth, some of the oldest stars in the universe were going super nova, exploding out carbon, hydrogen, nitrogen, oxygen, phosphorus and sulfur into space. Those elements should be familiar to you. They're considered the building blocks of life by scientists. They make up most of you and everyone on the planet.

I have had a lot of time to think on theories I was working on before all this happened. Those elements, carbon, hydrogen, nitrogen, oxygen, phosphorus and sulfur, should be the most effective magical materials, more than any crystal or other natural material. They should work better for the cost than any bronze coin ever could. Witches in the past have used gold and silver coins to great effect, but I don't believe anyone has experimented with CHNOPS intentionally. I want you to test my hypothesis and continue my research.

There is a chest in your father's parents' attic that hopefully they have not tossed. I enchanted the trunk so that only you will be able to open it using magic. It contains only one thing: a charge plate that belonged to your great-grandmother.

This charge plate has an address that you must go to as soon as you can. The property is legally yours, something I arranged with my mother before I agreed to seek help with her. We thought we were being paranoid, but we were just being prepared. The door will be locked, but has been enchanted so that it will open for you, and only you will be able to pass the threshold.

This is a safe space that has been protected with multiple protection spells that do not need to be recast. This house has been in our family since 1898, when it was purchased by your great-great-grandfather after the move from Germany. There's a caretaker, Lloyd Auden; he's able to enter the house as well. He checks up on the house and makes sure all utilities are still in working order. His sister was a very close friend of my mother's after she returned to Memphis. I hope she's been able to forgive us.

You will find a safe behind a mirror in the master bedroom. The deed to the house is in there, along with other important documents. Also in that safe are the most ancient secrets our family has held onto. These are all that is left of our family's cumulative knowledge. All our family's knowledge is safe there, waiting for you.

Go there and stay there. Please do not risk your life. Preserve yourself and our family line. Stay safe.

With love forever,

Theresa

Rachel had struggled not to cry while reading, but all the emotions from the day crushed down at her as she finished. She wept, her face wet with tears of sadness, then anger, and finally determination. She was exhausted, but she knew what she had to do. She closed up the letters, put them back in their envelopes and put them in her back pocket. She got out her phone, sent a few texts, and then called a rideshare to take her to the Big Black Dog bus station at around 12:30 a.m.

27

She hadn't been to the Big Black Dog bus station before, but it was easy enough to take a rideshare and let the driver worry about it. The radio was turned low, but Rachel could hear an electric guitar melody set to hand drums. The sign on the back of his seat had said his name was Mohamed and that he was happy to practice his English, but she didn't feel like talking.

The driver was a friendly man who greeted her with a smile when she got in the car. He didn't say it, but he was relieved to pick up a sober person. The last passenger had been too drunk to speak coherently. He had been afraid they were going to throw up in his car. This woman seemed sad though. She had obviously been crying. It wasn't his business, he reminded himself. His business was transport.

"We're going to the BBD downtown, yes?"

"Yes, thank you," Rachel said.

"What music would you like to listen to?" he asked. "You can use Bluetooth if you would like to choose."

"This is perfect, Mohamed," she said.

They drove for a few minutes before they got to the highway. When he checked his mirrors before changing lanes, Mohamed noticed the woman looking at her phone. He glanced again once he had merged smoothly. She didn't look like she was hurt, so he felt better about minding his own business.

"Could you please turn it up?"

He adjusted the volume so she could hear the hypnotic electric guitar picking and riffing better. Then he headed north to I-471.

She didn't understand the lyrics, which sounded French. But she didn't need to know another language to recognize the

melancholic emotions evoked by the songs. The singers' soulful
vocal melodies, persistent but gentle drums, and mournful blues
guitar spoke to what she was already feeling. She found some
solace in the shared sorrow.

She focused her thoughts on the view. As they passed under
the yellow arched bridge over the Ohio River, downtown
Cincinnati loomed on the horizon. In the dark, most of the
buildings were umber obelisk shadows against the navy sky. The
tallest structures were lit on top almost like beacons, their
brightness muting any starlight but illuminating the city enough
to keep it serviceable at night. Aside from the warm glow of
street lamps, the only other light came from the windows of the
third shifters and nighthawks hoping to earn an early worm.
These scattered lights on otherwise unlit buildings made the city
look dazzling at night, like stars among steel.

They took the 6th Street exit, following it until they turned
north on Broadway and then east on Reedy Street. They followed
Reedy as it curved across Eggleston Avenue before straightening
northward. They finally turned east on Court Street, driving
behind the mammoth garage and casino complex that faced
Central Parkway where it turned into Reading Road. The gray
concrete and glass behemoth towered over the neighbor at its
rear.

She was dreading what she was about to face at the bus
station, and she was having trouble ignoring the creeping terror
that threatened to overtake her. Some uncomfortable truths had
come out while planning with Emily and Morgan, and they were
going to use them in a bid for time. It was a gambit that had to
work. Her life and probably Morgan's life depended on it,
although she still wasn't sure Emily would be safe.

The rideshare driver pulled into the parking lot of the red
brick bus station and up to its entrance doors. She realized as
they were pulling in that she hadn't said a word since they left
Highland Heights.

"What have we been listening to?" she asked as they pulled up
to the doors of the bus station.

"Desert blues from Mali. Mostly Ali Farka Touré. This song is
'Masitéladi' by Amadou and Mariam," he said. "Are you ok,
ma'am?"

"Yes, thank you," she said to his kind brown eyes in the rear view mirror.

She didn't want to go. She wanted to ask what the song meant and to pay him to take her somewhere else. To keep driving and listening to Malian blues all night. Anything but this, she thought, but she opened the door and got out of the van. She reminded herself that they both had work to do. He had other, friendlier passengers to pick up, and she had to keep moving. She paid, tipped, and rated him highly on the rideshare app on her phone as he drove off. Then she went through the closest set of double doors into the lobby of the bus station.

Emily had offered to drive her, but they knew the plan would work better if she went alone. They had to assume now that they were always being watched when they weren't in protected spaces. They had argued the entire drive to Emily's house from Crystal Crescent. Emily had even shouted at her before slamming her front door. She had been terrified that Mike's group would prevent her from leaving. Her worst fear was that she would be the only one in the station when he showed up, but fortunately there were several clusters of people in the building.

She scanned the late night crowd, fearful he was already waiting for her. But she didn't see his face with his stupid dimples. She felt like a fool, but she checked her phone. Nothing yet.

The station was longer than it was wide, with dull yellow flooring throughout. Thirteen red metal doors were set in the white walls of the building with large black numbers painted over them. These portals normally led outside to waiting buses. At this time of night, only a few of the doors at the far end of the building were active.

The three doors at the back had metal stanchions aligned in front of them joined with retractable rope. Some people were standing in line between these posts, but most people in the station were sitting on the gray metal benches clustered toward the front and back of the station. She checked one of the monitor screens bolted to the ceiling. Then she walked closer to the door she would exit through, taking a seat on the closest bench to the door she would hopefully go through.

In the middle of the bus station was a cardboard cutout, around 5 feet tall. There was a cardboard cutout underneath. The anthropomorphic cartoon dog mascot of Big Black Dog Transportation was a black St. Bernard, whose gleeful eyes peeped out from a mop of dark hair. His big pink tongue hung out in a perpetual pant, and in most of the ads, he wore a small wooden barrel on his red collar.

This particular BBD prop had the usual happy expression, but under his barrel were three rows of acrylic pamphlet holders. They were all empty, but presumably had kept brochures about baggage restrictions or bus routes. But without the pamphlets, they were just empty plastic rectangles punched into cardboard.

"I wish he really had some bourbon in his little barrel," she thought, making herself smile by picturing a little spout on the barrel prop for community whiskey. *"Although I'm sure it'd be empty at this time of night too."*

Then she sighed. She looked again at the message she had sent Mike on her phone. He hadn't responded, but it was marked as "Read" right after she sent it, so she knew he had seen it. Hopefully he reacted like she thought he might. She looked down at the mustard yellow tile floor and waited.

It was nearing time to board when Mike entered the bus station. He scanned the crowd until he saw her, and then strode toward the back. She couldn't read his face, but he seemed anxious. She tried to look surprised that he was here, getting up and walking toward him. They met halfway across the building, adrift in a sea of yellow tile between the islands of the front cafe tables benches and the now crowded seating at the back of the station.

"Emily and I had a huge fight. Going to Memphis to get some space from her and scout second locations. I'll be on the 1:30 a.m. BBD to Memphis tonight but will be back Wednesday afternoon," was the text she had sent him before leaving her house.

He hugged her when he saw her, and she squeezed back in equal measure. Touching him felt wrong and right at the same time, but she couldn't think about that now. She had to pretend to be in love. It couldn't be that hard, she thought, he'd been doing it since they met. When they broke away she smiled at him like she was glad to see him, but she couldn't hide the sadness in her eyes.

He touched her face, and she almost winced. She let him stroke her jaw before kissing her.

"Is everything ok?" he asked. "I got here as soon as I could."

This wasn't true. He had gone first to his mother's house to ask her advice, only to find her awake and waiting for him. She knew Rachel was heading to the bus station in that weird way she sometimes knew where people were. She had told him what he needed to know and do. He had to make sure that she was still wearing the earrings and ask questions about what she was up to without making her suspicious.

He had to keep his girlfriend from running off, that's all. He wasn't supposed to bring up anything about the group. Just get her calmed down and try to get her to stay. The three Level 5 men who walked in the station before and after him and now idled around the cafe tables were there for a worst case scenario he wasn't high up enough to know details about. He just knew they would take her away if she looked or sounded like she was bolting because of the group. He knew his mother wanted her to be with the Level 5's on the night of the solstice, and she always got what she wanted for the Level 5's. And if they had to take her, it would make a scene, and his mother would never make him a Level 5.

Worse than that, she would be gone from his life. He had spent the last week imagining what their life would be like together after the solstice. He knew they needed some of her blood after his mom had used the handkerchief from the festival to make love charm. He had been uneasy at first, thinking it was a violation of consent until his Mom assured him it wasn't. She told him the charmed objects, especially the earrings, would only augment her natural feelings toward him.

Before he left to meet her at the station, he had asked her why she wanted Rachel so badly and what the other Level 5's were doing. She wouldn't tell him everything, but she finally told him some Level 5 information. It was what he had hoped. They were meant to be together and to rule the group as husband and wife after his mother passed and he inherited her power.

She told him Theresa had fled because of their plan to marry off her daughter, and they would stop at nothing to make sure Rachel didn't flee too. She was very powerful, and too strong to have as an enemy. If she was fleeing, it might be because she thought they had hurt her mother or heard disinformation about the group. He assumed the Level 5's discreetly accompanying him were there to start the debriefing process if things were really that bad.

He recognized there was some moral ambiguity about their plans, but he told himself that as long as she stayed with him, they wouldn't hurt her. He hugged her tightly at the bus station, hoping she'd have the right answers to his questions. When she pulled back from the hug, he could see that she had been crying. Her face was puffy and the white of her eyes was laced with pink, accentuating her green irises.

"Everything's OK," she said. "Emily and I have never fought like this before, but we'll be fine."

"What were y'all fighting about?" he asked. He brushed her hair behind her ears with his hands and was relieved to see she was still wearing the earrings. He moved to her side so he wasn't blocking the view of her from the obvious cult members so they could see there was no issue.

"It's my fault. I've been slacking off on finding a market for our second location," she said. There was a pitiful sorrow in her voice, and he felt his heart ache for her.

"That's not so bad," he said.

"It is though," she said. "I set a goal of finding at least three locations, but it's weeks after the deadline I set, and the only ones I've come up with are in Memphis. And I only thought of Memphis because of you. Emily says I've been distracted."

"Distracted?"

"I'm sorry, I know this is a lot, but there's something I have to tell you," she said. "You're all I've been thinking about lately. Emily pissed me off by saying I've been distracted from my project since we met. She said you sidetrack me from my goals."

She took in a staggered breath. He hoped she wasn't about to cry again. He put a reassuring arm over her shoulder and tried not to show his hurt pride on his face. He thought about when she had sent him and his surprise breakfast away. Had he been distracting her from her own goals?

"She hates that I've only been looking into a new location in Memphis, even saying I'm just copying your business. I can't help it if you inspired me. But what hurt the most was when she said that I'm turning my back on our business plans. I just need some space from her, so I'm going to check out a few spaces in Crosstown and Midtown Memphis. I know this is crazy, but I won't tolerate behavior like that from her. If I stick around, she'll think she was right. I'll never hear the end of it.

"I hope this doesn't scare you off, because I don't want anything to slow down between us. I love you, Mike. I'm ready to be with you. I just need time away from Emily before she and I strangle each other."

Mike felt tears of his own threatening to spill, although he wasn't sure if they were joyous at her declaration of love or tears of commiseration. He could understand wanting some space from Emily, who sounded like a real bitch. He wondered how much of the awful things she said had been about him.

"I love you too, Rachel," he said. "Are you sure this can't wait?"

"I can't stand to see her right now," she said, clenching her fists. "The people closest to you know how to hurt you the worst, and she said some terrible things. So did I. Things we can't take back. Oh, Mike, I'm so sorry. I know this sounds crazy."

He hugged her close again.

"I don't think it's crazy at all. But are you sure I can't convince you to stay?" he asked.

"I don't want to go, but I need some breathing room from her," she said, pressing her ear against his chest. "It'll only be for a few days. I'll keep busy with research when I'm not looking at locations, and it'll be next Wednesday before you know it."

"When do you get back?"

"Wednesday at 2:30 pm.," she said.

"Can I pick you up?"

"I'd love that," she said.

"I love you," he told her, taking her by the shoulders and looking into her eyes as he said it.

"I love you, too," she said. Even through her sadness, he could see the love in her eyes. He was sure it wasn't just from the enchanted handkerchief in his pocket or the jewelry in her ears.

Boarding for her bus was called. They kissed passionately and embraced one more time before Rachel went to the back of the line. He waved when she walked through the door, looking one last time back at him to smile tenderly. When he turned around, he noticed the Level 5 guys that had been eavesdropping had disappeared. There was a text on his phone from his mother telling him he did a good job.

He felt his heart swell with pride. Twice within the same day his mother had told him he'd done a good job. And the beautiful woman who would be his partner one day loved him back. Everything was coming up roses. He was sure that when he got her to the solstice, Karen would make him a Level 5.

***

Rachel tried to sleep on the bus, but her thoughts wouldn't stop racing until they left the city. She closed her eyes and tried to think about her mother's letter. She hadn't had time to process everything she'd learned before she had to deal with Mike. She felt gross after that exchange, but it had been necessary. If she started thinking about the things she said to him, she started seeing flaws and mistakes she had made. She started thinking he had seen her mask slip. She recognized the thoughts as unhelpful and tried to switch gears. She tried to think only about the letter her mother had sent.

"Let's start with the CHNOPS business. OK, so that sounds like good news. An alternative to killing myself with magic. I sucked at chemistry in school, but I'm pretty sure you can't get hydrogen on its own unless you're a scientist. You'd have to separate it from water or the air. Some of those elements. Jeez, if I tried to buy a load of sulfur and hydrogen, I'd end up on a fucking watch list. But still. Carbon. That's in everything, right?

"Thinking about chemistry just makes me feel ignorant. I'll have to do some research. At least it doesn't make me feel as stupid as finding out Rosemary Crantz was my grandmother this whole time. My family is so screwed up I didn't even know the name of my own granny. I barely even remember her. God. And she was involved in whatever cult killed Mom!

"God damn it, what is wrong with witches? Why can't they just stay home or stay in a cabin in the woods and keep to themselves? We're like moths to a fucking flame. No wonder we're rare. It's like we're dying to die. We must be easy pickings for cults.

"But this cult of Mike's had my mom and probably killed my grandmother too. My mother not only said they found a god, but that she was somehow the offspring. That it had given her strange destructive powers she couldn't control. I thought it was scary and beautiful when I found out magic was real, but gods? That's too frightening. When people say 'gods,' we usually mean unbridled and unquestionable power. Would gods even have a cost for their magic? Or would it be limitless? Would I have to face this god?"

Her thoughts were racing again, and she knew it. She took slow deep breaths until they were out past the city lights, visualizing her runaway train of thoughts as cluttered leaves in a clogged stream. Some of the leaves were blocking the rest from floating away on the current.

"You're going to die. They're going to kill you," said the big yellow clump of leaves. Fear of death made sense but was unhelpful. She was heading to the city that was their stronghold, but if she made it to the safe house in Memphis, she'd bunker down there. If she did her research and found no safe plan for return, she'd stay indefinitely. That was the worst case scenario, even if death seemed preferable to self-induced exile. That lonely road ended in paranoid madness or starving after running her bank account dry on delivery services.

She reminded herself that they let her leave Cincinnati, so her deception of Mike seemed to have worked. She was in a good position now, and there was no use putting the funeral cart in front of the horse. She watched the mass of golden leaves break away and drift down the stream out of sight, acknowledging to herself that they were only thoughts.

"They're going to kill Emily to make you come back, or they'll kill Morgan instead of you," said a clump of dark brown leaves. This one was easier to process. Morgan could stay put in her protected family home. And Mike's group had no use for Emily, especially if they thought they weren't friends anymore. That part of the plan would be hard on them both emotionally, but if she had to, she'd sacrifice their friendship to keep Emily alive. She told herself that they'd done what they could to protect themselves, and anything more was out of her control.

She watched the glut of rotten leaves float away. The stream's flow picked up. Only one other glut of leaves remained.

"Mike figured out you were acting, and he's going to be waiting for you in Memphis," whispered a bright red leaf. She knew that was just fear talking. She watched it float away, just a harmless intrusive thought.

She visualized the stream clearing, picturing the water flowing at a comfortable speed. She needed her thoughts to be clear, for leaves to float down the river smoothly. For a little while, she watched the clean stream flow past her. Satisfied she had calmed herself enough, she tried to sleep. It was a long road to Memphis, and she had almost 11 hours to think about everything. She needed to rest first.

Rachel felt exhausted, but she jumped in her seat when she heard a sudden crash of thunder. They were driving through a storm. She looked at the weather radar app on her phone and saw it would rain most of the drive to Memphis. She shuddered and crossed her arms before closing her eyes again. She managed to doze for a couple of hours, haunted by nightmares of knives and sacrifice.

She woke suddenly when lightning touched down not far from the bus as it hurtled down I-65 South towards Memphis by way of Nashville. She sat up from her slightly inclined seat and rubbed her stiff neck. She looked out the window as lightning arced across the sky. She shook her head at her own fright, and laid back down, watching the rain blur the view outside into watery darkness.

She saw lightning further in the distance. No, something else. Something small and a lot closer. At first it was just a streak of light, but as she watched it grew next to her window. Her eyes opened wide. She saw it was a hand, or something like a hand, made of light. The fingers seemed impossibly long and luminous as they reached through the glass to her. The tips of the fingers were sharp, and as they reached toward her face she wanted to scream.

She gasped and sat bolt straight. The hand was gone. Rachel looked around, but her neighbor was asleep. No one else seemed to notice what had happened. Rachel took a deep breath and sighed, relieved it had just been another nightmare.

28

After picking up the rental car and stopping for lunch, it was nearly 2 p.m. when she reached the address on the charge plate. She had slept uneasily all night and was looking forward to getting somewhere safe. Morgan had tried to use magic to see into the house, but it hadn't worked. She had been assured this was a sign that it really was a protected space, but she hated having to count on something so uncertain.

There was no driveway, so she parked her rental car on the street in front of the house. There were a few other cars parked on the street, but otherwise there didn't appear to be anyone around. She took a coin from her purse and held it in her hand as she looked out the window at the house. She concentrated on seeing the protection on the house, and it appeared for her.

She couldn't see the house through the shield. The house was concealed in a dome similar to the one she had made around her house. It was made of glowing light like her own, but the strands had been bundled into thick rope that had been chained together tightly to form a complex pattern of geometric shapes. She was reminded of the Epcot building, although this structure was made of triangles, pentagons, and heptagons. She was satisfied, so she let go of the spell and got out of the car.

She got her suitcase out of the trunk and looked up and down the street. She tried not to let her wariness show on her face. She had been unable to stop herself from considering the possibility that Mike's group had overtaken the old house and that she'd be walking into an ambush. Even the obviously sturdy bulwark couldn't abate these fears. All night her dreams had been of the hooded knife wielder and the long, thin claw reaching for her.

There was nothing unusual going on down the street. The sun was bright overhead, but there were still streaks of wet pavement from the night's storms. It had only stopped raining an hour ago, and most of the water that had dried from the street was still hanging in the humid air. She heard the drone of cicadas and the white noise of traffic on Poplar Avenue just a few streets over. There were no other cars parked near the house. She wondered where they would hide if they were going to take her now.

Then she sighed, recognizing she was being paranoid. She closed the trunk and glanced up at the house. She supposed she should feel overwhelmed by memories, but she only felt tired and scared. She didn't know if Morgan and Emily were safe. She was supposed to avoid contacting them until next Saturday. Morgan was staying put at her house. Emily was going to keep her head down until the middle of the week, running the shop like nothing had changed. But once it got close to solstice time, she would move to Rachel's house to keep safe until her return.

She stepped onto the sidewalk and looked up again at the house. It was larger than Rachel expected. It was in the middle of an historic district in Midtown Memphis, one of many houses built in the late 19th and early 20th century. The style of it was similar to its bungalow and craftsman neighbors. It was a boxy house, almost a perfect cube except for the covered front porch that ran the full width of the house. The house itself was mostly made of red brick, trimmed in white and roofed in gray asphalt shingles that looked new.

The porch was held up by four stout white columns rooted in short brick pillars built into the perimeter of the porch. White fencing joined these anchors to serve as a railing, open only where the stairs led up the porch to the front door. The roof on the second story was pitched low and its border created an overhang around the house. The house appeared to be two or two and a half stories. A small roofed dormer jutted up from the front of the roof, facing its short windows to the street.

"*That must be the attic,*" she thought as she stepped off the sidewalk and onto the brick path leading to the porch. "*The house looks like it's been taken care of. The paint even looks fresh. If I see Lloyd while I am here, I'll have to thank him and make sure they're receiving some money for their work.*"

She walked up the wide cement steps of the porch and past the windows of the front of the house. Two empty wicker rocking chairs at the far end of the porch seemed to move as her eyes passed over them.

"You really need to get some sleep," she thought to herself.

She found the door knob turned as though the door was unlocked. Even though she had looked at the shield around the house, she couldn't help but imagine Mike on the other side of the door. They had made it here first and were waiting for her.

As she pushed the front door open and began to see inside, she held her breath. Only when the door was all the way open and she saw no one inside did she step in. It occurred to her that they could be waiting further back in the house. They could even be in the backyard, where she couldn't see from the street. Other wild theories presented themselves to her until she saw the photograph on the table to the left of the entrance. When she saw the picture, she stepped inside, sat down her purse and closed the door, locking it before turning back around.

The entrance opened onto a small white tiled vestibule decorated only by a small table to the left of the door. On the table was the framed photograph. She picked it up, examining the photograph of her mother and an older woman whom Rachel now remembered was her maternal grandmother. Rosemary Crantz. They were on the porch of this house, her grandmother sitting in one of the wicker chairs that was still outside. Her mother was leaning on the cement railing that lined the porch. Her father was there too, sitting in the other rocked and holding a small bundled baby. He was holding her.

Memories of her grandmother and her father returned to her upon seeing the picture, and she realized she remembered the house she was in. Her grandmother had lived here. Her father had taught her how to ride a bike on this street. She had trick or treated here every year until the year before they had moved, when she declared to everyone that would listen that seven was too old to dress up as a princess anymore. She only wanted to dress up as scary things for Halloween from then on, like witches and vampires. She smiled remembering how her mother and grandmother had giggled but taken her seriously. She had been a swamp monster that next Halloween. She remembered that her childhood home had been just around the block.

She remembered how one day her Dad didn't come home from work. There had been an accident on his drive home, and suddenly Rachel didn't have a father anymore. Remembering how it had felt at first sent a sharp knife of mental anguish through Rachel's brain. The feeling of loss was immense and visceral, even 24 years later. She'd been pushing the thoughts of loss away for so long that she had pushed away the good memories too.

She welcomed the memories now as they came to her suddenly. He had taught her to ride a bike when she was five years old. She had wanted to give up, but he wouldn't let her. He had always tried to teach her things. She remembered when she had been about six years old, he asked her to sweep up the garage while he tinkered at his workbench. The next day he had her help him organize the tools, and he let her draw chalk outlines around the tools suspended on the wood pegboard.

"This way, we'll always know what's missing and where it goes," he had said.

The next weekend, he had helped her design and build a birdhouse. She had painted it white and had given it as a gift to her grandmother, who had promptly hung it up in her backyard. Sometimes they sat and watched for birds to go into it. But then they noticed birds began flitting out around it and not going in it.

Rachel noticed one afternoon that a lot of birds were singing in the yard. She had thought their song was a little weird, so she stepped closer to hear. All the birds were chirping frantically, even different kinds of birds had joined in on the cacophonous chorus. She had watched one bird fly close to the birdhouse and peek its head in before flying off, chirruping madly.

She had gone out to the yard and had taken the bird house off the shepherd's hook and opened the lid on the birdhouse, sliding the piece of wood out of the groove she had watched her father lathe. She had slid back the piece of wood and peered in, expecting to see birds nest. What she saw instead had made her drop the wooden box.

A thick snake inched its way out of the birdhouse and into the yard. Rachel was furious. The snake had holed up in the birdhouse and ate birds who thought they had found somewhere safe to roost. Rachel ran and picked up a rock bigger than her small fist. She bashed the snake until it was just a red mess on her, the rock and the grass. She remembered she had cried the whole time, yelling that it was a bad snake. Her grandmother had come out near the end and stopped her.

Her grandmother didn't yell at her. She didn't remember getting in trouble for killing the snake. She remembered they had repainted the birdhouse a neutral gray color, and that she felt it was her fault for painting the house white. She remembered her mother telling her that nature was like that sometimes, and the best they could do was learn from their mistakes.

That was when a forgotten memory from the night of the fire came to her unbidden.

Remembering it felt like brushing dirt off a stone marker to find writing hidden underneath. Slowly the details rose to the surface clearer than they had since she was a child. Hearing her mother scream had woken her. Finding her mother in the hall and thinking they were both going to die. She had wanted them both to be safe. She had wanted it so intensely that when she suddenly found herself shivering outside her home and holding her mother's hand, she hadn't questioned it. She hadn't had time to either, although she couldn't remember what had happened once they were outside. All she remembered was that it was nighttime, and her mother had teleported them outside.

Then she thought her mother had teleported them to her grandmothers. But now there were fuzzy memories of firefighters coming into focus in her mind. The big red truck and men bustling in large, heavy looking jackets to uncoil a long white hose. How had she forgotten? She remembered having a blanket wrapped around her because she was cold, even though her home was literally burning up in front of her. She remembered sooty handprints on the door handles of her mother's white Honda Accord. They had driven to her grandmother's house. And then she was separated from her mother. That had been the last night she had seen her.

The first teleportation had been real, hadn't it? Did they make it happen together? She didn't want to think about it anymore. Thinking about that night made her skin feel like it was too tight. She took a deep breath. Rachel set down the picture, then yawned and stretched. She decided to do a sweep of the house, just in case. The vestibule opened onto a short hall that offered several doors. Rachel decided to tackle them one room at a time.

There was a room to the right of the entrance at the beginning of the hall, so Rachel started there. The room was lined with white built in bookshelves that were packed full. In the corner of the room were two pale blue wingback armchairs separated by a telephone table with a stained glass lamp on the top. A dark blue cushioned stool was set to the right of one of the arm chairs. The scene made her smile as she remembered how enormous the chair had felt when she was small, reading her Goosebumps books after school while her Grandmother read in the other chair. Sometimes her mother would read with them too, and that's when Rachel would sit on the stool.

She walked out of that room across the hall into the living room. She stretched and looked around, finding new memories flickering to life as vividly as though they had never been forgotten. She found it strange that the house looked almost the same as her memories, as though it had been frozen in a moment in time. The same brown upholstered couch sat against the front window, and she remembered many hours spent reading there while her mother and grandmother visited. Her grandmother's favorite armchair looked almost the same as she remembered, if not more worn.

She ignored the temptation of a quick nap in the armchair. There would be time for a nap after she searched the house to make sure the coast was really clear. She moved on. The living room opened onto the dining room, which was connected to the kitchen via a walk-through pantry. Rachel was not surprised to find that there was no food in the house, and made a mental note to go get groceries after she explored. She went through the backdoor to the screened in porch. There was no one in the backyard, so she went back in.

The entrance hall off the front vestibule ended in the kitchen, but branched off to the right before then into stairs. Rachel walked upstairs, where she found four large bedrooms. One was empty of all furniture, but the rest were furnished like she remembered. She felt a little paranoid going up to the attic. There were a few small stacks of cardboard boxes, but it was mostly a clean, empty space. She went back to the second floor, exhausted but satisfied that she was alone.

The largest of these bedrooms she knew had been her grandmother's. She remembered the dark wood furniture, and before she turned on the light remembered how spooky the room had seemed when she was a child. It had been off limits to her, except when she could get her grandmother to play hide and seek. She remembered hiding under the queen sized sleigh bed, peeking through the eyelets in the border of the crocheted white quilt her grandmother had always kept over the bedsheets.

She ran her hand across the quilt, feeling the little bumps of the stitches that decorated the blanket with a rose pattern. It was softer than she remembered. The sheets under it were smooth and felt clean.

She thought about getting her purse from the vestibule and changing into pajamas but decided against it. She was deliriously tired. All the doors were locked, and she was alone in the safe house. Her family home. She flipped the lights off. Then she took off her shoes, socks, and shorts before slipping under the covers and closing her eyes.

"I'll only rest my eyes for a minute," Rachel thought. *"Then I'll unpack and find that safe."*

29

It was dark outside when she woke up. She had napped for hours when she meant to sleep maybe an hour at most. But she didn't wake up because she was rested. No, she knew why she was awake.

There was someone else in the house.

She didn't know if she had heard something that woke her up or if this was intuition clanging the alarm bells in her mind, but she was certain she wasn't alone. She didn't know if they were in the room with her, but she couldn't help picture the hood from her dreams: The figure was towering over her, a knife in one hand and a chalice in the other. She'd open her eyes, and it would be the scene from her nightmare for the last time. She'd feel the blade against her throat. In the nightmare, she always felt it sting as they started to slice just before she woke up. This time she wouldn't. She waited to feel the cold blade press on her neck. But it didn't happen. If there was someone standing over her, they were waiting for her to wake up. She didn't want to give them the satisfaction.

She felt frozen with fear, but she took inventory of herself while trying her best to keep her face still. She didn't have a gag in her mouth. Her hands didn't feel tied down, and she could feel her fingertips. In a moment of childish panic, she slowly lifted her eyelids the smallest amount possible, trying to look asleep while peeking out into the dark room. She couldn't see much in the darkness aside from her own trembling eyelashes, but there was no hooded figure above her.

She opened her eyes and looked. There was definitely no one in the room with her. She was in her maternal grandmother's bed. Zaza's bed, in Memphis. Weak light from the street filtered through the blinds of the window above her. She couldn't see them, but her shorts were crumpled on the ground next to her. Her cellphone was a lifeless brick on the nightstand next to her head. It had been at 10% when she laid down, and she hadn't plugged it in. It was dead. She knew it had to be around 9 p.m., because the sun was down.

She also knew there was someone in the house.

She held her breath and tried to listen, hoping desperately that she was wrong. She told herself it was impossible. This was the safest place she could be. Her family home, protected with an impenetrable magic shield.

She told herself that all houses make sounds, no matter how old they are. Especially in the summer, when wood and metal cool and contract after a long hot day. She wondered if she had heard a sound she wasn't familiar with, and that's why she had woken up so frightened. She listened for pops or creaks. She heard silence.

She took a long, deep breath. In and out. Her heart was beating fast in her chest, and she tried to calm it with slow breathing.

Then she heard footsteps downstairs. Heavy boots on the polished wood floor. It sounded like it could be coming from the entrance hall, but she wasn't sure. It could be in the room below her. The reading room, where she had forgotten to turn off the light.

"*Fuck,*" she thought, and then a ray of hope broke through her thoughts. "*It could be the caretaker.*"

She heard whistling, clear and shrill in the silence. He was whistling a song she knew.

He was whistling the vocal melody from "Don't Fear the Reaper" by Blue Oyster Cult.

It was Mike. She could see Mike in her mind. He was downstairs. Getting ready to kill her. He knew she had lied about loving him. They had let her leave so they could take her here, where they already had figured out how to get past the shield. Or maybe they used her to break through the shield. She had walked into a trap and laid down to rest.

The copper coins were in her purse, which was sitting on the floor of the vestibule right next to the entrance to the house, all the way downstairs. She was lying on the left side of the bed, closest to the door. She reached her left arm down to try to reach her shorts, trying not to let the mattress springs make a sound. If Mike was down there, he didn't know which room she was in. But he would know as soon as he heard the mattress springs or the floorboards cry out.

She wouldn't be caught with her pants down. Staring in the dark at the closed door on the opposite side of the room, she gradually stretched her left arm down the left side of the bed as far as she could. But she couldn't reach her shorts. She relaxed her left arm, and her hand moved closer to the bed. Her thumb tapped against the bed frame, and the sound was so soft it was almost inaudible.

He was moving now. He was right below her, still whistling Blue Oyster Cult. He really had been in the reading room. She heard his steps as he walked back into the hall. She held her breath as she waited for the steps to creak, for him to come upstairs. He had heard her. A bolt of panic pierced her.

"*Fuck fuck fuck,*" she thought.

He walked down the hall to the kitchen. She heard him open the back door and close it. It was only closed a few seconds before she heard it open and close again.

She took a long deep breath.

"You're not scared," she said. "You are a witch. You don't need coins to transmute your fear into courage like lead into gold. You already are brave. And if you get closer to your coins you can do almost anything."

It helped a little, even if her heart sounded like it was drumming along to "Don't Fear the Reaper."

Then a dark thought crossed her mind: If she couldn't reach the coins, she would sacrifice herself rather than be murdered. She would take them both out if it came to that. She wondered if he was wearing a hooded cloak down there. She took another slow, deep breath and tried to relax her body in preparation for what she was about to do.

The footsteps were heavy. Had he always worn boots? She heard the pantry door open. He was going to walk through it to the dining room. This was her chance, while she could hear him whistling on the other side of the house.

She had to move slowly so as not to make a sound. She would get out of bed. She would put on her shorts. She'd open the door

and turn right immediately. Then she would make her way down
the stairs to the vestibule. She didn't know if she needed to see
her purse to use the coins she had, but she would get as close to
them as she could. Then she would use magic to freeze Mike in
his tracks. She could get some answers after she disarmed him.

"*Your left arm is already out of bed,*" she thought to herself.
"*That's good. You need to slowly transfer your weight out of the bed and onto
the floor. As quiet as you can, so you can find him before he finds you.*"

She slowly lifted the covers off herself with her right hand,
focusing on keeping her heart rate down. There was nothing she
could do about the gentle shush of the sheets as they rubbed
together, but she didn't think it was loud enough to alert him. She
laid the bedding on the right side of her body so that she was
totally uncovered. Then she steadily lifted her left leg up off the
bed and brought her knee up to her stomach. She slowly moved
her bent leg left and then stretched her foot down to the floor.
She waited until the bottom of her foot completely met the
ground. Then she slid her hips slowly left until her left foot was
firmly supporting most of her weight.

Breathing deeply, she moved her right leg next to her left. She
couldn't touch the floor with it yet, but that was fine. She used
her stomach to sit up as slowly as she could, and when the
springs made a low shuddering cry, she tried not to do the same.

She stood up. The floor didn't creak under her feet, but
downstairs it was squeaking under footsteps that were moving
slowly around the bottom floor. Had he always sounded so big?
Maybe he had sent someone else to do his dirty work. Whoever it
was, it sounded like he was whistling in the dining room now.

"At least he's not right under you," she thought.

She leaned toward the window above the nightstand and
peered through the blinds. The street was completely parked up
now. Her rental car was tightly sandwiched between a black
pickup truck and a faded blue Volkswagen. But that didn't
matter. If she could get to her coins then she wouldn't need to
leave.

"Stick to the plan and don't panic," she told herself.

She quickly put her shorts on. She started to pocket her phone
but decided to hold it in her right fist like a brick. She could
bludgeon him with it if she had to. It occurred to her that there
were metals in her phone, like lithium and carbon graphite in the

lithium ion battery. But she had no way to know if it would be enough to do anything.

Her heart was a rapid double stroked bass drum, beating too quickly now for "Don't Fear the Reaper." It made her think of Emily. Just two months ago they'd been jamming out in her truck to "Children of the Grave" by Black Sabbath. Now her own heart was pounding like Bill Ward was tearing it up.

She took another deep breath. Emily believed in her. She believed in herself. She wasn't going to let herself die tonight. She took a deep breath. She could do this.

She slinked to the door, bracing her stomach to strengthen her core, walking as lightly on her feet as she could. She firmly grasped the doorknob and slowly turned it. Then she opened the door quickly, thinking a loud groan would be worse than a short bark from the hinges. But it didn't make a sound as she pulled it open.

She couldn't hear him in the dining room. She tried not to think about what he was doing down there, but her mind quickly supplied a worst case scenario, like if he had taken her purse and thrown it outside when he opened the back door.

She recognized the worthlessness of that thought and told herself that she could do this.

She peered out of the doorway and looked right. She could see right down the stairs to the empty landing between the first and second floor. She crept down the stairs as stealthily as she could until she was on the landing.

The dark wood floor creaked under her feet and she froze, listening. He was heading toward the living room, which opened onto the hall. He wasn't whistling anymore. He was humming. It was still "Don't Fear the Reaper," so either he hadn't heard her or he was toying with her.

She didn't have any time to spare. This was it.

She took a deep breath and stole down the stairs, tearing into the hall and turning left. She ran to the door. She saw her purse. Then she whipped around to face the dark living room. He wasn't whistling anymore. He was in the entryway that separated the dining room from the living room.

"Who's there?" he shouted.

It definitely wasn't Mike. This person's voice was deeper. She couldn't see his face, but he was around her height if not taller.

This man in the shadows was maybe 6 feet tall, with broad shoulders and a wide, muscular build. He stepped through the entryway and into the living room, heading toward her. She thought about the bag of coins and what she wanted in exchange for them.

He started to raise his hands.

"You are unable to move," she said loudly and firmly into the dark hallway.

He froze as still as the cardboard cutout of the Big Black Dog mascot, but he didn't look friendly at all.

She turned on the light and looked at the hulking man in the living room. He had dark brown eyes and close cropped black hair. She hadn't thought about him in decades. She was devastated to see that her old babysitter, the teenage boy who had taught her how to throw a football, was now a contract killer working for a cult.

30

"Sam, I don't know what you're capable of, so I'm going to make sure you're not armed before I let you move," she said.

She walked out of the hall and around the sofa and came to where Sam stood almost as still as a statue. She felt awkward about it, so she quickly checked the pockets of his jeans. He didn't have a weapon. He only had a wallet and cell phone on him.

She thought about the coins in her purse again before she spoke.

"You are able to move your head. Tell me who sent you. Was it Mike?"

Sam eyelids fluttered a few times before he opened them normally. He opened and closed his jaw a few times before he spoke.

"No one sent me. I come here every other day. Rachel Miller?" he asked. "I never thought I'd see the day. But it's you. I always knew you'd grow up big and strong. I hope you went out for sports."

"No jokes please. I heard you whistling all creepy and stomping around looking for me. Who sent you?"

"My family has always had an arrangement with yours. Your great-grandmother Eleanor hired my granddad as a caretaker for this house because she thought her daughter was a flight risk. Rosemary ran off after Eleanor died, and my dad took over looking after the house while she was gone. Rosemary made the same arrangement with my father, Lloyd. I took over for him. Aunt Ashley didn't want anything to do with the house after Rosemary left the second time and broke her heart. Are you ok? I'm sorry if I scared you, but you scared me too."

"Why should I believe you weren't here to hurt me?"

He frowned and lowered his brow, and Rachel wondered if his concerned expression was a tactic.

"Answer the question," she said. "Why were you stomping around? Why 'Don't Fear the Reaper'?"

"I just like to whistle, and it's a good song. I can see how that'd sound creepy, but I didn't mean anything by it. These are steel toed boots though, so I'm sorry if I frightened you. It's not my fault I'm such a big guy. That's just genetics. I honestly didn't know you were here until I heard you run down the stairs. Then I thought you were a burglar.

"But I'm really sorry I frightened you. I come here almost every day, like I said. Usually at night. Sometimes I read in that front room, because it's a shame that a beautiful house like this has just sat empty for ages. It's silly, but I figure it's good to keep a little life in it sometimes. Keeps it from feeling haunted."

It felt like he was telling the truth, but Rachel reminded herself that she'd been fooled before. Mike had slipped her magic earrings that had affected her perception. She couldn't risk anything like that happening again. She thought about the coins in the bag in her purse, and then she spoke.

"Any enchanted objects you have on you are now powerless," she said.

"I don't keep anything like that," he said. "The key Eleanor gave my granddad is by the door. I usually keep it in the gun safe. Don't like having magic things on my person. That'd be like running around with a chunk of graphite with Chernobyl, wouldn't it? Ashley always told me magic was dangerous for people that weren't like your grandmother. That it would drive a normal person crazy."

Rachel wasn't sure that was true, but it didn't feel like he was lying. She couldn't decide if he was trustworthy, but she realized she also couldn't keep him frozen like this forever.

"Do you promise no funny business if I let you move?"

He nodded.

"You are able to move."

Just like that, he stretched and rolled his shoulders. He shook out his hands.

"That was weird," he said. "Lloyd had said Rosemary did something like that to him when she came back. He never mentioned it feeling like your whole body fell asleep."

Rachel was glad he didn't run off or try to attack. He just looked concerned.

"Where's he now?" she asked.

"He passed last year. Ashley a few years before that. Lloyd kept up watch every week for as long as he could manage. Ashley never came to this house after Rosemary left."

"Why?"

"You don't remember? They were practically married. Probably would have been if it was legal then. Ashley was heartbroken when Rosemary left. She begged her to stay, but she wouldn't listen. She managed better as she got older, but she never wanted anything to do with this house."

"I'm so sorry," she said.

"Yeah, well, it's not your fault. You were just a kid. Why are you here anyway? Are you back for good?"

Rachel considered what she should say. She still wasn't sure she trusted him, but she couldn't help wonder if that was paranoia. Her hands were still shaky from the scare he had given her, but it was nothing compared to her fear of what would happen if the rest of the week didn't go as planned. She had no choice but to fill him in so that he wouldn't mess up the plan.

"There's a man I've gotten close to who I've found out is a member of a cult that I think is responsible for the death of my mother and my grandmother. Probably others too. I was meant to be next, but I fled here to keep my head down until after the solstice next Friday. I'm pretty sure they're monitoring me, since they've been ahead of me this whole time. But they can't see into this house because of its protections."

Sam nodded solemnly, and Rachel realized why she felt so strange. Nothing seemed to faze him. He kept his cool. She wondered what kind of stories he had heard about her family.

"Let me know what I can do to help," Sam said. "You'll need groceries. If you want to make a list, I'm happy to get them for you."

"That's very kind of you, but I think I need more covert help than that. If they're watching me like I'm sure they are, it'll look weird to have a guy coming in and out of the house."

"Why? You don't make friends with men?"

"That's not it at all. I just have a feeling Mike will get jealous. This guy has been manipulating me this whole time. I have to keep him thinking that things are secure between him and me until Wednesday or Thursday. I know if they think I'm on to them that they'll do whatever they can to get me. I'm afraid they'll hurt my friend Emily or another witch I know. If they think anything is going on with you, they may hurt you too. Right now our only chance right now is waiting out the solstice."

Sam nodded. His expression had shifted from concern to compassionate anger.

"That's not acceptable at all," he said, shaking his head. "I want to help. You can say I'm temporarily renting the house to you, if you need to. What else can I do?"

"Don't mention to anyone that I'm here," she said. "I'm going to do research here to figure out what happened and what needs to be done."

"Understood," he said. "And I can steer clear."

"That'd be good for now," she said. She thought a moment. "Come by on Saturday. If I'm still here we can talk before I head back up to Cincinnati. I want to make sure you're paid for your services."

"That was set up a long time ago, but I'm happy to discuss. Are you sure you don't need anything else?"

"No, you've done more than enough. Thank you for keeping up with this old place for us," she said.

Mike picked up a key from the side table as he left. It was attached to a tan leather keychain that was covered with tight, wedge shaped writing on it. He turned back to Rachel before he left.

"Good luck," he said. "I hope to see you Saturday."

"Me too," she said.

After he left and all the doors were locked, Rachel plugged in her phone. When it was charged enough, she checked her messages. She had four missed texts from Mike, all asking how the trip was going. One message was just three heart-eyed emoji.

"Hey handsome. I fell asleep when I got to the rental," she texted. "Just woke up because the landlord came by to make sure I was settled in. I'm going back to sleep so I can get an early start

tomorrow. Checking out a space near your alma mater tomorrow
:)"

He texted her back immediately, saying he loved her. She sent
back a text message saying the same, and although she had
grimaced at his quick response, she added heart emoji. She locked
the doors of the house, checked all the windows, and did another
check on the protective spell over the house. Everything was
secure. She grabbed her purse and thought over what she would
be doing for the next week as she went back upstairs.

"You have a plan. You have a safe space and a book to study.
There'll be more to read in the safe. You can stock up on
groceries after you check out that rental space near the
University. Just find retail-zoned rental spaces to look at every
day. Take notes and pictures at each one. You have to assume
they're watching. You just have to keep up the charade with Mike
until Wednesday. Preferably Thursday. The less time they have
before the solstice to figure out that you're not going to be there
on Friday, the better."

She walked into her grandmother's bedroom and plugged her
phone in, leaving it on the nightstand. She sat on the bed and
looked at the heavy wood dresser tucked in the corner between
the closet and the door leading out of the room. She didn't want
to wait any longer to open the safe.

She went to the dresser, reached her hand up to the mirror,
and pressed against it until she heard a click. The mirror pulled
open easily, swinging from a discrete hinge. Behind it was a built
in safe with a dial combination lock. There were no numbers on
the dial. Instead it was covered in tiny triangular marks, some
stacked on top of another, forming cuneiform-like lettering like
what she had seen on Sam's keychain.

There was a warning written in tight, plain handwriting on a
white card taped to the safe's face:

"Only those chosen by this family may open this safe.
Interlopers may find themselves dismembered."

Rachel took her wand and a coin from her purse. She held the
wand at arm's length, pointing at the safe's dial. She pictured the
safe door opening, and then she spoke.

"You will open for me," she said.

It did as she willed. The dial didn't spin, but the symbols
around it changed from dull white to iridescent, bright light

before dimming again. She reached for the handle, and the door opened easily.

Inside were keys to the house, two leather bound books, and a folio filled with papers. Rachel looked through the papers to find property documents, including her grandmother's and her mother's wills, both of which gifted her the house and referred to several accounts at local banks. Everything was notarized by Ashley Auden. One of the books was written in her mother's handwriting. The other two were much older.

Rachel stacked the books under the one Morgan had given her. She'd spend the next week studying their contents until she was ready for stage 2 of the plan. Morgan had told her there were spells in the book she had lent her that would let her see into the past. But she knew it'd be a lot harder to pretend with Mike once she knew what he had done to her mother and grandmother. She had to wait until after the solstice.

31

By Wednesday, June 19th, Rachel had made a total of eight outings to different parts of Memphis. She spent maybe 5 hours driving around. When she wasn't pretending to search for a second location, she was studying. She tried not to worry about Morgan and Emily, reminding herself that they had safe places to bunker down.

She was studying in the front reading room around noon on Wednesday. She had learned that any chemical element could be used as magic material. There were notes from Rosemary and Ashley Auden on experiments they had conducted with different minerals.

Since all ordinary matter is made of chemical elements, Rosemary and Ashley had studied and experimented to determine that some elements worked better than others. Efforts to only use the oxygen or hydrogen in the water as magic material resulted in dangerous chemical reactions. They had noted that they couldn't find an affordable or efficient way to separate water cleanly into hydrogen and oxygen, so they studied oxygen and helium. Rachel was relieved to realize both were available commercially.

Theresa had joined their work before things spiraled out of control. Her mother had filled pages of one of the books with her theories on CHNOPS and other elements, suggesting that the more abundant an element was in the universe, the more useful it was for performing magic.

She had recorded some experiments with sulfur, but her earliest work was on silicon and oxygen. Specifically, she recorded the results of studies on quartz. There was a lot of theorizing about the abundance of quartz on earth lending to its power as a magical material. Rachel learned that many crystals she had thought were unique were all varieties of quartz, including citrine, jasper, amethyst and rose quartz. Their chemical formula was the same, but different growing conditions like irradiation, pressure or heat resulted in structural changes that made something new and beautiful.

"*Grace under pressure,*" she thought to herself.

She still wore the rose quartz earrings, and she touched them now and sighed. Then she closed the book, deciding she couldn't put it off anymore.

"I missed my bus," she said in the text. "I have to wait for the next one, which doesn't leave until after midnight tonight. I should be back Thursday around 12:30 p.m. I'm sorry. Miss you. :("

She didn't set her phone down. He always responded quickly to her messages. Within a minute, the application showed that he was writing a response.

"That sucks! But I'll see you then. Can you send me your measurements? I'm buying that dress and having it tailored for you so we don't run into unexpected bumps in the road on Friday."

She grimaced at the request, but she sent him some measurements she found online. She acted thrilled about it in her response.

"Can't wait to meet your coworkers!" she texted next, picturing a crowd of hooded people around the hood from her dreams. Then she sat down her phone.

"Only a little longer now," she said to herself. "Emily is going to bunker down at my house. Then I just have to 'miss' the bus tonight and tomorrow. I can stop responding to this creep once it's obvious I won't be back in time, or if he offers to buy a plane ticket."

She opened back up her book. Her grandmother had filled pages with her thoughts on magic. Reading her words, Rachel regretted she had so few memories of the woman. She had been brilliant. Morgan's words about force of will being key to magic was echoed in Rosemary's entries.

She wrote that the most important part of magic was confidence and belief in oneself. She had also railed against the idea of gods being required as part of magic, calling theurgy the practice of conmen and grifters. She said that belief has a place in life for some, but that "any goodness rots when humans attempt to evoke divine beings or replace belief in themselves with that of spirits."

She believed that the universe was created with the big bang, and that as it expanded after that it began to fracture, splitting into parallel universes. Some of these universes subducted under others, and it was energy from those sunken universes that witches harnessed. She believed that travel between adjacent universes was possible, but probably fatal, writing that "The human form has adapted to live in this universe alone."

Rosemary believed a witch's life was an ascetic life, spent studying, meditating and staying out of the public eye. Rachel remembered what had almost happened to Morgan. It certainly didn't seem safe to be a witch any other way, she thought and sighed.

***

It was nearly midnight on the Thursday before the summer solstice. Emily was in Rachel's kitchen servicing her handgun. It had been a quiet evening, save for the drone of cicadas thinly drifting through the window behind her. She found the sound calming, and it had turned her activity into a kind of meditation. She'd done it many times, but focusing on each step of the process helped her clear her thoughts of everything else.

She hoped she wouldn't have to use it on anyone, but she wanted to be prepared. She had just finished reassembling the weapon when she noticed the bugs outside getting louder. She finished her work and then stood up from the kitchen table. At first she thought it was her imagination, but as she listened she grew sure of it. The cicadas definitely were getting louder, and the crickets were chirping faster.

She went to the backdoor and stepped outside onto the cement patio. It was much too loud outside. Frogs screeched in an out of sync and discordant chorus, while the katydids added their chittering treble percussion. It was eerie, but not as discomforting as what she was seeing floating around the sky.

At first, she thought it was a sign that she was going to have a migraine. She'd been waiting for one to start ever since she saw

the floating dots of light at Rachel's house. When it hadn't come,
she counted herself lucky. She had migraines with auras growing
up, where she would see bright twinkling lights with her left eye.
They didn't last long, and usually, about an hour after, the worst
headache in the world would start. But she hadn't had a headache
after seeing the lights at Rachel's when they did the map spell.

Those few points of light had happened so quickly that she
hadn't checked to see if she saw them with both eyes. But this
time, the lights were lingering. She closed her left eye for a
moment, but she still saw them. They were hovering in the sky
around the house, sparsely twinkling in the sky like nearby stars.
But as strange as the too bright stars looked, it was the light at the
back of the yard, behind the trees that interested her. There was a
thick cloud of the flashing lights near the back fence.

She felt afraid, but Rachel had assured her that the house was
a strong hold as long as she didn't let anyone inside. So she
stepped off the porch and walked through the dark yard to where
the lights were concentrated. She wanted to see what was going
on. She hadn't expected the increase in heat, but as she walked
toward the back of the yard, she couldn't help notice it was as hot
as it had been that morning. It was even hotter near the fence,
where the lights swarmed.

The crickets were chirping maniacally fast around the mass of
light against the back fence. Emily didn't blame them. What she
saw made her own pulse race as she headed past the few trees in
the back of Rachel's yard. Dazzling flashes of light were pulsating
at the fence line in a massive cluster, swirling like a miniature
galaxy.

It might have been beautiful if the center didn't have a
silhouette in it. She could just make out the shape of a crooked,
long fingered hand. It was pressing towards her as though it was
blocked by a window screen. It was hard to see against the
background of swirling flecks of light, but she had enough time
to see the fingertips looked sharp.

Then it was gone.

All the lights around the fence popped out of sight, but a few
lingered, leaving her in near darkness. The sounds around her
dropped back to normal volume as the bugs resumed their usual
song, with only the crickets near the fence maintaining allegro
speed. She turned around and ran back to the house, afraid that

there might be more than one attempt to break through. She sat in the dark with her gun at the table in the kitchen watching the fence line in the dark for a few hours, but she only saw lightning bugs.

***

Mike tried to call Rachel 16 times on Thursday night. He sat at the BBD bus station and waited in case she came in on the late bus, but she didn't arrive. He didn't want to believe that she had fled. But when she hadn't responded at all by Friday morning, he couldn't ignore her absence anymore.

He didn't know what to do, and he couldn't put it off anymore. So he went to his mother.

She was in one of the basement conference rooms meeting with the level 5's. She excused herself from the meeting and sighed before walking out of the room to talk with Mike. Before she closed the door, Mike saw that all the Level 5's were looking at him. One of them smirked. It was a bartender he had hired. Mike tried to ignore the feeling of being left out, telling himself he'd be a Level 5 when he was ready.

He followed her down the long oak paneled hallway to another empty conference room. He sat down in one of the black mesh chairs at the long black table in the room. Karen sat to his left at first, and she smirked as she asked him to tell her what was on his mind.

"Rachel is gone. She said she was going to be out of town on business until Wednesday. I think the love spell wore off and when her feelings changed she thought she didn't love me anymore."

Karen slapped him, and while it wasn't the first time she had hit him in the face, it was with much more strength than he ever remembered her having. He fell out of the chair, narrowly missing the heavy wooden conference table's edge. His face stung, and when he put his hand to his face, it came back with a spot of blood. She had been wearing the brass ring.

"Get up," she said with contempt. "I already know. We've cancelled the ritual for today because it's been clear since she didn't get on that bus that she wasn't returning. She hasn't left that house since last night. This is your fault for letting her go, but it's not the end of the line. I said get up. Don't look at me like that. If you want to cry, go do it in your office."

Mike got up shakily, bracing himself on the table as he stood. He was angry. He wished she'd never done any love spells on Rachel. The feelings felt bitter in him, and he couldn't keep them inside. It felt like poison.

"No. This is your fault," he said. "If you had let me get to know her the way I wanted to, things would have worked out. But you have to control everything! I don't think you ever want me to find love. I don't even know if you love me. You're an unfeeling monster."

She raised her hand again. She took a deep breath and then curled it into a fist before lowering it to her side. The way she looked at him now made him afraid. Her eyes seemed to brighten, although he was sure that was his imagination. Her brow lowered over her hard stare, and she looked like she was ready to shout at him. Her mouth turned small and square. He felt like a child. He sat back down and put his hands in his lap. Vertical lines appeared between her eyebrows, and she stood up from the table.

"Do not ever speak to me that way again," Karen said in a low voice, enunciating each word carefully. "I think you have forgotten your place in all this. Not only am I your mother, but I'm the head of this organization. You are nothing. You are my son, but that doesn't mean you have any authority. I gave you this club to manage, and I gave you one mission with Rachel. You've failed me. You've failed this organization, and you've failed Nephilor."

Karen let the words hang in the air for a moment to make sure Mike understood how guilty he should feel. She laced her fingers together, popping her joints. She felt on fire with anger that she had to continually teach him the same lesson. All he had to do was what she told him to do. That was it. She couldn't understand what was wrong with her son. She walked around the table toward him, trying to control herself. She wanted to throttle him, but she knew that wouldn't help. She made things so easy for him, she thought. Why couldn't he just do the right thing?

"You're only lucky you're my son," she continued. "If you want to continue having a job, you will do as I say. I make the plans, you follow. If I say jump, you jump. Get it?"

Mike nodded, his gaze not leaving the ground. He knew she wasn't done.

"Do you remember the golden rule, Mike?" Karen asked. She was standing over him now. Since he had sat down, it felt like getting yelled at as a child all over again. He felt frozen.

"Yes, ma'am," he said.

"Tell me the golden rule," she said. Her voice was low, and in the shadow she cast he felt suddenly very alone. Rachel was gone. It was his fault. All he had was his mother. Again.

"Mike, I know you heard me," she said.

He winced and then said what he knew she wanted to hear.

"She who makes the gold makes the rules," he murmured, trying to look into the fibers of the carpet. He wished for just a moment to be the size of a carpet mite. The thought seemed nice enough, to be so small as to be inconsequential to the woman in front of him. He hated her. He had learned about the phrase in a marketing class in college. It was meant to explain that the customer was always right, but his mother had twisted the phrase into something more narcissistic. He had learned the original phrase was "Do unto others as you would have them do unto you," but he wasn't taught that at home.

"*It's all about her and her plans,*" he thought. "*It always has been and always will be.*"

"Speak up. No Maples has ever been a mumbler," she said.

Mike wanted to say that he wasn't a Maples, but he knew she would lash back harder. Karen had changed her last name several times over the years to avoid suspicion. It was Smith when he was born. But she always referred to them in private as Maples, after Frank. Mike remembered his father cowering under her like this when he was small and for a moment, he felt incredibly angry and wanted to strike out. He looked up at her.

"She who makes the gold makes the rules," he said, putting all the strength and anger he had into his voice. He was glad he spoke before he met her eyes. There was a kind of anger there that he had never seen before. She looked like she truly hated him in that moment. Hated him enough to do something permanent about it, even. His mind reeled off ways she could hurt him: she could fire him, bankrupt him, take his car and his apartment. All of it was in her name.

He had stuck with her all his life, turning down other opportunities after graduation in order to join her business. She had promised him the opportunity of a lifetime. Managing a club on his own did seem just that. Since his future had been guaranteed to him since he was born, he didn't keep any of the old contacts from school. He never kept a business card, never went to a networking event, never even came up with his own business ideas, his inner critic quickly supplied. In that moment he felt trapped and useless, like there were no other options.

But he felt torn inside. He really had loved Rachel, maybe even more than he had let himself think. He had been heartbroken when she had stopped texting and had waited to tell his mother out of more than just embarrassment. The plan had been for him to seduce her into joining the group, and it seemed that he had failed completely. He was not sure what his mother had planned next, but he didn't want Rachel to be hurt.

But he felt that his best chances were under his mother's wing. He thought she was right. He couldn't run a club like that on his own. What would he do? Would his mother even give him a reference to work somewhere else? He had messed up. He needed her.

"What are you going to do?" he asked.

"Get out of my sight. I need to decide, and I can't think while you're whimpering," Karen said.

She stalked away. Relieved to be out of her shadow, Mike took a deep breath and then left the room. He knew she'd give him orders when she was ready, but he knew whatever she was going to do wasn't going to be good for Rachel. He thought for the first time that Rachel's life might be in danger, and that it might be his fault. What did he think she was going to do with her? Take a little blood sample and welcome her to the family? He cursed himself mentally for his naiveté.

As he walked out of the clubhouse, down the long cement steps down to the street where his car was parked behind a Tesla and a Maserati, several ideas occurred to him at once.

"*I don't think she was ever going to make me a level 5,*" he thought. "*She's never trusted me like that. She's been talking to me like a child my whole life. She's fucking nuts, and I don't want to help her murder the only woman I've ever loved. It was one thing when I thought she was going to leave the organization to Rachel and myself. I can't believe I bought that lie.*"

He started his car, and more things occurred to him as he backed up, switched gears, cranked the wheel and drove out of his parallel parking spot and up the hill out of the valley the Trettle neighborhood was in.

"I've been fooled," he thought. *"Would she even have kept me alive after the rapture?"*

A cold thought occurred to Mike. She had told him that when the rapture happened, their group would be spared. He remembered the fright he had the first time she had told him about the rapture, when he was 18. He had been afraid for her because of that look in her eyes when she talked about it. Her eyes had seemed to shine like they had in the conference room. He thought it was drive toward an impossible goal, but now he was beginning to suspect it was madness. It had to be, he thought.

The thought that his mother might be crazy brought other memories to Mike. She had always yelled at him a lot, something he hadn't given much thought to since it was all he had known. As he had grown up, it hadn't gotten any better. It occurred to him that her temper had worsened since he was a child. Her mood seemed to swing wildly these days, based only on Nephilor. For the first time, he wondered if the Nephilor creature his mother worshipped might be hurting her more than it helped her. All of her employees treated her with respect; would anyone say otherwise if she lost her mind? Or would they keep following her orders, no matter what they were? Would he?

His phone rang. His car's display told him it was Karen.

"Think of the devil, and she'll appear," he thought, pressing the button on his steering wheel that picked up the call.

"Are you going to follow orders I give you?" she asked over the car's speakers.

"Yes ma'am," he said automatically. As he did, he thought of Rachel and how beautiful she had looked in that black lace dress on the night she came to the club. A rebellious thought floated through his mind, and he smiled. He would help Rachel, he decided. The thought connected in his brain in a way that felt so right, Mike felt ashamed he hadn't thought about it before. He could help Rachel while under his mother's wing.

"Then listen, because we are going to have to act to get her back here," Karen said. "If you complete this for me, I will make you a Level 5 as soon as you return with what I need."

Mike listened as Karen began to lay out a plan. It was outrageous and part of him wanted nothing to do with it. He hung up after the call and began driving north to see the owner of a shop called Crystal Crescent.

32

Early Saturday morning, Rachel woke up in her grandmother's bed to the sound of a text message. She got out of bed and peeked through the blinds. There was a black SUV sitting in front of the house. The car was idling, and there were people sitting in the passenger and driver's seat. They were wearing black polo shirts.

She got dressed and checked all over the house, making sure that all the windows and doors were locked. Once she was sure everything was secure, she looked at her phone. She had one message from an unknown number:

"We have your friend. Get in the car out front. It will take you back to Cincinnati, unless you want Morgan's blood on your hands."

Rachel brewed coffee while she thought about how to respond. She ground some whole beans, hoping the smell would wake up her senses. She needed to think as clearly as possible. She pressed the button on the grinder to pulse the beans a few times. She poured ground coffee into the filter. It was gritty and much too coarse. She couldn't help thinking it looked like the bags of graveyard dirt at Morgan's store. She shook the coffee back into the grinder and pressed until the blades whirred and blended it smoother.

She wasn't sure if this was Mike who was threatening her or another member of his order. Clearly they couldn't storm the house she was in, but they had got hold of Morgan somehow. Maybe while she was at the post office, although she couldn't think why Morgan would stray from the plan. She started the coffee brewing while she weighed the pros and cons of the approach she was going to take.

Finally she wrote her response:

"I'll return on my own. I have arrangements to make at home that will take a few business days. I have made a magical device that will turn my blood into dirt. If you interfere or hurt Morgan, I will not hesitate to use it. Name your meeting place and time."

She hit send and then she waited, staring at the screen. She hoped her bluff would work. It was desperate, but it was all she could come up with. She poured herself a cup of coffee and tried not to think about how her hands were shaking. It was a few minutes before a response arrived, but she breathed a little easier when it did.

"We agree to your terms. You have until midnight on Tuesday. We will be at Church waiting for you."

She set down her phone on the kitchen table. She didn't have much time at all, but she knew what she had to do. She had to find out what had happened to her mother and grandmother and hope it gave her the information she needed.

She went upstairs and looked out the window of her grandmother's bedroom. The black SUV was gone, but she was sure they would still be watching her as soon as she left the house. She pushed the thoughts aside and focused on what she needed to do.

She took the sack of coins, her mother's scarf, and the rose quartz orb out of her purse. She took them along with Morgan's book to the empty bedroom on the second floor. Then she got a safety pin and rubbing alcohol from her purse. She pulled the blinds closed tightly, shut the door and turned off the lights. It was dim enough so that she could still read the passage she opened the book to.

"Crystal balls have been used for centuries by seers and charlatans alike, but only the witch may truly see into the past and present. The future will always be uncertain, which is why it's impossible to divine," the book read. "As already stated in these pages, any material with enough surface area can be used for scrying. The cost is significant, but if you need to see where or when you cannot, it is a price well paid."

Rachel got on her knees and spread the purple scarf out on the wooden floor. She set the rose quartz orb on its stand in the center and surrounded the orb with the rest of her coins. Then she read the incantation from the book aloud as she lightly traced the tip of the sanitized pin across the meat above her inner elbow on her left arm. When she was ready, she carefully pressed the tip down until it punctured and drew blood.

She held her arm out and let the blood dribble onto the orb until it started to bubble on the surface. A silver iridescent smoke rose from the orb as the blood boiled off. The vapor dissipated into nothingness.

Rachel sat back and quickly placed a bandage on the wound. She watched as the milky pinkness of the rose quartz orb began to fade. The stone's occlusions and imperfections in the stone vanished, and it grew transparent until it seemed to disappear entirely.

"I'd like to see the past. I want to see who is responsible for the death of my mother," Rachel said, holding her right hand above her heart and squeezing the wrist with her left hand. She felt slightly nauseated, and the feeling came so suddenly that Rachel was sure it was part of the spell's cost. She thought some of the sick feeling had to do with her question as well.

She pushed the thoughts aside as an image appeared in the crystal ball. It was of her mother, tied to a chair in what appeared to be a cave. Rachel looked closer.

Behind her mother stretched a cement block wall lit only by flickering torches carried by the group gathered there. The floor looked like the dirtiest old cement Rachel had ever seen. Rusty circles stained the ground around the chair Theresa was tied to, indicating this was far from the first blood sacrifice to take place there. Rachel swallowed a dry lump in her throat, fighting the feelings inside so she could see what she was up against. As Rachel watched, a group of hooded figures walked in a circle around her mother, and then stood in a horseshoe around her. One of the hooded figures was very short, and as she walked up to Rachel's mother, she lowered her hood, shaking loose long black hair.

Rachel recognized the woman at once and gasped, feeling a rush of anger at her betrayal so strong that she stopped paying attention. The woman was Karen. Mike's cousin and business partner, she thought so hotly she thought her blood would start to boil out of her pores. She wondered which of the 8 hoods behind her was Mike. Karen was yelling at her mother, so Rachel quieted her own outrage to listen.

"We've given you long enough to help us, Theresa. I'm very disappointed in you. It's been nearly 22 years since you first came to us. You were pretty well behaved for the first nine years, but you've been nothing but trouble since. I know you think it's funny making your blood evaporate when we take it from you, but I'll give you one more chance to start donating blood to help our organization again."

Rachel's mother began making a guttural retching sound, and Rachel leaned forward, her face stricken. Then she sat back as she watched her mother spit a loogie at Karen.

"Go sit on it, you ugly bitch. You'll get yours. Is this what you did to Rosemary too?" Theresa asked. She added in a louder voice, addressing the hooded figures behind her. "Funny when one of your original founders shows up after decades and then just disappears, huh?"

This set off some murmurs among the hooded figures.

"Silence!" Karen yelled, and the figures obeyed. The quiet was eerie. Rachel could only hear her own breathing as she watched. Karen sniffed, and then responded to Theresa. "This is just another one of your juvenile attempts to stir up disorder. Your mother had a heart attack. It's pathetic that you would defile her memory with such crass suggestions. She is honored in our garden of remembrance. You will have no such glory. You will be sacrificed to Nephilor. Your blood and soul will be his. An honor, really. Do you have any last words?"

"Bullshit. You killed her. Just like you're going to kill me. For the power. You're going to feed whatever creature it is you've found. I expect he's told you that once you make him happy, he'll be planting gardens and helping clean up highways?" Theresa asked. She scoffed and rolled her eyes.

Rachel began to wonder if her mother had counted on her using witchcraft to witness the moment of her death. It seemed like her mom was provoking Karen as much as she could to get her to spill information.

"How many have you killed for him, Karen?" Theresa asked. "Has he told you it makes you stronger? Have you believed him?"

Rachel watched as Karen hunched her shoulders up for a moment, and then relaxed them. She realized that Karen was taking a deep breath. Her mother had gotten to her, if only for a moment. Rachel found herself wondering how many people Karen really had killed. It hadn't occurred to her that it might be more than just her family that was involved. She watched as Karen responded.

"We know where to find your daughter, Theresa," Karen said. "It doesn't matter what you say. We even have a bronze ring that we can use to confirm she's got witch blood. She'll work just as well for our purposes as you could have. Better even, since you've proven your worth over the years. Mentally, physically, spiritually: You're useless. Even now, you are wasting your breath and my time. Now, I asked you if you had last words."

At this, Theresa looked resigned. She looked out for a moment, and to Rachel it seemed that she was trying to sense something. Then, for just a moment, it seemed like Theresa was looking right at Rachel.

"CHNOPS," Theresa said, pronouncing it "cha-nops." Then she closed her eyes and sat back.

Karen looked puzzled at first. Seemingly taking her silence as submission, she picked up a knife and goblet from the altar.

Rachel felt her stomach turn over and her mouth water as if preparing her to throw up. The knife and goblet were the same as the ones that had been in her nightmares. Rachel wondered if perhaps the nightmares had been an omen for this moment. Rachel watched as Karen advanced on her mother.

As she watched, Rachel's mother's mouth moved silently. Karen circled behind her and began aloud a strange and vulgar incantation. Rachel watched, rigid in her chair. She felt herself getting hot and flushed with anger, but she couldn't pull her eyes away. Her mother's lips formed words that repeated in what looked like an incantation.

In the moment before Karen drew the knife across her throat, Rachel saw it. It was like the shadow of smoke. The shadowy vapors poured out of her mother. Judging by the lack of reaction, not one of the hooded figures could see the strange mist. It reminded Rachel of *I Dream of Jeannie*. When the genie would emerge from the bottle, there was always a triumphant pillar of neon pink smoke that would pour out of the genie's bottle before she would appear.

This mist wasn't pink, but a strange kind of colorless that wasn't quite gray. As it poured out of her mother and as Karen held the knife against her mother's throat, Rachel saw the ghostly figure of her mother step up from the chair. She looked exactly like she did the night of the storm when Rachel first saw her. She seemed to look right at Rachel, and for a moment Rachel felt that she really was connected to her mother across time. The shadow smoke wafted around the figure of her mother, who held out her hand as though reaching out to Rachel. Rachel reached her hand out to touch the crystal ball. It was so cold that it burned her fingertips. She withdrew her hand but held it as close as she could stand.

"I love you, Rachel," her mother's ghost seemed to whisper. "I'm sorry."

"I love you too, Mom," Rachel said. She did not cry, but bit her lip and leaned forward.

She had just enough time to see that her eyes and nose had grown to look just like her mother's. Then the ghost of her mother disappeared.

She was surprised to see the scene in the crystal ball continued, although it was clear that her mother had left her body behind. Karen had held back her mother's head, and must not have noticed how her body had sagged slightly as her spirit had left it. She slit her mother's throat, and dark hot blood sprayed out, wetting the front of her mother's white gown, the ropes she was bound with and the floor in front of her. Karen held out the silver chalice under the stream until her cup was full and running over onto her fingers. Then, leaving the body to bleed out, she walked the few steps to the white marble altar.

"Nephilor!" Karen shouted down to her followers.

The 12 hooded figures echoed her cry, and then Karen took a gulp of the hot blood. Rachel felt bile rise in her throat, her salivary glands pumping spit into her mouth to prepare her for the coming upchuck. She was sure she was going to be sick, but she didn't dare turn away.

"Nephilor!" Karen shouted again. There was a red ring of blood around her mouth, but she didn't seem to notice or mind. She pulled from the cup again as the other hooded figured chanted "Nephilor."

This continued for a total of seven times. Rachel watched in horror while Karen drained the cup. With each swill, Karen would throw her shoulders back and look up, an exultant look on her face. At the seventh sip, Rachel noticed an almost opalescent gleam to Karen's skin. It lingered for a few seconds, but then it was gone.

When she was done, she set the cup on the altar and left the room, her cape trailing behind her. At last, the clarity of the scene dulled until the ball was no longer transparent but a milky pink rose quartz once again.

Rachel stood up shakily, then staggered out of the dark room into the hall to the bathroom. The old house had only one, and fortunately it was on the top floor. Rachel made her way to the toilet, then got down on her knees on the white tile floor in front of the commode. She gagged a few times into the toilet, but found she couldn't actually throw up. She sighed and stood back up.

"If that didn't make me sick, then I can take more. Who else has Karen killed?" Rachel thought. *"How long has she been killing witches? Did she kill Rosemary too?"*

33

Rachel made sure there were still plenty of coins around the orb, and then she took the pin in her hand again. She dug the tip into the flesh above her right elbow. She let the blood drip slowly on top of the crystal, and then watched as the orb hissed, smoked, and turned clear again.

"Show me what Karen did to Rosemary in 1997," she told the orb as she bandaged the wound.

The first scene it played was of Karen talking to her grandmother. Karen was opening a bottle of wine on one of two marble topped islands in a high-ceilinged kitchen. Rachel figured it had to be one of the clubhouses Mike had talked about. She wrinkled her nose in disgust remembering how he had bragged.

"You did the right thing calling me," Karen said. "We'll be able to help her get back to normal. It'll take some time, but with the right effort she should be ok."

Rosemary didn't turn around from the window. Rachel watched as she poured 2 glasses of wine. Rachel's eyes widened as she saw Karen add a white powder to one of the glasses of wines. The white powder dissolved without a trace.

Rosemary was looking out the window of the kitchen at the grounds. The clubhouse sat on a very well manicured lawn, but the backyard was full of manicured shrubs and bushes shaped like animals. The sun was just beginning to set, and the golden light made the foliage look even more beautiful.

"I hope so," Rosemary said. "You know, I wondered all my life what happened to you and Frank. I'm glad y'all made it ok. What's done is done, and I don't have many regrets, but I always wondered if I had made the wrong decision."

Rachel noticed the admission seemed to have surprised Karen. Karen had been walking toward her holding the two glasses of wine. Upon hearing this from Rosemary, Rachel noticed Karen lowered the wine glasses and stopped walking toward her, staring at her back. Her shoulders slumped. Rosemary turned and smiled kindly at her, a woman who looked young enough to be her granddaughter, and Karen straightened up and extended a wine glass to her.

"If you had stayed, we would have gotten a jump start on helping Theresa. And you would look as good as I do," Karen said. She winked at Rosemary when she said this, and Rachel felt her skin crawl. She didn't understand the strange dynamic between the two at all. It didn't make any sense. Her grandmother seemed unsure how to take the wink. She opened her mouth, closed it, and then she smiled weakly at Karen before responding.

"I left because I had to in order to raise her as a witch," Rosemary said. "But I never stopped wondering about you. How have you been? It's so strange. You look the same as when I left."

Rosemary took the glass of wine, but she did not drink from it. She held it in her hand, and Rachel watched with such frightened excitement and attention that she was almost holding her breath to listen as the two women talked. The things they were saying were strange, and Rachel didn't want to believe it, but the pieces were coming together. Was Karen much older than she seemed? It sure sounded that way, Rachel thought, and as if Karen heard, she confirmed it with what she said next.

"It's been a really long time since 1958. I started to think we'd never see you again. I know Frank would have loved to see you," Karen said.

"Where is Frank?" Rosemary asked. "I'm surprised Mr. Maples hasn't popped up to say hi after 44 years. Does he look like you do? Young still, I mean?"

At this, Karen looked uncomfortable, if only just for a second. But Rosemary and Rachel both saw the flicker of emotions play on Karen's face—a look of guilt, followed by a look a grief—before she composed herself into the brisk, business-like friendly smile she had worn before.

"He passed in 1995. Heart Attack," Karen said before changing the subject. "Would you like to step out on the porch? I think I'd like a cigarette."

"*I bet she killed him,*" Rachel thought. The flicker of certainty was strong, and looking at Rosemary's face, which now looked pale, Rachel thought she might have had the same feeling. She tried to focus on the scene, but couldn't shake the mental image of the empty spaces around Frank Maple's and Rosemary's grave.

"I don't smoke. I'm surprised you do, honestly," Rosemary said. Her eyebrows were furrowed and she didn't look at Karen. "I mean, it's 1997. Most folks agree it's hardly healthy."

Rachel watched as Rosemary lifted the wine glass to her lips. Something must have changed her mind, as she didn't drink from it. Rachel thought Rosemary might know something was going on.

Rachel wasn't wrong. Rosemary's intuition had started screaming at her when she arrived with Theresa. Rachel's experience with intuition was limited, but when a witch is threatened, that well of power begins to rise, opening up precognitive senses. The trouble with intuition is that when you're surrounded by threats, it can become impossible to distinguish one from the other. The waves of certainty about Theresa being a threat to society and herself were what Rosemary was focusing on. The belief that Karen was up to something hadn't crashed down on her until the two of them were in a room together, but Rosemary couldn't tell what Karen's intentions were. She wasn't being forthcoming.

Karen shrugged.

"Smoking hasn't bothered me since 1958," Karen said.

Rachel at first thought that must be some kind of catchphrase. It seemed like nonsense. Was it? Her own intuition was beginning to crackle with the beginnings of a belief that she immediately pushed away. But hadn't her grandmother said "young still" as though that was the case? It was impossible for her to really be that old, wasn't it? But here Karen was, looking exactly the same as she did in 2019 back in 1997.

Karen showed Rosemary to the door to the patio off of the kitchen. They walked out, and the view in the crystal ball followed them outside to the flagstone patio. The patio was paved with stones in shades of gray. On the patio were two black

8 person wrought iron tables and chairs. Each of the chairs had an ecru cushion, and Rosemary took a seat at one of the chairs at the end of a table. She set the wineglass in front of her.

Karen walked past Rosemary to the edge of the patio, where she leaned against the railing and lit her cigarette. She turned around to Rosemary, puffing the cigarette in a way that seemed almost nervous.

"When you left us," Karen started, but faltered. A nervous expression crossed her face, and then she took a long drag from her cigarette. Her expression changed once more to the business smile, and then to a more enigmatic expression. Rachel thought this must be her poker face.

"How does Karen know about her involvement?" Rachel asked herself, not wanting to believe the answer her intuition was trying to give her. She increasingly felt sure that Karen was much older than she looked, but found it so illogical as to be impossible. Surely the cost of magic like that is much higher than anything else, she thought. There's no way immortality is possible, she thought, and felt certain of that much.

"I did what I had to do for my child, Karen," Rosemary said. "Just as I'd do anything to help her now. Do you have any children, Karen?"

"I do. You weren't the only one to have a child with Frank. Frank and I weren't sure how long we'd be able to keep running the business, so we had a son. Little Mikey. He's about the same age as your granddaughter," Karen said. "Maybe they'll get along as well as we did once."

Rachel felt a wave of unreality sweep over her. It had never occurred to her how much Karen and Mike looked alike. She could see them in her head, the day that they had met. The day Karen's ring had pinched her hand so hard it drew blood. She felt like screaming. For a moment she tore her eyes away from the orb as her eyes watered with tears that threatened to spill.

"*Mike is Karen's son? How old is Karen? How is that possible?*" Rachel thought. "*How much have I been lied to? Jesus, she said...Oh fucking Christ, does this mean I'm related to Mike?*"

Rachel already felt nauseated using the crystal ball and watching the gruesome scenes she was calling up, but the family tree repainted itself in her mind before she could stop it, and the idea that she had almost fucked her uncle broke her attention.

Rachel realized she was clutching her cut hands so tightly they hurt. She was breathing in shallow, short breaths and her heart was racing. She wondered if it was the orb or her own reaction to the news that she had been dating the son of the apparently immortal woman who killed her mother.

She realized she was letting herself get excited, and that she was reacting instead of paying attention. Excitement wouldn't help anything, she told herself, but it would definitely do the opposite if left unchecked. She reminded herself that she had learned this lesson over and over in life. It was a good thing she had, because she was able to see what she was doing to herself. Realizing she needed to get control of herself, she pinched herself on the leg. She needed to pay attention. If not for her, then for her mother. For her mother and her grandmother, she decided.

She took a deep breath, and turned her attention back to the orb just in time to see Rosemary take a sip of the wine. She saw that as soon as Rosemary began drinking the wine, Karen loosened up. She told herself then that she had to be strong, for she was sure that Karen had killed more than just her mother and grandmother.

34

Rachel watched as the two women talked on the porch about their time together, and about the time they could have had together. Rachel learned that the clubs had been built as fronts for Karen's organized religion, and that Karen had started the church after Rosemary had left.

She watched as her grandmother began to look first tired and then drunk. It didn't take long after the first sip. Soon her head lolled over, and Rachel wondered if she was dead.

Things moved quickly after that. Rachel watched as Karen called some men in black polos who carried Rosemary out of the porch. She was set in a wheelchair, and an IV was attached to her right arm connected to two clear bags. One person took blood from her, filling several vials. They took the red tubes into a different room and didn't reappear.

Rosemary was transferred in the back of an SUV to a half built construction site in an area that Rachel thought looked almost familiar. Karen and a muscular man she recognized from Church transferred the sleeping Rosemary from the street surface through a network of tunnels down to a massive underground cellar. Once he had tied her to the chair, he left Karen and Rosemary alone.

After a little while, Rosemary slowly woke up in the same position her daughter would die in, tied to a chair in a dusty underground chamber of some sort.

"Where am I?" Rosemary asked, after she woke up sputtering. Rachel listened closely.

"Trettle street station," Karen said. "Far enough underground where no one will hear you."

She stood at the altar, alone. There was no crowd of hooded figures with her this time. Rachel wondered if the murder of an elderly woman was something the rest of the group would frown upon. She held onto the thought. Maybe Karen was the bad seed the whole plant had sprouted from.

"You know, I mourned you for decades, you old bitch," Karen said. "Just to have you come back and suggest that maybe you made the wrong choice. I wanted to strangle you right then. You have no fucking idea what I've been through since you left."

Rosemary shifted in her chair, tried to rock it and finding herself unable to get free, she sighed loudly. Rachel saw that Rosemary was not resigned, but steaming angry.

"That was a lapse in judgement, saying that. An intrusive thought. I'm glad I left you, you crazy cunt," Rosemary said, her voice startlingly calm. "I bet you keep on this path until it kills you. You never could control yourself. You're an obsessive. I hope Theresa sets this whole fucking place on fire."

"Nice language for an old maid. No, Nephilor has told me just what we need to do to keep her under control," Karen said. "Until we can get her to join up, that is."

"She'd never agree to any of your crazy shit," Rosemary said. "You're fucking with something you don't even understand. Don't you get it? Gods aren't needed for magic because there are no gods. I've told you this before. Whatever it is, he's been deceiving you. You're too full of yourself to see that."

Karen scoffed. She left the altar to stand in front of Rosemary, leaving the knife and chalice. She looked irritated, and stood with her arms crossed in front of the elderly Rosemary.

"Your memory must be going. You told me many times that gods weren't needed for magic, yes, but suggesting that there are no gods is something you hardly have the authority to say when there's an actual fucking god talking to me," Karen said. "Especially when you heard him yourself. Especially when you yourself have powers! "

Karen took a deep breath, then turned her head up and sniffed, looking up as though she was peering through the cement and dirt to the building above them.

"It's ok that you're being obstinate. There's nothing you can actually do to stop us. When we get your daughter to comply, we'll be able to summon him fully. Then the rapture will begin.

Frank will be restored to life. Maybe your daughter and grand-daughter will be spared, if Theresa works with us. Spared for a while anyway. We're going to clean the slate, Rosemary. It'll be a whole new world once Nephilor is corporeal. He can bring you back then, but I don't know if I want that anymore. Frank will be returned to my side, and he and I will be Nephilor's most favored servants. We will cleanse the Earth in a rapturous iridescent fire. I've seen it in my dreams so many times.

"We've already been helping people, you know. We do more than just run a club. Many of our staff members have had problems helped by Nephilor. They may not know that's what happened, but they believe in our organization, and that belief goes right to sustaining Nephilor.

"If things had gone differently, you could have been right by my side too. You know, I never would have met him if it weren't for you. I'll always be grateful for that. That's why I brought you down here alone.

"I think it's time you met him too. I want a practice run for this anyway. You see, first you're going to sample my blood, taken from me while Nephilor's spirit is in me. Then once Nephilor comes through, he will take your blood. Witch blood strengthens him. You're doing good here, really."

Karen pulled a piece of chalk from the pocket of her cloak. She kneeled on the floor and began writing words and symbols in a circle around Rosemary.

Rachel leaned forward, her eyes wide. This was the moment of truth, it seemed. Karen felt so confident that she had spilled her plans to Rosemary. Rachel was horrified to find out Karen was planning a kind of rapture, but she couldn't believe Karen had the power to do such a thing.

"Who or what is this Nephilor? How is he helping her?" she thought.

Karen went back to the altar. She cut her own hand while murmuring a low chant to herself. She held her hand over the cup and watched as blood dripped into the cup. Once she was satisfied with the amount, she wrapped her hand in a bandage she took from a pocket in her cloak.

Then, to Rachel's horror, Karen forced Rosemary to drink her blood. The blindfolded woman tried moving her head, but Karen held the cup to her face and held her head still with one arm

wrapped around her head, holding her chin. She forced
Rosemary's mouth open and the blood inside. Rosemary spit it
out immediately, red staining her teeth and lips. Rachel watched
as a single drop of blood wound down from her lips to her chin
and then dripped onto the front of her blouse.

"Doesn't matter. That was enough, I think," Karen said. She
tilted her head as though listening to something. "He says as long
as the blood is on you, it is enough. Good."

She removed Rosemary's blindfold and walked around to face
her. She sat down on the ground in front of Rosemary and began
another murmured incantation. As Karen spoke, she seemed to
go into a trance. Her eyes rolled back in her head, her eyelids
fluttered over white eyes, and then she passed out on the floor,
falling on her back, her head lolled over to the right. Rosemary
looked in horror from the out cold Karen to the space in front of
her. It seemed the air was beginning to shift and move in a
strange way.

Rachel wasn't sure what she was seeing at first. Five white
dots appeared on top of Karen's stomach. Karen began
convulsing as the dots began emerging from her, but she didn't
seem conscious.

Rachel thought they weren't quite white, as color flashed in
them as they grew. She leaned closer, her face almost against the
crystal. She sat back when she saw the dots were quickly getting
larger. They were grouped together, and as they emerged they
looked like 5 sharpened and crooked tree branches.

As the palm emerged, it became clear they were five very long
and sharp fingers, pinched together. Rachel held her breath. It
was the same ghostly hand she had seen on the bus and in her
nightmares.

"Stop! Stop this!" Rosemary shouted. "Karen, please!"

Karen was unresponsive. She was out cold, but her body was
shaking, the tremors racking her body in waves from the point in
her abdomen where the white hand reached out. Twists of red,
blue and purple light flicked up from the spot, licking up the base
of the white arm. The hand stretched its fingers out as the wrist
appeared. It was impossibly long and large, and it reached for
Rosemary. Rachel saw that it wasn't just white, but iridescent.
Streaks of color flashed magenta and teal as the long fingers
stretched out to touch Rosemary. The long white hand grew

closer and closer to Rosemary as the forearm began to emerge. Rachel didn't want to know what would happen if the hand touched Rosemary, but she wouldn't look away.

"No!" Rachel cried, and she realized Rosemary cried it at the same time.

Something was happening to Rosemary. Her face was dark red, almost plum color, and sweat was pouring off of her. She looked like she was gasping for air, but then she began to yell.

"No!" Rosemary shouted again. "I won't let you get to this world! I bind you! I bind you back to your world!"

The fingers were almost touching Rosemary's face when she said this. They seemed to hesitate but then continued to reach forward. The longest of the fingers touched Rosemary's face, tracing her jaw. Rosemary screamed. Where the fingers had touched, the skin turned gray and withered before hanging loosely, as though all muscle tone had been stripped. Soon the hand had her face in its grip, pushing her cheeks forward around her mouth. Rosemary struggled and opened her mouth again, her cheeks pressed hard against her mouth

"With all the life that I have, I bind you!" Rosemary screamed, spit running from her mouth as the ghastly hand tried to squeeze closed her cheeks and face. Her voice rang out loud, its echoes reverberating off the station walls. The color drained quickly from her face, and she slumped forward.

The hand disappeared instantly. The ball began to lose its clarity, and became once again a rose quartz sphere. Rachel shivered. She wasn't sure if what she had seen was a god or not, but she doubted it. She knew that whatever it was using Karen, whether she realized it or not. It was hitching a ride with her, somehow, and she didn't seem to know. If she did, it seemed like she thought it was good for her. Maybe eternal youth had severely clouded her judgement. But nothing seemed mutually beneficial about the seizures she had while the thing had reached out of her. It looked like it would kill her for it to break through.

"*It's like a parasite*," Rachel thought, thinking of Massospora fungus. "*Karen's like one of those half-eaten cicadas that doesn't even know it.*"

Something in her stomach groaned and twisted. Rachel felt a wave of hot, unstoppable nausea sweep over her. She got up quickly and ran for the bathroom, falling to her knees in front of

the toilet just in time. She vomited into the toilet until her
stomach was empty, then gagged and dry heaved for another few
minutes. With a shaking hand, Rachel flushed the toilet and then
laid down on the cold tile, staring up at the white ceiling. She
could feel her heart pounding in her chest, and she thought she
could hear it in her ears. Her whole body was sweating, and she
laid there on the cool tile for half an hour trying to think.

"*Mike is my uncle,*" she thought.

In that moment she felt disgusted and betrayed on a level she
never thought possible. Did he know? She wasn't sure it
mattered. She knew her mother and grandmother had been killed
by his mother, who had killed 10 other women besides them in
the last 6 decades. Rachel couldn't help associating Karen with
the salt-shaker bugs again as she thought about how Karen had
seized while that creature had reached out of her.

There was no doubt in her mind that the creature would kill
Karen when it was done with her. Rachel wasn't sure what
Karen's rapture entailed, but she knew it would be horrible. How
many would die when Karen finally let that creature loose?

Rachel knew she had to stop her. She shakily got up from the
bathroom floor and made her way back downstairs to find her
phone. She found her phone, and dialed Emily's call phone
number.

"We're kind of fucked," Rachel said when she answered.

35

"Yeah that does sound like some kind of parasite," Emily said. "Gross. Why would anyone let something do that to them?"

"She thinks it's a god. I don't think she knows how bad it is for her," Rachel said. "Maybe it really is like Massospora. I'm not saying Karen was a good person before she got mixed up with Nephilor. My grandmother called her an obsessive. Evidently she was obsessed with finding a god, even though there was a witch with actual powers telling her there's no such thing."

"I'm trying to put myself in her shoes," Emily said. "I mean, we all wrestle with the notion of the afterlife. I came out an atheist just like my parents, but I've definitely flirted with religion because it seems so comforting to believe in something more. Imagine believing with all your heart that there are higher powers, and then being with someone with actual magical powers who's an atheist."

"Yeah," Rachel said. "And then your husband gets that person pregnant, and they run off. I'm trying to feel sympathy for her, but it's hard. Who tries to get their son together with his niece? And what kind of monster murders people and drinks their blood? It's got to be Nephilor pulling the strings."

"Nephilor hijacking her brain is the only thing that makes sense," Emily said. "There's no reason or logic there. But there's got to be something good left in her. Did you want to talk about Mike?"

"No," Rachel said. "I think eventually when we're on the other side of this I need to see a therapist, but I've done nothing wrong. They've made enough victims out of my family members. No matter how I look at it, Mike was manipulative. It doesn't matter how much he actually knew. He knew enough to try to trick me into joining their organization.

"And Karen...I want to hurt her for what she's done, but I can't ignore that it's been Nephilor behind the wheel," Rachel said. "If she's not directly controlling her, she's been brainwashed. But this rapture...she wants to unleash Nephilor on the world. She probably thinks it's good for her. Whatever it is, it's getting her to murder witches for their blood, and it's not going to stop if it gets me."

"We need to go to the cops," Emily said once Rachel finished telling her what she had seen in the rose quartz ball. As soon as the words were out of her mouth she knew they'd be laughed out of the police station. "Fuck."

"I know," Rachel said gravely. "We don't have any proof. They sent me a text from an unlisted number, but it's not explicit enough to connect Mike and Karen's group to the murders. And we don't have any evidence at all of the murders. We're going to have to do something ourselves about this."

"I doubt Mike will turn. You know he mentioned his mother on that day I met him at the festival? He said he liked listening to occult rock music to piss her off. I'm so angry. I just thought he was a little juvenile, not an accessory to murder. If he hadn't been dosing me with some kind of love spell, I might have realized something was going on sooner."

"Don't blame yourself," Emily said. "Guilt is a waste of time. You know that. If we have to do something about this ourselves that we regret, we can talk about it then. We can find ways to atone. They can't. Not after what they've done. "

"I know. Karen said witch blood strengthens Nephilor. I think whatever Nephilor is, he must be giving her the drop on where to find witches," she shivered, picturing the long fingered hand reaching for her. "I've been seeing its hand in my nightmares. It looked just it did in the orb when he grabbed Rosemary."

"I think I saw him," Emily said. "Nephilor. In the backyard on Thursday night. He couldn't get through your protective spell, but I saw his hand as he tried. It was like you said. Long, sharp, crooked fingers. It reminded me of a spider."

"I'm so sorry, Emily," Rachel said.

"There's more," she said. "I don't know how to explain it, but I saw lights everywhere in your backyard. Especially around

Nephilor's hand. I saw them the other week when you found Rosemary on the map. These aren't like my migraine auras. It's got something to do with magic, I'm sure of it."

Rachel felt guilt worm its way into her stomach. She remembered what Sam told her about magic being dangerous. Her grandmother's wife Ashley had believed it could drive you to madness if you weren't a witch. She had to ask Sam what else she had told him about that. Nothing like it was written in any of the books from the safe, which made Rachel wonder if it was based on stories Rosemary shared about Karen. Even still, Rachel wondered if she had contaminated her friend somehow.

"Rachel?" Emily said.

"I don't know if it's good for me to do magic around you anymore, Emily," she said.

Emily was quiet for a moment. But when she spoke, she sounded irritated.

"Well that's fine," Emily said. "After we figure this out, you can stop. Right? I don't feel any different, but if I'm not dead in a few days I'll start saving for a CT scan."

Rachel thought about it.

"Right," she said hesitantly before deciding not to share more until she'd spoken with Sam.

"But until we figure out what to do so that neither we nor Morgan gets murdered, I don't want to hear any more guilt from you. Ok? These are intrusive thoughts. We need to think like this is business," Emily said. "We need to focus on what's most urgent and important. Stopping this rapture and finding Morgan."

"Right," Rachel said with more firmness. "You're right. Ok. Thursday night was when you saw Nephilor attempt to break in. They must have picked up Morgan between then and this morning. I've tried calling her in case it was a bluff, but answer. So I tried to use the orb, but wherever she is it's too dark to tell and I don't have enough coins left to see into the past again. I think she's in that basement space. I just hope she's ok."

"Me too. Although I don't know how they could have taken her. Especially if they couldn't get through the shield on your home. She said she wasn't going to leave. Hold on," said Emily. "I'm going to put you on speaker phone. I'm grabbing my laptop."

"I've already got mine open. I told them I'd be at Church on Tuesday, so I'm going to book the next flight back. There's one that leaves tonight, so I should be back at the house before the sun rises on Sunday."

Emily's response sounded far away, like she was ten feet from the cell phone.

"Do you think they'll let you leave?"

"I negotiated," she said. "I said I'd come to them. I have until Tuesday at midnight. Karen mentioned Trettle street station. Get this. When I search 'Trettle Street Station' online, it shows me where Church is, at the corner of Trettle and Central Parkway"

"That sounds so familiar," Emily said. It sounded like she had settled back near the phone.

Rachel could hear the clicking sounds of Emily typing on her laptop. She put Emily on speaker phone and finished purchasing the ticket for her red-eye flight. It was only around 1 in the afternoon now, but time was precious.

"It's part of the subway they didn't finish!" Emily yelled over the phone.

"What?"

"Yeah. The city used to do guided tours once a year," Emily said. "They stopped a few years back. I remember reading about the tunnels in the paper when they shelved that big light rail project a few years ago. Just found a map. I'm sending you a link right now."

"Ok, got it. That's right! I remember hearing about this when they put in that streetcar system downtown," Rachel said. "What I'm looking at says it's two and a half miles long, so there's got to be access points that they don't control."

"I did an image search. I'm looking at pictures of the tunnels, and they're covered in graffiti," Emily said. "If street artists can get in, we should be able to if we're careful. But how do we do it without getting detected and how will we get through the wall?"

"We've got to break in," Rachel said. "I've got some ideas. Do you still have that sledgehammer?"

"From the renovation? Yeah, it's in my garage. It took forever to knock down that wall in the shop. You don't think that would work do you?"

"With the right enchantment I think it might," Rachel said. "I have an idea for a plan where no one gets hurt. But we should be prepared for anything."

***

Rachel was almost hopeful until after she hung up the phone. Then she thought about what Emily had said about seeing Nephilor's hand and the strange lights. She tried to push the thoughts aside. She packed up the things she had brought with her and sat in the reading room for a while looking through the books from the safe.

It was around 4 p.m. when Sam came by to see Rachel. She invited him in and told him that she wouldn't explain what she was going to do or what she had learned, but that she was leaving. She also said she was making another pot of coffee and asked him if he wanted any.

"Sure, thanks. Are you coming back?" Sam asked.

"I don't know. Maybe. Is magic really dangerous for non-witches? You mentioned Ashley said something about it driving people crazy," Rachel said, handing Sam the mug.

"Yeah, she always said that, but she was sharp as a tack up until the end," he said. "I think she harbored a lot of bad feelings about how things ended with Rosemary. They had a giant fight the day Rosemary and Theresa left. She said some really nasty things to her, and then she never saw her again. I tried to get her to talk about it, but she always refused."

"What'd she say about magic?" Rachel said. "There was nothing in the books about magic being harmful to anyone else. My friend is telling me she's seeing things. Did your aunt ever say anything like that?"

Sam sipped his drink and thought about it before speaking again.

"Once. I overheard her and Lloyd talking about seeing spots of light upstairs in that empty room. It didn't use to be empty. They hauled a bunch of stuff out of there and buried it in the backyard. A bunch of files and things she said they had made together. Little wooden things and boxes of crafts.

"When I took over for Lloyd, she'd told me not to linger in this house," he said. "But that was only after Rosemary left.

Before then she was here almost all the time. They were happy. So I don't know how much credence to give any of that. I've never noticed anything too weird here, but I don't take chances with magical objects. That's why I keep the key locked up when I'm not here."

"What'll you do if I come back?" Rachel said after taking a sip of her coffee.

"I guess I'd have more free time. I've got a real job," he said. "This is just glorified house sitting. There's an account that was set up that you'll probably want what's left in it. There's a lot. This place hasn't needed much repair over the years. Are you going to stay?"

Rachel sighed.

"No," she said. "I've got business to take care of in Cincinnati. But I might come back. If I don't, what happens to the house?"

"Eventually it becomes Auden property," he said. "But that's not for another hundred years. The contract is kept in a security deposit box at the bank if you want to look at it."

"That's ok," Rachel said. "Thank you. For everything."

"You're family," Sam said. "Nothing to it."

36

They found an entrance to the subway tunnels, but due to its location right off Central Parkway, they opted to wait until night time to start their efforts. They left the truck off of Trettle, at the edge of the parking lot of a Baptist church. They parked close to the street but out of view of Church and its shining red pentagram window. They had driven past it, and it looked even eerier without the crowded parking lot.

She had hoped to find a neighborhood nearby, so that if things went south they could knock on doors or scream for help, but the whole area around the former Trettle Station was commercialized. Although parking out in the open felt compromising, they felt safer having the truck closer to the entrance to the tunnel entrance in case they needed to make a hasty exit.

It was Monday night, three days after the summer solstice and 24 hours before she agreed to come to them. The plan was to break into through the tunnel, rescue Morgan and take pictures for evidence. Then they'd head straight to the police. They weren't unprepared for other eventualities, but they hoped it wouldn't come to that.

They loaded up with what they had brought, hopped over a cement embankment, and then crouched next to the highway. The grassy cliff was steep and banked sharply down to the highway, but where they walked had a path worn into it from years of service and patrol units visiting the tunnel. The grass gave way to gravel after a few yards.

It was almost midnight, and traffic was sparse going into the city, but they weren't afraid of being spotted. Rachel had cast a few enchantments, running through nearly all of the coins she had. In addition to what they carried with them, she had cast a half hour spell. This was the lowest cost of the spells she cast that night, as it was only camouflage. To the drivers on the road, they were unremarkable, shadowless and gray like the cement behind them, but to each other they looked like themselves, dressed in all black like cat burglars.

"Let's do this," Rachel whispered to Emily as they both crept along the embankment as close to the wall as they could. She could see the door to the tunnels ahead of them.

The two walked down a broken gravel path that led to the entrance, where dark green weeds had overgrown the left side. Tangled weeds spilled in front of the doors, adding the only color to the industrial gray oversized canvas of the windowless metal entrance doors to the tunnels. The path crooked to the right after the entrance, and peering around the side, Emily saw the path continued for a few yards before it was overgrown with weeds. A second pair of doors were covered by vines. That door led to the right tunnel. They could go through either as the tunnels were connected inside by a concrete barrier, but the more trafficked door would be easiest to open.

Rachel had watched videos online posted by geocachers, history buffs and urban explorers on accessing the tunnels, but standing in front of the entrance she was surprised by the size. Gray windowless metal doors almost twice as tall as house doors covered the entrance, above which four feet of rusted metal grating cut a half moon into the cement.

The doors were nearly twice as wide as they were tall and were not a uniform gray color. Age had mottled some of the color, and water dripping from the grates above the doors had worn the paint off the top two feet, eroding to reveal the dark gray-blue steel beneath. Water stains painted swaths of shading on the doors. The false shadows made the doors look battered, as though a beast had beaten on them from the inside. But the metal doors were smooth except for the roughly 12 inch square box attached to the right door, lapping a few inches over the middle onto the left door.

The doors themselves were roughly 10 feet tall, and the box was in front of Rachel's face. She took her wand out of the backpack. Pointing it at the box, she thought with serious intent about what it was she needed and how to word her request.

"Unlock, but if you are connected to a security system, only show yourself as locked. Leave no trace of our entrance or exit this evening," she said, and then slipped her fingers under the curve of gray metal box.

She pulled the heavy door open, and as she did, they heard a short bark from the metal hinges. The gaping darkness of the tunnels gobbled up the sound, and as it echoed down into the tunnels, it distorted into a low hollow moan. Rachel looked back at Emily, who tried to hide the apprehension she knew she was wearing on her face. Rachel returned a wary smile. They walked in and closed the door behind them, sealing themselves in the tunnels.

They had known it was going to be dark inside the tunnels, but the dank humidity combined with the inky darkness created an atmosphere more chokingly cave like than Emily had expected. She walked in front of Rachel, and sat down what she was carrying. Rachel sat down hers as well.

Emily took a lantern out of her backpack. She turned it on, and the LED lights winked a few times before staying on and shining bright blue-tinted light all around them. The lantern created enough light for them to see about 10 feet ahead of themselves. They were surrounded on all sides by gray concrete walls stained with almost a hundred years of dripping condensation. The wall to their right had holes at regular intervals through which one could see or step through to the neighboring tunnel. Beyond the lantern's light, the darkness of the tunnels beckoned as a rich black void that gaped in front of them.

Rachel took her wand out of her backpack. She looked at the stick for a second, reflecting that it had once been an ordinary branch and was now a magical tool. She too felt changed. She pointed the tip of the crooked length of burnt birch at each of the beige metal tanks that Rachel and Emily had carried.

She dragged the tip up in the air, and the tanks lifted off as if plucked up by an invisible hand, hovering three feet off the ground. She walked forward, and the containers obediently moved before her. She knew that using magic was shortening her life, but that the point of her life seemed to be waiting for her in the tunnels. Everything had to go according to plan, Rachel thought to herself, or no one would be able to stop Nephilor.

Emily looked back over her shoulder to see, and despite her fear she smiled at the curious sight of the tanks floating gently to the ground. She turned back around, and looked at the tunnel walls around them in the lantern light. The light was bright, but the darkness of the tunnels was so deep that there was a perpetual black hole yawning in front of them as they walked.

It was comforting to know that Rachel could perform such magic and Emily had faith in their plan, but she only felt apprehension when thinking about the encounter ahead. If the creature had been watching them, she could only hope it didn't know of their plans. They had made sure to only discuss their strategy while in protected locations, but it occurred to her that protection might not extend to telephone lines. It was a chance they had discussed but decided they had to take.

Emily wondered what Karen might do if she found them before they were ready. After what Rachel had shared with her, including learning she had shook hands with a serial murderer, Emily didn't care to be caught by surprise. She held her pocket knife in one hand with her thumb against the side of the lock, ready to call it into action. Her handgun was holstered to her side, although she was hopeful she would not have to use it in the tunnels.

She wasn't sure how thick the concrete was down here, nor how a bullet might act in the tunnels. She was also nervous. She had fired the handgun plenty of times at the range, but she wondered if it would have any effect on the creature Rachel had described. If she had to use it. Rachel had done something to them that she said would work. But Emily shuddered thinking of the hand made of light that she had seen in the backyard. Not knowing what the hand was attached to made it difficult, but she had to believe in Rachel's power after everything she'd seen and heard.

They walked without seeing a soul. They had expected to see at least a patrolman or maybe a homeless person or two, but they didn't even see rats in the tunnels. There was evidence of life in the graffiti covered the gray cement walls of the tunnels. There were classic graffiti gossip lines and public warnings, like "Marge isn't Cincy!" and "Wes wuz here" as well as the usual bubble lettered tags, simple graffiti names, and stylized S's made of connected lines.

There were simple numbers and shapes spray painted throughout the tunnels, as well as construction orange stenciled instructions for a Rapid Transit project. There were murals where graffiti artists had clearly spent hours on detailed signatures, working like monks on their illuminated manuscripts to produce something so detailed and barely legible, Rachel was sure only other graffiti artists could read the wild jumbles of arrows, drips, and curves.

"Why's there no one down here?" Emily whispered, finally breaking their silence half a mile into the tunnels.

She peered through one of the door sized holes in the thick concrete wall that divided the two tunnels. Graffiti was just as prevalent in the other tunnel. Litter and shattered glass covered the floor, and drips from pipes echoed through the wide cement corridors like footsteps. The evidence of life was all around, but not a soul breathed in the tunnels.

"The locks, I guess. But I don't know. It feels weird, right?" Rachel said.

Emily agreed. She thought the abandoned subway tunnels were going to be creepy, but they were more than that. They felt haunted. A car driving by on the road above them zipped past, creating a ghostly echo in the tunnel. The sound reverberated down the tunnel, whooshing past them into the darkness further down. There were 2 and a half miles of tunnels, but they only had to reach the first station. Roughly a quarter mile walk. The dark tunnel ahead of them continued for miles before reaching its dead end, creating a chamber in which sounds were distorted.

"It's kind of a feeling like being watched," Rachel said. "Although no one can see us, I'm sure of it. I also know there's no protection spell. I guess they didn't think it was needed since they're sealed in."

"Either way, it's claustrophobic enough in here for me," Emily said. "Let's try to get this over with quick."

Rachel agreed. They picked up the pace until they were outside the sealed station. Rachel used the wand to gently drop the tanks against the cement bricks. They landed with a muted metal sound. Then they pulled two smaller tanks out of their backpacks and laid those next to them. Rachel cast a spell to ensure they would go unnoticed, reducing the cost by putting a time limit for their invisibility. She only needed them to be camouflaged for the next 24 hours, so that she'd be able to access them if they took her to their sacrifice chamber the next day or if things went wrong tonight.

Rachel pulled the sledgehammer out of her backpack. She had enchanted it to be three times as powerful for just an hour. They just had to hope that no one else was in the station, or that it was at most a guard that they could overpower.

The eerie darkness was forbidding, but something about the invisibility spell she had cast on them seemed to separate them like a diving suit from the atmosphere. Despite the separation, she couldn't shake the sense that something else was in the tunnels with them. They were ready if that were the case, but it wasn't time to worry. It was time to get to work.

37

Emily laced her fingers together with her palms up so that Rachel could boost her way up onto the wood runner along the walled in platform. Rachel set the hammer down and then helped Emily up onto the wooden edge. Then she handed her the sledgehammer.

Emily had grown up on a farm in rural West Virginia, so she knew how to chop wood with an axe. She had proved her skills swinging hammers during the renovation, so she had volunteered to bring down the wall. Rachel was hopeful it would only take a few swings, but before they started she said a spell for an illusion that would keep the wall looking solid to anyone else but them.

Rachel watched as the hammer connected with the concrete, which began to chip away immediately. The first hit made a small hole, roughly the size of a dime, but it shattered the concrete around the hole. The broken concrete fell to the ground in shards, producing thin gray dust in the air.

Emily swung the hammer as best as she could, finding her rhythm on the third sideways hit. They planned on creating a hole big enough to crawl through, but as she kept swinging the hole grew wider and wider. She moved to the left and struck against another spot. This last strike connected with a powerful crack, and roughly a third of the wall fell all at once, creating a wave of gray dust. The dust exploded out past them, creating a haze of pulverized concrete in the air. Rachel squinted her eyes into the dust and saw Emily backing up towards her.

Rachel backed up, but the wooden runner was old and rotten. The edge gave way under her left foot. She lost her balance and threw her arms out in an attempt to stabilize. Emily turned around, her face gray with dust, and grabbed her right arm. She hauled her back up onto the sturdier part of the runner, and they looked through the large hole together.

"Get out," a voice croaked, barely above a whisper in the darkness beyond the wall.

As the concrete dust settled, Rachel could see into the formerly sealed in station. It was a long room, only a portion of which Rachel had seen in the crystal ball. She looked to the right, but couldn't see to the back in the darkness. It occurred to her that she had never seen a subway platform, and that they were much bigger than she had expected. Peering into the darkness, Rachel felt a shiver as goosebumps peppered her arms.

"Did you hear that?" Emily said.

"Shh," said Rachel. She lifted the lantern through the hole and gently stepped over the broken concrete. Emily followed her into the platform.

There was a metal armed chair and an altar situated roughly in the middle of the platform Rachel could make out dimly. Seeing the site of her mother's murder made her want to throw up, but she had prepared herself for this. She took a deep breath and pulled her eyes away from the chair, pulling out her phone and taking photos blindly. She looked long enough to make sure she captured the dark stains on the ground around the metal armed chair.

She could also see a metal door not far from the altar, one with an electronic keypad. Rachel had felt apprehension as much as Emily, but she felt a fresh kind of horror as her eyes adjusted and she saw what was on the left side of the platform. On the far wall, there was a cage, larger than a dog kennel, but not by much and made out of chain link fence. Morgan shivered in the cage.

"You need to get out of here," Morgan urged, her voice hoarse. "They know way too much about us. They can lock you out of your power. Get out while you still can!"

"*She can't see or hear us*," Rachel thought. She quickly got out her wand and undid the spell.

To Morgan, it was as though the two had suddenly popped into existence in front of her.

Rachel figured the strange expression on her face must be one of cautious relief, but it looked almost like guilt. Rachel batted the thought away, naming it a distraction.

"*Of course she looks strained, she's in a cage*," Rachel thought.

She raised her wand to unlock the cage, but Emily stepped in front of her, readying her hammer.

"Back away from the bars, Morgan," Emily said as she moved her right hand to the front of the hammer haft and her left hand to its rear. Emily adjusted her stance, pointing her right foot toward the cage. Morgan stepped quickly to the back of the cage. Emily swung, aiming for the lock. The hammer knocked the lock off and dented the door significantly, but it opened when Morgan pushed at it.

"We need to leave right now," Morgan said. She thrust her arm at Rachel, who noticed a brass cuff around her wrist. "Unlock this please."

Rachel unlocked the cuff, which fell to the floor. Morgan rubbed her wrist and smirked gratefully.

"I made a huge mistake in thinking I could take them alone," she said. "But I don't think we're a match for them either. We need to flee."

They all heard the small, polite beeping sound of an ID scanner, followed by the turning of a metal door handle behind them.

"Oh, not yet," said a woman's voice dripping with sarcastic hospitality. "You just got here. Stay a while."

38

Ten hooded figures in dark green cloaks filed into the station quickly. Some of them were tall and others short, but they all hid their faces except for one. Karen smiled as she walked towards the three of them in the middle of the station, her hood down, dark hair coiffed and eyes sparkling.

Behind her and flanking out on either side were nine others whose hooded faces she could not see. She had thought it would be Karen alone, when they were ready. She had been wrong. What else had she mispredicted? Unease prickled over her as it occurred to her that it might be Mike behind one of those hoods.

"*Does he know?*" she thought. "*Did he know the whole time?*"

"We're as ready as we'll ever be," Emily whispered, and Rachel noticed that she was holding the hammer as if ready to swing. Rachel nodded. She was right.

"Get out of here unless you can help," Emily hissed at Morgan.

Morgan nodded and ran to the wall, feeling around where they came though until she found and went through the hole. Rachel wondered what part she had played in all this. Why hadn't she stuck to the plan? She brushed the thought aside, focusing on the advancing group. It was time for the big plan.

"Karen, I know what's going on, and I want to help you," Rachel said. She heard her voice echo back at her. Emily and Rachel didn't move.

Karen's eyes were shining like a kid's on Christmas, but when Rachel spoke her countenance shifted warily. Was she curious? She wondered if Nephilor was doing all the driving now.

"How do you mean help?" Karen asked. "Are you handing yourself over?"

"I know about Nephilor," Rachel said. "I know what he's done to you over all the years. And I know how to stop him."

Rachel raised her wand, pointed it at herself and then at Karen. She thought of the tanks of helium on the other side of the wall, mentally acknowledging they were the cost for the spell she was about to cast.

"If you kill me, it will kill you as well," she said. She spun the point of her wand in a circle, then back at Karen and stopping at herself again.

When the wand was still, there was a crunching sound on the other side of the wall like crumpling metal. It was the tanks. The spell had taken the helium in the tanks, leaving a vacuum behind. Each of the tanks had crushed into themselves, malforming the beige metal canisters into flat shards.

Karen stopped in her tracks. One of the hooded men behind her bumped into her and then quickly backed up. The others stepped back to join him, leaving Karen in front of them.

"What the fuck did you just do?" she said, in a voice angrier than any Rachel had ever heard.

"You heard me. If you kill me, it will kill you as well. That means bye bye Nephy, as well as your host."

"I don't believe you," Karen said. "I've been watching you when you haven't been in protected spaces. That's a big ask that I'm sure you don't have the cost to cover."

"You don't sound sure," Emily said. Rachel could see Karen's grimacing face flash frustration, anger, and hate, but Emily was right, the confidence was gone. What now? They had speculated she might fly into a rage or that she might flee. Looking at Karen now, whose anger seemed to be only increasing, Rachel's hope that she would run was rapidly diminishing.

Karen turned around, and she must have given an order, because two of the hooded figures rushed forward toward them, rapidly closing the 10 feet between the two groups. She saw the lantern's light catch something shining in their hands. They have knives, she thought.

Emily stood her ground, and as one of the men ran at her, she swung the hammer at him. He stepped back quickly, but the hammer's head caught his left hand that then jerked toward himself. Emily adjusted her stance, pointing her right foot at him. Her eyes were on his feet under the robes. She saw he was going to advance again. She brought the hammer up like she was going to split a piece of wood. She knew where he was going to be, and she was right. He came at her again, trying to move away from the hammer while he jammed the knife at her. The tip of the knife caught her sweatshirt, and she felt it scratch against her stomach. Lucky break, she thought.

The man moved enough out of the way so that the sledgehammer didn't connect with the top of his head. If it had, it would have ran right through his skull, shattering the bones and cratering a deep indent in his brain. Instead, it connected with his right shoulder, and the sickening crunch assured Emily that she had destroyed his shoulder and any other neighboring bones. The knife dropped out of his limp hand, and he fell to his knees. He gripped frantically at his right arm with his left, as if feeling to make sure it was still there, before he collapsed on top of it and stopped moving.

Rachel had raised her wand, and flicked it just enough to cause the knives in the attackers' hands to fly into the dark of the back of the station platform before the grim figures were upon them. The one who ran at her knocked her to the ground. The wand clattered out of her hand. He quickly wrapped his hands around her throat, and he tightened his grip until the edges of Rachel's vision violently blurred.

Rachel started to panic as mental klaxons started ringing in her mind. She tried to breathe, but couldn't get any air into her lungs. She frantically reached for the wand, felt the tip of the stick near her right hand, but her fingers only brushed it further away.

Krrack! She saw the head of the sledgehammer connect with the side of the hooded stranger's head, fracturing his jaw. Rachel wheezed for breath and finally found some as the man on top of her clasped uncomprehendingly at his slack face. His jaw had been pulverized. He fell to the side and slumped on the ground. Rachel found she didn't care if he was dead. She just was glad to breathe again. She grabbed her wand and quickly tried to get up. Dizzy, she stumbled, but Emily grabbed her right upper arm and hauled her up.

Karen and the seven hooded figures behind her hadn't moved, except two of them now were on either side of Karen as though they had to hold her up. Rachel almost smiled, realizing her spell had worked. She hadn't seen Karen falter, but she was sure she had when Rachel was being choked. She managed a bitter grin. Her mother's theory on CHNOPS was proving itself. She had to guess at how much helium it would take, but she would have been guessing blindly if it hadn't been for the tables her grandmother had put together in her lab journal. Helium, the second most abundant element in the universe, was easy enough to buy with next-day shipping from Danube Online.

"Figured out I wasn't bluffing?" Rachel said.

Karen scowled. Rachel noticed her face was contorted into a hateful mask. It was more than anger. It was terrible, almost inhuman how her eyes seemed too bright for the room. She wasn't sure how much Karen was left, but she felt determined to try to help her.

"You said you wanted to help," Karen said. "Tell me what you meant. Enough of this."

"I want to help you, Karen," Rachel said, tightening her grip on the wand. "I don't know if there's any of the woman left who was in love with my grandmother, but you need to leave her alone, Nephilor."

"You can't hurt me without hurting yourself. It's sympathetic magic. And I do feel sympathetic for Karen but not for Nephilor. But I'll give you a chance, because it's the right thing to do. If you leave now, peacefully leave and go back to whatever dimension you came from, I'll let you go. I'll do everything I can to help you get back to where you came from. It's your best option."

Rachel and Emily had talked a lot about this part of the plan. They knew Nephilor needed Rachel, but that it would err toward self-preservation. They had thought it would take their offer. They had hoped.

Karen laughed. She whooped with big belly laughter. Rachel glanced at Emily, but Emily didn't look put-off. Rachel took a deep breath, taking advantage of Karen's theatrics to pull herself together. Karen's laughter stopped as suddenly as it began. She straightened up and began to yell.

"You fucking Crantzes," Karen yelled. "First Rosemary fucked things up by giving this body depression for fucking decades and running off with my child, then your bitch Mom couldn't stop lighting things on fire for 2 fucking seconds. Did you know that nine times out of ten, her blood would actually boil off when we tried to take it?

"Karen gave up fighting me a long time ago. She and I have killed 12 witches now, and I have grown stronger with each bloodsupping. But of course you want to be a roadblock, just like your mother and grandmother. I'll finish you the same as I finished them."

Rachel said nothing. She held onto her wand tightly, loosening only when she realized she might break the stick in half.

She saw one of the hooded figures pull down his hood. It was Mike. He looked shocked at her words. She couldn't know this was the first he had learned of his mother's murders, but that's what the look on his face told her. Her heart sank seeing him hurt, and when it did, she felt disgusted, remembering what she had learned about him. Then she grew angry. Nephilor had done this to Karen, she thought, and to him too.

"Mike, that's not your mother anymore," she yelled. He tried not to look at her. "Don't you see that thing's taken her over?"

Karen laughed again. She turned toward Mike.

"I told you she'd try to trick you," she said. "Remember?"

Mike nodded, but Rachel could see the uncertainty in his eyes.

"Why don't you help her, Rachel?" he pleaded. "She doesn't even need your blood at first. She just needs some of her blood on you, and then Nephilor will be free. Then Nephilor only needs some of your blood to make him corporeal. She said he might leave you unharmed, so you can be with me in the world after."

Rachel sighed.

"Mike, she's been lying to you since you were born," she said. "That's not your mom anymore. Did she tell you that my grandmother conceived my mom with Frank?"

"What?" Mike said.

"You're my uncle, Mike," Rachel said. "She used you. She used you to get to me."

Mike looked at Karen. Her smooth face broke into a wide, eerie smile. The whites of her eyes sparkled in the dim light of the lantern.

"That's right," Karen said.

Mike flinched away from her. He looked back and forth between Karen and Rachel and began backing away. Karen turned toward her son. Rachel saw movement in the long sleeves of Karen's robes. She raised her long, crooked stick wand, pointing it at Karen.

"What are you doing?" Rachel said.

"I'm going to hug my son," Karen said and stepped toward Mike.

The six hooded figures behind them stepped back, almost in unison. They huddled together whispering a few feet behind the mother and son, then stepped back further.

Rachel tried to keep her alarm in check. She wasn't sure what Karen was up to, but she knew it wasn't going to be good.

"Why?" Mike said. "Why didn't you tell me?"

Karen smiled and stepped closer to him.

"Come give your mother a hug," Karen said.

Mike realized with alarm that his mother hadn't hugged him since he was a child.

She stepped closer to him, and he stepped back, backing into the six others who still had their hoods up. One of them pushed on his back, shoving him at Karen, who quickly joined her hands together under the robe. The fabric of the sleeves fell away for just a second, but it was enough.

Rachel saw the glint of the knife in Karen's hand and raised her wand. The knife flew out of her hand and into the darkness on the right side of the station. Rachel felt a small wave of relief knowing Karen was disarmed.

Mike tried again to back away and was shoved toward his mother again by the group of hooded men. Karen reached out to him, and for just a second, Rachel thought her hands looked iridescent. They pulsed with light in shades of pink, teal and orange, but mostly they were dark red with blood.

Rachel panicked seeing the blood on Karen's hands as she reached for her son's face while he pulled away.

"No!" Rachel screamed, but Karen had laid hands on Mike. Her hand landed with a slap on the right corner of his mouth, leaving a bloody handprint on his lips and jaw.

Karen instantly fell to the floor, her body spasming in convulsions more violent than the ones Rachel had seen in the crystal ball. Her tongue lolled out of her mouth and as her body jerked, her head shot up and then down, violently shutting her jaw on her tongue, the tip of which she bit off. Blood began pouring out of her mouth as the soft pink lump of meat fell from her mouth to the floor.

39

There was no slowness in Nephilor's escape from Karen's body this time. Perhaps the rage or the power he had gained in the intervening decade had given him the strength he needed.

Rachel felt frozen in fear watching the iridescent figure revealing itself. She knew she wasn't the only one. Everyone in the cavernous platform had froze in their tracks, unable to look away. Even Mike had stopped in his retreat, backed up yet again against the five others in his group. Bewildered but unable to look away, he watched in horror as the creature in his mother shed her like a coat.

The iridescent hands shot out of her body first, as easily as a diver into water, followed swiftly by long arms that were twisted at the elbow into spikes. Then the full arms shot out, two ghastly nacreous long limbs that bent and placed its hands on the ground on either side of Karen's shaking body, bracing itself as it pulled itself through.

She had not expected the second set of hands. They came through as easily as the first, iridescent long claws sliding out of Karen's abdomen, followed by spiked elbows and long forearms identical to the first set of arms. These hands snapped out and grabbed at Mike where he stood just a few feet away in front of the group of hooded figures. Most of the hoods stepped back, but one, the same one that had pushed him before, pushed Mike toward the snatching claws. Mike stumbled and was pulled on top of Karen by the arms, which held him as he screamed in pain. Now the top of the creature's head began to emerge, and for the first time since she hit the ground, Karen began screaming.

Rachel realized she had started to scream as well once she saw the creature's face. She had thought it would have looked like a human after seeing the hands, but even in its luminescent state, she could see the head was like a wasp's. Two giant eyes on either side with two long trailing flaps on top that, once emerged, stiffened and stretched above its head like prehensile horns. Its head popped out of her abdomen, revealing sharp mandibles, followed swiftly by the upper half of its body, which shimmered with rainbow iridescence.

Karen's eyes were wide, and blood continued to pour out of her mouth as she screamed, her yells now of terror and pain, choked by blood. The blood sprayed on Mike's face as he looked down at his mother, her face only inches from his increasingly pallid expression of pain and fright, now misted with dark red.

Rachel saw movement in her peripheral vision. Emily was reaching for her gun.

As the creature emerged, it held Mike aloft, so now instead of being face to face with his dying mother, he was several feet off the ground, kicking and screaming as much as she was. Nephilor seemed unbothered as he continued his rapid egress.

His backend was larger than the first half of his body, and it seemed to glow with red and blue light that swirled in strange patterns. Two more pairs of arms were attached to the backend, ending in hands as long and sharp as the others. It was with this last pair of hands that the creature reached up to Mike, held above its head now, nearly against the ceiling of the station.

Rachel could see from where she was that Mike looked dead or at least unconscious. His skin had turned a stale shade of gray, and he was no longer screaming. The last pair of hands that emerged from Karen grabbed his head and removed it with a meaty crunch. Mike's blood poured over the creature, and the iridescence the creature seemed to be made of gave way to a dull gray color in the dim lighting of the station.

Only a few minutes had passed since Karen had slapped her son with her blood, and here the creature was. Mike was dead. Rachel looked at Karen, who lay motionless on the ground. There were no exit wounds since the thing had been made of light when it left her, but Rachel was sure she was dead. She had stopped moving, but her eyes were open and stared with horror.

Emily's hands were shaking but she had the now corporeal creature in her sights. She had grown up hunting and had shot animals that had moved swiftly before, but this creature was unlike anything she had ever seen. The reality of the being now that it was corporeal was terrifying. Standing on two pairs of its 8 long legs, it was nearly ten feet tall. She aimed for its head, where two giant compact eyes stood out on either side like engorged blackberries, gleaming and swollen in what little light Rachel's lantern still put out. Below its eyes two mandibles clicked together rapidly,

Emily took a deep breath and focused, and as she exhaled she took the shot. One of the blackberries exploded, and black liquid sprayed down on the group below. Nephilor lurched but was unfazed, and he reached for one of the hooded figures cowering below him. Karen's top tier cult members had fallen to their knees in a worshipping position, but the person who had pushed Mike still stood.

"She's got a gun!" the man yelled, taking off his hood long enough for Rachel to see his face. He was an old white man, with gray-white hair and a wrinkled face, wrinkled even more by the expression of rage he wore. Nephilor grabbed him up with four of his hands, and Rachel saw that the ends of his fingers were more than just sharp. Each of his fingers ended in a small pointed hook. Those hooks dug into the man he grabbed, who screamed in surprise and indignation. Those who were worshipping scrambled to their feet.

Emily took another shot, but this one missed, striking the concrete wall behind the creature. Rachel finally felt herself free from the paralysis that had held her in place with fright.

"*Mike's dead*," she thought, and her left hand went to her ears. She was still wearing the rose quartz and diamond earrings he had given her. She felt within herself a thrum of energy, and quickly removed the earrings, holding them in her hand with the wand. They were icy cold in her hand, and as she thought about what she was going to do, they began to burn in her palm.

"I want to help you!" the old man screamed as Nephilor pulled him up into the air. He tore the man in half. Blood and guts poured on top of Nephilor, staining crimson the dull gray carapace that covered the two sections of his body. He dropped the empty torso and legs which landed wetly on the cement. He reached for the next closest worshipper, catching only their cloak as they jumped back.

The cloak pulled off of the man, who was revealed to be a young blonde haired man who Rachel recognized as one of the bartenders at Church. The bartender with the striped chevron tattoo. Rachel realized now it was a spider. The hands came for him again, four long fingered hands with claws as sharp as needles. He pretended to run to the right, and then took off for the left, barely catching up to his three friends as they rushed through the metal door on the other side of the cage. They slammed the door behind them, and Rachel was sure they had locked it.

"*It doesn't matter,*" Rachel thought. She stepped forward, raising her wand and pointing it at Nephilor.

"Last chance to die or get the fuck out of our universe," Rachel said.

It was just the three of them on the platform. Rachel's eyes flicked from the large hole in the wall to her right and back to Nephilor. The hole was about three yards away from her, and maybe four yards from Nephilor, who crouched on his eight hands in front of the altar where he had been worshipped, his head close to the ceiling.

It seemed to be their only exit. His as well once he sees you leave, she reminded herself.

"You don't really think you have a chance against me, do you?" Nephilor said, and as it spoke its mandibles moved aside and Rachel saw in horror that it had a mouth. Blood from its eye was still pouring from the gaping wound on the side of his face, and it had trickled down onto its teeth, giving them an oily black stain. There were no lips, only sharp teeth that seemed to perpetually smile. It grinned at her from across the few yards between them, and then it slowly began to advance. It moved slowly off the altar, one leg at a time. It moved like a spider, and Rachel was sure it could have easily closed the distance in less than a second if it wanted.

"*It's trying to intimidate us,*" she thought, and then a new idea occurred to her. "*My spell still works, or it thinks it does. He's feeling it out to see if it's safe to attack me.*"

Emily fired another shot. This one landed in the middle of the creature's thorax, a foot above where his mandibles clacked violently, but the bullet didn't penetrate the chitinous shell. The force did push him backward a few feet, but then he began his slow advance again.

A voice sounded from the hole in the wall, and Rachel turned, lowering her wand as she did.

"I hope you like snakes, fuckface!" Morgan screamed, and as she did several giant black snakes poured in from the hole, slithering in quickly and surrounding Nephilor.

"Morgan, you don't have the cost for this! Get out of here!" Rachel shouted.

"I don't care!" Morgan shouted. "I've got me!"

Morgan stepped over the hole in the wall and rushed toward Nephilor, screaming. It stepped back, and one of the largest snakes, which looked to be about 20 feet long, raised up and hissed at him. Green venom dripped from its fangs, and Nephilor began scuttling backwards against the back wall. One of the snakes lurched forward, and it bit off one of Nephilor's hands, spitting it on the ground where the hand curled up like a dead spider.

"The lights!" Emily shouted.

She tried to keep her focus on her target, but what she saw made it impossible. There were more lights than she had thought possible, and they were everywhere, bumping into each other and igniting as they collided with an audible pop. It seemed like every inch of air was packed to capacity with the flecks of light, and as they rammed into each other they grew brighter. The temperature in the room was rising quickly.

"Something's not right. There's been too much magic here!" Emily yelled, and she raised her gun and tried to aim for Nephilor. Squinting to peer through the spaces between the flickering lights, she could barely make him out against the back wall of the platform, cornered by the snakes. She shot, and the bullet spun out of the barrel and was dissolved in the air by the lights just a few feet in front of her. She quickly holstered her gun, bent down and picked up the sledgehammer again. "We need to get out of here!"

Rachel knew Emily was right, and realized with an alarming certainty that if they didn't get out soon, they would never leave alive. She couldn't see the lights, but she could see the fear on Emily's face and hear it in her voice.

Rachel raised her wand again at Nephilor, but then she felt Emily's hand on her wrist, squeezing her tightly.

"No more magic!" Emily yelled.

Morgan either didn't hear her or did not care. Morgan raised her hands, and as she did, the snakes rose up and reared back to strike.

Things quickly descended into chaos as the lights became visible to everyone in the platform. The lights really were everywhere, Rachel thought. She could no longer see past a few feet in front of her. They had permeated the air, and more and more of them kept colliding and igniting. Rachel felt sharp pain on her arms and legs, and looking down saw red pock marks sizzling on her skin.

Emily grabbed Rachel's left hand and yanked her hard, running to the hole. They ran through to the other side, jumping down from the platform onto the space below where tracks would have been if the subway had been completed. Rachel turned back to see through the haze of lights if Morgan or Nephilor were following them. She couldn't see through the lights, but realized she had left her lantern. Emily again yanked Rachel away from the hole. They jumped down from the splintered wooden platform onto the cement trackbed below.

"Run!" Emily yelled, and they began to run the way they had come. Without the lantern, they had no light to see in the darkness. They had gone only about three yards when they heard more of the wall come down. Rachel stopped and turned around, and so did Emily. They could see the flickering lights pouring out of the hole in the wall, and it provided enough light for them to see that there was no movement.

There was silence.

Then they saw something fly out of the hole. It struck the far side of the tunnel wall with a sick thud and then fell on the ground. Rachel could see it was Morgan's torso, and she saw in the dim light that Morgan's eyes were opened wide, her mouth open as though she was still screaming.

Then Rachel saw the tanks. They had crushed in on themselves, but they'd still hurt if they were thrown, she thought. Before she could raise her wand to move them, she saw movement on the wall Morgan's body had struck. She realized she was looking at Nephilor's shadow as it felt its way out of the hole in the platform wall. One appendage, now just a stump dripping blood, came out and waved around in the darkness as if feeling for them.

"Mike's dead. Morgan's dead. Karen, Mom, Rosemary, and we're next if we don't get the fuck out of here," she thought. *"All the wolves are gone, but they left a monster behind."*

Rachel was furious.

Nephilor crawled through the hole and turned to face them. Whatever he had done to Morgan appeared to have strengthened him, or at least emboldened him enough to take another run at them, Rachel thought. She couldn't make out his face in the darkness but she was sure he was grinning at her again.

"You will be mine," Nephilor said in a whisper that gave Rachel chills. There was once again less than ten feet between them.

The lights that had flowed out of the platform were slowly filling up the tunnel, and Rachel noticed it was becoming much brighter where they were. She could see he was indeed smiling at her again, and then he spoke again.

"You've made a lot of trouble for me," Nephilor said, rubbing his mandibles together. "But I'm free now. And as soon as I kill you I'll have all my power restored."

"Oh yeah?" Emily asked. "Even though it's not the solstice? Why?"

Rachel saw she was holding the hammer loosely in her hands. Emily had shifted and wasn't holding the hammer like she was going to swing it. She had the head pointed toward him, but was holding the aft loosely in her hands, parallel to her body. She caught Rachel's eye and raised her eyebrows.

"I would have returned so much stronger if you hadn't left," Nephilor said pridefully. "I was a human witch once. I attempted to travel to the unseen dimension. It didn't work. I was neither here nor there, like a witch ghost on the astral plane but with enough being to still think. It was only when I found Karen that I realized a plan to return to my natural form. It was easy to fool her into thinking I was a god when I couldn't maintain a form anywhere aside from her dreams. It took a long time to find a form that I could maintain.

"But I will only have this wretched shape a little longer. And I will have all of my power again once I kill you. I've destroyed 12 witches before you. Including pathetic Mike, whose will I've spent the last 31 years undermining. To think that he would have inherited my power infuriates me still."

"You sure? That sounds an awful lot like wishful thinking," Rachel said.

Nephilor snarled and started to move toward them. Rachel took the opportunity to quickly point her wand at the sledgehammer and then straighten her arm with a jerk at Nephilor. The sledgehammer flew out of Emily's hands so quickly she later had splinters deep in her palms. The hammer shot through the air, connecting with Nephilor in the space where his thorax connected to the abdomen. He shot three of his hands and the bleeding stump toward the hammer, wrapping his long arms around it. The hammer kept going, and Nephilor went with it. They heard the thud a few seconds later, but the echo made it impossible to tell how far he had been thrown back in the tunnels.

40

They didn't wait around to find out. Emily and Rachel fled, running as hard as they could, splashing in darkness for the quarter mile back to the entrance. They quickly shut the door behind them. Panting, Rachel pointed her wand at the door.

"Lock, and stay locked," she said between gasps for air. "Lock all the tunnel doors so that they will not reopen."

She felt the rose quartz burn in her hand. Surprised by the sharp pain, she accidentally dropped her wand. Her right hand had two round burns in it, forming a kind of figure eight in the middle of her palm. The rose quartz was gone, but the diamonds remained. She hurriedly picked back up her wand and shoved it and the diamonds in her pocket on the front of her sweatshirt.

They ran as quickly as they could back to the truck, which they drove away as quickly as they could, peeling out of the church parking lot. The tires squealed as they swerved into the right lane on Trettle, speeding toward Central. Once they got on the parkway, Rachel finally felt comfortable driving only 10 over the normal speed limit.

"Fuck fuck fuck fuck fuck," Emily said.

"We're panicking," Rachel said.

"Yeah, we're fucking panicking," Emily said. "It's still down there, and it knows where we live. I don't...I don't know what we're going to do."

Rachel was silent. She considered her options in her head as she barreled down the street. She knew Emily was right.

"We could go to Memphis," she said. "There's a house there where we'd be safe."

"Like how Morgan was safe?" Emily asked.

"Look, we can't," Rachel started, but stopped when she looked in the rearview mirror. Emily saw it too, and she whipped around in her seat and watched the road behind them.

In the rearview mirror, the asphalt began to buckle violently. Rachel realized her mistake and sped up, focusing on the road and not looking up when she heard the explosion as Nephilor burst out of the road behind them.

In her panic to get the hell away, she had gotten on the nearest highway. She had gotten onto Central Parkway, the highway built on top of the tunnels. She wasn't sure if Nephilor had sensed her or was just trying to get out of the trap she had caused by sealing all of the tunnel's doors. She looked to her left and saw they were passing the nearly city block sized red brick edifice of the Cincinnati Music Hall's backside. The pointed gables weren't as numerous as the front, but it was unmistakable. They had almost made it to where the tunnel would have ended, the sharp turn downtown above what would have been the Race Street station.

Chunks of asphalt rained down on the truck. One piece broke the back windshield, landing in the backseat of the cab. The glass shattered, creating a large hole that the night air began rushing into as if it too was fleeing for its life. Further ahead on the road she saw a cop car pulled over on the side of the road turn on its lights and whip around to face them. Driving the wrong direction, she thought. She flew past the cop car and heard its siren whine scream as it passed her and barreled down the road toward Nephilor.

Emily screamed, and Rachel looked up at the rearview again and saw that Nephilor had crawled out of the massive hole he had created. In one of his hands he held the sledgehammer she herself had enchanted. He looked down the road at them. Rachel was sure his one good eye had met hers, although she didn't know if it was fear or intuition telling her they'd been seen.

The cop car had swerved behind them and stopped, and the officer had gotten out with his weapon drawn. She could only hope he had radioed for backup. There was 30, then 40, then 50 feet between her car and the monster now, and only a policeman between them.

She saw the flash of gunpowder in the rearview as the cop opened fire, then flicked her eyes back to the road, trying to keep in her lane.

"It didn't see us. It didn't see us. It didn't see us," she thought, hoping, but dreadful certainty in the pit of her stomach told her she was wrong.

Emily screamed again, and Rachel looked up just long enough to see that the cop car was flipped over. She barely saw the hands of the cop underneath the car, palms open, the pistol he had fired dead on the ground. Her eyes were on Nephilor, who confirmed her fears of being seen. He was chasing them again. His long appendages, no longer cramped by the tunnels, were stretched out on all sides of his body, and he was running quicker than any spider Rachel had ever seen. She saw he was running on the stump, and it frightened her that it didn't seem to bother him at all.

She flicked her eyes back to the road. Rachel realized she was driving North again, that Central Parkway had turned into Reading Road and that they were about to pass the casino on the right, a massive modern glass and concrete building.

The distance between them was closing rapidly, and seeing his face in the rearview mirror, Rachel stomped on the gas, pushing the truck as fast as it would go to a dangerously roaring 95 miles per hour that kept the tachometer firmly in the red zone. But still Nephilor ran faster, scurrying along the street behind her until he was nearly on top of them. Rachel was sure he was going to reach his sharp hands through the broken glass and grab her. She realized she was running out of options.

Rachel stomped on the brake. The tires squealed and the car swerved toward the entrance to the casino, toward the metal poles in front of its entrance meant to keep things like cars from barreling into the glass entry of the casino. Rachel quickly let go of the brake, jerked the steering wheel left and then straight, and then stomped again on the brake. The truck slid to a stop, halfway on the curb in front of the metal poles in front of the casino.

Nephilor couldn't stop himself fast enough, sliding to a stop about 30 feet in front of them. He quickly regained his bearings. Raising his body off the ground on his long legs, he scurried to them, closing the distance in what felt like seconds. Rachel quickly got out of the car, never taking her eyes off him. Emily slid over into the driver's seat, buckled and tried to take off, wincing as she wrapped her splintered hands around the steering wheel.

Nephilor grabbed the front end of the vehicle with two of his hands, and lifted it over him. Chunks of asphalt that had fallen into the truck bed when Nephilor burst out of the road fell down onto his head and around him. He swore before casually tossing the truck 15 feet into the flat green space on the side of the casino. Rachel heard Emily scream, then the horrible crunch of metal and glass as the truck landed on its side. Then there was silence.

41

It was just Rachel and Nephilor on the road now, and Nephilor was grinning at her again. The bleeding from his eye had stopped, and in the light from the streetlights she could see just how sharp his teeth were, each tooth sharpened to a nail point. He rubbed his mandibles together over his grin like he was savoring the moment. He was holding the sledgehammer in one of his back legs, and she could see he was ready to swing it.

Rachel grabbed in the front pocket of her sweatshirt for the diamonds, but it was empty. She realized she didn't have her wand either. She saw the light from the streetlights was glinting off of objects on the pavement and quickly realized she couldn't tell if it was glass or the diamonds. It was then that she felt truly fucked, in every possible way.

Nephilor seemed to sense she was out of options. Maybe it was the look on her face when she realized she had nothing left to defend herself with on her person. He started to laugh, big confident chuckles as he stepped slowly toward her. He didn't see the need to rush anymore, she thought.

"I've been waiting a long time for this," he said. "You almost ruined everything with that spell of yours. It's too bad you didn't realize Mike was always the backup option. Why else would I have let Karen have a child?"

He smiled at her and clacked together his mandibles over his wicked grin in what Rachel assumed was good cheer.

"Oh, lost your magic tools? Here, take some fucking rocks," he said.

With one hand he picked up one of the chunks of asphalt that had fallen from the truck. He threw it at her. It was about a foot long, and Rachel was almost able to dodge it. It scraped her left calf as it whizzed past her, and she winced with pain. He picked up another smaller chunk and threw it, hitting her right thigh. She buckled for a second, and he stepped closer to her again. He seemed to be having fun, she thought, seeing how he waved the sledgehammer back and forth in one of his back hands.

Rachel took a deep breath as Nephilor came closer to her. She felt her own fear, remembering what he had done to Mike, how gray he had looked before he had ripped him apart. He hadn't looked like the Mike she had known at all when Nephilor was done with him. She thought of all those he had wronged. He had taken her mother and her grandmother from her. Karen's life was ruined by Nephilor, so was Mike's, Morgan's, and now Emily's. Rachel thought for a moment that Nephilor was right, that she was alone.

She looked up at him then, not bothering to hide the mournful look on her face. He was so close to her now that she could see into the wound where his eye had been and his blood stained teeth. She could smell his hot breath, reeking of iron and sulfur.

"That's right. You should just give up. Hold still, and maybe I'll make this quick and painless," he said, snickering. He reached out a hand toward her face and traced the tips of two of his hooked fingers from under her ear to her mouth. She felt the claws on his fingers scratch into her face. They were so sharp that it was barely painful, but she felt the blood drip down her chin. Rachel jerked away.

Suddenly, with a clarity almost as painful as the loss she felt, she knew what she needed to do. Nephilor didn't seem to notice the change in her demeanor, and if he did, perhaps he thought the determination on her face was that of someone who knew they were about to die. Rachel raised her hand to her face, feeling where the blood was coming out of the wounds he had traced on the right side of her jaw. She looked at her hand, red and wet with blood.

She saw him put his hand in his mouth, tasting her blood. He smacked his teeth together with a terrible clacking sound, and Rachel realized he thought he had already won. He was pulling the sledgehammer up in the air now, slowly, as if savoring the moment.

Rachel took another deep breath, pulling from her diaphragm the deepest breath she could take. She pictured herself drawing up every ounce of power that was in her. She wanted to use everything she had.

Rachel screamed as loud as she could, a guttural war cry. She pictured all her fear leaving her as she did, leaving her with just power and hate. She started to walk toward him as she screamed.

Nephilor had been only a few inches from her face when she screamed, and it had startled him backwards. He scurried to his feet and tried to loom tall over her on his long legs, stretching up to his full height, roughly 14 feet tall. He seemed to have forgotten the sledgehammer and was standing on it.

"What are you doing?" he boomed, but Rachel noticed he didn't advance.

So she did. She ran forward toward him, clapping both her hands together, spreading the blood on her right hand to her left, and she reached out for him. He scuttled away, quickly putting ten feet between them.

"What are you doing?" he shouted again, bewildered.

She had never felt such hate in her entire life, nor such power, and the two seemed to mingle and roil within her. She felt strange. It didn't hurt, but it felt like her whole body was humming and vibrating with energy. Suddenly she remembered what exactly what had happened in the hall the night of the fire. It had been her. It had felt something like how it felt now. More than pins and needles or feeling like her limbs were falling asleep, it was like inside she was made of white noise and steadily stinging static.

Nephilor, over his initial startle, began to gather his wits. He must have thought she was bluffing, as he began running toward her, waving the sledgehammer in one of his long arms.

She wanted to be on the other side of him, and she focused on a point down the road past the casino. Just like that, she was standing where she had looked. There was a smell like ozone all around her, and she was so cold that her skin was covered in goosebumps.

She watched as he struck the ground where she had stood with the hammer with all the force he could muster. It cracked the pavement around where it landed. He looked down at where the hammer landed, and Rachel almost laughed seeing that he had picked up some human movements from the decades he spent inside Karen. He had raised one of his hands to the back of his head in confusion.

He must have heard her, because he whipped around, and though startled and confused at what had just happened, he charged at her again. This time he left the hammer. Rachel waited until he was close, and then willed herself to where the hammer stood in the cracked pavement.

"Stop that!" Nephilor screamed.

Police sirens cried out like banshees heading toward them.

"Fuck you!" she yelled, and she picked up the hammer with her bloodstained hands. She held the sledgehammer like a small baseball bat. Grounding herself with a staggered stance, she watched as he ran the distance between them. "I want you to fucking die already!"

She waited until he was nearly upon her, and then she swung.

42

The hammer connected with Nephilor's abdomen with a crunch, and he was thrown backwards. He landed on his abdomen, rolled and then fell flat before struggling to lift himself.

"No!" he screamed as he crawled slowly back towards her.

He faltered, collapsing on the ground before pushing himself halfway back up. He reached out with three of his long arms and grabbed her around the waist, sinking his claws into her. She could feel the hooks in her hips and sides, pulling the skin there taut as though he was going to tear it from her body. He pulled her towards him, tearing at her flesh. It was excruciating, but nothing else mattered now.

She raised the hammer again and repeated her curse.

"Fucking die!" she screamed as she brought the hammer down on his abdomen one last time.

There was a loud crack as the hammer struck.

Nephilor didn't scream, but Rachel felt his hands go slack in her sides. The blood smeared, gray carapace that covered the two sections of his body cracked. Fissures spread out from the points where she had struck him. At once, these fractures widened, revealing dingy white meat underneath. Seeing the morphing and heaving body under her, Rachel dropped the hammer to her side. She scrambled to remove the three hands hooked into her, yanking them out of her flesh with a clenched jaw scream.

Keeping pressure with her hands on the bleeding wounds on her sides, Rachel scrambled back from the body, but tripped over another of Nephilor's arms. Landing on her ass on the pavement, she stumbled to her feet. Strange flesh was ballooning up from the cracks in Nephilor's casing, bubbling up like a plague of boils.

The skin on these protrusions was so taught that Rachel could see what looked like milk swirling inside.

Nephilor's corpse burst like a thunderhead, drenching Rachel with oily, black blood that reeked of sulphur. Unable to see, she spat out some of the slick liquid and gagged at the rotten egg taste in her mouth. She wiped at her face with the sleeves of her shirt, but only succeeded in spreading the black fluid thinner around her eyes and mouth. It stung in her eyes and blurred her vision. Nephilor's thick blood clung like a coat to everything and in unexpected places. There was slick black grease in her ears, nose, under her nails. Everywhere was black except for the red stains from her own blood on her palms.

There was nothing left of his body except chunks of greasy gray flesh in her hair and spread on the concrete around her. Part of his head lay on the wet ground, its ears curled all the way to the crown. The jaw was obliterated. His left mandible remained attached, but only the front three pointed teeth remained, their points resting on the sidewalk. One eye remained, staring at her. She lifted up her foot and crushed the compact eye, which popped under her sneaker with a final burst of black gore.

The sirens that had started wailing when Rachel struck Nephilor were getting closer. She looked at the bloody hammer and the mess around her. Then she looked in the distance to the wreckage of Emily's truck. She ran to it, leaving sticky black footprints in her wake. She heaved the driver side door open.

Emily was buckled in upside down and was hanging upside down. Her face was dark with the blood rushing to her head. She was bleeding from cuts and scrapes on her arms, head and neck. Rachel took one of her Emily's limp hands and felt frantically for her friend's pulse. Feeling a weak throbbing, Rachel gasped in a jagged breath.

"Please be ok. Please be ok," Rachel repeated mournfully. She cupped Emily's face in her hands, leaving two red and black smeared handprints on Emily's cheeks.

Seven cop cars pulled to a stop in front of the casino, and she heard a voice on a megaphone tell her to put her hands up. Cops in black uniforms poured out of the cars, surrounding her with weapons drawn. She raised her hands, red palms in the air.

"Hold fire!" a voice shouted.

"Keep your hands up!" another officer shouted. "Get on the ground slowly!"

***

Emily was rushed to the hospital, and Rachel was detained by local law enforcement. Rachel had enough money to make bail, as well as enough to hire a good lawyer. In the United States, if you have enough money, a good lawyer can be almost magical.

It was a few days before Rachel was debriefed and released from police custody, but without her lawyer it would have been weeks. Rachel had disrupted an undercover investigation that had been operating for almost a month when she and Emily brought down the wall on Trettle Station. They had suspected human trafficking, but were in the early stages of discovering the scope of the crimes committed by Nephilor's group. As part of the deal, Rachel told them everything she knew about the group, including descriptions of the Level 5 member she recognized with the chevron tattoo.

The investigators agreed that Emily was not going to face any charges as long as she agreed to keep quiet about what happened. Rachel was required to leave town within 30 days of the agreement. The unofficial representative for the city told her no charges would be pressed on the condition that she would never return to the city of Cincinnati.

Her lawyer told her it was mostly theatre, since they couldn't enforce it. He would be in touch with her again but wanted her to take time away to cool down. So she's taken the deal for now and was considering moving to Memphis. He would call her when the city found itself needing a witch.

She didn't think it would be the end of her dealings with Nephilor. The police were investigating leads on the remaining cult members, and one of the detectives gave her his contact information. He told her he already had hers.

The first call she made after legal matters were finally settled was to her therapist. She called and made an urgent appointment on her way to Morgan's house. There were some things she needed to take care of there before the local law enforcement figured out Morgan's connection to everything.

When she was done at Morgan's, she went to see Emily. Emily was still in traction, but she was healing quicker than expected. She was experiencing an increase in migraines and visual disruptions that she said were not magic related. The doctors weren't finding anything wrong with her eyes, and imaging results were inconclusive. Despite Emily's assurance that she was fine, Rachel didn't like hearing that she was seeing auras. She felt like her blood or Nephilor's blood on her hands might have made everything worse, and it made her feel guilty.

Rachel wanted to talk to her therapist about everything that had happened and what she had learned about her past. More than anything, she needed help figuring out how to tell Emily and her grandmother that she had to leave. She made it early to the appointment so she'd have more time to think.

The waiting room was almost full, but Rachel picked a chair in the corner after she signed in. She tried to think for a while, looking at her bright orange low-top sneakers and deciding how to phrase the questions she needed to ask. She was leaving, but she wasn't sure where yet. She knew she would go to Memphis, but after reading the note Morgan left her, she didn't know if she could stand to stay there. It felt like going back would be repeating the same mistakes others had made. She had to pick a different course.

She teared up thinking about Morgan's letter. She'd left it on the counter of her shop for Rachel to find. She took the letter out of her purse and read it again.

Dear Rachel,

Your wolf is waiting outside. I asked him to let me prepare a few things while he waits on the porch. He's not the smartest one, and he's a terrible liar, but you shouldn't fault yourself for falling for him. It's easy to be fooled when they're charming, and even easier when they're misleading you in the first place.

I know this is impulsive and I might regret what I'm about to do, but I can't stay in this house forever. Being under lockdown like this has made me realize that I don't want to do to a child what was done to me. I can't force another person to bunker down here the rest of their life.

Working with you made me feel like I had more purpose in life. Before I was just placating suburbanite egos with friendly Tarot readings and selling black market goods to make ends meet, I grew up in a house haunted by long gone legacies. I've hidden too long and avoided risk all my life. This is my chance to change all that. I'll destroy them for you, even if destroys me. At least then I'll have done something aside from hiding.

Witches have been isolated from each other for far too long. Find more of us. I want you to take everything that's in the library. If you (and only you) slip this letter under the door of the library, it will open. You'll find everything in there that my family has worked on for years. Take it all and grow from there.

With Love and Faith in Your Future,
Morgan Wilso.

A door opened, and her smiling dark-haired therapist stepped into the waiting room.

"Rachel Ogden?"

"That's me," she said, stood up and smiled.

Made in United States
Troutdale, OR
02/23/2024

17935504R00192